WAITING FOR SPRING

R. J. KELLER

PUBLISHED BY

amazonencore

Printed in the United States of America.
This book was self published, in a slightly different form, in 2008.

Published by AmazonEncore
P.O. Box 400818
Las Vegas, NV 89140

ISBN-13: 9781935597551
ISBN-10: 1935597558

This book is dedicated to Mom and Betsy,
whose backyard holds a secret mushroom cemetery.

And to my husband. You always warn me about the ants,
but never discourage me from going on the picnic.
And that is why I love you.

PROLOGUE

They say actions speak louder than words. Maybe. But words do a hell of a lot more damage. Even well-meaning words spoken by well-meaning people.

People like Sister Patricia Mary Theriault. She was my catechism teacher when I was seven years old. Until she ruined my life, I loved her more than anything, because—unlike the other nuns at Saint Isabel's—she was pretty and nice and she always smiled. Her favorite subject was the Power of God's Love. We once spent an entire ninety-minute class answering the question, *When Does God's Love Seem Most Real to You?* Other kids talked about playing with their pets or spending time with their parents or waking up on Christmas morning. Not me.

"When I open up my big box of seventy-two Crayola Crayons."

The other kids laughed at that but Sister Patricia smiled and asked me why I felt that way. I said, "I don't know," even though I did know. She would understand, and I could tell her after class, but not in front of the laughing kids. The reason was actually very simple even if they were too stupid to get it. There wouldn't be colors called *Burnt Sienna* and

Hot Magenta and *Aquamarine* if God didn't love us. There would just be brown and red and blue.

My mother, raised to worship God with fear and trembling, did not approve of Sister Patricia. She called her the Hippie Nun, which, of course, made me like her even more. The first time I dropped acid—this was later, long after catechism classes and church and even prayer had been a part of my life—I had a vision of Sister Patricia holed up in her Nun Sanctuary Bedroom, or at least what I imagined it to be: dark and dreary with enormous posters of the Blessed Virgin taped to her wall, glowering down at her, scary and accusing and bitter. Her one small window faced north, toward the cold, letting in only cold light, cold air, cold love.

In my vision she was wearing a beautiful tie-dyed habit, kneeling on her stone floor, head bowed, praying to God. There was a light rattling, tapping, rustling sound at the window that startled her out of her meditations. She floated to the window and opened it up and when she did it let in a rainbow, pure and just as vivid as my crayons had once been. The beauty of it enveloped the cold, dreary room and filled it—filled her—with the Love of God. I was nineteen, holed up in my one-room apartment with some guy I'd met two hours earlier. I still can't remember his name, but his hair was Goldenrod and his eyes were Sky Blue.

But when I was still seven, before I knew anything about the wonders of psychedelic drugs and Pink Floyd and casual sex, I only knew that Sister Patricia was the coolest person I'd ever known. I felt that way right up until she taught us our final lesson for the year. It began innocently enough:

"Your heart is like soil. Love grows there."

The parable of the Sower planting seeds. The Sower is God, the seeds are His Word. They fall here and there, some on Bad Soil and some on Good. She told us first about the Good Soil, where the seeds can take root and grow. That's what she—what God—wanted our hearts to be like. Lovely and soft and fertile. Ready for planting. Just like spring. Every one of us knew what she meant, because there were lots of big, smelly, fertile farms in Brookfield, Maine, with acres and acres of soil.

Then she told us about the Bad Soil. There was probably more than one type of bad soil in the parable that she explained to our class that day. In fact there must have been, because she talked about it forever. But the only bad soil I heard about was this:

"As the Sower was scattering the seed, some fell along the path; it was trampled and—"

Path. Trampled. Bad soil.

I thought of the path that my older brother Dave and I had worn down through the field beside our house that led over to where Dave's best friend Jason lived. Years of travel, back and forth. Hard ground, packed tight. Grass and wild flowers grew all around it in the summer, tall and beautiful and untamed. But not on the path. Nothing grows on hard ground.

I came back around when she was saying, "'Those sown on the path are the ones out of whose hearts the devil takes the word so that they will not believe and will not be saved.' Don't let your hearts become trampled down, children. Keep them soft and fertile so you can feel God's love inside of you."

Seven years old. And already I knew I was in some deep shit. The kind that even Sister Patricia couldn't do anything about.

Backseat. My mother driving home. Irritated. Her hour and a half of freedom was over. Dave sat up front because he was nine. And because he was Dave. His First Communion was only a week away and my parents were *very, very proud of him* because *it's a very, very big step.* All it meant to me was that next year he would get to stay home and watch *Superfriends* on Saturday mornings and I'd have to ride home from catechism all alone.

He was telling us what he had learned that morning from Sister Margaret. They had talked about Jesus's trial and execution. It seemed to have touched something inside him, like the parable of the soil had done to me. Only Dave didn't seem scared like I was, just angry. Because Jesus had been taken from his friends in the middle of the night, accused of a crime he didn't do, and there was no justice to be found for him anywhere.

"Pontius Pilate was the magistrate and—"

"What's a magistrate?"

"That's sort of like a governor. But he's like a judge, too."

"Oh."

"And he thought Jesus was innocent, but he let the crowd talk him into having him executed anyway."

"Why?"

He shrugged. "Because he was weak, I guess."

"Can I see your book, Dave?" The magistrate's name sounded familiar.

He handed it to me. *Pontius Pilate.* Then I remembered.

...He suffered under Pontius Pilate; was crucified, died and was buried...

Not Ponch's Pilot. Not like *CHiPs*.

I liked it when things clicked.

I gave him back his book and looked out the window at the scenery as he rambled on about Injustice. I didn't want to hear about Injustice. I was thinking about soil. Thinking about it, not talking about it. Because I knew she wasn't going to ask me what I had learned that morning, even after Dave stopped talking.

Home. Play clothes. Walking to Jason's house.

"What are you doing?" Dave asked. "We're supposed to be there by now."

"Planting."

"You can't plant anything there. It won't grow."

"Shut up."

"I'm going without you, Pest."

I didn't care. Well, I cared a little. But I cared more about proving that I was right. That I was all right. Good things could grow on the path; I knew it. All I had to do was make the ground soft and fertile. Just like spring.

I scraped and scratched with my fingers, my fingernails, imitating the huge machines that grated our road every year. I uncovered a rock, just below the surface, the size of my hand. Couldn't budge it. I took off my plastic Forest Green headband, my brown hair spilling everywhere, and used it as a shovel. It snapped in half, which was even better. I dug and dug and dug some more. Dirt wedged underneath my fingernails and crusted in between the teeth of the headband.

The rock came out. It left behind a gaping hole, a crater, and that was perfect. I just had to fill it up, fill it in. The beginning of June was too early for wildflowers, so I settled on grass and dandelions. Used my headband shovel, dug underneath the soil beside the path; good soil, good roots and dirt. Filled in the hole. Packed it down. There was no water nearby, so I spit on it. And spit again. Kept spitting until my mouth was dry.

That would do it.

I ran to Jason's house and took turns doing swingset races. I lost. My legs were too short. Oreos and milk. More races. I lost again. Then the rain came, a light drizzle that would turn into a downpour. I ran back toward our house, right behind Dave, but stopped halfway.

My little garden was still there. I smiled at it. Because I was right. I was all right.

But the next morning I went out bright and early before breakfast, before church, and my garden was gone. Just a hole and it was half filled with sticky mud. The grass and dandelions had been washed away. Somewhere. Out of sight. Gone. Within three days it was completely filled in, more dirt and pebbles, and by the end of the week it was trampled down again. Hard ground. And I couldn't tell that there had ever been a garden there at all. Couldn't even see the crater.

Hard ground. Where nothing would grow.

CHAPTER 1

Nine steps from the door of the courthouse down to the sidewalk. Granite? Probably. Marble was too much to hope for. Brookfield was too small for that. They were some sort of grayish stone and it didn't really matter what kind of stone. They were solid, slick with ice in spots, crunchy with salt in others. I focused on that sound, my boots crushing the salt, because it was better than hearing the judge's gavel echoing in my brain.

Coat pocket. I felt for my keys with mittened fingers, still crunching along. Twenty-one steps from the bottom of the stairs to the parking lot. Thirty-three more to the car. I turned the key in the ignition, turned on the front and rear defroster before I realized I hadn't been gone from the car long enough for it to frost over. Even though it was only twenty-eight degrees outside.

9:17 a.m.

Eleven-and-a-half years of marriage. Took only minutes to end it. And Jason hadn't even bothered to show up. Probably he was at work right now. Was he looking up at the clock at this very second? Waiting, nervous, wondering

1

if it was finally all over? Only four-and-a-half miles away from where I was sitting right now. Or maybe it was forty or four hundred. And-a-half.

I pulled onto the main road, headed toward Hillside Café for coffee and a newspaper. And, with luck, maybe a little pick-me-up.

I was in luck. The sign beside the road was lit.

I walked inside and the place was empty like I knew it would be midmorning on a Wednesday. By lunchtime it would be packed. Specials: turkey club, cheeseburger basket, spaghetti with meat sauce, and for dessert—of course— the latest gossip. Hot and juicy and fresh. I'd be gone long before then anyway, either asleep or floating on a cloud. Or both.

The shelves on the far wall were filled with basketball trophies, pictures of champions. Glory days. Jason was there, King of the Champions.

He was everywhere.

"What the hell do *you* want?"

I jumped. Coach Poulin. Why was he here so early?

No cloud today.

"Black coffee. Newspaper."

Hard eyes. Silver stare. And I was there alone. Small. He gave me a cold smile.

"You fucking whore. Go get it somewhere else."

Too tired for rage, too empty. Too cold. Not even a flicker. And in that land of numbed unreality a dispassionate realization. I did the backwards math.

He'd been waiting for eighteen years to say that to me.

Congratulations, Coach. Job well done. Another trophy for your shelf.

I turned away from the silver man, walked to my car. Lost count of the steps after sixteen. I drove to the Qwik Stop where there were curious stares but no open hostility. I brought the paper to the car and snapped it open right there in the parking lot. A bold, black-lettered headline on the front page read:

Murder in New Mills.

I skimmed through the story, only vaguely interested because—

Brutal slaying...small lakeside community shocked...home invasion...rampant drug problem among local teenagers...

—while it was tragic, this wasn't the reason I'd bought the paper. But one sentence jumped off the page.

The victim, Catherine Arsenault, 42, operated a local cleaning service...

Cleaning service. Small community. How many cleaning services could one small community support?

Section D. Classifieds.

New Mills: One-bedroom apartment. Affordable. Rural setting. One mile from lake.

One more question. I opened my glove compartment and dug out my Gazetteer. New Mills was sixty-two miles from Brookfield. Sixty-two glorious miles. From my mother. From Jason. From everybody. It seemed like the closest thing to a sign from God that I could ever hope to receive. Sober at least.

I dug out my cell phone and dialed the number. An old man answered, very thick Downeast accent. "Ayuh. The apartment's still available."

He quoted the price. Cheap. Almost too cheap. What was wrong with the place?

"Nothing. It's small, but it's a good little house. Me and my wife raised our family there. Cut it in two after she died. Oh, 'bout fifteen years ago that'd be now."

Duplex? In the middle of nowhere? Sounds good, Mr. Baxter.

"Call me Charlie, please. I can give you a tour tomorrow. Can you be down here 'bout…ten thirty?"

Sure could. Might as well, even though a tour was a formality. The only thing that would prevent me taking the place would be a rat infestation.

I hung up the phone and hurried back to my brother's house. I'd held it down long enough and I knew it was coming. Better to have the breakdown in private. At least, as private as I could with my sister-in-law at home.

Deep breath. That's it. Good, you're ready. Now, walk into the house. Just. Like. That.

"Hey, Kim," I said.

"How did it go?" Sympathetic eyes. Sepia eyes.

Will the baby get those eyes?

I shrugged and gave her a brief smile, then trudged on to the bathroom. I closed the door silently and leaned back against it, closed my eyes so I wouldn't see Jason's face. It didn't work. It was still there, blonde and blue, covered with the trim, gorgeous beard that I had always loved. I could still remember the way it felt beneath my fingertips, on my face, my breasts. Scratchy and rough and perfect and…

Oh, God. Here it comes.

4

I turned on the exhaust fan to drown out the noise, then dropped to my knees and—

He didn't show up.

—vomited quietly. Vomited forever.

I washed my hands, brushed my teeth and tongue vigorously, relishing the mint, then bleached the toilet clean and washed my hands again. Lavender soap. Mint and lavender. They danced together in my mind, more colors than scents, and that was even better.

I looked at my reflection, practiced my smile, and walked back out into the living room. Kim and I talked for a few minutes about infant car seats, then I excused myself. I wandered to the guest bedroom, my home for the past five months, lay down on the bed, and fell asleep in my clothes. Slept forever.

CHAPTER 2

"You're not driving sixty miles on those roads."

I sipped my coffee.

"*Tess...*"

I could do that, too. I cocked my head and gave a scowl. "*Dave...*"

"I mean it."

I looked over his head, out the window. I'd slept for nineteen hours. During that time a foot and a half of snow had fallen. Winter had waited until March to start. Global warming probably. It was melting ice caps and making all the polar bears drown so why shouldn't it fuck with my life, too?

"I'll call and reschedule," I said.

He nodded. Proud. Big brother, heap big man. Kim said nothing, only smiled.

"You're not eating your breakfast." His victory had made him overly confident.

"That's because you made eggs. Eggs are an ingredient, not a meal."

"You need some protein. You're pale."

"I'm pale because I don't eat eggs?"

He didn't answer. Defeat. Can't win 'em all. He finished his coffee, wiped his mouth then stood up. All six foot three of him. Then he left, with a quick kiss for Kim and another stern look for me. Off to battle Injustice. He won most of those.

I brushed my teeth and headed back downstairs. Kim was lying on the couch, practicing her breathing. I poked her big, fat stomach and was rewarded with a kick. "How's Hezekiah doing today?"

She glared at me. She hated being poked almost as much as she hated hearing me call her son Hezekiah. I couldn't blame her.

"He's restless. I wish he'd hurry up and come out."

I shook my head. "He's still cooking. Two more weeks?"

"Twelve days."

"Ah."

"Is your cell phone charged?"

I checked. "Yep."

"Drive slowly. *Please?*"

I nodded. "I'll see you this afternoon."

The roads were slick. The speed limit on the interstate was down to forty-five and I set my cruise accordingly. Life sucked, but it was better than the alternative and I felt better than I had in months. I knew why. Sleep. It's like sex. You know it's good, but you don't know just how good until you're not getting any.

I got into New Mills at ten o'clock. I was half an hour early and the apartment was only five miles outside of town—if what I was driving through could be called "town." New Mills was, indeed, a small lakeside community. In addition to its apparent rampant teenage drug problem

7

and a brutal slaying, New Mills was known for having once been home to a textile mill and a shoe factory. Hence the horrid name. Both plants had closed their doors, like most mills and factories in the state, and those jobs were now in the hands of people who lived south and east of town. Very far south and very far east. By people who spoke Spanish and Chinese and were willing to work for a few bucks a day.

Most of those former mill workers had lost their homes to foreclosure and back taxes. They'd been sold to foreigners who were only too happy to buy up a lovely, small Maine community so they could have a pretty place to spend their summers. Foreigners from south and west of town. They spoke English—if Massachusetts, New York, and Connecticut accents could be considered English—and had surnames like Talbot and Caldwell and Pratt. They were foreigners nevertheless. Still, former mill workers didn't hire cleaning ladies. Talbots and Caldwells and Pratts did.

I glanced at the notes I'd jotted down twenty-four hours earlier. Typical rural directions: very vague with only landmarks as a guide.

...turn left at the sand shed...another three miles out...turn right onto the road across from the big lake...about a mile, first mailbox on the right...

The place was hidden from the road by thick, bushy pines and naked maples. The driveway was a little rough but already plowed, which was a good sign. The house itself was white. Two stories. Small and very old. Old enough to explain the low rent. Enclosed porch with lots of windows. There was no garage or barn, but there was a decent-sized shed beside the house. It was white, too, but looked

8

much newer than the house. And beside that stood a little orchard with five bare, snowy apple trees.

There were no other vehicles in the driveway. I parked facing the orchard, kept the car running. Stared out the window at the trees. The heater was running at full blast. I still shivered. I'd been shivering for five months.

No. I'd been shivering longer than that.

My heart was Titanium White. Arctic Wasteland. Hard, trampled soil covered with ice. The frozen orchard seemed to say that it always would be and the tears came. Finally. Stinging and bitter, but quiet like always, and I looked away from the trees, looked down at the dashboard. Oil light flashing, neon red. I stared at it, tried to imagine my engine: tired, hot, low on precious blood. The neon light liquefied, blurred, floated as my eyes filled past the point of choking it all back. I glanced up to let them spill over, hoping I'd be able to dam up what would want to follow. Squinted my eyes against the tears.

And that's when I saw it.

Bare, icy trees, eerie and still. They almost looked dead, but they were really only sleeping. Waiting for spring. The red light caught in the pool of tears, refracted, projected, and I could see it. I could see what the orchard would look like covered with blossoms. In the spring. Alizarin Crimson, Dusty Pink—starry, superimposed on the wintry scene. Like covering a photo with a clear sheet of plastic then drawing on it with dried-out marker: shadowy and transparent. But real. So real.

God, I know it's been a while and I hate to ask, but...please... please let me be able to paint the orchard. The way it looks right... now...

Two streams, hot on my cheeks, and the blossoms disappeared. I wiped my face, took a deep, deep cleansing
breath, and checked my reflection in the rearview mirror. Cleaned up the makeup. Righted the mirror. Saw,
coming at me, a big yellow plow attached to a bigger
red truck. I took another deep breath then practiced my
smile. I thought about the orchard and the smile didn't
feel fake.

I hopped out of my car and examined the truck beside
me. It didn't seem possible that the clunker managed to
hold onto its plow, let alone that it was strong enough to
use it to push aside snow and ice. There was faded black
lettering on the door:

LaChance Builders. And a phone number.

The driver got out and strolled toward me. I wondered
how many of the calls he got were actually work-related
and how many were local women hoping to reach out and
touch someone. He was tall and sturdy. His eyes were Van
Dyke Brown. So was his hair and it almost touched his
shoulders. Probably mid-twenties, twenty-seven at the most.
He was good-looking and he knew it, but not arrogant, the
same way a person knows they've got blue eyes or big boobs
or straight teeth. Genetics. Luck of the draw.

He nodded his greeting. I nodded back and said, "Shit.
I've got the wrong house."

He laughed like it was the funniest thing he'd ever
heard. And then I saw it. Something other than Van Dyke
Brown in the eyes. I recognized the Something right away
and it made me smile again.

He smiled right back. "Tess Dyer?"

I cleared my throat. "Yeah."

"Brian LaChance. I live downstairs." He held out a hand and I slipped off my mitten to shake it. Bare, warm, calloused. "Charlie's running a little late so he wants me to show you around till he gets here. Not," he added, "that it'll take that long. It's kinda small."

I liked his voice. Deep. Maine French. Probably called his grandparents Memé and Pepé.

He led the way. Cozy porch. Two doors. His was on the right, mine on the left. He unlocked my door then looked back at me. "Don't worry. I don't usually have this key."

I just nodded.

We clomped up the stairs. He was three steps ahead of me. I knocked some snow off my boots while he unlocked the top door. I heard it open and looked up.

His ass was right there. Right. There.

I missed the step, slipped, grabbed the railing. I hung on with both hands and got my feet underneath me. He reached down and grabbed my arm.

"You okay?"

I nodded, then tried to explain away my clumsiness: "Icy boots."

He helped me up the rest of the stairs, let go of my arm once I reached the top step, and I followed him inside. He was right. It was kinda small. Kitchen and dining area to the left, living room to the right. All open. Tiny bathroom. Small bedroom. But lots of windows and an extra storage closet. No tiny turds in the cupboards. No mold or mildew in the bathroom or on the window sills. Only one problem I could see.

"How does he feel about his tenants painting the walls?"

"Well, you can paint 'em any color you like. As long as you like white."

It's what I'd figured. Jason and I had been forced to keep the walls in our apartment beige. Beige was even worse than white.

"He's a good guy, though. Pretty easygoing about most things. Oh, come here."

I followed him over to the living room closet. He closed the door and pointed to the wall. There was a gash there from the doorknob.

"You show him that. Tell him you'll fix it and he'll let you in without a security deposit."

"I don't know how to—"

"I'll do it for you. Slap on a coat of mud, let it dry, sand it. It'll blend right in. Piece of cake."

"Ah. Well…I'll think about it."

He nodded, and his gaze fell to the brooch that was pinned on front of my coat. He examined it for a few seconds then said, "Do you know you've got a stone missing?"

"Yeah."

He stared at me for a few moments, waiting for an explanation, but I didn't feel like giving him one. Fortunately I was rescued by a heavy clomp, clomp, clomping from the staircase. I looked out the window and saw a newish-looking blue truck sitting in front of the porch steps. It made Brian's seem even more dilapidated than it had before.

"Sorry I'm late, Mrs. Dyer." Charlie Baxter, huffing and puffing. Looked about seventy. He had a red face, white hair, and a big pot belly. Bigger than Kim's.

Ho ho ho.

12

I shook his hand and debated on whether or not to correct the *Mrs.* The reasons for and against such a correction were actually only one reason and he was standing right behind me.

It's only been twenty-four hours, Tess. Don't fuck the nice neighbor boy.

Twenty-five hours. And-a-half.

I left the *Mrs.* uncorrected.

Brian tossed Charlie the key and left us to dicker. I decided on the No Security Deposit Plan and wrote him a check for first and last months' rent. Yes, white was the only acceptable wall color; yes, I could move in this Sunday; and yes, I could plant a flower garden in the spring, so long as I kept it weeded.

Charlie left and I looked around the apartment again. Alone. Damn.

I trotted carefully down the stairs. Brian was loitering on the porch.

"So. We're gonna be neighbors."

"Yep."

"Need any help moving in?"

"Oh. Uh…"

Light bulb. *He's wondering about the Mrs.*

Well. He'd find out sooner or later. Why not sooner?

"I'm living with my brother, Dave, right now. He has a truck and most of my stuff's at his place anyway. My dad's not really up to lugging shit upstairs—"

Completely untrue. But if he came then my mother would come.

"—but I think Dave and I can manage okay."

I could see him tallying the score. Brother: check. Dad: check. Husband: nope. Then he gave me a big smile. I gave him one right back.

Twenty-six hours, Tess. Cut it out.

Then he looked at me a little dubiously. "What are you? Five-foot-three?"

I scowled. Almost literally. "Five-five."

With my boots on.

"Yeah. Tell your brother I'll be here to help Sunday morning."

I walked out the door without answering. My car was frosted over just a little. I started it, turned the defroster on high, and stepped outside again for another view of the orchard. Bare and icy.

Not for long, Tess. Spring is coming...

On my way back through town I stopped at every business I came to, full of sympathy over the recent loss of their beloved cleaning lady, Mrs. Arsenault. I handed out three pages of references at each one. The doctor, a real estate agent, and an insurance company all hired me on the spot, happy to have me start cleaning their offices next week. Because, naturally, all my references were glowing ones.

I might be Brookfield's town whore, but I could sure scrub the hell out of a toilet.

CHAPTER 3

All of my worldly possessions—aside from my easel and art-work—fit neatly in the back of my brother's truck. It wasn't a fact I was proud of. My mother surveyed it all with cold, blue eyes as Dave and my dad covered it over with a tarp. I braced myself. Clenched my jaw. My hands. My stomach...

"You should have kept the bigger table, Theresa."

You should have worked things out with Jason.

"That one wasn't mine. It was his before we got married."

I don't take things that aren't mine. Or keep them when they're not mine anymore.

"You should have bought a new table for yourself, then. A bigger table."

Too bad you don't make enough money to buy yourself some decent furniture.

"My new apartment's too small for a bigger table."

I'm not a materialistic bitch like you.

"Then you need a bigger apartment."

You really are pathetic.

"Just so I can have a bigger table?"

It was weak but it was the last word and that, at least, was something. Because that's when Dave said, "Ready to go, Tess?"

You're goddamn right I am. "Uh, yeah. Let me just go say goodbye to Kim."

She was in the living room, sitting on the rocking chair. She was a beautiful woman, even though she was puffy with pregnancy weight. Black hair, olive complexion, and eyes that always reminded me of old-fashioned photographs...

I hope the baby gets those eyes.

She stretched noisily and grimaced. "Everything packed?"

"Yep. Back hurting again?"

"Not again. *Still.*"

"Only nine more days."

She groaned, struggled to her feet, and looked at me silently for a few moments. I knew what she was thinking. She said it anyway.

"Dave's worried about you moving so far away."

"He shouldn't be. I'm thirty-four, for Christ's sake."

"I know, but...just promise me you'll take care of yourself."

So he doesn't have to.

I nodded and let her give me a hug. Even though I hated being hugged. And when I turned around my dad was there. I didn't have to worry about having to endure a hug from him. He was the very personification of New England Reticence. Even so, I could see that he—like Dave—was Worried About Me. He waited until Kim, recognizing her cue, left the room before he said, "How are you for money?"

"I'm all set." I wasn't, of course, and Dad knew it. Jason and I had spent more than thirteen years together with nothing tangible to show for it. No kids or pets. No real estate or anything of actual value. All we'd had, really, was our joint savings account: several thousand dollars that we'd saved toward a down payment on a house. No house in particular. Just, *Someday We'll Buy a House.* Because there's always Someday. Except that, of course, there wasn't.

Instead there were lawyers and papers to be signed. Things to be divided. A savings account to be split. And that's where things got tricky. Because I wouldn't take a penny of it, even though I had contributed nearly half. My lawyer could never understand why. It had puzzled even Jason, who sent me frequent messages—through the law-yers—that I should quit being so stubborn and take the damn money. But I was firm. I didn't want money. Didn't care about it. I only wanted what was mine. Not his. Not ours. Mine.

"Tess—"

"No, really. I've been living with Dave rent-free for five months. He wouldn't even let me give him anything for food or—"

"I still want to help."

"I appreciate it." I said it, even though I really didn't. "But...I'm all set."

He said nothing, just stared at me with tired, pale-green eyes. They were the only things he'd ever been stingy with, letting my brother and me inherit Blue from our mother. Well, he'd been stingy with his affection, too. But he was still a good man. And you can't have it all.

"Dad, I need to go."

He nodded his goodbye. And I nodded right back.

I pulled out of the driveway, smiled as I saw my mother shrinking in the rearview mirror. We had to pass by Hillside Café on our way to the interstate and I noticed, with sudden longing, that the sign outside was lit up. I couldn't stop, though. Even if there was no Coach to worry about, there was a Dave right behind me.

No cloud today.

Once we hit the interstate I divided the time pretty evenly between glancing at the road and watching the miles tick by on my tripometer. At mile thirty-one, exactly halfway between Brookfield and New Mills, I pulled into the passing lane to let a string of cars merge into traffic. They were coming from Westville, population eighteen thousand; the closest thing to a city this part of the state had. Its highlights included a Walmart, a McDonald's, a bar, a hospital, and a State Police station. Everything an area swarming with Displaced Workers could possibly need.

Another thirty-one miles and we were there. My new home. I pulled in beside Brian's truck and Dave backed up close to the porch steps. He met me near the tailgate and we untied the tarp. Then he nodded toward the clunker.

"You didn't tell me this guy's in construction."

I coiled the four short pieces of yellow nylon rope around my hand, tied them tightly together, and tossed the wad at Dave. "I told you he's about as tall as you and wouldn't have a problem helping you carry my shit up the stairs. What else did you need to know?"

The first question people insist on asking a new acquaintance is: *What do you do for a living?* I hated that. Insecurity, probably, because I'm not a lawyer or a doctor or any of those other professions that make people say, *Oh...* in that reverent, awestruck way. And anyone unlucky enough to ask me that fatal question without preceding it with at least two others—for example, *what books have you read lately* or *who's your favorite ballplayer*—was answered with:

"I'm a lumberjack."

Because any person with a greater interest in what it is I do to earn enough money to afford rent and music and beer and food and jeans—rather than in the fact that I think Bill Lee is the coolest guy ever to climb onto the pitcher's mound—deserves to think I spend my days in the woods cutting down trees.

The porch door slammed shut and the man in question trotted over, zipping up a red hooded sweatshirt. He gave Dave's truck a quick once-over. "That's all you've got?"

"Hello to you, too."

He grinned. "Why, hello, Tess. I sure hope you had a nice drive down."

"Oh yes. It was lovely."

"So...that's all you've got?"

"Yep."

Dave cleared his throat. I made the introductions and held my breath. He reached for Brian's outstretched hand, gave him a long, hard stare, then fixed me with one. The look on his face was identical to the time when, at the age of twelve, he solved his Rubik's Cube half an hour after he brought it home from the store. I gave him a sideways kick and said, as sweetly as I could, "Dave's a lawyer."

Brian raised his eyebrows, awestruck, and said, his voice appropriately reverent, "*Oh.*"

"So, Brian. Do you own this place?" Dave was in full Big Brother Protector mode and I did my best not to laugh at the image that was probably haunting him.

Hey, Mr. Landlord, I'm afraid I'm a little short on the rent money this month.

That's okay, baby. I'm sure we can work something out.

Brian saw it too. "I...uh...*no*. No I don't. I just rent the bottom...the downstairs. The apartment downstairs."

Dave gave him a grim nod, then turned to open the tailgate. They had, maybe, a half hour's work ahead of them. With Dave in his present mood I decided it would be kind to throw Brian a lifeline. I got his attention and mouthed, *Fishing*. Did my best cast-a-rod impression, in case he misread my lips. He nodded, grateful. I grabbed my bucket of cleaning supplies from my trunk and made my escape upstairs.

They made three trips up and down before Brian noticed what I was doing. Told me all about the recently departed Cathy Arsenault. Charlie had hired her a week before she died and she'd cleaned the whole place. Kitchen, bathroom, floors...everything is spic and span, Tess. Nothing to worry about.

That interested my brother.

"She died?"

"Yeah," Brian said. "Last week. A couple of teenagers broke into her house. She was home sick with a stomach flu and when they found her home they freaked out and... uh, killed her."

I wrung the dirty water out of my rag and prepared myself for the onslaught.

"You moved to a town where they're killing cleaning ladies?"

"Don't get your panties in a bunch. *A* cleaning *lady*. It's not like there's a Clorox Serial Killer roaming the streets of New Mills."

Brian laughed. "You're a cleaning lady?"

I gave him a hard stare. "Do you have a problem with cleaning ladies?"

"No...I just mean...is that why you moved here? Because you heard about Cathy?"

"Well, we all gotta eat."

"Yep. That's true enough."

Dave was ready to get us back on topic. "They broke into her house and killed her?"

Brian nodded.

Brutal slaying. How had she died? The newspaper hadn't said. Had those kids shot her? Beaten her to death? Stabbed her? Did she live long enough to know what was happening to her? Already miserable from a stomach flu that was bad enough to keep her home from work. Lying on the couch, watching *The Price Is Right.* Then...the door bursts open. Or the window breaks. Then there's fear. Pain. Calling for help, her husband, her mother, calling for anyone. What about her family? Had her kids discovered her body? Get off the school bus, run to the front door. Expecting hot chocolate and a *how was your day* and some help with homework. And there she is. Dead. Brutally murdered in their own home.

Is that the last thought that floated in front of her before she died? *Please, God, don't let my kids find me like this...*

I looked up at Dave. He was glaring at me. I hated that. Then he looked at Brian.

"They were on drugs. Right?"

Brian nodded again. "They tried Cathy's house because her husband died of cancer a month or so ago, and they figured she'd have some Oxycontin left over."

"You moved into a town where there's a drug problem."

"'A *rampant* teenage drug problem,'" I quoted.

He glared even harder. We are not amused.

"Dave, please point me in the direction of any town where there isn't a drug problem. I'll be very happy to settle there instead. Besides, New Mills is a pretty small town. How bad can it possibly be?"

I looked over at Brian for support and saw something else instead. The truth. It was pretty bad. He tried to come to the rescue anyway.

"Those kids leave us alone over here. They're usually too busy breaking into the camps on the lake looking for stuff they can sell."

I chuckled. "Well, at least that's something I don't have to worry about."

Dave said nothing to that, because what can you say? He just shook his head and went back downstairs, with Brian on his heels. By the time they were done unloading the rest of my stuff, the kitchen was clean. And Dave was ready to leave. I knew why. Even though he didn't say it. Even though I'd spent the morning trying not to think about it.

Jason.

He was at the house waiting for Dave to get back. Or on his way there. Because they had repair work to do, lots of it. The kind they couldn't do during the winter when they'd really needed to. Not with Tess the Pest hanging around. So I smiled. Thanked him for the help. And then I paused. The great debate. Because what I wanted to say next was:

Make sure you ask him why he didn't come to court. Didn't even show up. Couldn't spare a goddamn half hour from his busy fucking schedule. He's the one who ended it. And he couldn't even show his face. Couldn't see the thing through to the end.

But there are some things you just can't say. Not to your brother and not to anyone. And so I was stuck with:

"Don't forget to call me when Kim goes into labor."

He gave me a half-hearted smile and said he wouldn't forget to call. Thanked Brian for the help. Then he lingered at the door. Finally looked me in the eye and I saw what Kim had warned me about. Worry. More than that. He was nearly frantic. I could almost feel it coming off of him. But he said only, "You're sure you're okay?"

Of course I'm not okay. It's all new. Everything. And I'm all alone now. For real.

But I couldn't say that, either. He'd already told me not to leave so hastily. *There's no rush, Tess. Stay as long as you need.* And I knew that he'd really meant, *Stay here with us, where you're safe. Or at least stay close by. Where I can watch you. Where I can keep you from messing up your life.* Because he knew, of course, that I probably would. But I'd said, *Nope, it's time to leave now.* And it was, really. He'd protected me from myself for five long months. He looked it, too. He and Kim needed their home back. Their life back. So. Here I was.

"I'm fine."

I wasn't, of course. And he knew it. He looked over at Brian again and then back at me. Because he knew something else. But there wasn't anything he could do about it. So he said, "Well, I'll see you later." Then he closed the door before I could say goodbye.

And so I was alone. For real.

Well, not really. Not yet.

I turned toward Brian but couldn't look him in the eye. Not right away. Because I knew what he'd see in mine. And I knew that it was pathetic. Knew that I was pathetic. I took a deep cleansing breath, like the kind I'd been practicing with Kim, and it worked. I looked up at him and managed a smile. He smiled back and said:

"First baby?"

"Yeah. First grandchild in the family, too."

"You guys must be excited, then."

I only shrugged.

Silence. But he still didn't leave. And that meant it was my turn to make a contribution.

"Sorry about the way he acted when we first got here. He can be a Neanderthal sometimes."

"I've got a sister, so I know where he's coming from."

More silence. He looked at the boxes littering the floor.

"Want some help unpacking?"

"No, I'm all set."

"You're sure?"

"Yep. Not much here, really."

There wasn't, really, and I couldn't let this guy rummage through my coffee mugs and underwear. But I didn't want him to leave. Didn't want to be alone. So I let my gaze fall on my stereo and speakers. The television. The cheap, unassembled pressboard entertainment center I'd bought only days before, still in the box. Then I looked back at him. Because I knew already.

Mr. Fix It.

He smiled, took off his sweatshirt, and went to work. I left him to it and started on the kitchen boxes. But before I was halfway through my precious collection of coffee mugs, I heard him laughing. I turned around to see why. He was looking inside a plastic shopping bag. Inside it were the wires to all the electronic gizmos. Each of them was neatly coiled, held together with a little bread-bag twist tie. I always saved those things because *you never know when one might come in handy*.

"Why is that funny?"

"Oh, it's not. It's not funny at all."

"Shut up."

He didn't, of course. He talked while he worked. A lot. About skyrocketing property values and how unfair it was that people whose families had lived in New Mills for generations couldn't afford to buy a decent home. About a television show he'd seen recently about paparazzi pho-tographers who stalked celebrities and how *there oughtta be a law against that sort of thing*. But he seemed most upset about an article he'd read in the paper the day before about campaign contributions and he wondered what had happened to the principles of having a government that was of the people, by the people, and for the people rather than of, by, and for big corporations.

I nodded a lot and made very intelligent replies like *yeah* and *uh huh* and *nope* while I unpacked my dishes. Finally he said, "Well, I'm all done here. Bring me a CD and I'll adjust the sound levels for you."

My music collection didn't impress him.

"Everything in here is at least twenty years old."

"You say that like it's a bad thing."

"That's because it is."

I shoved Neil Young at him.

"Uh…no." He looked through the box again and settled, without any real enthusiasm, on Bob Dylan. Once the music started he busied himself, pushing buttons and adjusting levers. "Does that sound better?"

It didn't sound any different to me than it had before he'd made the adjustments, but I nodded anyway and said, "Sounds great."

He shrugged. "You can't do much to it with this kind of music. You're gonna need something with lots of bass and a beat to really do the job."

I had never listened to anything with lots of bass and a beat. I didn't need to start now.

"You can't really dance to this, either," he said.

"I can't dance, so it's just as well."

He smiled. "I bet you can and you just don't know it."

I stared at him. At his eyes. They were fucking gorgeous, but it's not why I stared. There was something there again, a Something that scared the shit out of me. The words, of course, were an invitation. I knew that. I'd been waiting for it. It just wasn't the invitation I'd been expecting. Because his eyes didn't say *why don't you just forget about these boxes for a while so we can fuck all afternoon*. Not that dance. They said Something Else.

The other dance.

I looked away, because I knew what it was my eyes were saying. Then I forced my mouth to say, "I'd better go unpack the bathroom."

He wasn't deterred. "Are you hungry?"

"Nope."

"Liar. I'm meeting some friends for lunch in a few minutes. You should come with me."

"I'll eat later. I've got too much to do right now."

He nodded. Looked around the room. "Maybe. But I don't think any of those boxes have any food in them. Are you planning on eating packing peanuts or what?"

"I'll run into the market in a little while."

"Great. You can do it after we eat."

I really was starved. What was left of the coffee and toast I'd eaten for breakfast wouldn't be enough to keep me going long enough to finish unpacking. But.

That dance?

I looked at him again and sighed. Food. Meet new people. Groceries. I did need that. Needed all of those things. And so I followed him into town.

CHAPTER 4

His truck sputtered and stalled but somehow managed to make it into town. We drove right past two restaurants that were both very sorry for being closed for the season and pulled instead into a diner called Fran's.

He opened the door for me and I walked inside, feeling assaulted in every possible way. The air was heavy with the smell of pizza sauce, deli meats, and fried things, and there was a general commotion of kids screaming and laughing, arcade games beeping and, most noticeably, a loud juke-box pounding out the beat of an unfamiliar pop tune—the exact sort of music that would never find its way into my CD collection. My empty, growling stomach was the only thing that prevented me from making a beeline for the door.

A thin, petulant girl who appeared to be in her late teens stood behind the counter. Her dark brown hair was streaked with white-blonde chunks and pinned up into an intricate up-do. It made me more self-conscious than ever about my own sloppy, gray-rooted locks. Brian gestured to her and whispered, "That's my sister."

I looked at her more closely and nodded, noting the resemblance. She caught sight of us walking toward her and rolled her eyes. They were Van Dyke Brown, like her brother's, but so hazy and bloodshot that I had to smother a jealous grin. She raised an eyebrow at Brian and said, "Don't you ever cook?"

"Nope. Jeff and Laura here yet?"

"Nope. Zeke's out back in the bar. He wants to see you."

"How come?"

"How the fuck should I know?"

He gave her eyes a hard stare. "Uh huh."

"Just go talk to him and get it over with." She nodded toward me. "Can't you see I've got customers to deal with?"

He sighed and gave me a quick, "I'll be back in a sec." Then he walked down a long hallway and through a set of double doors.

She grabbed her pen and notebook from the counter. "What can I get for you?"

"Veggie Italian. Diet soda."

She shuddered, hollered back my order and took my money. And stared. I hated that. When she gave me my change I pocketed the coins and shoved the bills into her tip jar. I'd been on her side of the counter so I knew. You can't live on minimum wage. That cheered her up a bit and she managed a real smile as she said:

"You're Tess."

I glanced at her nametag. She'd pinned it on upside down. "You're Rachel."

She glanced back toward the doors her brother had disappeared through and asked, "So. What do you think of him?"

The question caught me off guard even though it shouldn't have. I stumbled through a variety of vowel sounds before managing, "He's…I think he's nice."

She laughed loudly at that. I wasn't sure if she was laughing at me or if everything was funny to her in her present condition. Once she recovered she gave me a smirk and said, "'Nice.' *Right.* I'm sure 'nice' is the first adjective that popped into your head."

I knew this game. I returned the volley with, "Actually, the first was, *wicked hot.* Then came, *sweet ass.* So I guess that makes *nice* number three."

That got another laugh. "I'm sure he'll be glad to hear it."

Home: 1. Visitors: 0.

She handed me a ticket, number 76. Just like the Bicentennial. I shoved it into my pocket and headed for the restroom. I inspected the toilet and decided I could wait until I got home. Washed my hands and examined my hair. It sucked. I shook it out, twisted it into a half-hearted ponytail, then opened my purse to debate my lipsticks. Red or pink. I looked up at my tired reflection and decided on Chapstick instead. Heaved a great sigh and entered the arena again.

Brian was leaning back against the counter upon my return, but Rachel was nowhere in sight. "Howdy." He said it just like a cowboy.

"Hi."

"My friends are here." He gestured toward the corner booth. His posse waved. "I've already told them all about you."

All about me? What did he know? Cleaning lady. Foul mouth. Big tits. Big, obnoxious brother. Can't climb stairs. "Lead me to them."

He guided me through the obstacle course of the dining area. Red and white checkered plastic tablecloths, white and brown plastic salt and pepper shakers. Families out for a nice lunch. He nodded a greeting to nearly every table, singled out husbands and kids, diplomatically ignored staring wives.

Then, his table. He made the introductions and I took turns shaking their hands. The Burkes. They were dressed up. Probably came here right from church. Jeff had sandy hair and was big enough to be a football player, but wore dark-framed, deliberately nerdy glasses. The contrast made me like him immediately. Laura was skinny and pale, but very pretty, like a porcelain doll. Lots of wavy hair that was too auburn to be natural and her makeup was Just So. She seemed genuinely friendly, like someone who was used to working with the public and liked it. I took off my coat, slung it across the back of my chair, and sat down.

Brian looked around the room. "Their daughter is running around here somewhere. Where is the little pinhead?"

Laura said, "She's playing video games in the other room." Then she turned her attention to me. "So, how do you like New Mills?"

"It's a pretty town." I hadn't been here long enough to add anything of substance to my review.

"It's a lot smaller than Brookfield, isn't it?"

"Brookfield isn't exactly a huge town."

Jeff laughed. "Maybe not, but your boys still manage to kick ass in the basketball tourneys every year."

I managed a *we sure do* that made it sound like I was sufficiently proud of the Hometown Heroes. Basketball was a sore subject with me but Jeff had no way to know that. He was just making polite conversation with the woman who'd been forced on his family's lunch.

We continued on with the small talk, because that's what you do when you make a new acquaintance. Jeff sold cars at his dad's dealership in Westville. He could give me the names of some businesses he knew of there that hadn't yet found a replacement for the recently departed Mrs. Arsenault. I thanked him and nodded, because it was a nice gesture, and didn't tell him that I wasn't interested in traveling that far for work if I could help it. I didn't want to set the world on fire. All I really cared about was making enough money for rent and music and beer and food and jeans. Maybe enough to put aside for the oil bill in the winter.

But when Laura told me she worked at a hair salon right in town that was still looking to hire someone to clean I was interested in more than just the work. The salon back in Brookfield was Gossip Central and I'd avoided the place all winter long.

"I'm so overdue for a trim," I said.

She cast a quizzical eye over my hair and I could see she agreed wholeheartedly. She handed me a business card that had her hours written on the back and told me to pop in. Soon.

Rachel's voice boomed our order numbers over the loudspeakers. I stood up but Brian waved me back down. "Me and Jeff'll get it."

I gave Laura an awkward smile and tried to think of something to say. She returned the smile, apparently as inept at small talk as me. After about thirty full seconds of silence, she turned toward the counter and I followed her gaze. Brian and Rachel were in the middle of what was obviously a heated exchange. Laura and I turned to each other simultaneously, relieved that a topic for conversation had presented itself. Laura started.

"Zeke—that's Rachel's boss—told Brian that he's going to suspend her for a couple days if she comes in stoned again."

I didn't ask why the boss had bugged Brian about it, only nodded sympathetically. Brian was still upset when they returned a minute or so later, accompanied by the Burkes' daughter. She introduced herself as Cassidy Rose Burke. She was eight years old and very proud of it. She had auburn hair that proved Laura's to be natural after all and something about her was familiar. Not just because she looked like her dad. It was something else, someone she reminded me of, but I couldn't quite place it.

Brian handed me my sandwich with a shudder. "Veggie Italian? What the hell?"

"Shut up."

And then things were quiet for a few minutes while we ate, at least as quiet as they could be inside a crowded family diner, until Cassidy pointed to my coat. "Your pin is broken. Did you drop it?"

I finished chewing a cucumber and said, "I bought it that way. Last summer at a yard sale."

"You bought a broken pin on purpose?"

I nodded, unfastened the brooch from my coat and handed it to her to look at more closely. It was an odd-looking piece of costume jewelry, oval-shaped with four pieces of round, cut glass. A fake emerald, fake amethyst, and fakes of whatever gems were naturally orange and light blue. One stone was missing. I liked to think it had been a fake ruby.

"Why did you buy it if it's broken?"

"Because the lady I bought it from told me a cool story about how it got broken."

She bounced in her seat. "Ooh! What's the story?"

I was exhausted, and not really in the mood for Storytime. But she looked so excited and she was so damn cute. And she reminded me of someone. Who the hell was it? I wiped my mouth, took a sip of my diet soda and cleared my throat.

"The lady I bought it from, her grandmother had just died and the pin belonged to her. She got it when she was young, back in the thirties, from her boyfriend—"

"Didn't they call them *beaux* back then?"

"Uh...I don't know. Maybe."

"Scarlett O'Hara called her boyfriends *beaux*."

That didn't go over well with Jeff. "How the hell do you know anything about Scarlett O'Hara?"

"Grammy let me watch *Gone With the Wind* at her house last week."

Jeff rolled his eyes and shot Laura a look. She only shrugged. I waited a few seconds before I went on with the story.

"The *beau* bought the pin for the girl because he knew she liked colorful things, and she loved it. More than anything. Time went by and they got engaged, but a month before the wedding the *beau* lost his job."

"Did he get fired?" Cassidy asked.

She probably didn't know what the Great Depression was, unless Laura's mom had let her watch *Grapes of Wrath*. I didn't want to go off on another tangent so I told her that the mill where he worked closed down. She nodded to let me know it was a concept she was familiar with.

"The girl's parents wouldn't let them get married until the guy got another job. So he packed his suitcase and headed to New York City to look for work. The poor guy was only there a week and he got mugged. He didn't have a whole lot of money to begin with and they took what little he had left. So there he was. Stuck in New York with no money and no job and no place to live."

That sounded fair to Cassidy. "That'll teach him to go where the Yankees live."

"The girl's parents apparently thought so too, because when they found out about it they made her break the engagement and set her up with someone else, some guy they'd wanted her to marry all along. And in the meantime the first guy, the *beau*—"

It really was the silliest word in the English language, but she literally squealed with delight every time I said it.

"—found out about his fiancé marrying another guy and he became determined to get rich. Just to show the woman and her family what was what. And that's just what he did."

I took another sip of my soda. I wasn't used to talking quite so much.

"He got a job at a furniture store in New York. And he worked really, really hard and after many, many years he opened his own store. And that got bigger and bigger until finally he had lots of stores all over the East Coast. He was very, very rich and he got married to a really rich woman—"

"I'll bet he didn't really love *her*," Cassidy said, her eyes gleaming merrily. "Rich people never marry for love."

"True. Anyway, he came back to Maine with his new wife so he could say—"

Fuck you and the horse you rode me out of town on. It's what I would've said.

"'How do ya like me *now?*' And by that time the woman's husband had died, but when her *beau* came back into town she was—"

Pissed because she missed out on the gravy train.

"—broken-hearted that he was married to someone else. And that's when she knew: They'd never be together. Ever. And so she grabbed that pin right out of her jewelry box and flung it against the wall. And it busted right... there. And the fake ruby fell out."

If I was going to tell this story I might as well do it right.

"She burst into tears when she saw what she'd done and tried to fix it, but she couldn't. But she kept it anyway so she'd always remember her *beau.*"

It really did sound better than *boyfriend.*

"She hid it in a shoebox along with a diary and a bunch of letters he'd written her. And her granddaughter found it, and that's how she learned the Story of the Broken Pin."

It was a little anticlimactic, and I wasn't the world's greatest storyteller, but it made her smile anyway. Every freckle on her face seemed to pop right off. And that's when I knew.

Anne of Green Gables. That's who the kid reminded me of.

"So," Laura asked, "who was the *beau?*"

"Beats me. Just some rich furniture guy. It couldn't have been anyone famous or she would've sold the pin to a dealer somewhere instead of sticking a three-dollar price tag on it for her yard sale."

Brian laughed. "You only paid three bucks for it?"

"Nope. A dollar. I talked her down."

"But it's an antique."

"Well, yeah. But it's broken."

"So you like it because it's broken, but because it's broken you only paid a buck for it."

"One buck, three bucks. It's all the same. I talked her down because it pissed me off that she was selling it. She should've kept it and handed it down as a family heirloom or something."

I went back to my sandwich. I'd neglected it and now the bread was a little soggy from the oil. I choked down a bite anyway.

Cassidy gave me back my pin. Then she asked, "Are you Brian's girlfriend?"

It had been a long time since anyone had made me blush. I snuck a quick peek at Brian. His face was burning up, too. I cleared my throat. "No, I'm not."

"That's too bad. Because you're nice."

Laura gave her a kick underneath the table.

"Well, she is."

"Uh, thanks. I think you're nice, too."

I finished my sandwich quickly and stood up to leave. Muttered a sincere *it was nice meeting you* to the Burkes and a *see you later* to Brian. He only nodded.

* * *

Small-town market. Narrow aisles. Customers who appraised me with expert eyes. Nice coat, but not new. Old boots. Worn-out, inexpensive jeans. Verdict: She's from out of town, but she's not From Away. And then they'd nod. That meant approval, a novel thing for me, so I nodded right back. I had a clean slate here. Best to take full advantage of it.

Checkout counter. I stood behind a young woman and her son. He was maybe five or six years old. Both of them were dirty. Smelly. Old, ripped clothes. Her groceries: a candy bar, a gallon of milk and a half-gallon bottle of Allen's Coffee Brandy. I clenched my teeth, because I knew. Even though it's wrong to judge a book by its cover. Even though I'd been judged—unfairly—too many times to count and knew better than to do it to someone else. I judged her anyway.

And I was right.

I'd never had a problem with the concept of State Aid. Food stamps or MaineCare or even welfare. Because sometimes people fall on hard times. Sometimes people work hard and still can't afford health insurance. Sometimes they roll out of bed one morning and find that their job has been shipped south or east. And that's when they need a helping hand. A little something to see them through the rough spots. I'd been there myself.

Then there were people like this woman.

She paid cash for the twenty-dollar bottle of liquor. Used her food stamp card for the candy bar and the milk. The milk that wasn't for her son. He wouldn't drink it with his supper tonight or dip any cookies in it for dessert or pour in onto his breakfast cereal in the morning. He looked up. Gave me a huge smile and I smiled right back. He had greasy blonde hair and big blue eyes. Probably the kids picked on him at school because his clothes were dirty. Because he smelled. Because his front two teeth were black and rotten. But underneath the dirt he was a beautiful child.

I wondered how much longer it would be before he realized exactly what kind of family he'd been born into. Before he understood that the twenty dollars his mother was using for liquor should have been used instead for soap and shampoo and laundry detergent. Would he grow up resentful? Bitter? Would he rise above it, determined to make a better life for himself? Or would he grow up thinking that it was normal to live that way?

The woman turned back, too. Glared at me. She knew what I was thinking and I didn't care. I wanted to say something to her. Wanted to tell her to go get some fucking help. Tell her that twenty bucks would buy a bar of soap and a bottle of shampoo and a box of cheap laundry detergent. Or maybe tell her about all the childless couples out there—out *there*—who would gladly take that little boy off her hands and give him a good life. A life that was filled with baths and toothbrushes. With leafy green veggies and cold milk. The kind of milk that was poured over breakfast cereal and not mixed with coffee brandy.

I didn't, of course. Because right now—right now—the boy was at least somewhat content. Living with a mommy who probably loved him at least a little. And he loved her. That much was obvious. Bad days were coming for him. I knew that, too. But right now, to him, today was the Day Mommy Bought Me a Candy Bar. I couldn't turn it into the Day Mommy Yelled at the Mean Lady in the Grocery Store. I couldn't do that to him. So I gave the woman an almost-friendly nod. Waved goodbye to the boy and watched them walk away. The little boy was holding his mommy's hand. Because right now he still loved her.

Then it was my turn to face to Agnes, the nosey cashier. Older than the hills. She quizzed me about my life while she scanned my groceries. Personal questions that no one except priests and very old ladies could get away with asking. I gave her cryptic answers and smiled politely. Even though I didn't feel like smiling.

Then home. I drove quickly because I was already tired and I had to finish unpacking. Brian was still out, and I remembered that Jeff had said something about a poker game. That meant silence. It meant I was going to spend the evening alone, for real. And, worst of all, it meant I was stuck lugging the groceries up the stairs by myself. Four trips up and down, but it was good exercise and I needed it. I'd spent the winter a slave to Kim's cake cravings and gained thirteen pounds in two months, most of it in my ass. It had taken me three months to lose eight of it.

I wanted to sit down for a break but I couldn't. Too much to do. I started by hanging my art up on the walls, which made it feel more like home. Even with the white paint. Then I tackled the remaining boxes. It didn't take too long to unpack every box but one, and that made it feel less like home. And then, finally, the bed.

I'd saved it for last—except for the box that I didn't want to open—because I knew. Temptation. The kind that would have whispered for me to leave the damn boxes for later and just get some sleep. I put the frame together. Box spring. Mattress. Hopped on it a little to make sure it was sturdy. It squeaked loudly in protest and that's when I remembered: this was once Our bed. Mine and Jason's.

And I tried not to remember all the things we'd done in it. Made love and cuddled and laughed and talked and fucked and made plans for The Future.

Sheets, blankets, pillows. And that was when I heard Brian's truck heading toward the house, maybe half a mile away. And that meant temptation, too. The kind that didn't whisper. I ran out into the living room and snapped off all the lights. Locked the front door then peeked out the window. He was just pulling into the driveway. I ran back into my bedroom, stripped naked and slipped between the sheets. Listened quietly.

His truck door slammed. Porch door, open and shut, then his front door. A muffled cough, a little banging around and another door closed, somewhere. Then nothing, for a long time. I felt myself fading. Drifting. Until…

…a sharp, wet snap, then a hiss. It scared me so badly that I bolted upright in bed. My heart bolted, too. Jumped into my throat, then back into place, and pounded against my chest. Then there was bubbling. Gurgling.

It's just the pipes, you idiot. Old house equals old pipes. Noisy pipes.

And then, of course, the other realization.

He was in the shower.

I lay back down even though I knew I wouldn't get to sleep right away. Not now. I tried anyway but the noise was still there. He was still there. In the shower. And even after the noise was gone I listened, still. I heard the door again—must be the bathroom door—and then another one. Bedroom door? Probably. Then silence once again. And still I didn't sleep. And so I gave in.

He'd been out of the shower for a long time, but in my mind he was still in there. Wet and naked and soapy. The hair on his chest was Van Dyke Brown. There was a little guilt, just a little, because he was right downstairs. And guilt, of course, because this was once Our bed. Mine and Jason's. Even though, now, it really was mine. But the guilt didn't stop me. And when I was done I rolled over. And finally slept.

CHAPTER 5

I woke before dawn to the sound of the weatherman bleating cheerfully from my radio alarm clock. Unseasonably warm, highs in the mid-sixties. I groaned out loud, because I knew what that meant: melting snow. It meant I'd waste the sunrise vacuuming rugs and scrubbing floors at a doctor's office and an insurance company, only to have them tracked up by clumsy, careless, muddy boots. And after half an hour it would be just like I hadn't been there at all. I went in anyway, of course, because it had been a week and a half since either place had seen a dust rag or a toilet bowl brush. It looked like it had been longer.

When I was done I hopped in my car, looked at my reflection in the rearview mirror, then drove to the salon where Laura worked. She gave my hair a thorough examination, shook her head, and hacked off three inches. Then it was time for hair color choices. I looked at the price list on the wall and did some quick math. It would be tight for a while, but I needed it. And while I sat in her chair with my hair covered in goo, Laura filled me in on the LaChance Family's History.

Brian and Rachel's mother was diagnosed with cancer when Brian was only ten, Rachel four. They had an alcoholic father who was never home. Went off to work then stayed out nights, drinking too much and cheating on his wife. Just like a country song, Laura said, but without the twang. Neither of us laughed because it wasn't funny.

She was sick for about two years. Chemotherapy, radiation the whole nine yards. And it didn't work. So one night she had to tell Brian that she was going away. That he had to look after Rachel. He had to be strong, even though he was still just a boy. Even though it wasn't fair. Because his father wouldn't do it.

"He's not going to stay," she said.

She died a week later. Brian was almost twelve. He dropped out of school at sixteen and started working with his father. Watched and worked and learned and waited. Waited for his mother's prophecy to come true. And it did, the day after Brian turned eighteen. As though his father had been waiting, too. Waiting until it was safe for him to leave. Even though he'd never really been there at all.

And so Brian took it all on his shoulders for real, even though he'd already been carrying most of the burden for years. He and Rachel moved into the apartment that Brian was still living in. Charlie took pity on them because he knew their situation well enough, let them rent it for practically nothing until Brian was able to turn his dad's business around. Because he'd left that in shambles, too.

Brian still carried it, all of that burden. Especially Rachel. Because she was on the verge of screwing up her life. Even though she was nineteen and on her own now, she was still his to look after. Probably, Laura said, he'd always feel that way.

I nodded and gave her a sympathetic smile. I knew why she'd told me the story even before she gave me a look that said:

He's had it rough. So be nice to him. Okay? Don't use him. Don't hurt him. Because he deserves better than that...

And she was right. Because, of course, we all did.

Then it was home again. Seventeen steps from the car to the porch stairs, four of those. Six to my door. Fourteen stairs up, into my apartment. First time I'd noticed.

I stumbled into bed and slept until six thirty. After a long shower I grabbed two beers from the fridge, took them into the living room and plopped them down on top of the big plastic bin that was sitting in front of my couch. It was clear with a lime-green cover and held all my sweaters except for the red one I was wearing. It was serving as a temporary coffee table, remarkably similar to the coffee table I'd had in my very first apartment. I'd constructed that one myself. Spray painted three white plastic crates in various neon shades and tied them together, lengthwise, with wire. Then I made two end tables for a matching set. At age eighteen plastic furniture is a symbol of freedom. Independence. It shouts, *Fuck you, World, I don't need any help.* At age thirty-four it whimpers, *I'm fucking pathetic.*

I made it quickly through my first beer and cracked open the second. Halfway through, I stared at the box I still hadn't opened. It claimed to contain three 182 ounce jugs of Clorox bleach. Because when you're a cleaning lady you buy your bleach in bulk. If I shoved the box into the back of my bedroom closet, right now, then in three days time

I'd have myself convinced that it really was a box containing three bottles of bleach. In a month or so I'd buy a real coffee table, scoot my plastic bin of sweaters in front of the bleach box and, the day after that, completely forget that the box of bleach was there.

I finished beer number two. Walked over to the box of bleach. Picked it up. And that's when my illusion was shattered before it even had a chance to begin. Because of one word. Jason's writing. Bold block letters on top of the box. Black permanent ink: **PHOTOS**. He had packed the box on his fateful last trip to our apartment then given it to Dave to give to me. I had shoved it, along with everything else, in Dave's garage. And now—apparently—it was Mine.

I chucked it back onto the floor, sat down beside it. Picked at the tape with my fingernail, loosened it with shaking fingers, then yanked quickly. It released the scent of fresh cardboard; the scent that seemed forever linked in my mind with goodbye.

"Oh, fuck that, Tess," I told myself. "Be a man and get it over with."

I crumbled up the tape, tossed it aside. Blindly grabbed a handful of pictures. Leaned back against the couch. And started to look through them.

It was a mistake.

Because there we were, Jason-and-Tess, captured in time. Trapped on dozens of four-by-six pieces of paper. I was holding our last vacation in my hand, our tenth anniversary weekend in Bar Harbor almost two years earlier. I flipped through the pictures slowly. Flipped through the memories. I closed my eyes and I was there again, surrounded by it. All six senses. The sharp, tangy scent of the ocean. Laughter—his and mine mingling together—as we imitated tourists' accents in the gift shops. His hand, strong and warm, resting on my leg while we drove around Park Loop at sunset. His trim, gorgeous beard, rough and hot against my cheek, my shoulder, my breasts; the sweet sting of the carpet on my back as we made love in our hotel room, ignoring the soft, giant bed...

I was almost there. Almost on the verge of tears. I could feel them threatening again, and this time I knew I wouldn't be able to stop. But then I heard it. Brian's truck, about half a mile away. I wiped my eyes and listened. Waited. Hoped.

Truck door slammed. Porch door. Then his footsteps up the stairs and a knock at the door. I chucked the pictures onto the coffee table, ran to the door, and greeted my rescuer with a sweet smile. Then I remembered my silent promise to Laura's silent plea and toned down the enthusiasm. If the sudden change in my demeanor surprised him he didn't show it. He just cleared his throat and said:

"Your hair looks good blonde."

"It's not blonde. It's..." Laura had called it 7NA. I called it Honey. "It's just a lighter shade of brown."

"Um...okay."

I nodded to the bag he was holding. RadioShack. "What's that?"

"This," he said, grinning, "is everything you need to get free cable TV."

"Amazing. And I thought it was just a bag."

He dug inside and pulled out two packages of wires. The kind that weren't coiled up and held together with bread-bag ties. "I've got the cable run through the wall from downstairs, so all I have to do is hook it up to your TV with these." He noticed my uncertainty. "I do it for all the upstairs people. The last couple took off with the splitter, so…" He held up one of the packages. "I had to get a new one."

"We won't get in trouble for this?"

"Nah. The cable guys never come all the way out here unless there's a problem, and when they do I disconnect everything until they leave."

"But is that fair? I get free cable, but you have to pay."

He shrugged. "I have to pay for it anyway."

"At least let me split the bill with you."

"Why? No one else ever did."

"I'm not a freeloader. I either pay for half or you don't hook it up."

He gave me a scowl and waited. Probably thought I'd change my mind if he did it long enough. I folded my arms and scowled right back.

"Fine." He sauntered past me, into the living room.

"You're going to do it right now?"

"Why, is it a bad time?"

"I guess not."

He went to work. Pulled the television out a little and fiddled with a few wires. Fiddled with some more. And when he was done he gave me a tour of the channels. There were almost a hundred of them and only five of them jumped out as something I'd actually watch. I thanked him anyway.

"That really is a nice sound system you got there."

I nodded. Jason had bought it three years earlier. It was ostensibly a birthday gift for me, though, and therefore Mine.

"Have you played anything on it since I hooked it up?"

"Yep. Neil Young sounded great while I was unpacking."

He rolled his eyes. "You know what you need?"

"Uh…"

"Gunshots and galloping horses—"

That was my second guess.

"—so I can fix the surround sound for you. And you're in luck, because there's a John Wayne double feature on tonight."

"John Wayne."

"Don't you like John Wayne?"

Chauvinistic He-man with a heart of gold. What's not to like? My dad had every one of his movies, which was pretty funny. I really should brush up on my Freud.

"I do, actually."

"Cool. *True Grit* starts at eight." He bounded over to the couch, taking the remote control with him. He set it down on the makeshift coffee table and picked up the pictures that I'd left out. Out in the open. Like an idiot.

I held out my hand. "Give them here. I'll put them away."

"You don't want me to see them?"

I considered for a few moments. What was the harm? They were just pictures after all. Slices of life trapped on dozens of four-by-six pieces of paper. Nothing to be afraid of.

I sat down beside him and shrugged. "Go ahead."

He stared at the photo on top. I leaned over to see what it was. Windy-Haired Tess on Cadillac Mountain.

"This is a real good picture of you," he said. He sounded sincere.

"Thanks."

He flipped to the next one. It was Golden-Haired Jason. His eyes were beautiful: clear, bright blue like the sky behind him. It was my favorite picture of him because he was smiling. It reminded me of how I used to live to see him smile.

"Your husband?"

"*Ex*-husband." It was the first time I'd said it. Ex. It tasted sour.

Brian studied the photograph for a few more seconds then continued through more of the Doomed Dyers' Bar Harbor Weekend. When he was finished he set them down gently on the bin and asked, "What does he do?"

I couldn't say *lumberjack*. Not about Jason. Because, like Dave, he didn't have the kind of job that was just a means to an end. Not only a way to earn money for food and rent and all the rest. It was his passion. His life. Who he was.

"He's a teacher."

Brian nodded and I looked at my bare feet, wishing I had painted my toenails instead of opening the box of bleach. Finally he asked, "What happened?"

"To what?"

"I mean…why didn't it work out?"

I cleared my throat. "Isn't it time for the movie to start?"

"Still got half an hour."

"Oh."

I chucked the pictures back into the bleach box. Glared at the plastic bin, as though it was to blame for all my troubles instead of just a representation of them. I looked at my toes again, praying for inspiration. A topic for conversation. Anything. And my eyes fell on my two empty bottles. I asked him if he'd like a beer and he gave a reluctant nod. We drank in silence for a while while he scanned the canvases on my walls. He'd nod at one, smile at another. I followed his slow gaze until he got to the last painting. We shivered at the same time.

"Isn't that Mount Kineo? On Moosehead Lake?"

"Yep. Have you ever been there?"

"A long time ago." He pointed to its reproduction. "It doesn't look spooky like that during the day, though."

I nodded and we fell silent once more. I finished my beer and got another for each of us. They weren't doing the trick. I was still seeing blue eyes.

Brian cleared his throat. "I saw a nature show last week about these chimps in the Congo. I can't remember what their real name was, but they called 'em hippie chimps because all they do, pretty much, is just have sex all the time."

He waited for me to respond. I didn't, of course, so he continued.

"It was kind of sad, though, because they're almost extinct. You'd think with all the sex they're having that they'd reproduce quicker'n rabbits, but there are these poachers who—"

"What?"

"Poachers. I guess the meat on those chimps is pretty tasty, because—"

"I meant, what the hell are you talking about?"

He shrugged. "I don't know. I just don't like awkward silences."

"Monkey sex is better than an awkward silence?"

"Definitely."

"Ah."

He looked at his watch then picked up the remote, because—finally—it was time for the movie. *True Grit*. A grizzled U.S. Marshall and an arrogant Texas Ranger help a spunky teenaged girl track down her father's murderer. Justice and revenge. No better way to spend an evening. Brian interrupted the movie several times with "important trivia" and a very bad impersonation of the Duke. I'd forgotten Glenn Campbell was in the movie and, under the influence of more beers than I could count, sang the chorus to *Rhinestone Cowboy* every time he came onscreen. The second movie—which I kept forgetting the name to—passed by in a haze of galloping horses and gunfire. By the time it was over there were ten empty beer bottles in my sink and eight more littering the living room floor. Brian and I were both sprawled out, heads back against the couch, our feet propped up on the lime green coffee table.

He rolled his head toward me and slurred, "Your hair looks good like that."

I was going to tell him he'd said that already but I didn't. Didn't tell him that I thought his hair looked good, too. That I liked the way it curled behind his right ear but not his left. The way it almost touched his shoulders but didn't. Not quite. And that I wondered if he always kept it long or if he had it cut short during the summer. Because he probably worked outside a lot and long hair might be too much in the heat. I didn't say any of that, even though I was thinking it, because talking and thinking about hair reminded me that I'd promised Laura something.

"What did you promise Laura?"

"Did I say that out loud?"

"Yep."

"Well, I promised her I'd use the conditioner she made me buy. I have to use it every day." That wasn't a lie. Because I really had promised her that.

"How was she today?"

"She was good."

"Did she tell you all about my sad, terrible childhood?"

"Yep." I said it before I remembered that I'd planned to feign ignorance about his sad, terrible childhood.

He gave me a grin. "In that case you owe me."

"Owe you what?"

"I don't know anything about you. Nothing real, anyway."

I rubbed my eyes and yawned. Wondered if I could do a convincing impression of the Woman Who Passed Out From Drinking Too Much. Probably not. Because I'd been drinking too much. "You want to know something about me?"

"Of course."

I sighed. Bit my lips. They were numb. Then I told him the story, because I was too drunk to care if he knew—even though I wasn't drunk enough for it not to hurt—about the Doomed Dyers. It was the edited-for-television version.

"So...he left you because he wanted kids and you didn't?"

"Yep." It wasn't the only reason, of course, but Brian didn't need to know everything.

"Didn't he know that you didn't want kids before you guys got married?"

"Yep."

"Not too bright for a teacher, then, is he?"

I shrugged. Nobody's bright when they first fall in love. Everything is laughter and fun and sex; a nonstop, barefoot, giddy romp in thick, green, sunny meadows.

Who cares about tomorrow? Or the tomorrow after that? Especially Jason and me. So many yesterdays, a whole life-time of them before our Us even began. More than most people started with. So what's there to worry about? Why worry when *he'll never change* and *she'll change her mind some-day* and, especially, when *everything will be Just Fine.*

Why wouldn't it be?

Tess, I want you to know something. And don't ever forget. I have loved you forever.

"I think it was more that he had too much confidence in his own ability to win me over to his side of the issue."

"Oh." He looked at me, bleary-eyed. "Why don't you want kids?"

"Well…it's sort of a scary idea, isn't it? There's no start-ing over if you do it wrong. You screw it up, and it's screwed up."

Just like that little boy at the grocery store. What if the state came in, right now, and took him away. Put him with a family with milk and soap. Would it make a difference? A real one? Or would he still be screwed up? Was there such a thing as Too Late?

He pondered that for a while. "I suppose. But I think most people are scared of that before they have kids."

Were most people scared? Were Dave and Kim scared? Right now?

"Maybe. But I'm too old for it all now anyway."

"No you're not. Why? How old are you?"

I laughed. "Let's just say I'm not twenty-five anymore."

"So Laura told you everything about me."

"Not really. I just paid attention." And backwards math is my specialty.

He propped an elbow against the back of the couch, leaned his head on his hand and cocked an eyebrow. "So… what is it? Forty?"

I kicked him. "I'm not forty, you shithead."

"I know." He grinned. Looked at me. Carefully. And his eyes were Van Dyke Brown…

"Um…thirty?"

"I'm not telling you."

"Come on. Tell me. You can't be any older'n thirty. Not that it matters to me if you are. Honestly. It doesn't matter at all."

I smiled. Stared at his lips. Lingered there. They were fucking gorgeous. And I wondered what they tasted like. How they'd feel on mine. How they'd feel all over me…

He smiled back. He could see it there, all of it. And I didn't care.

He reached for my face. And missed. The smiles faded.

Shit. Are we too drunk? Too drunk for this? Because you've been here before. Drunk sex equals bad sex, and if it's bad then what's the point?

I shook it off. So did he. He tried for my face again and got it this time. His hand felt so nice on my cheek. It really did. Warm and strong and calloused and, *oh God,* it had been so long since I'd felt a man's hand on my face. Let alone anywhere else. I leaned in a little closer, close enough to feel his breath on my face, and waited for him to kiss me. I rested my hand on his leg. It was smoldering away just like a woodstove. I looked away from his lips, finally, up. Into his eyes. And that's when I knew why he wasn't kissing me. He was searching my eyes. I knew what it was he was looking for. And I knew that he wasn't going to find it.

He pulled his hand away, gently, and sat back. Because he knew it, too.

"You're still in love with him."

I yanked my hand off his leg. "No. I'm not."

He shook his head and started to get up. I grabbed the waistband of his jeans, pulled him back down beside me and clutched his hand. "I'm not. Really."

Don't leave. Please.

He squeezed my hand and smiled kindly. I knew what it meant, so I let it go. Let him stand again. I stood up, too, and walked him to the door.

"Well, thanks for…hooking up the cable."

"No problem." He opened the door to leave, then sighed heavily, closed it, and turned to face me again. "I'm not…" He stopped. Mulled it over. "I'm not just looking to get laid here. That's not all I…want. Okay?"

And there it was. Out in the open. Just. Like. That. Even though I'd known it already. If that's all he wanted he could have gotten it the day I'd moved in. Hell, he could get that anywhere, anytime…

"I know, Brian, but…I'm just not ready to start anything new. Not anything serious, anyway." The beer let me add, "Not yet."

I looked closely at his face to gauge his reaction. To check for signs that he was weakening, faltering, anything that said he might stay. And I saw it. A spark in his eyes. I could see it, actually see it…right there. And I knew— *knew*—that I could make him stay. Reach right up, put my hands on his face, pull his mouth onto mine and that would be it. All it would take. He'd be mine for the night, and maybe even longer. For as long as it took to make this

56

god-awful ache in my heart disappear; to fill up the craters eroding my soul...

But I didn't. Because I had promised Laura I'd be good to him. That I'd be nice. Just like he deserved.

He took a deep breath. And the spark was gone. "Okay. I can understand that."

"So I guess I'll...see you around?"

He smiled. "You better believe it."

I waited until he'd safely navigated the staircase, waited a little longer until I heard his door shut. Then I went to into my bedroom. Stripped naked. Slipped between the sheets. Bunched up my blankets and extra pillow and snuggled in close. It didn't do the trick, of course. Because there was nothing solid there. No strong arms around me. No rough beard against my cheek and shoulder and breasts. No sweet whispers that told me...that told me...

...I have loved you forever...

But not anymore. I'd felt it all slipping away, all of it, for months and months. Hope and happiness and love. Slipping away. Drifting. Slowly. Away. And now...it was gone. He was gone. He hadn't even shown up in court, and it was probably just as well. Because I was drunk enough to remember that I'd planned to beg him to take me back.

Please, Jason? Please? Five months apart and that's long enough. Long enough to know that it's stupid to throw everything away. All those years together. A whole lifetime of love. We can't just give up on it. It can't be over. Please, Jason...

Please?

I was going to beg him. To take me back.

Too late. It really was. But I still missed him. Still. Even as I drifted off to sleep. Even in my dreams...

When I woke up in the morning he was there. Mine again, all of him. Golden beard. Blue, glowing eyes. Hands and lips everywhere, all over me. Hotel carpet. Sweet whispers that told me I was safe and loved. Even if it was just in my mind. One more time. One last time.

It had to be the last. Because when I was done there was no guilt. None at all. But I had to bury my head in my pillow, the one I'd spent the night pretending was him, to hold back the tears. Because that's when I knew. For real.

He wasn't mine. Not anymore. Not ever.

CHAPTER 6

Dave called while I was eating supper. Kim was in labor.

"Isn't it too soon? I mean, doesn't she have six days left?" Kim had told me that there was something to worry about when a baby came too early…something about lung development…

"She's fine. Her water broke anyway, so we don't really have a choice."

"Oh. Okay. Well, I can be there in about half an hour."

There was a long pause. Too long, and it made me nervous. Finally he said, "Tess, Jason's here. He's in the waiting room with Mom and Dad."

I sat down. Fell, really, onto a kitchen chair. It let out a small screech as it scooted a few inches across the floor. I knew just how it felt.

God damn it.

I'd just spent five months with them and their stupid fetus. I'd helped Kim decorate their nursery, painted it for her because Dave didn't want her inhaling the fumes. Practiced breathing exercises with them until I thought I'd hyperventilate. Folded clothes and washed bottles and helped organize all of their baby shower gifts. And what had

Jason done? Why did he deserve to be there? He couldn't be bothered to come to court, but he had no problem with making himself at home with my family while they all waited for my nephew to be born.

And why not? Dave had been his friend forever. Why shouldn't he be there?

"What…Dave, what should I do? Should I come up too, or just wait here?"

There was no answer, and he was right. He wasn't going to play the bad guy. Wasn't going to play Solomon with his unborn son. He had a wife to worry about, to breathe with; had to watch her suffer and scream for hours and hours. Had to worry about ten fingers and ten toes and…

God damn Jason. God damn that fucking bastard.

I took a breath, a deep one, just like hundreds that Dave and Kim would take over the next few hours. And then I tried for Laid-Back Tess. Nonchalant.

Everything is fine. Nothing wrong here. What could possibly be wrong?

I managed a yawn that sounded convincing and said, "Dave, I really am tired. In fact, I'll be honest, I'm fucking exhausted. Moving and unpacking took more out of me than I thought it would. I've been working too, so…I'm really wiped."

That was the story he could tell our mother. She'd believe it, even if she didn't like it.

"And I wish I could be there for you guys right now, I really do. I'd love to be there the second Matthew is born. But I don't think I can handle being in a waiting room with her for hours on end. I really don't."

That was the story he could tell everyone else. And they'd believe it. Kim and Dad and even Jason. Because it was true. Even if they knew it wasn't the real reason.

"I'm really sorry, Tess. I was with him at lunch when Kim called and—"

"Dave, it's okay. Just get back to Kim. Go do the whole Lamaze thing. Did you remember to bring that stupid stuffed elephant?" It was her focal point, her favorite toy when she was a kid.

"Yes."

"Well, then go. I'll head up in the morning."

I hung up before he could say anything else, because he needed to go take care of his wife. And because I needed to not talk to him about it anymore. But what I really needed was to not think about it anymore. To not think about anything.

I jogged to the fridge, grabbed the remaining six bottles of beer, then settled down on the couch in front of the television. Tried to drink myself into oblivion. It didn't work. I could still see Jason's face, pleading with me. I could still hear his words.

But, Tess…this is what you want to do when you love someone.

Oh is it? So, if I really love you then I'll be your incubator?

No, that's not it. That's not what I mean at all…

Here it was, over a year later, and I still didn't know what it was he'd meant. At all. Because he had talked about starting a family just once before we got marred. Threw it out there, wrapped up in a Someday. And I'd let him know, very clearly, that it wasn't going to happen. Not with me.

Just the thought of being a mother makes me sick to my stomach.

Okay, Tess.

No, don't give me "okay." I mean it.

And he never mentioned it again after that, not even a hint; never even hid it inside a Someday. Not until the day after he turned thirty-five. And then he never stopped talking about it. He tried everything. Calm explanations, just like I was one of his students, one of his slow students, who needed him to spell it all out for me. Logical reasoning, as though he was Spock and I was McCoy and the problem could be settled in a battle of wits. And, finally, Positive Reassurance.

Tess, you'd be a great mother. You're so creative and funny and warm and...

I hated that most of all. Because it made me feel weak. Damaged. As though I *needed* reassurance. But I didn't tell him that. I just said the same thing I'd said to all his other tactics.

"No."

And what I told myself was: *It's just a mid-life crisis. That's all.* And it was better than having him out screwing some young blonde or buying a bright red sports car. And finally, in the spring, I started to see signs of the old Jason, like he was waking up right along with the trees. And by the time summer vacation started he was back for real. Jason. My Jason, the one I'd fallen in love with.

Then came the middle of July. We spend a hot, humid afternoon in Dave's backyard. Barbecue and croquet and beer. And an announcement from Kim.

We're going to start hearing the pitter-patter of little feet around the house...

Pitter-patter.

I smiled with the rest of them, tried to be happy for them. But I knew. The other Jason was back. I could see the change already. I could actually see him doing the math.

She'll see the baby in March. Nine months after that: Fatherhood.

Sure enough. He put his arm around my shoulders and pulled me close, kissed me so tenderly that his beard barely touched my cheek, because he knew how much I loved that. Then he whispered, "Just wait till Dave's baby gets here, Tess. You'll see. You'll understand then."

It was the middle of July, hot and humid. I shivered anyway. I'd just gotten him back, back from That Place. I didn't want to lose him again. I couldn't. So on the drive home I said it.

It.

"Thank God Dave's finally giving my mother a grandchild. Now she can quit bugging me about it."

It was bullshit and we both knew it. My mother had never—not once—bugged me about grandchildren. She wouldn't care if I never had kids, or if she never had grandchildren at all. I knew it. And Jason knew it.

He knew it. Got the message loud and clear. Finally.

It ain't ever gonna happen.

The next morning was still hot and humid. Ceiling fans whirring in every room. Cereal and fruit and coffee.

Silent breakfast.

He brushed his teeth and got dressed. Headed for the living room. Hand on the doorknob.

Errands.

Errands? Jase, you don't have any errands to run today.

Obviously, Tess, I do.

We didn't have any plans to do anything together, nothing specific, but it was Summer. Our time. No school, no students, no tests to correct.

Our time.

Swimming, movies, bike rides. Whatever we felt like doing when we woke up in the morning was what we did during the day. But he took off, left, couldn't wait to bolt out the door, to be as far away from me as he could get.

Well...okay. I love you, Jason.

I'll see you tonight, Tess.

He didn't say it back. He didn't say it again.

I love you, Jason.

Good night, Tess.

Barely got a kiss on the cheek again. Didn't have sex again for almost two more weeks and then it was quick, so quick I thought he must be half asleep. He woke up in the middle of the night with a hard-on, rolled over and I was there, so sure, why not?

And then...nothing.

No baby, so no sex. Punishment.

I shivered through August.

The first week of school he signed up to teach night classes. First time he'd ever done that. The week after that he took up playing basketball with his buddies on weekends. And I knew what fall and winter would bring. More basketball. Because he was the coach now.

Jason Dyer, Patron Saint of Basketball.

I'll just eat supper out, Tess.

Okay. See ya tonight.

First time I didn't bother to say it. Didn't say it again. Even though I did still love him. He probably didn't notice the omission. He didn't notice when I said it, didn't notice when I didn't say it. So what was the point?

What's the point, Tess?

He didn't want me anymore so it didn't matter. He couldn't even look me in the eye. He didn't love me, didn't want me and someone else did. Why should it matter? Nothing mattered after that. Nothing. So I fucked the Someone Else. His name was Chris.

And I spent my fall and winter at Dave's house. Then came divorce court. Because that's where you go when the love runs out…

And he didn't even bother to show up.

What was Jason thinking about, right now, while he was sitting there in that waiting room with my parents, and Kim's parents, too? Probably he was thinking I was a coward, and he was right. I was. An even bigger coward than he had been when he hadn't show up at court. And what about Kim? Right now, right this very second, she was in pain. Lots of it. Worse than anything she'd ever gone through. Grunting and breathing and focusing on a relic from the past to forget the agony of the present. All so she could give birth to her Future. And here I was. Thirtysomething miles away from it all. Drinking myself into oblivion. Focusing on nothing. Doing nothing.

Nothing…

I fell asleep and didn't know it. My cell phone woke me up at just after six in the morning. I sat up and blinked rapidly, surprised that I wasn't hungover, and gave Dave enough time to go to voice mail. Then I trudged into the kitchen to listen to his message. Matthew David Bellows had arrived at last.

I took a shower, threw on my coat, grabbed my purse, then clomped down the stairs. The driveway was wet and soupy with thick, brown mud, and I had to take slow, deliberate steps so my boots didn't get sucked off my feet. When I finally made it to the car I tapped them lightly against my tire well, but it didn't do any good. They were still dirty, and now the car was, too. Dirty and tired and gray, just like me. I kicked the driver's side door, hard. Kicked it again and left behind a small, muddy dent. I kicked it two more times, for good measure, before I heard Brian's voice, directly behind me:

"Tess?"

I hadn't heard him come outside and it scared the shit out of me. I shrieked so loudly that it bounced off the house and shed and trees, like a thousand startled little girls screeching at us from every corner of the yard. Once they fell silent I turned to face him, armed with profanity, but the words never made it to my lips. I had expected to find smug amusement on his face. I saw honest concern instead, and my nerves were so raw that it almost made me cry.

He noticed and it threw him a little. "Oh. You're..." He reached out and touched my arm, gripped it gently. Not a strained, awkward gesture; it was genuine, natural. Just like he was supposed to be touching me. "Tess, what's wrong?"

"Nothing's wrong."

"Look, why don't you come on inside. I can—"

I shook off his hand, opened up my battered door, and got into the car without another word. I checked my rearview mirror as I pulled onto the road. He was still right there, watching me drive away.

The hospital elevator stank and so did the music. Disco, which is the last thing sick people and their relatives should be subjected to. The door opened onto the maternity ward. The hallway was empty except for me, so I waited a few moments to prepare myself, even though Jason was long gone.

I opened the door of the waiting room a crack, peeked in, and groaned. My parents were still there. I thought I'd waited long enough. They were sitting on opposite ends of a sofa, my mother reading a book, my dad watching CNN on a television that was bolted to the ceiling. I clenched my teeth in what I hoped passed for a smile and strolled in.

My father and I nodded our greetings. My mother looked at me, snorted, and said, "What on earth made you decide to go blonde?"

"It's not blonde. It's light brown."

"You can call it what you want, Theresa, but you look atrocious. Your complexion is much too sallow for that color. Especially since you put on all that weight over the winter."

"Thanks." I gave my father a quick glance. He had turned his attention back to the news and was pretending to be absorbed in it. I hung my coat on a peg next to his jacket and sat down in a chair across from them. "So, where's the baby?"

My mother gave me an icy stare. "The baby is with his parents where he belongs."

"Well, how do I get in to see them?"

"David should be back out in just a few minutes. He's been checking for you all morning."

She turned her attention back to her book and I stared at my boots. They were caked with dry mud and it made me wish I'd stopped into the restroom to wash them before I'd exposed myself to my mother. She'd report my appearance and demeanor to anyone who would listen once she got back to Brookfield. It wouldn't be favorable.

My dad came to life at the commercial break. He asked about work and my new place. If I was all settled in. Smiling. Excited. Like I was nine years old and on my way to summer camp. But he meant well so I smiled back and told him that everything was just fine. Work and the new place were fine. Met some new people. Everything is fine. Great.

My mother listened, too, and when I was done she said, "Jason stayed with us here all night. He stayed awake, like your father and I did, like Kim's parents did, and he didn't leave until he had the chance to hold the baby."

"And now he's hard at work, filling young minds with knowledge and dreams of a happy and productive future. And all with no sleep. Heroes can do that."

My father knew what was coming and had no stomach for it. He stood up and excused himself. Grabbed his coat and said he was going to get himself a cup of coffee from the cafeteria. He said it even though I knew he was really going outside to have a smoke. Because he liked to pretend that he'd quit years and years ago and I liked to let him pretend. The same way he liked to let me pretend that everything in my life was just fine and great. No problems, Dad. Nope. None at all.

I took in a deep breath, a silent one, in through my nostrils so she wouldn't hear it. She sized me up with blue, piercing eyes and I had to look away. It was just like looking into some sort of warped mirror, with an older, more confident version of myself staring back.

I didn't have to ask what it was she saw when she looked at me.

"Theresa, there's no need to take that tone. Jason—"

"Look, I think it's great he was here. He's a great guy and all that other bullshit. But it would've been awkward for both of us to be here. The day was supposed to be about Dave and Kim and their baby. Not about me and Jason, which is what would've happened if we'd both been here. He got here first and I bowed out. I'm sure he would've done the same thing if I'd gotten here first."

It was a lie and we both knew it. He would have come anyway.

"But it doesn't matter, really, what I do," I said. "I'm always gonna be the bad guy."

I flinched, because she had me and she knew it. She even closed her book. And smiled. My mother hardly ever smiled. "That is your own fault, Theresa. You made a mistake. A big one. And now you have to pay for it."

I gave her a bitter chuckle. She was the expert at making people pay for their mistakes. But I couldn't say that. She carried a can opener around with her just waiting for me to bring out that can of worms.

"Tess!"

I jumped. So did my mother, and it did my heart good to see it. It was Dave. Smiling. Excited. As though it had been light years since our last meeting. As though I hadn't chickened out and stayed away from the scene of the birth of his firstborn child.

"Hi."

"Ready?"

God damn right I'm ready.

I followed him out the door without bothering to throw back a goodbye. She wasn't expecting one.

"Did everything go okay?"

He nodded. "They're both doing great."

We turned a corner and I shuddered. The corridor walls were a boring off-white and the waiting room a soothing sage green, so I wasn't prepared for the Pepto Bismol Pink that greeted me in the maternity ward. It was the most disgusting thing I'd ever seen.

Dave noticed my discomfort. "*Christ,* Tess. It's paint. Get over it."

I did and followed him into Kim's room. She was lying in bed holding the baby in her arms. He was cocooned in a striped blanket. I tried to hide my astonishment at her appearance. She looked like she'd been through a boxing match. I remembered a picture on one of her baby shower cards that showed a radiant, glowing new mother lovingly cradling her newborn. She had the loving and cradling part down, but she was far from radiant and glowing. She was pale and tired, and she had circles under her eyes that were so dark that if I hadn't known better I would have assumed Dave had been using her as a punching bag. But she managed a smile and said:

"Would you like to hold your nephew?"

I hadn't come all this way just to endure my mother's contempt and stare at a striped blanket, so I nodded. Backed up so that Dave would have to make the relay, took the bundle, gingerly, and looked closely at its face.

"Dave...he looks just like *you.*"

"Don't sound so surprised. He is my son."

"I know, but…" I looked at Matthew again. His eyes were sort of murky, instead of blue, and he had a head full of black hair, like Kim's, but he definitely looked like my brother. Same nose and lips. Even a little cleft chin. I had expected some sort of generic Gerber baby, not something so…familiar.

They were waiting for me to continue, so I covered with, "I expected him to take after Kim's side of the family." I hadn't expected any such thing. I hadn't thought about it at all. But I had heard so many people say it while Kim was pregnant—some bullshit about dominant Italian genes— that it came out sounding natural. It seemed to satisfy them at any rate and I turned my attention back to the baby.

He was stirring just a bit. His little forehead puckered and so did his lips and he let out a small noise that was almost a squeak. I held him a little more firmly in my arms and kissed his forehead. It was warm and soft and he smelled so good, almost like aloe. It made me smile, because I'd always like the scent.

And that, of course, was the moment. The one I'd been warned about months earlier…

You'll see, Tess. You'll understand then.

I did. I felt it. Something inside of me shifted, just like changing gears without the clutch engaged. Grinding and noisy and painful. I clenched my jaw and steadied my knees, pulled the baby a little closer, closed my eyes against the slightly spinning room.

Oh my God.

What if I'd come last night? What if I'd held the kid this morning with Jason standing in the same room? Breathing the same air. Smelling the same aloe. It's why he came, why he stayed. He was waiting for me, waiting to see it. And what if he had? Would it have changed anything? Would he have taken me back? Or would it have only been an opportunity for *See, Tess, I told you. I was right after all...*

"Are you okay, Tess?"

I looked up at Dave. He was blurry. "Oh. Yeah. I'm fine. He's just—he's beautiful, Dave. Even if he does look like you." I gave him back his son. "I'm really happy for you guys."

"Thanks."

The room was stuffy and much too warm, and without Matthew's scent to disguise it, the odor of hospital disinfectant seemed even stronger. I felt suddenly confined. Nervous. And I needed to get away. Get the hell outta there.

Deep breath. Through the nose. Silent.

"You look like you could use some sleep, Kim. No offense."

"None taken. I'm really tired."

"Well, I'll get going then. Give me a call when you're settled back in at home and I'll come up and visit."

She gave a vague nod. Her eyes were closed before I finished the sentence.

When I made it back to the waiting room my parents were gone. I grabbed my coat. Got into the elevator. More disco; the Bee Gees. They thought I should be dancing. Their advice made me laugh, so hard I had to grab my stomach, and I didn't stop laughing even after the door opened on the fourth floor and a sad-looking family joined me. The woman next to me, the mother from the looks of her, took a step to the left. Away from the crazy laughing lady.

"Don't worry. It's not contagious."

I finally stopped when we hit the ground floor. I let Sad Family out first then followed. Out the front door. I tried counting footsteps but I kept losing track after thirty-four. Parking lot, parking garage, car. Reached into my pocket for my keys. I pulled them out...and a small envelope came out with them. My name in my father's neat handwriting. Inside was a brief note on white lined paper:

Tess, it's been a rough few months for you. I know how you feel about accepting help, but please take this and use it. Dad.

Five one-hundred-dollar bills. I looked at them. At Benjamin Franklin. He stared right back at me. Five times. His lips were pursed, his left eyebrow raised in silent condemnation. I wondered where his bifocals were.

I tucked three Bens inside the envelope and put it back into my pocket, stuffed the other two into my clean, empty ashtray. Drove over to the McDonald's drive-thru and ordered a coffee. Paid with an Abe Lincoln from my purse. Shoved the change and the extra two Bens in the Ronald McDonald House collection bin and headed for the interstate.

I switched on the radio and turned it up loud. Counted the miles as I drove along. Counted until I reached the sign that said *Welcome to New Mills.* My new town. My Starting-Over town. The sign that meant that everything had changed.

CHAPTER 7

First Wednesday in April. Three weeks since I'd moved to New Mills. Jason's face still haunted me most nights. But it was starting to fade.

Brian's television was on downstairs, a cop show by the sounds of it. I knew his schedule by now and was surprised that he was home. He usually went out to supper with Rachel on Wednesday nights. Chinese food in Westville, All-You-Can-Eat buffet. He always brought home an order of egg rolls and heated them up for breakfast on Thursday mornings. The smell made me nauseous. Every Thursday morning. My own schedule was much easier to remember than his, because it was always the same. Weekdays: Work, then home alone. Weekends: Home. Alone. For three straight weeks. And I was sick of it. Sick of being alone.

But here it was, Wednesday night, and Brian was home watching television. Alone. So I scribbled out a check, padded my way down the stairs and knocked on his door. When he opened it up he had a huge smile on his face and I knew why. We'd only exchanged brief nods and a *hello* every now and again since he'd caught me kicking the shit out of my car, and now: *here she is.* He looked at the check in my outstretched hand and the smile faded.

"What's this?"

"Half the cable bill."

He grabbed it, gave it a once-over and said, "This is too much money, Tess."

I liked the way my name sounded in his voice.

"I know what channels we get. That's half the cost."

"You can't just let me be nice, can you?"

"Sure I can. As long as you let me pay for half the cable."

He rolled his eyes. "Well if you're gonna make this all about business, then come in here so I can write you a receipt."

I followed him in and stood beside the kitchen table while he disappeared into a room that looked like an office. First time inside his apartment. It looked very much as I had imagined: comfortable, masculine, informal. The walls were white, like mine, and there was no real décor. The furniture looked very functional and inexpensive, like he'd gotten most of it at yard sales and department stores. The place was basically clean but very cluttered with piles of papers and empty bottles and his supper mess. He had eaten two mini pot pies. At least he'd eaten the beef, crust and gravy. The vegetables were pushed to the side of each aluminum plate.

Loud footsteps.

"Here you go, *ma'am.*"

I pocketed the receipt without even looking at it.

"I'd feel better about taking your money if I thought you were actually watching the cable. I never hear your television going."

"I watch it."

"What do you watch?"

"Stuff."

He raised an eyebrow. I knew what he was thinking but didn't correct him. Better for him to think I spent my free time watching porn than for him to know I'd become addicted to True Hollywood Stories.

"You like cop shows?" he asked.

"Yeah."

"Cool. Stay down here and watch TV with me. This one's almost over, but—"

"No, I'd better get back upstairs." I said it even though it was the real reason I'd come down. Even though he knew it.

He pulled my check out of his pocket and regarded it with a mournful sigh. "I won't be able to accept your money till I know for sure that you're watching the cable. And there's only one way for me to be sure."

I pretended to think about it. "Fine."

He smiled and, tackling the big, white elephant head on, said, "I can get you a beer, too, if you think you can control yourself this time."

"I'll do my best."

He handed me a bottle and I followed him into the living room. Every surface was coated with a thin layer of dust, the coffee table was littered with newspapers and a half-empty coffee cup, and there was a huge pile of unfolded laundry on the floor. It answered that age-old question: he was a boxers man.

I sat down beside him on the couch. The credits were rolling, so he grabbed the remote from the coffee table, muted the television, and smiled at me. Apparently this time it was up to me to make sure there were no awkward silences before the next show started. I settled for that old standby: work. He said construction wasn't his dream job, but he was good at it and he made decent money. Now that he was finally out from under the debts and back taxes his father had left behind, he could start saving some money instead of living from check-to-check.

"But...if they were his debts then why did you pay them off? Even if you did take over his business...isn't that what bankruptcy is for? Or you could've started from scratch."

"Nope. Not with his name, and not with his face. Not in this town."

"Ah."

He had a crew of four guys working for him, because he'd recently hired two new full-time workers. He could have saved more money for himself if he hired only one, of course, but he could afford them both so that's what he'd done. Because, he said, the local economy was in the shithole. Lots of businesses were still leaving the state. So if you have the opportunity to create a new job then it's your responsibility to do it.

"How about you? I hear you've been getting lots more work."

"Yep." About half the businesses in town had called in the past week and a half. Because when one beloved cleaning lady dies it creates a demand. And when another moves in—one who never forgets to refill the toilet paper and doesn't leave streaks on the mirrors—word quickly spreads. Unfortunately it takes a while for the pay to follow, what with accountants and bookkeepers and office managers who always put the light bill and phone bill ahead of the cleaning lady bill. I wasn't too worried, though. It was what I'd expected and the money was due to roll in at any time. And in the meantime I still had my savings.

"Must be a good way to meet new people."

"Not really. Just gossipy receptionists and dim-witted file clerks."

I realized I'd said the wrong thing even before I saw him wince. Small towns. Gotta love 'em. Only three weeks in New Mills and I knew all about Brian's reputation. Gossip was still debating whether he'd been celibate or discreet while Rachel was living with him, but after she moved out, last fall, he was neither. He'd had a go at most of the local girls, those who were single at any rate, including the dim-witted file clerk who worked at the insurance company I cleaned for.

Her name was Ashley. She was young, maybe nineteen or twenty, and very cute. Curly blonde hair and clear green eyes, just like I'd always wanted. She had been nursing a crush on Brian since she was in junior high school with Rachel, so spending a night with him was something she'd dreamt about for ages. Then morning came and she realized that, to him, it was nothing. No big deal, just like all the rest of them. She still wasn't over him, and she wasn't smart enough to keep everyone in town from knowing it.

He grunted a response that I couldn't quite make out, then turned the volume up on the television. Typical cop show. Brutal murder. Investigation. Forensics. Reluctant witnesses. Irritated lieutenant, *just get the job done.* It was probably very interesting, but I tuned out after the first commercial. I tried not to stare at the coffee table, but even a dramatic shootout and the subsequent arrest of a murderous drug dealer failed to hold my attention above the six separate sections of newspaper strewn across the surface of the table. The cold, stagnant coffee in the cup. The dust. I could practically feel my skin crawling with it.

I sat up straighter. Crossed my legs. Picked at my socks, dug my nails into my foot to keep it from bouncing. I was finally rescued by another commercial break. Brian, apparently oblivious to my distress, hopped up off the couch.

"Be right back." Then he strolled into the bathroom.

The door shut.

I leapt up, gathered the bottles and coffee mug. Padded my way into the kitchen. On my way through I grabbed the pie plates and fork and quietly deposited everything in the sink.

The toilet flushed.

I skidded back to the living room, collected the newspapers, folded them quickly and deposited them in the empty magazine rack beside the couch.

The door opened. I sat, cross-legged once more, out of breath, waiting for his return. Instead he headed into the kitchen, hollered over his shoulder, "Want another beer?"

I swallowed and took a deep breath. "Yeah, I'll take one more."

He came back just in time for the show to start, sat down beside me and handed me the bottle. I glanced at him out of the corner of my eye. He surveyed the coffee table without a word then stared straight ahead at the television.

The vicious, drug-dealing killer was convicted. Life in prison. No possibility of parole. Dramatic music. Cue credits. That was my cue to leave, but I didn't want to go. Didn't want to be upstairs alone. Didn't want to be where he wasn't. So I asked about Rachel. About why he was home on a Wednesday instead of eating Chinese food with her. He smiled. It was a big one and I knew why. I knew his schedule. Then he said:

"Oh, she's pissed at me. She thinks I'm butting into her life too much."

I laughed. "Are you?"

He wasn't amused. "Someone needs to butt in. She's screwing up her life. Drinking. Smoking pot. Sleeping around."

Sleeping around. Typical older brother, double standard bullshit. But I swallowed my *look who's talking* and let him continue. She was smart, he said, but she was working a dead-end job instead of trying to Make Something of Herself. He'd tried to get her to go to college, or at least a technical school. Get a skill. Anything. But she didn't take anything seriously.

"She's still young. Just let her get it out of her system. She'll be fine in a couple years."

I waited for him to ask if I was speaking from experience, and the answer, of course, would have been *yes I am.* But he didn't ask it. Instead he told me a story. It was the same one Laura had already told me, but his was the DVD version, complete with the deleted scenes.

"I thought my mom was wrong, at first, because my father stuck around for a long time. Well, technically, anyway. He wasn't *really* around much and I took care of stuff. I made sure Rach did her homework and took her bath and ate her breakfast and all that shit. But he was still... there. So it was easy to pretend that everything was okay.

Then this one Friday night when I was sixteen I stayed out wicked late with my girlfriend. I didn't get home until way after midnight 'cause…"

He stopped and gave an embarrassed grin which made me laugh.

"Anyway, I knew as soon as I pulled in that he wasn't home, because his car was gone, but I figured that he at least got a babysitter or brought Rachel someplace where someone would watch her. But when I walked in…she was there. The bus dropped her off at three and she was alone that whole time. She was just sitting on the kitchen floor in front of the fridge."

He was staring at the wall. But he was looking at a frightened ten-year-old girl. Shaking his head, like he was seeing it for the first time. Like he was still shocked by it.

"My father was out, God knows where, and she was home by herself. In the middle of the night. And…she looked up at me as I walked in the door, with these big, big eyes. She was so tired and I could tell she was scared, but she was trying so hard not to let me know it. And all she said was, 'I'm kinda hungry, Brian.' Because the only thing in the fridge was pickles and ketchup." He rolled his eyes. "And plenty of beer. 'Cause my mom was right. Even if he was there, my father was never gonna be the Dad. He wasn't even man enough to make sure there was fucking food in the house. So I had to do it instead. I had take care of her. And she hasn't been the same since then. She hasn't been…right. And once he really left it got even worse, because she thought he was gonna come back. For a long time. She kept waiting for him to, even though I told her he was gone for good. And once she did realize it…well, anyway. I gotta keep an eye on her, Tess. Can you understand that?"

I just nodded and smiled kindly, because what can you say to that? He smiled back and it was almost real. Almost. Except for the eyes. They were filled with something that went even deeper than sadness and I wanted to reach for him. To hold his hand. Maybe even hold him, because it was what he needed. But I knew what it would probably lead to. And I couldn't bear having to hear him say *no*. Not again. So I stood up and told him that I should probably get going. He nodded and said he was glad I'd come down. Said we should do it again sometime. Soon. And I said that sounded like a good idea.

An hour later I was lying in bed, restless, just like I did every night. But this time I wasn't thinking about Van Dyke Brown. Not about naked showers or warm, calloused hands. I was thinking about my brother. And I wondered how often Kim looked into his eyes…and saw the same things I'd seen in Brian's.

CHAPTER 8

Second Thursday of May. I'd been in New Mills for almost nine weeks and I was nearly broke. I'd used up most of what was left of my savings to pay for food and rent and, of course, the cable bill. Everything else was waiting. Waiting for the offices to pay and for the Summer People to arrive and discover that they needed a new cleaning lady.

It was just as well, because any extra money would not have gone toward anything healthy. I'd discovered, without asking, that there were two sources of good weed in New Mills. The first was the asshole who dealt mostly in harder stuff and even if I'd had the funds I wouldn't have given him my business. The second was a sixteen-year-old boy, a straight-A high school student. His father was gone, his mother worked two jobs, and he was saving for college. It was a noble goal and one I would have given my whole-hearted support to. If I'd had the funds.

It had been a long time—too long—since I'd been able to float away on a cloud, since the day before I moved in with Jason. When you're living with a schoolteacher, there are certain things you can't do, certain things Superintendents and School Boards and Parents frown on. Smoking pot is one of them. And once I moved in with Jason there was no real need for the cloud. Most of the time.

But I needed it now. Needed something. I had just fifteen bucks in my purse so that Something was supper out. Fifteen bucks would buy me a meal and a beer and an evening away from home. It wasn't much, but it would have to do.

I strolled into Fran's, with my real destination being the sports bar in the back. People in town called it *Zeke's* as though it was a separate entity, because the bartender was a guy named Zeke. He owned the place, too, having inherited it from his mother, Fran, a few years earlier. When she was alive she ran the diner and he managed the bar. Now that she was gone Zeke did it all. Rachel was in her usual place behind the counter, waiting on a customer. He was a rough-looking guy in his late thirties with a very hard face. The way he eyed Rachel while she bagged up his order made it obvious that something else was hard, too. And when she looked up at him she smiled, apparently flattered by the attention. I rolled my eyes, walked up to the counter and cleared my throat. It did the trick. She jumped slightly and let out a loud squeal.

Home: 1. Visitors: 1.

"Oh. It's just you, Tess."

"Hey."

She gave the guy a sideways glance then looked back at me and plunged ahead with the introductions. "This is Tim."

I gave the pervert a brief nod of acknowledgment. The name sounded familiar but I couldn't—for the moment—remember why.

"This is Tess, my brother's, uh…neighbor."

"*Neighbor*. Gotcha." He laughed and gave me a slow up-and-down, the kind that made me wish the weather was still cold enough for my bulky winter coat. I glared at him, ready to do battle, but Rachel intervened.

"What can I get for you tonight, Tess? More raw vegetables?"

"Actually, I'm going into the bar to eat. But first…" I leaned my elbows against the counter and batted my eyes at her, "I'd like to hear all about how things are going with you. Brian was wondering just yesterday what you've been up to, because he hasn't seen you for a while. But since I just *happened* to run into you I can…" I nodded toward her admirer, "fill him in."

She clenched her teeth and narrowed her eyes at me. I returned the scowl, undeterred. I had more experience with this than she did. She finally gave up, looked over at Shithead and said, "I guess I'll see ya later."

He looked right at me and said, "Yeah, Rach. You will." Then he sauntered out the door. I watched through the window until I saw his car pull safely away. Bright red sports car. And that's when I remembered where I'd heard the name before. Tim. He was the asshole drug dealer; the one who didn't confine his inventory to just pot.

I whipped my head around to say something to her, even though I wasn't quite sure what it should be. A warning? Did I know her well enough for that? Maybe a threat to say something to Brian? But before I could make up my mind she said:

"It's not what you think, Tess. Honest. I just like to flirt with some of the customers." She grinned. "They leave bigger tips that way."

I had to laugh at that. I'd worked at a convenience store right after high school, and all it had taken was a snug uniform shirt and a friendly smile for me to get a *keep the change* out of most of my male customers. But my laughter faded when I remembered all the times I'd brought home more than just a big tip.

"Rachel, you need to be careful with that guy. Okay?"

"I will. You won't…say anything about this to Brian, will you?"

I mulled it over. Keeping overprotective brothers in the dark was a specialty of mine. But.

She hasn't been the same since then. She hasn't been…right.

"Well…as long as you *promise* me you'll be careful."

"Yes, Mommy."

"Shut up."

"So," she said, giving me an eyebrow, "what's Brian been up to?"

I shrugged. "Work, I guess."

"You guess."

"Yep."

She smirked, but let it go. "Well, I'll let you go back there so you can eat your supper with the grown-ups."

I nodded, said a quick goodbye, and headed down the hallway. My first trip through the double doors. It was a typical bar: dimly lit, dark wood paneling, New England sports memorabilia clinging to the walls. The bar stools were all empty, but the chairs that surrounded ten big, round tables were filled with sweaty guys and their dates. Most of them were watching the Red Sox game on the large-screen television that hung on the far wall.

I took a stool and nodded at the bartender. I knew it was Zeke without having to ask. I'd never laid eyes on him before, but I recognized him from the description gossip had given me. He was about my age, tall and thin with short brown hair and soft brown eyes. He was nice-looking, and single to boot, but he was unavailable just the same. Not just to me; to any woman. Apparently it was a favorite pastime for some of the local girls to come in and flirt with him. They had aspirations of "turning him." I could have told them that their mission was in vain, but who was I to get in the way of their dreams?

He grinned and said, "What can I do for you tonight, Tess?"

Apparently gossip had given him an accurate description of me, too. I grinned right back and said, "Well, for starters you can tell me something. Is your name *really* Zeke?"

He looked surprised at the question. "Yes, it is."

"Really? It's Zeke?"

"Yeah. Short for Ezekiel. I was named after my great-grandfather. Why?"

"It's just that it's a really cool name, so naturally the moment I heard it I figured you made it up and that your real name was Ralph or Joe or something boring like that."

He laughed. "I'm afraid not. So…can I get you a beer?"

"Yeah. And a green salad. No dressing." My cake pounds were finally gone and I needed to keep it that way.

He gave me my beer, hollered my order back to the kitchen, then came back over to me with a big smile. "I hope you don't mind, but I'm going be rude and bring up business."

"I don't mind."

"I'd like to hire you to clean my house. Once a week if you have room in your schedule."

"I have room."

"Good. I would've called you earlier but I was waiting to see what gossip had to say about your abilities."

"I take it gossip approves? I'm not used to that."

"The receptionist from Dr. Stephens's office was impressed that you cleaned in between the keys of her keyboard. I have to be honest, that impressed me, too."

"Q-Tips are amazing things."

"I'll remember that. And Brian told me you're a clean freak."

"I'm not sure that's a compliment."

"Well, I think he meant it as one. People tend to admire qualities in others that they themselves don't possess."

I laughed. "Where'd you get that boatload of crap from?"

"Fortune cookie. Anyway, I don't have time to keep my place clean, since I'm here all the time, so how about it?"

"Sounds good." We made arrangements for an estimate then he brought me my supper. I ate silently for a few minutes while he dealt with a rowdy table. When he came back he watched me shovel a few forkfuls into my mouth, then said, "If you don't like celery you could have ordered the salad without it."

I looked at my plate. "Oh, it's not that. It's my favorite part so I always save it for last."

He laughed. "Whatever works."

I barely heard the words over a sudden explosion of noise from my fellow patrons. Their drunken eyes were glued to the set and several voices—none of them in sync or in harmony—were chanting the batter's name amid banging fists and clanking beer mugs. I turned to watch the action. Bottom of the eighth. We were down by one run, but the bases were loaded with only one out. We held our collective breath as Our Guy took a swing...

And grounded into a double play. The banging and clanking stopped, but not the voices.

"*I* coulda hit that fucking thing!"

"Give *me* a million dollars a year and I'll get a man home."

"That useless shit gets *fifteen* million a year."

I shook my head, remembering that the *useless shit* had hit over forty homeruns last season, and turned back to my salad. Just celery now. I ate it slowly because I wasn't ready to leave. Not yet. Because once I got home I'd have to walk past Brian's apartment. Past his window. His door. While he was in there, wide awake and waiting for me to get home.

I'd lied to Rachel. I knew how exactly how Brian was doing, because we watched his cop shows together almost every night now. We took turns: his place, my place. We talked and joked and laughed. And flirted. Just the night before we'd sat on his couch as close as we could without touching, just like a couple of idiot teenagers. I sat there with my heart thumping in my throat, knowing that I could reach for him without having to worry about getting a *no*. But I didn't. Because I knew what it would mean if I did. And I knew it was time I figured out what the hell I was going to do about it.

I was startled out of my meditations by a voice that asked, "Can I buy you a beer?"

I looked up from my celery. I hadn't noticed that a man had taken a stool a few seats over from me. He was about forty or so. Good-looking but arrogant. He'd done the bar a favor by walking in and the stool an even greater one by sitting his precious ass down on in. And now he was about to do me the greatest honor of all. The kind of guy who I knew, from bitter and disappointing experience, would be shitty in the sack. Then there was another thing. The insignia on his baseball cap. Even in my present mood, even if there was no Brian dancing in the back of my mind, the man would never have stood a chance.

I hid a smirk. "No thanks. I'm all set."

"Just one?"

"Seriously. No thanks. I'm heading home in a minute."

"Not all alone, I hope?" He let his eyes slip down a little farther south than they should have and let them linger there too long.

"If the alternative is going home with you, then I'm better off alone."

He rolled his eyes. "You don't think you're getting a little too old to be so picky?"

New in town. First time at Zeke's. Business to consider. Didn't matter. He had pushed every single one of my hot buttons and all in less than a minute. I sat up straighter in my stool and looked him squarely in the eye.

"Yep, I'm *wicked* old now. And I'll admit that life's been rough. So rough that it's left me with only two rules when it comes to men. One: I don't fuck Yankee fans. Two: I don't fuck assholes. I'm afraid you're disqualified on both counts."

He reached for his wallet, put a bill on the bar next to his untouched beer, gave his stool a kick and stormed out. Zeke, who had been watching the scene from the other side of the bar, came over to me with a hearty grin. "Good work."

I shrugged. "Who the hell was that?"

"Ted...something or other. He's from New York, as you could see, but his wife grew up around here."

"Wife? Wow, he really is an asshole."

"Yeah. He's some sort of useless executive in Manhattan. She's nice though. Her father died a few months ago and left them a house on the lake. Ted came up here to sell it."

"I'll have my people go put a bid on it tomorrow."

"Too late. He closed on it today. Half a million."

I stared at him, open-mouthed. "You've *got* to be shitting me."

"Nope. Some couple from Connecticut bought it."

I shook my head and finished my last mouthful of celery. Zeke put my plate into a plastic tub, then rested his arms on the bar and gave me another grin. I groaned out loud, because I knew exactly what was coming. The general topic, anyway. He knew I knew it, but he said it anyway.

"You know, Brian's not an asshole. Or a Yankee fan."

"I know he's not. He's a great guy. He's..." I sighed. "He's a great guy."

"You said that already."

I laughed. "I know. I...I'm just..." ...*just?* "I don't know. Just scared I guess."

It was a stupid thing to say to a guy I'd just met, but he only smiled and said, "Had a rough time of it, haven't you?"

I nodded. "Coming out of it, though."

I was, mostly. The sounds of Brian's shower, and the images that drifted up with them, had pushed Jason's face away almost completely.

"Good to hear."

"So," I said, grabbing my purse and trying for nonchalant, "what else did he say about me? Other than the whole anal clean freak thing."

He pulled out a dishcloth and wiped the counter—just like bartenders are supposed to do—and seemed to consider his answer. Then he looked up at me and said, "He says he has to fight to get more than two words in a row out of you, but that it's worth it when he finally can, so he's gonna keep right on fighting. He's trying to figure out why you like to stare at the trees beside the house, and someday soon he's gonna break down and ask you about it. And…he said you have the prettiest smile he's ever seen."

I stared at him long enough for his face to blur before I finally remembered to blink. And then all I could think of to say was, "Oh."

He tossed the dishcloth aside and smiled. "Can I get you anything else?"

"Uh…nope. I'm all set." I plunked down my fifteen bucks and told him to keep the change. Even though it wasn't much. And I made a mental note to leave a bigger tip next time.

When I got home I stared at the orchard again through the glare of the headlights. It was still too early for leaves or flowers. The trees hadn't even started to bud. But I could see the blossoms there, clinging to the bare limbs, just like

I had that first day. Even against the black, starry sky. Even if it was only in my mind.

Brian's living room light was on, but I didn't linger by his door. I rushed over to my own, ran up the fourteen stairs and into my bedroom. Looked, for a silent moment of eternity, at my easel. I'd been waiting for some signs of life from the orchard before I put it on canvas, something real to tell me that I'd been right about it; but I couldn't wait for the leaves or the blossoms. It had to be tonight. If I waited, for even one more day, it would be gone; whatever it was that had whispered to me.

...*Spring is here*...

Gone forever. I knew it. Even though I didn't know why.

CHAPTER 9

I was eight years old the first time I held a real paintbrush in my hand, the kind that wasn't big and awkward and dipped into plastic pint-sized containers of watery elementary school paint. It was at Jason's house, because his mother, Alice, watched Dave and me during summer vacation.

Alice was a potter. She had learned the craft from her mother and, after her husband died, she made her living by selling plates and bowls and mugs to gift shops all over the state. Every weekday summer morning, while Dave and Jason rode their bikes along the back roads of Brookfield, I would sit in Alice's workshop, drawing and coloring in my sketchbook while she turned cold, ugly lumps of clay into lovely souvenirs. Each piece was hand-painted with a small moose or a deer or a clump of blueberries, because that's what the tourists like.

But every once in a while, after her clay was centered on the bat, waiting to be formed, she'd stare out the window, out at her backyard. I never knew exactly what it was she was looking at, but I knew she wasn't actually seeing the backyard. And when her foot gently kicked the wheel into motion again her pale, blue eyes were soft and distant, like she was still in that Far Away place. Her strong, lean fingers would coax the wet clay, guide it; let it reveal itself to her rather than bending it to her will. And when the wheel finally came to a stop she'd survey her new creation with a smile and say:

"That's so I don't forget why I started doing this in the first place."

And one day I was brave enough to ask her, "Why *did* you start making pottery?"

She nodded toward my sketchbook. "The same reason you started drawing."

"Because it's fun?"

"Well…that's part of the reason."

Then she started up her potter's wheel and went to work on another mug. I went back to my sketchbook. I didn't bother to ask her what the rest of the reason was. I knew she'd tell me when she was ready.

She was ready two days later.

We watched through the window as the boys took off on their bikes, and when they were out of sight she said, "Tess, I have something for you."

She held my hand, led me out the back door and into her workshop. Standing in the corner was a three-legged wooden easel. Beside that, on a stool, sat an open wooden box filled with a dozen tubes of acrylic paint and a package of paintbrushes. I let go of her hand and ran over to it. Looked at each tube. Rolled the names of the colors around in my mind.

Cobalt Turquoise…Raw Umber…Phthalo Green…

And that's when she brought it out. A fresh, new canvas.

"It's so *big*, Alice. What am I supposed to paint?"

"Tess, there is no *supposed to*. You just paint whatever it is you're feeling."

"But...what if I make a mistake?" You can erase something you draw with a pencil, and even throw away something you colored with a crayon if you mess it up. But a canvas seemed so...permanent. There's no going back if you do it wrong.

"You'll just have to incorporate your mistakes into your painting." And then she strolled over to her wheel without another word. Leaving me alone. Alone with the canvas.

I looked at it for a good long time. It was white. Blank. Scary. I touched it, gently. Ran my fingers along the rough surface: thousands of little threads, woven together into a cloth, stretched over a solid, wooden frame. I looked away, out the window and into the backyard, to the place where Alice always seemed to get her inspiration. And it worked. Because I saw it, standing there, shining merrily in the hot, golden summer sun. Jason's swing set.

As much as I loved watching Alice in her workshop every morning, what I loved even more was what happened every day after lunch, after the boys were done with their bike ride. Swing set races. Every afternoon. Me and Jason and Dave. I always lost. Every time. But I never cared. It was the most fun ever.

Pump faster, Tess. You can do it! Faster. Now...let go!

Ever.

Jason's swing set was blue, nothing but cold, rigid metal poles. But in my painting it glowed with Cadmium Red and Yellow Ochre and the top bar was pitched, just like a roof. Because that's how it looked—how it felt—in my mind.

Warm and safe. It was my haven. The swing set, the backyard, the workshop, the house…all of it.

It was home.

And when Alice looked at it she smiled, too, because
she knew that it meant I loved her. And I smiled right
back, because I knew why Alice made her pottery. Not the
cookie-cutter trinkets she sold in gift shops to keep a roof
over her head, over Jason's head, to put food in their bel-
lies. But the vases and bottles that came off the wheel when
she wrapped her heart, instead of her hands, around the
clay. And the reason was this:

There are some things you just can't say out loud. Some
feelings you can't find any words for. They have to find a
different way to escape. A better way. A truer way.

That's the way it was with the orchard. Because it was
more than just five bare apple trees waiting to bloom. It was
a sign, a message. It was trying to tell me that everything
was going to be all right. That I was going to be all right.

I set a fresh canvas down the same easel Alice had given
me on that perfect summer day so many years before. It
was scratched, worn, stained with paint. I'd had to repair
the back leg three times in the past five years. But it was still
up to the job. Then I opened up my bedroom windows,
closed my eyes and inhaled deeply. Cool night air. Spring
air. Because it was here. Finally.

I picked up my palette, gripped it in my hand, loaded
it with color. I closed my eyes once more and remembered
the orchard the way it had looked that day, more than two
months earlier. Remembered the cold, bitter snow, the
even colder despair. The loneliness. All the other countless
emotions I couldn't put names to. Then had come the hot

tears that brought the flowers, even through the snow. The flowers that were really a promise. Something to cling to.

Hope.

I opened my eyes and let it come out. It surged out of me, a swift, hot current—right through the bristles and onto the canvas. All night long. I missed the sunrise, didn't even think to look out at what colors it was bringing to the morning, to the day. I just kept right on painting until it was done.

And by then, of course, it was time to get ready for work. Because there's always work. Even after you've spent the night pouring out your heart and soul and gut onto thousands of little woven threads. So I took my shower, got into my grubby work clothes, grabbed a quick breakfast and skipped down the stairs.

And ran right into Brian. He was wearing a great, big smile and I knew why.

"You're chipper this morning."

"Well," I said, "it's a beautiful morning."

It was. Sunny and green and almost warm. He held the door open for me and I skipped down the porch steps, too. Looked all around, at all the trees. The maples in between the pines that lined the road were starting to come alive. Newborn leaves of the palest spring green, the prettiest green of all. I turned toward the orchard, my heart nearly leaping inside of me, because I knew. It was time for it to come to life, too. Finally.

Except that it wasn't. The branches were still bare. All of them.

I looked back at Brian. "What...what's wrong with the orchard?"

"Uh...what do you mean?"

"Well, look at it."

He did. Then he shrugged. "Pretty nasty, huh? Charlie wants me to knock all those trees down. I'll probably get to it some time next weekend."

He said it like it was nothing.

"Knock 'em down? Why?" I asked it even though— really—I already knew. I just needed to hear him say it. To hear the truth.

"Well...they're just rotting away out there."

They were. They were dead. So I said the only thing I could say:

"Oh."

And I left for work without another word. I cleaned for the doctor and the real estate agent who both still hadn't paid me, then headed to Zeke's house. I gave him my estimate, which he accepted, and gave the place a good, thorough cleaning. Then I drove home. Showered away the stink of cleaning chemicals. And fell asleep on the couch. Dreamt—like I knew I would—about the orchard. It called out to me even while I was sleeping. Even in my dream I knew it was dead. But it still whispered:

Spring is here. Summer is coming. It's gonna be all right...

Then:

Tess.

And that made me smile. Even in my dream. Because it knew my name.

"Tess?"

Shaking, gentle at first. Then rocking. A hand on my shoulder. Rocking me awake.

I opened my eyes. Red hair. Freckles. Bright green eyes.

Anne of Green Gables.

"Cassidy?" I sat up.

"Brian wants to know if you wanna eat supper with us and play Penny Poker."

I cleared my throat. Focused.

Supper. Penny Poker?

"I'm supposed to tell you that he got one of the pizzas with just vegetables."

"Um, your parents are here, too?"

"Yep. Do you know you have raccoon eyes?"

"Do I? Thanks."

"You're welcome. So, are you coming?"

"Tell them I'll be down in a few minutes."

"Okay. See ya."

She ran down the stairs and I ran over to the kitchen window. Looked out at the orchard. Because in that land of barely awake, I couldn't remember if it was really dead and rotting away or if that was just part of my dream. But no. It was still dead. Which meant that, very soon, it would be gone.

I fixed my hair and makeup. Red lipstick. Just so. Then I changed my clothes. Tight, red button-up shirt. Low cut. Because I knew.

This is it. Tonight. It has to be. If it doesn't happen soon it isn't going to happen at all. And I need it to. I need him.

And not just sex. Although that would be good, because I needed that, too. But there was a Something that was inside of him that I wanted to have with me. Something in his eyes that told me it was all going to be all right.

And I really needed that.

I trotted down the stairs toward vegetable pizza and Brian and new friends. Hellos and chitchat. Supper and beer. Then Jeff dug out the cards. I had scrounged around in my coat pockets and all my drawers and came up with three dollars, traded it in for six rolls of pennies. I lost two hands before I caught Laura looking at my roots.

"I'll be in again soon," I told her.

She nodded. She heard what I didn't say.

As soon as I can afford it.

Brian must have heard it, too, because he said, "You got room in your schedule for another house cleaning job?"

Damn right. "Is it a one-time deal or a weekly thing?"

"Weekly. Remember your buddy from Zeke's last night? The Yankee fan?"

"How do you know about that?"

They all laughed and Jeff said, "You're kidding, right?"

"No. I'm not."

"Know about what?" Cassidy asked.

Brian smiled at her. "Hey kiddo, remember those tadpoles I told you about?"

She beamed. "The ones in the backyard?"

"Yep. Why don't you go check 'em out."

She hesitated for a few seconds. Looked at her parents, then me, then Brian again. The Great Debate. Tadpoles or adult conversation? She shrugged and ran out the door, headed toward the vernal pool on the edge of the woods.

Brian continued. "Tess, you holler out something like that in a bar fulla guys and...well, it's gonna get around."

"Jesus, that didn't take long." Not even twenty-four hours. So much for my clean slate. I looked at my cards and folded. My hand was shit.

"Hey, don't take it that way. You're their new hero."

"Well, what does the Yankee guy have to do with the job?"

"The couple he sold that camp to called me for an estimate today, to remodel the upstairs, and the wife was bitching about how filthy it is. She didn't exactly strike me as the type who'd do the job herself, so I gave her one of your cards."

"Oh. Well, thanks…"

Conversation lagged until Laura mentioned Zeke. He'd been in to have his hair cut the day before and she'd wanted to ask whether he was seeing anyone new, but didn't dare. I could have answered, but I let Brian do it.

"Nope. He's too buried inside that fucking bar of his."

It's what I'd figured. When you clean a person's house you get to know things about them. Zeke's house was the kind of mess that said:

I'm never home. And when I am I'm by myself.

It had been a week, he'd said, since he'd done any housework, yet the only dishes in the sink were seven cereal bowls, seven coffee mugs and seven spoons. Dust accumulated over the remote controls and books and the telephone. And the saddest clues: only one rumpled pillow, only one toothbrush.

Jeff shook his head. "The man needs to get a life outside that place."

"He won't. He's afraid to leave anyone else in charge."

"Control freak?" I asked.

"Not really," Laura said. "It's just that he and his mom almost lost the diner once. I think he feels like it's his responsibility to make sure that it doesn't happen again."

Brian scoffed. "The only reason they almost lost it was because of those church people."

Laura glared at him. "Don't you look at me like that. They weren't from *my* church."

"Your church, their church. It's all the same."

Jeff rolled his eyes, but said nothing. Old argument here, I could see, and one I wanted no part of. Still, not being familiar with New Mills's ancient history, I asked "What happened? Did people freak out when they discovered Zeke's gay?"

Brian nodded. "Zeke came out about ten years ago. The minister of the church Laura and Jeff *don't* go to told his followers that they should boycott the bar and the diner. I guess he figured Fran would make Zeke leave or something. All she did was say *fuck you* and stayed open anyway. She made Zeke stay open, too, 'cause he was gonna take off so she could save the diner at least." He shrugged. "But they all came around eventually."

"What made them change their minds?"

Jeff laughed as he dealt out another hand. "It's the only bar in town. The only place to eat out during the winter, too, unless you wanna drive to Westville."

"Funny thing," Brian said, "is that those same church people were in there every night getting plowed for years and years before their minister caused all the problems. And once the whole thing blew over they were right back there, at it again. Still are, too."

I was familiar with that brand of piety. "Bible buffet. Pick and choose which sins you're gonna pile on your plate. And I'm Catholic, so all I have to do is go to a priest and run it through the dishwasher so I can start all over again."

Brian laughed so hard that he choked on his beer. Jeff said nothing and Laura squirmed in her seat.

Rule number one when discussing religion with new friends: don't discuss religion.

"Shit, I'm sorry. I didn't know you guys were Catholic, too."

Cassidy picked that moment to wander back into the house. "You're Catholic, Tess?"

I nodded.

Her face lit up. "You should come to church with us on Sunday."

"I...uh, well thanks. But—"

"And then maybe Brian would come, too."

Brian shook his head and tossed a handful of pennies into the pot. "Nope. Brian wouldn't come even then."

Cassidy looked at him, a little wounded, almost teary-eyed. "That's what you always say. You don't believe in God. Do you?"

He considered for a moment, held her gaze. Silent. Torn. He loved her. Didn't want to make her cry. And he could stop it with a little lie. She'd probably know it was a lie, but sometimes we need it, need the lie. The struggle was plain on his face. He tried to smile, tried to say something that was kind, but he couldn't do it. He was too filled with some kind of bitterness that even she, as young as she was, could feel. And there was no way she could understand that it wasn't directed at her.

"No, Cass. I don't."

"But..." Real tears now. "But I don't want you to go to hell."

Laura stepped in to steer her daughter's boat to a safe shore. "Cassidy, Brian isn't going to hell. He's just mad at God right now. That's all. It's like when you got into that fight with Brittany last week. You were mad and you wouldn't talk to her even when she called on the phone. But then you realized that you missed her and you talked the problem over with her at school and now you're friends again. It's just like that."

Cassidy nodded and looked at Brian. He was looking at his cards.

We played four more hands of Penny Poker. I lost them all, even with Cassidy's help, and found myself two dollars and eleven cents poorer than I'd started the evening. Jeff was nearly five dollars richer. He stretched and looked at Brian. Then he grinned and said, "We'd better get going." He collected his cards while I collected the beer and supper mess.

I said a quick goodbye to the three of them and watched Brian walk out onto the porch to say his own goodbyes. Before she left Cassidy gave him a huge hug, wrapped her little arms around his neck. Tightly. Then she whispered something in his ear. He nodded and kissed her forehead. He stayed on the porch and watched silently until their car was out of sight.

CHAPTER 10

He wasn't surprised to find me still in his kitchen. Leaning against the counter. Waiting for him. But first things first.

"Are you okay?"

"Yeah." He gestured toward the porch. "Cass is just… yeah. I'm fine. You, uh, wanna stay for a while? For a drink or something?"

"Sure."

He made his way over, slowly. Smiling. He stopped directly in front of me and pointed to the cupboard behind my head. The one that held his liquor. "You know, you're sorta in my way."

"Yeah. I know."

He didn't say anything, just stood there. So close I could actually feel the heat coming off of him. Still smiling. Waiting. His eyes locked onto mine. He was going to make me say it. Even though he knew. He'd known it the second I'd come downstairs, just like I'd known the second I'd been snatched out of my dream that afternoon.

I cleared my throat. "I'm not really thirsty."

"Yeah," he said, and he was still smiling. "I know."

I was shaking, just slightly. I knew why. Nervous. Like I hadn't been the first time this had almost happened. Because this was different. I managed to smile, though, managed to keep my eyes focused on his. They were more alive than I'd ever seen them. He wasn't nervous at all, not even a little, and my heart started thumping, pounding out that ancient drumbeat. Because this really was it. It was all about to break loose and I was ready. Stopped shaking. Finally.

He noticed, had been waiting for the shaking to stop. He reached out, held my face in his hands with gentle fingers. Like it was something precious and fragile. Like it would break if he wasn't careful. It threw me a little, because I hadn't expected tenderness, wasn't prepared for it at all. Until that moment I'd been ready to dive right in and go for it. Wild hippie monkey sex, the kind where you wake up in the morning wondering where the hell your pants are. But his touch promised something even better. Something I hadn't had for a very long time and when he closed the gap, so slowly, and finally kissed me it was with a soft, warm mouth. Tender. Slow. Like he didn't care if it took all night. Like he didn't care if it took forever.

But then he stopped, just barely. Our lips were still touching but he didn't move. I felt him smile, opened my eyes to see his hovering there. Open, expectant, and I could see the question. He was waiting, again. Probably still half expecting me to break away, give him a quick *thanks, that sure was nice, see ya later* and run upstairs. I smiled back, my lips stretching over his.

Oh, it's happening, baby. Buckle up.

I found his belt loops, grabbed tight hold of them, but didn't pull him any closer. Opened my mouth, guided his lips into another kiss. But not like before. I had to let him know.

I *need* this.

I touched his tongue with mine, slid it slowly underneath his, coaxed it into my mouth. I wanted it all, needed it, and he gave it to me. It was hot, tasted a little like beer, and I knew mine did, too. And it was perfect.

But it wasn't enough. I needed to feel him, to touch him. Him. His body, his skin. I tugged, pulled his shirt out of his jeans and reached underneath it. He trembled at my touch but his hands were still gentle as he ran his fingers through my hair. I took my time, explored the new terrain slowly. His tight stomach. The taut muscles of his chest. It was covered with soft, damp hair and I slid my fingers through it, lingered there. It had been at the root of every fantasy I'd ever had about him and I was nearly overwhelmed by a sudden, swift flood of all of them: The sounds of his breath in my ear, his hot scent. His rough hands, all over me. The way he'd tasted. In my mind. All of him. It mingled with reality, with his lips and fingers and heat and tongue and I let out a brief moan, almost a whimper, then choked it back, embarrassed.

He let go of my lips and drew in a sharp breath. Looked at me with eyes that weren't quite focused, hazy with arousal, and I thought he'd finally reached his breaking point. The point when clothes got ripped off of bodies in a mad rush for the bedroom. But he only put his arms around me, firmly, and pulled me to him. I slipped my arms around him, still underneath his shirt, ran my fingers along the muscles of his back. He pressed me against him even closer, so close that I could feel my heartbeat against him, an echo of his, my breasts tight against his chest. Then he took my mouth again, held me in his arms on that hot, spinning carnival ride of wet lips and damp skin.

And it wasn't enough.

I knew he was holding back. I could feel it. Could feel him wanting to let it go. And I needed him to. Needed it. I slid my fingers slowly down his back, slick now and hot with sweat. Let them wander lower still. I stopped for a moment at the waist band of his jeans, pulled at it with my thumbs. Waiting. Waiting, my heartbeat ticking down the last remaining seconds. Gave him one more chance. Waited. Then...

I let go of the waistband and grabbed it. His ass. It was tight and round and perfect. Felt perfect, and I saw, behind my closed eyes, how it looked that day, that first day, climbing those stairs right in front of me, and now I was—

Oh my God, it's in my hands, here, right here, it's in my hands...

—actually touching it, I could *feel* it, finally, even if it was just through his jeans it was...

It's. Right. Here. Right here in my fucking. Hands.

My blood flowed hot through my veins, washed away all reason and thought; lost all track of his lips and his hands. The only thing in the world was his ass, his ass, and I grabbed it harder, squeezed it. Leaned back against the counter. Pulled him closer. Close as I could, so that his ass wasn't the only thing in existence. Even through his pants, even through mine, I felt him, hot and hard, and I still didn't let him go. I had waited so long, too long, and

I needed him, please, God, needed all of him, against me, on me, inside me...

He pulled his mouth away from mine again, gave a loud, deep groan. His hands were heavy on my shoulders, like he might fall over if he didn't clutch them. It made me smile. Into his shirt. While I struggled to catch my breath. His breath was quick and hot in my hair and on my forehead and finally I heard a husky whisper in my ear:

"Tess...if you don't let go of me...I *swear*...you're gonna get it right here. Right here in the fucking kitchen."

Oh God, yes. Please, please, please. Gimme...

I squeezed my eyes, fought to get control of myself again. Took a slow, deep breath, oxygen and coherent thought finally returning to my brain.

"Sorry." I let go, embarrassed again, my own breath still hard and shallow.

What the hell is wrong with you? It's been a long time, but you're not an animal...

"Don't be," he said, and his voice was still hoarse. "I'm not. I just want...I *don't* want..."

He took my face in his hands again, firmly this time with strong hands. Lifted it up toward his and everything else in the world melted away. Everything except for Brian. He was the most beautiful thing I'd ever seen. His mouth wet and open, his hot gorgeous breath on my face. His hair was damp and he smelled—God, he smelled sweaty and spicy and hot and so, *so* good. His eyes were wild and dark and burning, searching my whole face. I knew what it was he was hunting for. And I hoped he found it looking back at him.

He pulled me quickly out of the kitchen, through the hallway, into his bedroom. He snapped on a dim lamp, kicked the door shut, pushed me up against it and kissed me. This time his mouth was different—raw, rough, demanding. He pressed himself, his whole body, tight against mine, barely leaving enough room for breath. And I loved it.

I did that to him.

I pulled at his shirt and he broke away reluctantly, leaned back to let me slip it over his head. I caught a brief glimpse of an armband tattooed high on his right bicep. Once his head was clear of his shirt he came right back at me and I cursed myself for focusing on it, because I'd lost my chance of getting a good look at his chest.

He pinned my arms against the door, holding me in place. His open mouth was hot at my neck, sliding slowly down, slowly, and I was sure he could feel my pulse with his lips and his tongue. So slowly, until he got his first taste of cleavage. He lingered there forever, my shirt fluttering with each breath he took, then he finally released my arms and went to work on the buttons. He fumbled slightly with the first one, but the other three gave up without a fight and soon my shirt was dangling, not quite open, just waiting for him to unwrap his gift. Before he did he looked into my eyes. Clear, focused, ready. Making sure I was, too. I dropped my arms, let them rest at my sides, and smiled for him again.

Go for it.

He brushed aside the two halves of my shirt, just below the curve of my breasts, and stared silently for a few moments. Then he smiled and his eyes told me that he knew. And he was right. Red lace bra. I'd put it on just for him.

He gave me his mouth again as he slipped off my shirt and, with a few urgent tugs, my bra. My breasts were free at last, but only for a second because he was right there, exploring. First with tentative fingers, then boldly with his rough, warm hands. Finally his mouth left mine and he continued his research with those gorgeous lips, and his tongue, and—

...oh God his mouth is so, so, so fucking hot...

—he stayed there for a slow, hot eternity. I held his head in my hands, his hair wet in my fingers. Short gasps. Murky head, swimming dizzily. I felt myself losing balance, listing back toward the door. He pulled me back to him, firmly, back to his open mouth, but the rest of my body was burning and neglected, crying out for him to touch it. I took in a raspy breath and when I let it out it was a plea, practically a sob.

"Brian..."

He tore himself away and I waited, with my own mouth open, for him to kiss me again. Instead he smiled weakly, his face flushed and hot, and whispered a breathless, "Sorry."

I smiled back. "Don't be. I'm not."

I found his buckle and made quick, careful work of opening his jeans, pulled them down as far as my arms would reach, while he did the same to me. I stepped out of my pants and he whipped off his own. Finally we faced each other completely naked.

I looked at him, at all of him. I was going to touch that gorgeous body. All of it. Feel it on top of me, underneath me. Mine. And then, of course, the other realization. He was looking at me just as closely. Nothing to be too ashamed of, not really, but thirty-four isn't twenty-five and...

He shook his head and pulled me to him. His arms were gentle once again and it was just how I wanted him to be. Then he uttered the sweetest words in the world.

"Tess..." He was looking right into my eyes. "You are beautiful. The most beautiful woman I've ever known."

His lips were on mine before I could respond. Slow, hot, patient, just the way he'd begun. He backed slowly toward the bed, pulling me right along with him. Even as he lay me down on it, leaning over me, sliding me farther back, his mouth never left mine, not until I felt his pillow underneath my head. I looked again into those dark, dark eyes, and smiled up at him, waiting for him to start.

Instead he reached over beside the bed, yanked open the drawer of his nightstand and started digging around inside it. The drawer banged shut and I heard something crinkling above my head.

Welcome back to single life, Tess.

The words flashed like neon in my mind and helped me to focus. I thought of the prescription that I had taken for years, the one I'd been too afraid to cancel, even through a lonely fall and winter. And I wanted to tell him he didn't need to put it on, that we were all set. But then I remembered. His fall and winter hadn't been so lonely.

He finished quickly and lay down on top of me. I loved the feel of him. His skin, his heat, his weight on me. He brushed aside the bangs that had fallen over my forehead. Then he didn't move. Just gazed down at me with beautiful, glowing eyes. They told me what I already knew, what I'd known since the first time I'd seen them, and I had to close my own eyes; suddenly, stupidly panicking.

Just for right now, please Brian, just for tonight…let it just be about the sex. Please don't look at me that way. Please. I can't bear to think of how bad it will hurt when you stop looking at me that way. Please—please—just fuck me tonight and let me worry about whether I'm ready to deal with the rest tomorrow.

I opened my eyes. His were directly above me. Searching. Worried.

"Are you okay?"

I nodded and smiled up at him. He waited a few moments longer, still searching. Then he smiled back, swallowed hard and finally started; a slow, sweet, exquisite rhythm. He whispered to me, deep and soft. Hot, sexy, beautiful words that felt just like a song, and I lost myself in him. All of him. Completely engulfed by him—his touch and smell and sound and sweat. He was so tender and warm, nothing at all like I'd expected, so much better than I had ever imagined him, and I finally let go. Finally gave in to him, let him carry me off with him to where he was, where he'd been for so long, where I knew he wanted me to be. And when I felt it start, the slow spark that became hotter and hotter, one electric wave after another, it wasn't only my body, but all of me responding to him, and I surrendered to it—and to him—completely. His name started in some deep, secret corner within me and I wasn't sure I'd said it out loud until he whispered mine back, and when I heard it again, a final, searing moan, his eyes were wide open and looking down into mine.

He collapsed heavily on me, his breath quick and warm, blowing in my hair, his heart pounding against me. Mine hammered away, too, short, deafening blasts, each beat a cymbal in my ears. And it was full, so full of him, that

I thought it would burst. I tried to focus on it, to make my way through the ripples to find the sweet emotion at the center, but I couldn't. All I knew for certain was that everything had changed. Because he was still inside me. Still. And I didn't want him to ever leave.

He raised his head, finally, and looked down at me. I knew exactly what it was he was thinking—what he was feeling—because his eyes were still glowing with it. But he didn't say the words. He just caressed my cheek gently, kissed it, and said, "I'll be right back."

I listened to his footsteps thudding toward the bathroom while I stared at a tiny crack in the ceiling. His room was directly below mine. And I wondered, for the first time, how my own footsteps had sounded to him from down here. If he had ever lain awake, right here, right in this bed, listening to me.

He sauntered back into the room and plopped down beside me on his back, pulled me over to him. I rested my head on his shoulder, played with the hair on his chest while he caressed my back lightly with his fingers. It was the best feeling in the world. But there was a can of worms I had to open. The one I hadn't thought about until I'd heard crinkling above my head. I watched the clock on his night stand, trying to build up my courage. It glared back at me in bold red numbers for seven full minutes. Both of us were silent the entire time. Finally I was brave enough to get as far as, "Ummm…"

He waited for me to continue and when I didn't he asked, "Are you humming to yourself or are you trying to tell me something?"

I laughed. Told him about my prescription and he smiled. Then I asked him That question. And he was still smiling when he said:

"Yeah, I have been. And I'm clean. I've never done it without a rubber anyway."

It was all he said. And I smiled, too, relieved. Then there was something else.

Never?

It had been so long since there was something new. Even if it wasn't my something new. So I climbed on top of him and kissed him. Deep and hot. Then I smiled again.

Ready again. Twenty-five. Gotta love that.

CHAPTER 11

I woke up long before Brian did the next morning. I lay next to him for a long time, silently watching him sleep. He was lying on his back, one arm flung over his eyes, the other hanging off the bed, his mouth open, breathing softly. A faint, dark shadow covered his jaw.

He was almost too beautiful.

And then I remembered the tattoo. I leaned over him quietly, craned my neck trying to get a better view. It was a name. It was partially hidden by his pillow, but the letters *dy* were very clearly inscribed within an intricate black-ink armband. I wondered who she was, who had been so important to him that he'd gone through the pain and hassle and expense of having her name permanently drilled onto his body. And I braced myself for the ordeal of having to see it staring back at me every time he was naked...

"Don't worry, Tess."

His voice startled me so badly I nearly fell off the bed. He grabbed my arm just in time and pulled me to safety. I would've been more grateful if he wasn't laughing so hard. He made sure I was situated securely before he let go of me. Then he turned his arm slightly so I could see the whole name.

Wendy.

I nodded, still clueless.

"Wendy was my mom's name."

"Ah." Then I smiled. "You know…that's really sweet."

He grimaced. Manly men do not like being called sweet.

"Nice? Thoughtful? Kind?"

Nope.

"Studly?"

He rolled his eyes and opened his mouth to speak, but whatever the words were going to be died on his lips. Because that was when we heard the kitchen door slam shut. He bolted out of bed toward the door and I took a brief moment to admire his naked ass before I covered myself with a sheet. He cracked open the door, peeked out and hollered, "That you, Rach?"

"*Duh.* Who else has a key to this fucking pig hole?"

He groaned, grabbed a pair of jeans from a pile on top of his dresser and threw them on.

"I'll see if I can get rid of her." Then he jogged out the door, slamming it behind him. I knew my cover was blown when I heard Rachel cackling a few moments later, but I still waited for him to come back in and break it to me.

"I don't know how she knew it was you."

"Maybe because she's not an idiot."

He smiled, almost shyly, and that's when I knew the answer to the question that New Mills debated for years: He'd been celibate, not discreet. All those years and…no one; not until Rachel moved out. Even with a town filled with willing women. I wasn't sure if that was sad or sweet. It was probably a little of both. Just like the tattoo.

I rummaged through his pile of fortunately clean laundry and picked out a T-shirt that could have been a dress and a pair of sweatpants. I had to roll each leg up five times before I could walk.

I followed him into the kitchen. Rachel was busy at the stove, cooking bacon and eggs. She snickered when she saw my ensemble. I ignored her and headed for the bathroom. Did my business, washed my hands, surveyed my reflection, then stared at his medicine cabinet. Studied the hinges. They looked old, like they might squeak. I ran my tongue over my teeth and decided it was worth the risk. I flushed the toilet again, to cover any noise, and slowly opened the cabinet door. All that worry for nothing; it didn't squeak. And I found what I'd been hoping for: an extra toothbrush. It was brand-new, still in the package. Red handle, medium bristle. I tried not to wonder why he had an extra one lying around.

By the time I'd finished up in the bathroom, breakfast was ready. I poured myself a glass of orange juice and jellied a slice of toast. Brian dove right in, shoveling food into his mouth like he hadn't eaten for days. I had to avert my eyes when he dipped the corner of his own toast into a glob of runny egg yolk. Rachel shook her head.

"You're not a vegetarian, are you?" She made it sound like the worst of all possible offenses.

"No."

Brian laughed. "Then why don't you eat meat?"

"I eat chicken and turkey. And fish."

"That's not meat."

"Please tell me I'm not getting nutritional advice from the man whose cupboards are filled with Chef Boyardee."

The phone rang before he could answer. He looked over at it, then down at his half-finished breakfast. Ring number two. He gave a big sigh. Then: inspiration. He piled what was left of his egg and two strips of bacon onto his remaining piece of toast, folded it over and jogged to the phone. He answered, "Yeah?" then stuffed half the sandwich into his mouth. Chewed noisily, away from the mouthpiece. Swallowed. Listened for a long time. Closed his eyes, still listening. When he opened them again he gave Rachel an angry stare. Then he turned away from her, still silent. Still listening.

Whatever her transgression was, she didn't seem phased by his wrath. But she probably was. I took a quick peek at her eyes. They were clear. But it was only nine-thirty.

"You're not trying to impress him by not eating a lot are you?"

I smiled. I knew this game.

I'm about to catch hell, so I'll dish it out to someone else first.

"No. Why, does that impress him?"

"Nope."

"Good."

She twisted her hair into a tight loop at the nape of her neck, then let it go. It spun wildly and finally came to a rest over her right shoulder. "It sure took you long enough to finally get your shit together."

"Excuse me?"

"He's been following you around like a puppy dog since you first moved in here. I've been waiting for the 'Do Not Disturb' sign to pop up on the door here for weeks.

I figured you thought he wasn't good enough for you or something."

"Why would you think that?"

"I don't know. Maybe because he's in construction. But he's a real smart guy. He'd be doing something else if... Well, anyway, he's smart enough to be doing something else."

I love my brother. He's a good man. He gave up a lot to take care of me. Don't hurt him.

Fair enough.

"I scrub shit outta toilets for a living, Rachel. Do you really think I'm gonna be put off by a guy because he swings a hammer? Besides, I know it takes a lot of brains to run a business."

She poured herself a glass of juice. "What does your husband do?"

"My *ex*-husband teaches high school. English literature."

"So he's pretty smart, then?"

"Well..." I hesitated. "He's smart about English literature."

I finally got a laugh out of her. It faded when Brian slammed the phone down. He stormed back into the kitchen, still clutching the remnants of his sandwich. Sat down. Chucked the sandwich onto his plate. Glared at her. She glared right back.

"You were suspended for two days *without* pay?"

She shrugged.

"You go into work fucked up just one more time and Zeke's gonna shitcan your ass."

"He already told me that. He didn't need to bug you with it."

"Well, he did. Don't you *get* it, Rach? At all? The only reason you still have a job is because he likes you. Because he knows you're not *really* a fuck-up. And you're not. So quit acting like one."

He waited for her to say something. She didn't. So he cleared his throat and finished his lecture with:

"I told him it's not gonna fucking happen again. And it sure as hell better not." He gave her eyes the same once-over I had. Then his gaze dropped to her inner arms.

She pulled them back. "I'm not doing any of that shit. Jesus, I just smoke a little pot every once in a while."

"A little."

"It's not like you're perfect, you know."

"I haven't done any of that kinda shit in a long time. And I *never* went to work that way, Rachel. Never."

She didn't have an answer for that. He shook his head. Looked at her with frantic eyes that said, *I love you. Don't screw up your life.*

She was looking at her fingernails.

"What are you doing today?"

She shrugged.

"Wanna hang out here with us? We could rent a movie or—"

"Nope."

"—we could take off for the day and go to—"

"I said no."

"How come?"

"I'm going out."

"Where?"

"To see a movie."

"Who with?"

"With some friends." He gave her a suspicious scowl and she smirked. "Why? You lookin' to score?"

"Fuck you, Rachel. Quit treating this like it's a joke."

She stood up and shoved her chair under the table. It honked in protest.

"Wait. Who are you going to the movies with?"

Her hand was on the doorknob. "I told you. With. A. Friend."

"You said *some friends.*"

"Goodbye, Brian."

The door slammed behind her.

He glared at his plate. I knew he was itching to chuck it at the wall. I'd seen that look at least a hundred times before on a different face. I cleared my throat. "She wants you to know what she's up to. That's why she goes to work that way."

He looked up at me and sighed. "I know. And she wanted me to yell at her. That's why she came over here."

I nodded.

He nodded back. "Well, I guess that's settled."

Except that it wasn't, of course. But what can you do?

He had an idea. "Let's walk to the lake."

"The lake?"

"Yeah. It's less than a mile and it's warm out today."

We held hands as we walked down the road. The water was beautiful. Cold, dark blue—Prussian Blue. The spot he took me to was hidden from the road by thick clusters of newly-budding maples and white birches and filled in with lovely green grass. We spread out an old blanket and lay underneath the shadow of the trees.

We were silent for a little while, but it couldn't last. I was glad it didn't, because I'd already learned to love the sound of his voice. He didn't talk about Rachel. He talked about the lake. Not about its beauty, because he didn't have to. It was too obvious a thing to have to say. Instead he talked about endings. Only two more weeks before the summer people came to take over the town. Soon the lake would be overrun with jet skis and motor boats. And that meant No Trespassing. He was wistful. Resigned. About the lake. And about the other thing.

So I wasn't surprised when he pulled me on top of him and kissed me. Long and deep and full of need. A need that wasn't just sex, although it was that, too.

Because what is sex, really?

Sometimes it's making love. Hearts bursting with fragile emotion, two souls touching, closer than two bodies ever could. Sometimes it's fucking—passion and fun and wild release. Sometimes just an urge. Or an itch. A means to an end. A compulsion.

But whatever it is, it's really always the same. Mechanically. Sex is taking another person's body inside of yours, or giving yours to them. Even when that's not *all* it is, that's *what* it is. Always. And sometimes *that's* the need. The only one. To be inside, to hold inside, to be a part of someone else, to be connected to them. That's what he needed. And it's what I needed; but I needed something more than that, too. I rolled us over a few times. Off of the blanket. Onto the ground...

I rocked on top of him. Gentle, slow, deliberate. The grass was damp underneath my knees and underneath his

124

body. And underneath the grass and the dirt, inside the ground, were the roots of the trees that hovered above us. They were connected to the lake, too. Fed off of it. Part of it. The breeze rustled through the leaves of the maples and birches so that even the wind became a part of everything. The lake. The trees. The ground...

　　...and part of Brian and me.

CHAPTER 12

When I was six years old my family was snatched out of slumber in the middle of the night by a phone call. Dave and I sat in the upstairs hallway, rubbing sleep from our eyes, while my mother muttered indistinguishable sounds into the kitchen phone downstairs. On her way back to her room she saw us waiting. Said simply, "My mother died. Now go back to sleep." Then she walked into her bedroom and closed the door.

Dave obeyed her immediately. At least, he went into his room. I have no way of knowing whether or not he actually went back to sleep. Probably he did. But I stayed awake all night, sitting outside my mother's bedroom door, quietly listening. My father was sleeping in the den by that time, so I knew she was in there all alone. Like she was every night.

I didn't go back into my room until I heard her get out of bed and open up her dresser drawer at six-fifteen. She was getting ready for work. Like she did every morning. And for weeks afterwards I wondered why it was she didn't cry that night. There are times, even now, when I wonder about that.

So when Brian and I were snatched out of slumber one night, my first conscious thought was, *who died?* He reached for the phone and my next thought was that it must be about Rachel. And I hoped that she was just sick or in jail.

"Yeah? Uh, okay...yeah, no problem." He hung it up and fell back onto the bed with a small yawn. Or it may have been a sigh of relief. "Wrong number."

Good. It was someone else's bad news. I looked at the clock. **2:38** in glowing green numbers. Just over three hours of sleep left. I rested my head on his chest to settle back down to sleep. Then it hit me.

Green numbers...

I sat up. "Shit!"

"What is it?"

"This is *my* apartment."

"Yeah. So?" Then: "Oh."

The phone rang again. Because it was my bad news. Mine.

Second ring. Some things go away if you ignore them. A ringing telephone carrying bad news in the middle of the night isn't one of them.

It was Dave. "Sorry to wake you up, Tess."

"Is Matthew okay? And Kim?"

"Yeah, they're fine."

It was Dad, then. Or my mother.

Please, God. Please don't let it be Dad...

"Tess, I...it's Alice."

"No."

Dizzy. I knew. Already.

Gone. She's gone. How?

Please let her just be sick, God. Please just sick, not...

I swallowed. Tried to talk. I had to say it again—

No!

—but couldn't find my voice. I hadn't seen her in months. Spoke to her the day before I moved. She called me at Dave's house, begged me to come see her before I left.

I'll try, Alice.

I said it even though I knew I wouldn't. I should have gone to see her. Just to say goodbye. That's all she wanted. Just to say goodbye.

Please, God, please don't let it be too late...

I cleared my throat and finally managed, "Is she sick?"

"No, she's...she died. It was a heart attack."

"Oh my God."

"It started late last night. Jason was there at the house with her and—"

Hot tears. I pulled them back and flipped myself over, onto my belly. Let my feet dangle off the side of the bed. Rested my free arm on Brian's chest. Rested my chin on my arm. Cracked the joints in my toes. Ankles. Knees. Couldn't think of anything else to do that might drown out Dave's words. I tuned back in at:

"—they lost her once in the ambulance, but they were able to bring her back. When they got her to the hospital... well, she was just too sick and...it happened about an hour ago. I was going to wait till morning to call, but I thought you'd want to know."

I nodded, even though he couldn't see it. Closed my eyes and saw Alice's kind, lovely face; tender and patient and generous. She had always loved me, always. Never stopped. Even when she should have stopped.

Please, God, no...

I started crying for real, hot stinging tears that rolled down my face and landed on Brian's chest. He touched my cheek, wiped it dry, but it was wet again a second later.

I should've gone. Should've gone to see her. Just to say goodbye.

I wanted to turn toward him, try to make out the shape of his face in the semi-darkness, but I couldn't bring myself to do it. I stared instead at the clock and got control of myself.

"Did..." I closed my eyes again. "Did Jason get a chance to say goodbye before she...went?"

"Yes. He did."

"Good." His father died when Jason was only nine. Car accident. That morning Jason was sick and stayed home from school. He slept in late, so he didn't get the chance to say his usual goodbye. Their little ritual. Fake British accents.

Goodbye, Professor Dyer.

So long, young Master Dyer.

And he'd never really gotten over it.

"Can you...can you tell Jason that...can you tell him that I'm sorry?"

What a useless, empty thing to say. Meaningless. I tried to think of something better, but a hard, hollow bubble of sadness and guilt had swelled in my chest and for a moment I was afraid that I was going to break down. Lose it for real. I swallowed, squeezed every muscle in my stomach, managed to hold it in. Took a deep breath.

"I really loved her, Dave. Can you let him know that?"

"I'll tell him."

Then there was silence, except for background noise—a woman's voice paging a doctor. Dave was still at the hospital.

Was Jason standing near him? Listening to Dave's half of the conversation? Maybe I should ask to speak to him, let him hear my condolences personally. Instead of having them filtered through my brother.

Except that I was lying in our old bed. Naked. On Brian's chest. Also naked.

Dave sighed heavily. "Well I'll let you get back to sleep. I'll call you tomorrow afternoon—well, it'll be this afternoon, actually. Hey, Tess, is this your new phone number?" He rattled it off.

It was almost funny. But not quite.

"Yeah. Why?"

"Because I...I must have dialed a wrong number right before I got you. I woke up some...guy."

I wasn't in the mood for his little fishing expedition. "Whoever he was, he'll get over it."

There was a long, long pause, then: "Yeah. I'm sure he will."

He knew. The only question was whether he knew it was Brian he'd talked to or if he thought I'd just picked up some strange guy. A random hook-up. Which would he think was worse?

"All right then. I'll talk to you later."

I hung up the phone and sat up. Took in a slow, tight breath. Let it out even slower. Brian sat up, too, and switched on the lamp beside the bed. I hadn't expected it and had to close my eyes against the sudden bright intrusion. I blinked rapidly and focused on him, but he said nothing, only looked at me expectantly.

"That was my brother. My mother-in-law—my, um, *ex*-mother-in-law—died."

He still didn't say anything.

"Heart attack."

More silence. He was waiting for more. And I couldn't think of anything. Finally he asked, "You were close to her?"

"Um, yeah. We...uh, Jason's family lived on the same road as us when we were growing up, so I've known Alice since I was a kid, and...well, anyway. She's gone."

He reached for my hand and squeezed it. "What was she like?"

"Like?"

"Yeah. You know, what kind of person was she?"

I shrugged. "She was...nice."

Nice was a stupid word and Alice deserved a better one, deserved a thousand and one of them. And if she had been just a friend then I could've found all those words, used them to tell Brian all about her. Tell him about the sound of her potter's wheel, tell him about my easel. That she always smelled of ginger, even though she never baked. How she encouraged my impractical dreams when my own mother was too busy with work and money to bother even asking me what they were. Let me visit with her, long after I was past the age of needing a babysitter. Just let me sit with her in the workshop, and didn't ask questions, during my last two horrible years of high school, after my mother had completely given up on me.

I wanted to tell him all of it, and I knew he wanted to let me, probably wanted to hear about her. Because it would help him to know me better. And because he wanted to comfort me. But it would all lead back to Jason.

Pump faster, Tess. You can do it! Faster. Now...let go!

Make it clear to him just how deeply those roots went. He didn't need that rubbed in his face. And I didn't want to be reminded of it.

He finally said, simply, "I'm sorry."

I only shrugged again and wiped away another tear. What I really needed was to let it out. Have a good, hard cry. Because that's what you do when you lose someone you love, what you're supposed to do. Cry. Say goodbye. Move on. But the idea of mourning my ex-husband's mother in front of my new boyfriend didn't feel right. And, even worse, I had a sudden, creepy feeling that somehow Alice could see me now, knew that I was in her son's bed with someone other than her son.

Stop it. You're just tired. Just go back to sleep. Bury your head in your pillow and hunker down until morning. You can let it all out in the shower after Brian leaves for work. You can hold it in. Just a few more hours. You can do it. You can wait.

I tried to tell him I was okay, to turn off the light. I wanted to remind him that he had to be to work early and that he needed to get back to sleep. Instead the bubble finally burst. It burst with a horrible, sick yelp that I tried to swallow, but couldn't.

I struggled blindly to make my escape to the bathroom, to have my breakdown in private; but he reached out before I could and pulled me to him, held me tightly against him so I couldn't get away. I lay there with my face against his chest, trying not to cry, mostly succeeded. Just a few errant tears. A few dry, sickening sobs. And still Brian held me, whispered comforting words, stroked my hair. Told me, over and over, to just let it out, that it was okay to cry. But I couldn't. The guilt was too great, bigger than the grief.

I'll try, Alice. If I have time after I'm all done packing. I'll try then.
It was bullshit. Most of it was packed already. Just waiting to be moved. She knew it, too. Knew she wouldn't see me. Probably ever.

Coward.

And then there was Jason. He had lost the woman who was the most precious person in the world to him. He was— at this very moment—being tortured with a grief I couldn't even imagine. And he had no one to hold him like I did, to whisper sweet words of comfort and love in his ear, to make him feel safe.

And it's all my fault.

I fell asleep sometime, against Brian's chest. And when I woke up a few hours later he asked if I was okay. I told him, *yes, thanks for holding me, I feel better now.* And it was true. I did feel better.

I didn't feel anything.

* * *

True to his word my brother called me with details about the funeral.

"Do you think you'll make it?"

"I think it would be pretty awkward for Jason if I'm there. Don't you?"

He sighed. "I don't know, Tess. It's up to you."

I rubbed my eyes. Mulled it over. I knew already. Everyone would be there. Everyone.

"If I show up it will cause a fuss, and I don't want that. Everyone's energy should be focused on comforting Jason, not on gossiping about us."

"If you don't show up then they'll just talk about you anyway. It will all be about why you weren't there."

"Well if I'm gonna be in a damned if I do, damned if I don't situation I'd rather do the 'don't.' It won't do Jason any good having me there anyway. I bought a card for him this morning. I'll mail it to him and leave it to his friends to do the rest."

"I guess you're right."

"You sound exhausted, Dave. Did you get any sleep last night?"

"None."

"Well, try to get some tonight."

"Speaking of sleep, Tess…that wasn't a wrong number I got last night. Was it."

I'd known it was coming, eventually. I just figured he'd wait, maybe until after things had settled down. After the funeral at least. "Dave, I don't think this is an appropriate time to get into this subject."

"Really? And when would be an appropriate time?"

I sighed. Why not? What was the big deal anyway? I wasn't committing a crime. Hell, this time I wasn't even committing adultery. Why shouldn't he know? Why shouldn't they all know?

"I've been…seeing someone. It's just been a couple weeks, but—"

"That didn't take you very long."

"What the hell is that supposed to mean?"

"You don't think it's a little soon?"

"Is there a waiting period I'm supposed to observe? Shit, I guess I shoulda bought me some black dye to boil all my clothes in the day after Saint Jason left me so I—"

"Cut the bullshit, okay? I only meant…you just moved down there. That's all I meant." He groaned. "Jesus Christ, Tess. Who is it? That kid from downstairs?"

"It's none of your goddamned business, Dave. What a fucking double standard. And I never expected it from you. Jason started banging someone less than a week after he left me and all you had to say about it was some bullshit about how he was doing it for an ego boost. Here it is, closing in on a year later, and I'm starting an actual relationship, not just putting a few notches in my bedpost. And *I'm* the one getting shit? Is it because I'm a woman? Or because Jason's your best friend?"

"Goddamn it, Tess, it's neither. Just forget it. You were right. This isn't an appropriate time to get into it. I'm sorry I even brought it up."

I rubbed my forehead. It was throbbing. The sort of throb I knew from experience wouldn't fade anytime soon. Then I took a deep breath. I might as well tell him the truth. He was going to find out sooner or later; they all were. And I wasn't ashamed. I had no reason to be.

"It was Brian. And it's not what you think."

Silence. So much of it I began to think we'd been cut off. Finally he said, "Okay, Tess. Whatever makes you happy, I guess."

I snickered. I couldn't help it. Because I'd heard those words from him once before.

He remembered, too. "I mean…I just don't want to see you get hurt again."

"Oh." It was the first time he'd ever acknowledged that I'd been hurt, too. It was the first time anyone had.

He cleared his throat. "Don't forget to send the card, Tess. I think Jason will…it would be a nice gesture."

I checked the clock. 4:34. Just enough time to write a few lines, sign my name, and drop it off at the post office before work. Except for one thing.

"Dave…I don't know his new address. I always just had my lawyer—"

He gave it to me.

"Thanks. He should get it in the mail tomorrow."

"Good. Well…I'll talk to you later."

I hung up the phone and sat down at the table. Looked at the card. Orange sunset. Inside it was white. Blank. Scary. I'd always hated words. Always. Especially now. And this card didn't need any. The sunset said it all.

I looked up at the clock again. I was running out of time. I scribbled a few lines, read them over, added a few more, and read the whole thing. Read it again and groaned.

Then I drove to the post office. Bought a stamp from a tall, young brunette who told me, without much enthusiasm, to have a nice evening. I wished her the same, only with even less enthusiasm. She was one of Them. One of the local girls who'd kept Brian company over the winter. Like curly, blonde Ashley from the insurance company. And the pretty, dark receptionist at Dr. Stephens's office. And the curvy, red-headed cashier at the courtesy counter at the market. There were others too. They always seemed to be staring. Sizing me up. But there wasn't anything I could do about it.

I dropped the card in the mailbox outside. It told me that the last pickup had been at four-thirty, almost half an hour ago. But Jason would get a hundred cards in the next few days. If he bothered to open mine at all he'd only skim through the awkward expressions of sympathy…then he'd toss it aside. So what difference would a day make?

A big difference. Huge. And it wouldn't get tossed aside. I was too tired to fool myself, and that didn't happen very often. But there wasn't anything I could do about the postal service, either. And so I went to work. To start cleaning. Other people's shit.

CHAPTER 13

Something I learned about Brian in our first month together—because he frequently told me—was that he wasn't one of *those* guys. He meant, of course, that he wasn't a chauvinistic asshole who couldn't take care of himself.

"I'm not gonna let you do all the cooking, Tess. I'm not one of *those* guys."

A noble sentiment. What it actually meant was this: on Tuesday, Thursday, and Sunday he went through the strenuous effort of opening a can or two, and sometimes a box, for the microwave; on Monday, Wednesday, and Saturday he pushed vegetables and broiled chicken or fish around his plate with his fork, looking at me like I was Judas Iscariot. Our only night of refuge was Friday. That's when he treated me to supper at Zeke's. Things finally came to a head when I came home one warm Thursday evening in the middle of June to Spaghetti O's and fish sticks.

"You like fish."

"This isn't fish."

He grabbed the box from the freezer and looked at the ingredients.

"Okay, Brian, this is ridiculous. We need to start doing our shopping together so we can get some food we both like."

Saturday, late afternoon. Small-town market. Narrow aisles. Customers who appraised us with expert eyes and laughed. Because we couldn't even agree on hot dogs.

"I'm not eating tofu."

"They're not made from tofu. They're organic, but they're still made with meat. See…" I pointed to the package.

"Chicken hot dogs?"

"Look. Yours have nitrates. These don't."

"What the hell is a nitrate?"

"They're…it's…I don't remember," I admitted irritably. "But I know they're bad for you. And besides, they use real meat in these. Those hot dogs are just made from—"

"I really don't want to know what they're made from."

By the time we made it to the deli we both needed a break. I left him to fend for himself while I soldiered onward with the cart. I wasn't too worried. I'd been through this kind of thing before. I got Jason to quit smoking, so getting Brian to start eating healthier would be a breeze.

I stopped in Health and Beauty to examine a jar of eye cream that I'd seen advertised on TV. It was *guaranteed to minimize the appearance of fine lines and wrinkles.* I read through the list of ingredients then put it back on the shelf. It may very well have been a miracle product, just like the teenager masquerading as a thirty-something-year-old woman in the commercial claimed, but it was full of chemicals whose names were too long and had too many consonants for comfort. And when I looked up from the shelf I saw a mass of blonde curls coming at me that was too familiar for comfort. Ashley. I seemed to run into her everywhere I went. And today, of course, she'd hit the jackpot.

"Hi, Tess."

I nodded. Looked at her outfit. Short shorts. Tight T-shirt.

You're no Daisy Duke, honey.

She didn't have to be. She was young and thin and cute and blonde and had pretty, clear green eyes. And no wrinkles. But it really was stupid to be jealous of a little girl, so I smiled and managed to sound friendly as I asked her how she was doing.

She was doing great. Life was great. She'd just got a raise at work, her second one in six months. Her mother's new boyfriend had given her his old computer, which was very, very exciting, because she could surf the Web at her apartment now instead of having to go to her mom's house to do it. She had tickets to some concert, and it made me feel like a grandma because the band's name sounded only vaguely familiar...

She rambled on and on, from one inane topic to another. It was more than just polite conversation and I knew it, but I let her ramble anyway and surveyed her cart while she did. It was filled with beer and chips and just about every kind of liquor imaginable, and it made me wonder just what kind of raises they gave out over there at that insurance company. It might be time to raise my rates.

Finally, the moment she'd been waiting for. It was almost amusing to see her expression undergo its startling transformation as she caught sight of him. Her eyes lit up, her smile widened—in fact her whole face seemed to jump up and holler "Yee haw!" And I did the only thing I could do. Which was nothing. Except stand there and watch.

Brian was mercifully oblivious to the hell he was walking into, because his head was bent over several deli packages. "The lady back there said *these* are all full of nitrates too, but—"

He looked up and saw her. The transformation on his face was startling, too, but not at all amusing. Surprise, of course. Then embarrassment. Finally, there was shame. And that told me everything I needed to know.

He glanced quickly at me, wondering what, if anything, I knew. I just grinned. Then he looked away and tossed the lunchmeat into the cart. Ashley gave her curls a toss and got the ball rolling.

"How have you been, Brian?"

"Great." He still couldn't look her in the eye. "You?"

"I've been okay." She dragged the last syllable out until she hit nearly every note in the key of B flat. Then she brightened up. "Today's my birthday."

He nodded. Looked at her cart, examined the contents, then finally looked up at her. "Rachel's not twenty-one yet. She's not even twenty. You know that, don't you, Ash?"

I tried not to shudder at hearing him use her nickname. She, on the other hand, beamed up at him even more brightly than before.

"Yeah, I know. Rachel was a year behind me in school. Remember?"

And she'd be there anyway. She'd get plastered or high or both. Then she'd go home with some guy. And there was nothing he could do about it.

But Ashley had a suggestion.

"You can come, Brian. If you want. That way you can keep an eye on her."

He didn't even miss a beat. "Nope. We already have plans."

She looked at me and I gave her an eyebrow.

That's right, honey. While you're getting drunk and stoned with your little friends he'll be in my bed. Fucking me. Stuff that in your training bra.

And there it was. The secret to eternal youth: Jealousy and pettiness. I'd gone from grandma to ten-year-old in less than five minutes.

She shrugged and turned her attention back to Brian. "If you change your mind feel free to pop in. You know where I live."

Ah. Well, at least it hadn't happened in his bed.

She strolled merrily away. It hadn't gone too badly after all. And that meant that we'd have to do it all over again some other time. I studied my list. Crossed out three items I'd already crossed out. Looked at the cart and then my list again. I finally felt confident enough in my ability to speak. "What kind of toothpaste do you want?"

No answer. I looked up. His hands were stuffed in his pockets and his face was tense with what appeared to be defiance. I countered with a blank stare. Finally, he reached over, grabbed a tube of toothpaste, and threw it into the cart. I tossed the eye cream in on top of it.

He drove us home in silence. More silence while we split the groceries and took turns putting them away. First his cupboards. Then mine. We ate a silent supper in my apartment, a Brian-friendly meal of hot dogs and macaroni-and-cheese and a salad. By the time we finished eating he'd finally had enough.

"You're just gonna sit there all night not saying anything about her?"

"What's there to say? It's none of my business what you did before we got together."

What I meant, of course, was *who* you did. And he knew it.

"Haven't you ever done something stupid before?"

"Of course. That's why I'm not gonna say anything about her."

He nodded, but he was still irritated. He cleared the table while I brushed my teeth, then he helped me with the dishes. And after the final fork was safely tucked away inside the silverware drawer he said:

"Let's go out tonight."

"Sounds good."

"There's this dance club in Westville—"

He knew better than that.

"Oh, come on, Tess. Live a little."

"I can't dance."

He didn't push it. Even though he wanted to. "Okay. A movie then. I'll even let you pick it out."

It seemed a little strange that it was our first time out. Our first actual date. I chose an action flick that was a sequel to a movie I knew was one of his favorites. Car chases and explosions and very bad acting. A sex scene that showed the girl fully naked and the hero only shirtless. Didn't even show his ass, which wasn't fair. It was still pretty hot. Then there was the inevitable breakup followed by the inevitable shootout. The bad guys all died and the hero walked away with only a few scratches. And, of course, he patched things up with the girl. As we walked out of the theater I wondered if she'd be back for the inevitable part three or if they'd find the aging hero a newer—and even younger— love interest.

It was a perfect June night. Starry and warm and not muggy at all. He unlocked the truck door and opened it up for me and before I got in I stood up on tiptoe and whispered in his ear. Told him he should pull around to the side of the building where it was dark and deserted. Because, I said, the sex scenes had made me horny. And because of the novelty of doing it in a vehicle in a public place. And, I didn't say, because of the other thing.

I didn't have to ask twice. And it was great. Even better than the sex in the movie. And then he drove us home. It was almost midnight but neither of us were tired. We lay in my bed in the darkness, wide awake and silent, but not still. He fidgeted. Tapped his feet and hands on the mattress, along to some beat that only he could hear. Rolled over onto his side, then his stomach. Onto his back again. Finally he hopped up. Switched on the overhead light and ceiling fan, jumped back onto the bed, pinned me down and tickled me till I begged for mercy. Then he rolled off me, snuggled in close and, before I'd even caught my breath, said:

"Tell me something about you I don't know. Something real."

I didn't have to think too hard. The list was long but most of the items on the list weren't open for discussion. So I nodded toward the living room and said, "I painted all the pictures hanging on the wall out there."

He shook his head and started tracing invisible circles around my belly button with his index finger, in sync with the shadow of the fan. "I knew that already."

"How did you know that?" They were all signed, of course, but the signatures were all deliberately illegible.

"Maybe because I'm not an idiot."

"Oh."

"They're really good, you know. Have you ever sold any of your paintings?"

"Actually…" I could feel my face burning, even though the breeze from the fan was chilly. "I put one in a gallery a few weeks ago. Over in Hallowell."

I didn't tell him that I knew the guy who owned it. I'd had a quick fling with him right before Jason and I got together. My last fling. Nice guy, the kind you could settle down with. And someone had, because he was married now. At least as married as the law allowed. To another nice guy. Because despite my best efforts I wasn't able to turn him.

"Really?" He smiled. "What's the painting of?"

"The orchard that used to be out back." I braced myself, because I knew, from his beaming face, what was coming next.

"Let's go there tomorrow so I can see it."

I dropped my gaze, focused on his chest, on the dark, curly hair. "It sold already." I looked up at his face again to see his reaction.

"Oh." He tried to look happy, and mostly succeeded, but his voice sounded a little hurt. "What made you decide to sell it?"

…without letting me see it first?

"Well...I needed the money. My house cleaning jobs are the only ones that aren't behind and my savings was getting low—"

It had all but run out. There had only been five dollars left, the minimum amount to keep the account open.

"—and I didn't think it would sell. At least not that quickly. But I figured it was worth a shot and...anyway."

He waited a moment then ventured, "If you need money, Tess—"

"No. Let's not go there."

"Tess—"

"Look, I'm okay now. The checks are finally starting to roll in for work I did back in March and April. I should be fine from now on. You know how billing cycles and payment cycles work."

"Yes I do. But..." He sighed. "I think it's awesome that one of your paintings sold. I'm not surprised, because I think you've got a lot of talent. But I hate that you only did it because you were broke."

"It's not like it's gonna be a habit. I don't paint to make money. I just do it because I...well, not for money. Not usually, anyway."

It was the first time I'd sold one of my paintings. I knew it was supposed to feel like an accomplishment. Validation. But it only made me feel dirty.

"I've been doing some new sketches lately, if that makes you feel any better."

"Actually, it does. What have you been sketching?"

I smiled. "Our lake."

He smiled back. I thought he was going to ask if he could see what I'd done so far, and I prepared myself for having to let him down again. I couldn't let him see the sketches; not yet. I wasn't at all happy with them. As he'd predicted, the summer people had taken over the lake. It was constantly abuzz with motors which made it impossible for me to capture it with any accuracy. Heat and sadness and love and connection...

But he didn't ask to see them. Instead he brushed my bangs out of my eyes and said, "Tell me about Kineo."

"Kineo?"

"Yeah. That Kineo painting."

I shrugged. "There's not really much to tell. It's a painting of a mountain and a lake."

"Bullshit. There's more to it than just that." He propped himself up a little higher on his elbow and, for the first time since I'd known him, struggled to find words to express himself. "There's something about it, Tess, and I don't know what it is. I never saw a *place* that looked like that before. It's almost like the mountain is...like it's weeping. It's like a heartbreak or something. I don't even know how you *do* that with just a brush and some paint. Were you sad, or depressed or whatever, when you did it?"

"No. I wasn't."

I'd painted it during my first summer with Jason. Summer of Love. We'd gone to Moosehead Lake for a daytrip and had a great time. Mount Kineo was supposed to be the highlight of the day because neither of us had ever seen it. It was a beautiful, oddly shaped mountain. Narrow at the bottom, cresting high above the lake, then ending suddenly flat on one side, in high, flinty cliffs. At first glance, from a distance, it had reminded me of the whale from Pinocchio, and we had laughed about that.

"I wasn't depressed. But when I was up there I heard this story...a legend about a—" I pulled the sheet up and started playing with it, making little accordion folds. "It sounds stupid now, but it was about an Indian princess. Her husband went out on a hunting trip and he never came back. She waited and waited, for a long time, but...nothing. No word from him, not anything from him. He was just...gone. She was so...heartbroken that she jumped off the cliff and into the water, and killed herself. It was...it...I don't know. I guess it sort of stuck with me."

It had done more than that. The woman who had told us the story—she was a waitress in a restaurant a few towns over from where the mountain stood—had done so very matter-of-factly. It was obvious she'd told it a thousand times, and it didn't really mean anything to her other than as a minor point of interest for tourists. But it had scared the hell out of me, so badly that I couldn't eat my lunch.

Are you feeling all right, Tess?

Yeah, Jase. Just a little carsick. I'll be fine.

It was after sunset when we drove past the mountain again on our way home. It looked different somehow. Lonely. Forbidding. Rising out of the water like a haunted headstone.

We got home late, exhausted from the day and the drive, but I couldn't sleep. I lay awake for hours watching his peaceful, sleeping face. I couldn't stop thinking about the poor woman—who had probably never really existed—waiting for her husband to return. Sick with worry. Going over every horrifying possibility of what might have happened to him. Had he been killed in the forest by an animal? Come across a member of an enemy tribe or stumbled upon a white settlement? Maybe his canoe had capsized and he had drowned in the lake...

Or maybe he had just run off. Got bored or restless. Or fell out of love. And just...left her.

I shot out of bed, shaking so badly that my teeth actually chattered, pulled out my easel and poured everything out onto a fresh canvas. Dark, frantic, heavy lines. Foggy. Black and gray and dark, dark blue. But I wasn't sad, I wasn't depressed when I painted that picture. I was scared out of my fucking mind. Scared of losing that feeling I had only just discovered, for the first time in my life, of being in love and having someone love me back. Safe and completely, truly happy. Most of all I was scared because I could imagine, for a brief, fatigue-induced moment, why that Indian princess had climbed to the top of the steep, woody mountain. Looked over the edge. And jumped. Landing hard on the water.

Brian touched my cheek and I jumped, startled back to reality.

"All that stuff you're feeling right now? You got that all on the canvas, Tess." He ran his finger gently underneath both my eyes. I hadn't realized I was crying. "But I'm gonna make sure you never feel like that again."

I nodded, blinked back a few more tears, then gave him my best smile. It didn't fool him but he didn't say anything.

"It's pretty late you know," I said. "And you need to get up early in the morning."

"Nice try. Even I don't work on Sunday." He brushed my cheek gently with his lips. Then he whispered softly in my ear, "I love you. You know that, don't you?"

Just like that. Even though I'd already known it. So I said it back. "Yes I know. I love you, too."

He fell asleep with his arm wrapped tight around me. He was so close that I could actually feel his breath, warm on my shoulder, his heart beating against my back. It was telling me that everything was okay again, that I was safe and loved. But I stayed awake all night anyway, shivering. Because I'd felt that way before. And I knew. Even if Brian didn't.

Flying. Falling. Landing hard.

CHAPTER 14

"Six plates? Is that boy eating with us?"

I grabbed a fistful of forks and knives from the drawer. Took a deep breath. Handed them to my mother. "Yes. *Brian* is eating with us."

Kim hopped up out of her chair. "I'll go tell the guys everything is ready."

What she meant was:

Thank God. An excuse to get the hell out of here, even if it's just for a few minutes.

Fourth of July. It's normally a safe time for a Bellows' Family Day. Throw everyone outside with a plateful of barbequed chicken and corn on the cob, some coleslaw and potato salad. Give 'em each a couple of beers. Set up a horseshoe pit and a volleyball net and everyone has something to do. Something to keep them occupied. Very little opportunity for conversation, and that's important. This year it was more important than ever. Which is exactly why, this year, it was raining. It was coming down in buckets. And that meant we were trapped indoors. With nothing to occupy us. Except for conversation.

So far so good. Brian, Dave, and my dad were all out-side, standing underneath my dad's umbrella, peering under the hood of Brian's truck. Dave's idea. He'd said:

"Let's go take a peek at that alternator. Maybe we can figure out what's wrong with it."

What he'd meant, of course was:

Come on, Dad. Let's keep this poor guy away from Mom for as long as we can.

But he hadn't left me completely unprotected. He never did. He'd left me Kim, which meant my mother had played nice. But now Kim was leaving and Matthew was too young to do me any good.

The door closed quietly. I clenched my toes, my stomach, my heart.

"Just when it looks like you can't screw your life up any worse that you already have," she began, "you manage to top yourself."

I grabbed my mitts, opened the oven door and pulled out the chicken.

"Just how old *is* he? Twenty?"

Set it on the counter.

"What exactly is your plan this time, Theresa?"

On a hot pad.

"It's all well and good for you to go back to playing your little games, but—"

I pulled the aluminum foil off the pan and inhaled deeply.

"—this one lives right downstairs."

The smell of barbeque sauce made my mouth water. I opened the oven again and shoved the chicken back inside to brown.

"You couldn't manage to stay in the same *town* as Jason when you were done with him."

I grabbed the potato salad from the fridge and set it on the counter.

"So why do you think you can live upstairs from this boy when he's through with you?"

Then the coleslaw.

"Does he know what you did to Jason?"

I took the lid off the steaming stockpot and looked inside at the corn. The great debate: Transfer it to a platter now, and risk letting it getting cold?

"Does he know that he can't trust you around his friends?"

Or let it stay inside the hot water and get soggy? Because if they didn't hurry up and come inside soon then it would. Get soggy. Soggy and gross instead of crisp and tender and sweet. It would be ruined. Ruined and, god*damn* it, what the fucking hell was taking them so long?

"At least the boy is self-employed. He doesn't have a boss he'll need to keep an eagle eye on whenever you walk in the room. Or worry about whenever he leaves the room. Too bad I wasn't so lucky."

Bull's-eye. I could actually hear my nerves snap. I spun on my heel, lid in hand, mouth open, ready to let her have it. But that's when the cavalry arrived. Dave came through the door first. He checked my face, then my mother's, and then mine again. Damage report. I gave him a brief smile that said, *I'm okay.* Even though I wasn't. He was followed by Kim, who headed directly for her still-sleeping baby, then my dad, who avoided eye contact with both my mother and me. And finally Brian.

He strolled right over, gave me a quick kiss on the cheek and asked, "What can I do? And don't say 'nothing.'"

I took in a shaky breath, then did a quick inventory. Something was missing and I couldn't think of what it was. I rubbed my left temple. It had been aching for three days, in spite of all the Tylenol I'd taken. Brian had finally taken the bottle away from me because, he'd said, taking that much was bad for my liver.

Liver...

"Beer."

He nodded and went to work. Emptied two bags of ice into a huge metal bucket. Filled that with the beer bottles. I watched him, still rubbing my temple. Pressed down on the spot that throbbed the worst. My mother noticed, sauntered over and put a hand on my forehead. I pulled away.

"I'm fine."

Fuck off. You don't get to play the role of Concerned Mom.

She backed up and gave me a small smile.

Suits me just fine.

Everybody grabbed a plate, filled it, and settled around the table. For a few minutes the only sounds were those made by clinking silverware and sloshing beer. I snuck a glance at my mother. She was sneaking glances at Brian in between mouthfuls. He was sitting beside me, happily stuffing his face with potato salad. It had been a few weeks since he'd eaten a carbohydrate that wasn't high in fiber. I looked over at Dave, who was already looking at me. Waiting for his signal. I gave him a brief nod and he cleared his throat.

"Brian, what's the fishing like down here?"

He wiped a glob of dressing off his mouth with his napkin before he answered. "They stock the lake real good every year. Trouble is you can't get on it anymore unless you got a house down there, and those are all bought up."

Dave nodded sympathetically. It was getting that way all over the state. Then he told Brian about the place where he and my dad frequently fished, about an hour west of New Mills. It was too far into the woods for tourists to know about it, but easy to get to with a truck. Then he asked Brian if he'd like to join them for their annual Labor Day fishing weekend. He accepted the invitation, surprised but happy.

After a minute or so of silence Brian picked up the slack with the safest of all possible topics. He nodded toward Matthew and said:

"You guys have got a great-looking baby there."

It wasn't safe enough. My mother had been waiting for an opportunity to strike.

"How many children do *you* have, young man?"

I glared at her, but she ignored me and fixed Brian with an icy stare. He gave her an eyebrow of his own.

"I don't have any children, Mrs. Bellows."

"Has Theresa told you that she doesn't like children?"

"No. She didn't. She told me she doesn't want any kids of her own. But from what I've seen she *likes* 'em just fine."

My mother was undeterred. "Don't you want children of *your* own someday?"

He gave her a sweet smile. "Only an idiot would get involved with a woman who doesn't want kids if he does. *I'm* not an idiot."

Dave's ears turned red, my dad choked on his coleslaw, and Kim snickered, then covered it over with a cough.

My mother gave Brian a dirty look while she prepared her troops for the second wave of the assault. He was a formidable opponent, true, but she wasn't in the habit of retreating. I cast a frantic glance at Dave. He swallowed whatever it was he was chewing, washed it down with some beer and came to the rescue.

"Uh...Tess. How is—business going?"

Normally, of course, the subject of work was off limits. But I had called him earlier in the week and told him my good news. My business clients were all still behind but paying steadily and my housecleaning jobs were all up to date. For the first time in my life I was more than just self-sufficient. I was caught up on the bills and building a savings. Because I knew, of course, that once fall came and the Summer People left, my pay would be cut in half. It didn't matter, though, because I was planning ahead. Calamity foreseen and dealt with. For once.

And it felt good.

So I gave my mother a brief rundown of my weekly schedule. Busy, busy, busy. Out there working hard. Making Money. And when I finished speaking I fixed her with what I hoped was a pair of cold, blue eyes.

I'm earning my paycheck.

She pretended not to notice.

"Hey, that's great." Dave said. "It didn't take you long to get back on track."

It didn't take my mother long, either. She ran through the list of what the rest of the family did from eight till five.

"David is a well-respected lawyer in Brookfield—"

Brian knew that and, of course, my mother knew that he did. But she never missed the chance to savor the way the words rolled off her tongue. *My son, the lawyer.* So much better than, *Tess. She cleans toilets.*

"—John is an accountant—"

My dad despised his work and his boss.

"—I work as an office manager for Mike Poulin."

Here she paused for effect. Brian didn't know who Mike Poulin was and just nodded politely. I polished off my second beer and reached for a third. Finally she finished with:

"And Kimberly is a registered nurse in the cardiac intensive care unit."

Brian turned to Kim with obvious interest. "Really?"

My mother added, "She'll be going back to work in the fall."

Kim glanced at Matthew and said, "We'll see."

Brian plunged ahead. "When my mother was sick we hardly ever saw the doctor. But the nurses were *always* there. They took real good care of her. Me and my sister, too. They knew just as much about what was going on as the doctors did, and they were a lot nicer. If you ask me, nurses are *way* underpaid."

Kim smiled at him. Score one for Brian.

"Tess didn't go to college," my mother started.

"Neither did I," Brian returned.

"She wanted to go to school for her painting, but I told her that I wasn't about to *pay* for her to play with her paints. Not when she could fool around with them at home for free." She narrowed her gaze at me. "If you were really serious about it I'm sure you could have found...*some* way to pay for it on your own."

I finished my beer. Two thirds of a bottle in one long, noisy gulp. I plunked it down on the table and looked toward the big, beautiful beer bucket, sitting prettily on the floor next to the kitchen counter. I wondered if a fourth would do me more harm than good.

"She's much better off cleaning, anyway," my mother added. "She's *good* at that."

She'd finally managed to shock Brian. He sat silently for longer than I thought possible. Just staring at her. She held his gaze. Just waiting. And he said:

"Tess sold a painting last month. Obviously someone thinks she's good at *that*, too."

She only shrugged.

He set his fork down and rested his arms on the table. Leaned forward. "Don't you think she's a good painter, Mrs. Bellows?"

He thought he had her cornered. That he knew what she'd say, what she'd *have* to say. But he was wrong. He'd done it. And he didn't even know it.

He didn't know her.

She looked at me. At me, with those hard eyes. And I wanted to look away from them but I couldn't. So I sat there, staring back at her. Just waiting.

"No, I don't. And I think she's wasting her time and her energy and her money when she should be using them for—"

But she didn't get any farther. At the words, *No, I don't*, Brian grabbed my hand. I looked away from my mother and over at him. His eyes were filled with remorse. Because now he knew.

"Don't listen to her, Tess. You're a great artist."

I couldn't think of anything to say. Part of it was because I was a little foggy from having downed three beers in less than fifteen minutes. But most of it was because his words were still bouncing around in my brain. They echoed. Everywhere. Especially:

Artist.

It sounded good. Better than good. I especially loved the way it sounded in his voice. And I loved him for saying it, because it was the first time anyone had. Not just, *you do good work* or *that's a nice painting*.

Artist.

But even better than that was: *Don't listen to her.* Because what he'd really meant was: *She's hurting you. And I'm gonna make her stop.* Even though it wasn't true. Nothing, ever, would really make her stop. But at least it was true for a little while. And at least he was willing to try.

Dave cleared his throat and said, "Yes she is."

And that made my dad brave enough to ask about the painting I'd sold.

"Oh. Um, it was...it was just an orchard."

Hope. That's what I'd called it. In my mind. Then I sold it.

And that's when Matthew woke up demanding food. It was about time, too. Dave held the kid close to his chest while he him gave his bottle. The rest of us finished our meal in silence, then I cleared the table while the guys and my mother retired into the living room. There was plenty of room for everyone because now I had three new armchairs and a new coffee table. I'd paid fifty bucks for all four pieces at a yard sale the week before. None of them matched each other or my couch, and my living room was a little crowded now; but they were colorful and clean. And none of them were plastic.

Kim and I did the dishes while Brian and my dad talked politics. It was a topic I'd given him the green light to bring up, since they were pretty much on the same page. Dave interjected from time to time, but my mother said nothing. She just stared out the window. Out at the rain.

Once the dishes were done I sat beside Brian on the couch. He was holding Matthew on his lap, facing him. It was the first time I'd looked at his face since the day he was born. He still looked like Dave, even had the eyes. He was very fascinated, for some reason, with Brian's nose and he stared at it for quite some time. Brian attempted to hand him off to me, but Matthew took one look at my face, puckered his own and bawled for all he was worth.

Kim grabbed him and covered with, "He's just had too much excitement today, Tess. That's all."

They only stayed for another hour, because there's not much to do inside a small, crowded apartment on a rainy day with a cranky baby who's had too much excitement. I said my goodbyes from the living room and Brian walked them out to Dave's new minivan. I watched from my window while he waved at them from underneath my umbrella. When he came back upstairs a few minutes later I was still sitting down on the couch. He stood over me. Upside down. And still he was beautiful. He didn't bother with *are you okay?* Instead he went right to:

"He married her because he knocked her up. Right?"

I nodded. "They were both nineteen. Then I came along two years later and her life was really over." I was a Thanksgiving baby. Because God has a sense of humor.

"Is that what she told you?"

"Sort of."

He pondered for a moment, then said, a bit reluctantly, "That's more than just a mother-daughter thing. I mean,

I've seen Laura and her mother go at it before, and it's not pretty. But your mother…she doesn't like you. Does she?"

Nobody had ever said it out loud before and it felt good to hear it. But the truth was that it went even deeper than dislike. My mother hated me. She'd hated me even before I was born. And even though I'd always known it, she had confirmed it for me when I was fifteen. It was the weekend before Dave's eleventh-grade final exams. I sat across from him at the kitchen table, quizzing him on landmark Supreme Court cases for his history class, while she stood at the counter, hacking up vegetables for supper.

"Mapp versus Ohio."

"Nineteen sixty-one. Guards against unreasonable search and seizure."

"Gibbons versus Ogden."

"Eighteen twenty-four. The states cannot interfere with the power of Congress to regulate commerce."

"Commerce?" I rolled my eyes. "Bo-*ring*."

"Come on, Tess."

"All right, all right, all right. How 'bout…Roe versus Wade."

My mother snorted over the celery. "That one came two years too late for me."

I glanced up at her, then back at Dave's notes. And then I shivered.

Roe versus Wade, 1973. The Supreme Court recognizes a woman's right to abortion.

Two years too late. Not *four* years. Not just *too late*. Not Dave. Me. And what can you say to that? Nothing, except: "Hazelwood versus Kuhlmeier…"

I cleared my throat. "No. She doesn't like me. But then, the feeling is mutual. So it's really no big deal."

It was a big deal, of course. But it's one of those things you just have to let go, because there's nothing you can do to change it. And talking about it isn't going to make it any better. So he kissed me. Upside down. Then he plopped down beside me.

"Who is Mike Poulin?"

I blinked. "What?"

"Your mom said she worked for a Mike Poulin. Am I supposed to know who that is?"

"Oh. Uh…not really. He's a *well-respected* businessman back in Brookfield." I laughed, because it was a pretty good imitation of my mother. Then I cleared my throat. "He was a selectman for a while, too, so…well, it's a big deal for her to be working for him."

"Oh." He put his arm around me, then nodded to the wall with my paintings. "I meant what I said, you know. You're really good. *That's* what you should be doing, all the time."

I didn't say anything; just snuggled in close and rested my head on his shoulder. We sat there in silence. Looking out the window. Just watching the rain.

It was still coming down in buckets.

* * *

Later that night I lit a dozen tiny candles all over my room and we made love in my bed; slow and hot and beautiful. The room was filled with shadows. They flickered everywhere: on the ceiling, on the walls, on Brian's face as it hovered gently over mine. My heart was open wide, filled and overflowing with a thousand fragile emotions I couldn't even put names to. I stared into his eyes, eyes that were glowing with dark orange light. Glowing with love and heat and the reflected flames of the candles, and I was too overwhelmed for words or moans or sounds of any kind. I just gazed at him, at those eyes, his hot breath on my face, as he reached inside me and touched my soul.

And when we were finished, when I was lying in his arms, I looked into his eyes again and I said it. Even though I'd said it to him before, more times than I could count.

"I love you, Brian."

I said it to him again. Because it was the first time that I'd really meant it.

CHAPTER 15

Friday was always a busy day. Doctor's office. Real estate office. Zeke's house, which was still a lonely mess. Then I spent the rest of the day cleaning camps on the lake.

They weren't really camps, they were houses. Most of them were once owned by locals but they'd been bought up by Flatlanders, people From Away. The ones with names like Talbot and Caldwell and Pratt. These families generally fell into two categories: the couples who were in their late thirties or early forties who had teenaged children, and the May–December couples.

The husbands, December and otherwise, spent most of their time on their computers or cell phones, keeping themselves connected to the Real World. Business. Money. Important Matters. The May wives planned parties and swam in the lake and tanned their skinny little bodies in the sun, drove their cute little cars into the salon, the one where Laura worked, to have their hair and nails done. And they got together and gossiped. The forty-year-old wives did all of the things the May wives did, but they also set aside precious time from their busy schedules for Business. It wasn't the same kind of business that their husbands

conducted, but it was just as important. It was the business
of Staying Young.

They worked hard at it. Exercise and trips into Portland for Botox injections. Facials. Plastic surgery. Because
they knew all about the May–December couples. And they
wanted to make sure that their own husbands didn't turn
their own May secretaries or massage therapists—or a stray
waitress—into the second Mrs. Talbot or Caldwell or Pratt.
They even eyed their cleaning lady with suspicion, which is
why I always made a point to wear my oldest, baggiest jeans
and an oversized T-shirt when I worked on the lake. Even
though my May days had long since passed me by.

And then there were the teenagers, who were *bored out
of our fucking minds* because they were stuck in the boonies
all summer long. They spent their days swimming and sunbathing, driving their parents' cars and polluting the air
and water with their parents' jet skis and boats. But it was
better than how they spent their nights. I knew all about
that, more than their parents did, because the teenagers
gossiped about each other, too. They talked about sex
and money and drinking, even when I was within earshot.
Because the lesson they'd already learned is that you can
say anything you want to in front of your cleaning lady or
your cook or the guy who's fixing your roof. Because, of
course, they're not People. Not Real People. Not the kind
who have eyes and ears and brains.

I always ended Friday's work day with George and Tiffany Kendall. They were the couple from Connecticut who'd
bought the Yankee fan's camp, one of the May–December
couples. Sixty-four and twenty-two. The previous summer
he'd left his second wife, a former May who was now an

aging June, so he could marry Tiffany. And, if he lived long enough, he'd probably replace Tiffany before she turned thirty. If he didn't live that long then Tiffany, who'd been a waitress until a year ago, would inherit millions of dollars, several cars, a big house in Connecticut, and a nice lakeside camp in a lovely Maine community. But they paid well and on time, so what business was it of mine? And not just me. Brian had been doing work at their place since even before they moved in. They paid him well and on time, too.

I strolled in the side door, the kitchen door, like I did every Friday. Bucket of cleaning supplies in one hand, canister vacuum in the other, the hose coiled loosely around my shoulder. Three-thirty. On the dot. The cook, Mrs. Pelletier, watched me walk through the room. She was a very old lady, silent, protective. The kitchen was her space and I knew it. I nodded and she nodded right back. Then I pushed gently on the door that led into the dining room. And when I was finished in there I opened a different door, walked through a hallway and stumbled into the living room. Tiffany was sitting on the sofa reading a book.

"Oh, excuse me, Mrs. Kendall." It really did irritate me that I had to refer to her that way, but I was very careful not to let it show. "I didn't know you were in here."

She looked up and smiled. Like she was actually happy to see me. "Hello, Tess."

Tess. There were kids Jason had taught who were her age now, and some who were older, who would still call me *Mrs. Dyer* if they saw me.

"I didn't realize what time it was."

She bookmarked her page then looked up at me again, almost expectantly. I recognized the look and the need behind it. She was lonely. Stuck here in the boonies with nothing to do. Stuck with a husband who was old enough to be her grandfather and no women to talk to except for a flock of Mays, who were shallow and brainless and gold digging, and the older wives, who feared and despised her.

And she wanted a friend.

I knew I shouldn't feel sorry for her. She'd dug her own grave and now she had to lie in it. But I felt sorry for her anyway. Because she wasn't shallow or brainless, even though she was a gold digger. She wasn't outside sunbathing or spending her husband's money on a manicure or gossiping idly with another May about the older wives. She was inside on a sunny day, alone, reading *Zen and the Art of Motorcycle Maintenance*. So desperate for company that she was trying to strike up a conversation with the cleaning lady. But there wasn't much I could do for her. I wasn't really Tess Dyer while I was here. I was just the cleaning lady, The Help, so I had to wait for her to get the conversation rolling. Even though I wanted to ask her what she thought of the book. Even though I really was curious to know if she loved it, like Jason did, or if, like me, she though it was a repetitive pile of condescending crap.

I shifted my weight from one leg to the other. My load was heavy and a little awkward, but I didn't feel right setting it down until I knew which direction things were heading. She finally noticed and said:

"I'm keeping you from your work. I'm sorry."

"That's quite all right, Mrs. Kendall."

She stood up. Smiled again. Hesitated once more, but finally left the room, clutching her book. I heard the back door open and shut and knew she was heading for the back deck. The thing was huge with a gorgeous view of the lake. Brian had built it for them.

I got to work. Living room, hallway, master bedroom, master bathroom, guest bedroom. Then my favorite room. I knocked. There was a long pause before I heard *come in.*

The den. It reminded me of the room where my dad spent most of his time. Manly. Outdoorsy. Dark wood and leather furniture. Mr. Kendall was standing behind his desk. When he saw who it was *coming in* he smiled and said, "Why hello, Mrs. Dyer."

Fortunately, I'd always been a huge fan of irony.

"I thought you were my wife."

God forbid. I couldn't even bring myself to imagine the horrors that possessing that title must entail. But she'd volunteered for the job, so it was hard to feel too much sympathy for her in that regard. And he was a pleasant enough man. So I smiled back.

He lowered his voice and continued. "Her birthday is next week and I've got her present hidden in here."

I tried to make my *ah* sound interested. I must have succeeded because he asked:

"Would you like to see it?"

The answer was *No.* I didn't give a shit about the latest diamond-covered monstrosity he'd spent too much money on in order to compensate her for services rendered. I wanted to hurry up and finish so I'd have time for a shower before I met Brian at Zeke's. I couldn't actually say that, of course, or anything like it. Even if I was stupid enough to put my own job in jeopardy by telling off a client—and I wasn't that stupid—there was no way I'd risk Brian's job that way.

Most of the lake husbands, especially the Decembers, had been a little hesitant about hiring Brian. Letting him into their homes, getting all hot and sweaty around their wives. Of course, even if there wasn't a Tess in his life he wasn't stupid enough to put his business in jeopardy just for the thrill of banging a bored, lonely May or even a scared, lonely Botox Beauty. But the husbands didn't know that. All they knew was that he was a young, good-looking guy and that there were whispers of how his father had behaved in similar circumstances. It's why Brian always wore his oldest, baggiest jeans and an oversized T-shirt whenever he worked on the lake. Even though it meant he risked getting a farmer's tan.

George Kendall was the first of the Decembers to give Brian's work—and his character—a thumbs-up and it had opened a lot of doors for him. By now they all knew we were an item, which was actually a point our favor. But it also meant that any mistake I made with my big, fat mouth could risk both of us losing our best-paying clients. Consequently I responded with:

"I'd love to see your wife's gift." I even managed a smile.

There was a small bookshelf on the floor behind his desk. He pulled it out a few inches, reached behind it and pulled something out that was covered by a white sheet. Even before he unwrapped it I could tell what it was. A framed canvas. He looked at it and grinned proudly. Just like it was something he'd given birth to. Then he turned it around so I could see. And all I could say was:

"Oh…my God."

Because he had it. He had my painting. *Hope.* The room spun for a few seconds, just a few, and I had to force myself not to speak. Made myself wait until the room stopped spinning. Because what I would have said was:

Give it back, give it back now. It's mine. I'll work for it, work for free for the rest of the summer. Next summer, too. You can even keep the frame, find another painting for it. Just give me back my fucking orchard.

My orchard. Mine.

I couldn't say that, of course, because it wasn't mine. Not anymore. I'd sold it, traded it for one month's rent and a light bill because I was too proud and stupid to borrow the money. Now it was George Kendall's painting. He'd paid for it. Then he'd paid someone to put it inside a God-awful, butt-ugly frame, so he could give it to a bimbo named Tiffany. And I couldn't even tell him that the signature at the bottom was mine. Because nobody wants to hear that their artwork was painted by the cleaning lady.

I took a deep breath. Two jobs at stake. I had to smile. Had to do it. And it wasn't too difficult, not really. Because, after all, he'd bought my painting. He'd walked into the gallery. Saw it. Liked it. Paid money for it. That was a good thing. And so I smiled.

My reaction seemed to please him. "You like it, don't you?" he said.

I shivered, tried to ignore the hair that was standing up on the back of my neck. Then I said the only thing I could say:

"It's lovely." But still, I had to know. Because I'd never sold a painting before. "Why this particular painting? What was it that drew you to it?"

He smiled again, like he'd been hoping I'd ask. "My wife has been busy decorating the camp, as you know. And the leaves in this painting are almost an exact match to the wallpaper in the living room."

Wallpaper. Exact match. And that's when the room started spinning again.

"Um...excuse me, sir?"

Wallpaper?

"Uh...you...it..."

No. Shut up. Don't say anything. Close the mouth. Close it. Right now.

I did.

"You look surprised."

And he looked proud. So proud. I wasn't sure if it was because he thought he'd surprised me or because he'd managed to find a pretty little painting that exactly matched the goddamn living room wallpaper. Or both. But I managed a nod.

"I know it's true that men don't typically pay attention to decorating and colors, but I know how important it is to you ladies."

You ladies.

Focal point. Just like Kim's Lamaze class. Remember? Look at his glasses. They're crooked. Just a little crooked...

"So I brought a sample of the wallpaper with me to the gallery and searched until I found the perfect match."

Green wallpaper. Perfect match. It really was the reason he'd chosen it. Perfect. Match.

Crooked glasses.

I cleared my throat. "Ah."

It seemed to satisfy him. He covered the painting with its sheet and hid it once more behind the shelf. Then he looked at his watch. I looked at mine.

4:45. Shit.

"I'm sorry I've kept you so long, Mrs. Dyer. Why don't you let this room be until next week. It will keep."

I looked around. Dust. Lots of it. I hated that. But.

"Okay."

I turned to leave. Bucket of cleaning supplies in one hand. Canister vacuum in the other, the hose coiled loosely around my shoulder. He courteously closed the door behind me.

I walked down the hallway. Set the vacuum down and knocked on the bathroom door. It was empty. Sink, shower, tub, toilet. Mirror. Floor. Cleaned 'em all.

Because that's what I did. What I was good at.

I drove home quickly, but I lingered in the shower. Washed the stench of the day off of my body, watched it swirl down the drain. Then I did my makeup and hair. Just so. Put on my lucky Red Sox T-shirt, just like I did every Friday. There'd be no Pinstripes for us to boo at tonight, but Zeke's would still be busy. And that meant fun. And I needed that.

I hopped into my car and drove into town. Sure enough, the place was packed. I walked in through Fran's, instead of going in the back way, so I could say a quick hello to Rachel. She was there in her usual place behind the counter. And standing in front of it, slimy as ever, was Tim.

This time they noticed me right away. Rachel rolled her eyes and said, "Hey, Tess."

I nodded my greeting. "Is Brian here yet?"

Get this stupid fuck out of here before Brian gets here and sees It.

"Nope. He's not here. *Yet.*"

Go sit down before my brother gets here and sees you.

But Tim didn't move, apparently too stupid to get the hint. I looked at him. Raised an eyebrow. He grinned back.

Oh, I got the hint, all right. I just don't give a shit.

I could play that game, too. I stretched, loudly and leisurely, then leaned against the counter. "So, Tim. How's business?"

He leaned back against the counter, too. "Business is booming."

"Yeah, that's what I heard."

A month earlier a sixteen-year-old boy and his mother had been arrested. Cultivation and distribution of marijuana. Someone had called in an anonymous tip to the State Police. And when they were released on bail the boy was sent to a foster home, away from the Bad Influence of his mother. Even though she didn't have anything to do with the pot. Even though she'd been the only person in New Mills who hadn't known that her son was growing and selling it in order to save money for college. Because she was too busy working two jobs. Now, of course, she was working no jobs and the kid wasn't saving anything toward college. Even though she really was a good mother and the boy really was a good kid. They were both just doing what they thought they had to do in order to get by. Maybe even get ahead.

So now there was only one person in town to see if you wanted to float away on a cloud. If you wanted to escape into a haze. Or if you wanted something a little stronger. A bigger cloud. A hazier haze. Just one place, one-stop shopping, just like a convenience store. All because someone had called in an anonymous tip to the State Police.

Tim leaned in closer and whispered, "You interested in—"

"Nope." Even though, of course, I was. Just not from him.

He stepped back and shrugged. Then he looked at his watch, turned to Rachel and said, "Well I gotta go."

"See ya."

I waited until Fuckwad was safely out the door, then said, "You need to stay away from that asshole."

"Yes, Mommy."

"Rach, I'm not kidding." Because even though her eyes were clear and bright—right now—I knew that usually they weren't.

She nodded. Bored. The door gave a loud *ding* as it opened up behind me. I turned to look but it wasn't Brian, just a group of teenagers—locals, of course, not Lake Kids—with hearty hellos for Rachel. She returned their greeting with great gusto. And that was a hint for me.

Go away. Let me talk to my friends in peace.

And so I left her. Entered Zeke's to the usual chorus that greeted me. Several voices, none of them in sync or in harmony, called out:

"Hey Tess! I'm not a Yankees fan!"

"I know, but you're all assholes."

174

Having taken care of the formalities, I strolled over to
the bar. Zeke and my first beer were waiting for me. He
looked at my face carefully. "You okay, Tess?"

I wasn't okay, even though I didn't know exactly what
was wrong. There was something dancing in the back of my
mind, something about fear and love and insecurity and
loneliness. For a moment a vague image of Tiffany Kendall
floated before me. Sad. Desperate. Something in her face,
especially in her eyes, that spoke of misery and regret. And
I wanted to talk to him about it, to see if he could help me
figure it out. But the place was just too busy to get into anything real. So I gave him a smile and brought up a different
subject, one I'd wanted to for weeks.

"Zeke, we need to do something about your house."

That surprised him. "What's the matter with my house?"

I sighed dramatically. "I don't have enough time to go
into the subject in any great detail, so I'll just highlight
the obvious. It's an old lady's house. And the last time I
checked—well, not that I've ever actually checked—you're
not an old lady."

"Tess…it was my mother's house."

"I hate to break it to you, but she doesn't live there
anymore. And I never met the woman, but from what I've
heard she wasn't the kind of person who'd insist on making
you keep that place a shrine. I mean, do you actually like
plastic slip covers and lilac wallpaper?"

I finally got a laugh out of him. "No, but I don't have
the time to do any remodeling."

"Gimme a break. It'll take you less than an hour to walk
to the hardware store and pick out a couple colors. Less
than that if you're lazy and drive."

"You're just gonna paint every room in my house."

"Sure."

"And how much is that gonna cost me?"

"I'm not gonna *charge* you. Damn it, Zeke, I'm a cleaning lady, not an interior decorator. You just have to pay for the paint and brushes and the thousands of gallons of wallpaper adhesive remover it's gonna take to clean up those walls."

"I'm not letting you do it for free."

"Oh come on, Zeke. If you pay me it won't be fun, it will be work. And I need something fun to do."

I did. I needed something. Not fun, really. I needed some color, needed to be surrounded by it, by paint and brushes, to be creating something, even if the canvas was a just a wall. Because I hadn't painted anything all summer— nothing since the orchard. The lake was still dancing in the back of my mind, but there was still something not quite right about it. Something that went beyond the motorized intrusion. It wasn't complete somehow, wasn't ready. And nothing else was speaking to me.

"But I'll tell you this. I won't do white or off-white or beige or anything boring like that. Pick some real colors. Something hot."

I winked at him and he turned red with embarrassment, then gave me a scowl. But he'd give in. I was right and he knew it. He needed change, needed lots of it; the kind that didn't come from a paint can. There wasn't anything I could do about most of that, but maybe if he wasn't living in Grannyland he'd be more inspired to go out and find it. Because it would be a nice change for me to have more than seven coffee mugs to wash every week.

I turned my attention to my beer, nursed it slowly, waiting for Brian. And, finally, a body sat down beside me. I turned, prepared with a smile, but it faded quickly enough. Because it was Ashley. Green-eyed and blonde and young. And for a moment I wondered how many extra toilets I'd need to scrub before I could afford one or two of those Botox treatments.

"Hi, Tess."

"Hey."

She had a drink already in hand, some sort of sweet-smelling shit in a tall glass. "Are you waiting for Brian?"

"Yep."

"That's what I thought."

We each guzzled our drinks. She finished before me, but Zeke refilled mine first. Then it was her turn, but with a *that's your last one* warning. I looked at her more closely. Her eyes were fuzzy and she was swaying slightly on her stool. And it was only six-fifteen. She tapped my arm and gazed at me a bit unsteadily.

"Are you *really* in love with him?"

"Yep."

"Me too."

I sighed. I'd known this day was coming. But of all the places in the world, this bar—filled to capacity with sweaty men and their dates—was the last place I would have chosen for the encounter. And this was not the day I would have chosen, either. At the same time I had to feel bad for the girl. I'd been her. Spread 'em for a guy, thinking it was the Real Thing. Turns out you're nothing more than a Sure Thing. It sucks. Big time. It's the lesson all women have to learn. But what could I do?

Nothing. Except try to be nice.

"Ashley, I—"

"You sorta have a fat ass, don't you?"

"Uh…excuse me?"

"But some guys like that. And you've got big tits, too, so that evens it all out."

I looked around the room. Sure enough, her voice had carried above the din of sweaty guys and their dates, even above the ex-ballplayers and pompous sportswriters who were yapping away on the pre-game show, giving their opinions about a game that hadn't even been played yet.

I turned away from the chuckles and snickers, leaned in closer to her and whispered, "Ashley, why don't you let me give you a ride home and we can talk about this later. Or maybe Zeke can call someone for you and—"

She shook her head and shoved me. Hard. I hadn't been expecting it, naturally, and fell right off the stool. Barely managed to keep myself from landing flat on my big, fat ass. Even worse, I'd been holding onto my beer and it spilled all down the front of me.

I set the mug down on the bar and hopped back onto my stool. Because there was more, lots more, to come. I knew that much. And since we'd already caused a scene I figured I might as well get it out of the way. It would be better than having to endure another one later on. I took a deep breath, turned to face her and waited for the rest.

And she brought it. She rambled on and on about her magical night with Brian. Zeke tried to shush her, as though I didn't already know, as though everyone in the bar didn't already know, but she wouldn't stop. Told us all about it, painted it in beautiful, rosy colors. And when she was done I felt more sorry for her than ever. Because even though she hadn't said it, I knew. Just by the way she talked about It. About Him.

Brian had been her first. Because she'd had a crush on him—and in her mind it was love—since she was just a girl. She had loved him forever. She was thin and blonde and pretty, and she could have had any number of guys if she'd wanted them. But she'd waited, saved herself. For Brian. And to him it had been nothing special. Neither was she. Just another girl. A Sure Thing. It was close to being the saddest thing I'd ever heard and, for a fleeting moment, I wanted to track the bastard down and smack the shit out of him. But then she said:

"You know, one of these days he's gonna wake up and realize that he needs something more than just big tits, you fat old bitch!"

I swallowed. Took a very deep breath. "Okay, Ashley. I think—"

"He's gonna get tired of you and when he does he'll know where to go. I know what he *really* wants. And—"

"Oh, *please*, little girl. You don't know shit. I was playing with dicks when you were still playing with dolls."

She muttered something in response, but I wasn't listening. I leaned over the bar, grabbed a handful of napkins and tried to wipe the beer bubbles off my big, fat tits. It didn't help. My lucky shirt was still soaked. And I knew what it meant, even though I'd never admit it to another living soul. The Sox were jinxed for the rest of the season.

So I reached for my purse, rifled around inside, pulled out a big bill. My emergency fund. Then I finally looked up at Zeke. He looked amused and worried. Funny how guys could be both at the same time. Even the nice ones. He saw the money in my hand and waved me off.

"No, you're all set, Tess."

"Fuck you. I'm paying for my beer. And...whatever her bill is, too." I dropped the money onto the bar walked away before he could say anything else. Kept my head held high, like Wronged Heroines are supposed to do.

And I ran right into Brian.

He was leaning against the counter talking to Rachel and whatever the conversation was about I could see that it was, at worst, a neutral subject. He looked tired and sweaty, brown with dust and sun. But they were both smiling, even before they caught sight of me. And when they did it gave them both a big laugh.

"What happened to you, babe?"

I resisted the urge to start the story this way:

Once upon a time, you popped a girl's cherry...and broke her heart.

"Oh...I just had a little accident."

He laughed again, but I still didn't smack him. Even though, really, he deserved it. "I guess this means we should get supper to go?"

"Yeah. Why don't you head on home and I'll be there in a few minutes."

"Are you sure? I don't mind—"

"Nope. Go on. You look exhausted."

Rachel called back the order without having to ask what we wanted. Because we always got the same thing. Every Friday. Brian paid and said, "See ya, Rach." Then he gave me a quick kiss and headed out.

As soon as the door shut behind him I turned to Rachel. "I meant what I said about Tim. Stay away from him."

She wiggled her eyebrows. "Too late."

I had figured. Still, I'd been hoping I had figured wrong.

"Tess, I know what you're thinking. But I'm not into the shit he's selling. I swear. I'm just having a little fun with him."

"That's not the kinda guy you have a little fun with. Damn it, you're young and pretty and funny and smart. You deserve so much better than...*that*."

"Look around. There's not a whole hell of a lot to choose from."

She was right. Then I peeked over her shoulder. Fry cook. Blonde. Tall. Cute.

"There you go."

She looked behind her and smirked. "That's Donny. Been there. Done that."

"Jesus Christ. Well, do it again. Anything's better than that other fuckwad. Besides, why do you have to do anyone? Just...go out into the world and do some *living*. There's so much more out there for you than just...*this*. You could go to school or—"

But I didn't get any farther. The double doors swung open and Rachel and I both looked over. Ashley, barely vertical, was being helped out by one of the guys who was an asshole but not a Yankee fan. He was wearing a big smile. And a wedding ring.

"Hey!" Stern voice. Mean Tess. I was on a roll. "Don't even *think* about it."

"But—"

"Nope. You put her in my car."

Ashley opened her eyes and tried to focus. When she saw me she called me a fat, old bitch again, then sputtered, "*You're* not bringing me home."

I ignored her, glared up at the married asshole and repeated, "Put her. In *my* car."

He glared right back.

"If you wanna screw around on your wife, be my guest. But you're not doin' it with a girl who's too drunk to walk. So put her skinny little ass in my car. Right now."

I said it with conviction. As though I was six feet tall, instead of just a beer-soaked shrimp, and could actually back up what I was saying with some muscle. But he must have seen something in my face. Maybe it was the eyes. Maybe they were cold and hard like my mother's were. Or maybe he just had an attack of conscience. Whatever it was he wavered. Then gave in.

"Fine."

He dragged Ashley out the door. I watched out the window and nodded when I saw him heading for my car, then turned my attention back to Rachel. "Is my supper ready?"

She headed for the kitchen, laughing to herself, and when she came back she was laughing even harder. She set the bag down on the counter and said, "Donny wants me to tell you that Ashley's full of shit."

"Excuse me?"

"He said you got *curves,* not a fat ass, and that guys really *do* like that."

I looked past Rachel, into the kitchen. "Hey Donny!"

He looked up from his fry vat. "Yeah?"

"Fuck you."

He nodded. "You're welcome, Tess."

By the time I got to the car, Horny Disappointed Man was buckling Ashley's seatbelt. I hoped that's all he'd been doing, but it was too late to do anything about it now. When he saw me coming he slammed the door. He was horny and pissed now. I didn't care.

"Go home and fuck your wife instead."

He gave me the finger and walked back inside. I got into my car and slammed the door. Ashley glared at me.

"I want *Andy* to bring me home."

I sighed. "No you don't."

I drove to her apartment—the beauty of small towns: you know where all your boyfriend's exes live—and plopped her down on the couch. Partly because it was the nearest soft surface, but mostly because I didn't want go into her bedroom. Didn't want to see the bed where Brian had fucked her. I tiptoed into the bathroom, rummaged through her linen closet, grabbed a couple towels and a bucket, and placed them within puking distance of the couch. I locked the door on my way out and wondered if she'd remember who her rescuer was when she woke up in the morning. If it would make her hate me even more than she already she did.

Brian was in the shower when I finally made it home. I opened the bathroom door a crack and peeked inside. Saw his tall silhouette, fuzzy through the frosted glass door. He was washing his hair, singing to himself, happy as he could be. Naturally. What the hell was there for him to worry about?

I closed the door silently behind me. Leaned back against it, inhaled the hazy steam. Fought back a raw, sharp fang of fear. I'd been fighting it for a long time. Long before tonight. It had been there, poised and ready to sink in, since our first night together. I watched him still as he poured more shampoo into his hands. It seemed sweet and funny that he really did lather, rinse and then repeat; sweeter still that I was probably the only other person in the world who knew that he did. And I was overcome by a sudden, tired, primitive urge. A cold, desperate need. To claim him. To mark him.

Mine.

Because I'd had it with all the cute, young chickies hanging around him. Not just Ashley. All of them. The nameless faces that stared at him, at us. They were everywhere. Just like vultures. Waiting for him to get tired of me. To get it out of his system.

They'd had their turn. He was mine now, goddamn it.

Mine.

I peeled my clothes off, opened the shower door a couple of inches and watched him scrub his dark hair. Eyes closed. Covered in white, foamy suds: his chest and stomach and legs. He was still singing some song I didn't recognize. Even his voice was gorgeous. Deep and soft, echoing against the stark, white tile.

He finally opened his eyes. "Enjoying the show?"

"Sure am. How was your day, anyway? I never did ask."

He grunted and rinsed out the last of the shampoo. "Long day."

I stepped inside and he smiled.

"It's getting better all the time, though."

I didn't say a word, just put my arms around his neck and pressed my body against his. Let mine get slick with water and soap and leftover shampoo. Got an instant reaction from him. And it was my turn to smile.

I stood on tiptoe. Took his face in my hands, pulled his lips onto mine, and kissed him. Slowly. Full of fire and passion and tongue, the way he always kissed me, the way I loved it. He wrapped his arms around me, enveloped me in a warm, wet embrace, and I lingered at his mouth. Kissed him forever. Then I traced the line of his jaw with my tongue, gently nibbled on his neck. He pulled me even closer, pressed me tightly against his chest, and I could feel his heart hammering against me.

I slid my body down his, slithering slowly out of his grasp in the hot, steady downpour. Took some time to kiss the muscles of his chest, let the hair tickle my face, because I still loved that. More than just about anything in the world. Then I continued my journey downward. Paused at his stomach. Kissed it, too. Lightly, gently. Gave him temporary shelter between my breasts while I glanced up at his face. His eyes were closed, mouth open. Dreamy. Off in another world.

He really was too beautiful.

I smiled, dropped to my knees and took him into my mouth. He cried out suddenly, just like it had surprised him, even though he'd been expecting it. Even though he'd known what he was in for the second I'd stepped into the shower. I started slowly, because it's how he liked it, and his hands found the back of my head, but not to guide me. He didn't even try, knew he didn't need to. I could always tell by his breathing and his moans when he wanted me to speed up or to slow down. He just liked to touch me, loved to run his fingers through my hair, caress my neck, my face. To feel my mouth while it was going down on him.

He let out a quick, sharp breath. The muscles in his legs and abdomen locked, relaxed, and then tensed up again. He was getting close. I knew what he wanted before he said it, knew exactly where he wanted to be, where he wanted to end, because I'd made him want it; was making him want it right now, even more, by rubbing them gently against his thighs. I waited anyway, made him say it, and when he did it was more a command than a request. Desperate, vulgar, hoarse, rough and I let him go. Took him in my hands, shook my head as he reached down, trying to take over. I knew he was looking down, that he was watching, could feel his eyes on me as he gave me exactly what I wanted, even though he didn't know it.

My name in his deep, clear, ringing voice.

I smiled as he repeated it, as it echoed against the shower walls. I knew that he wanted me to look up at him, look into his eyes while it was happening. But I couldn't. I looked down at the floor of the shower instead, even after he was finished. Watched the drain as the water collected there, swirled slowly around, then disappeared; watched as the cycle repeated a few more times. I couldn't let him see my face. Not yet. I had to wait. Just a few more seconds.

I knew my smile would give me away.

You're mine, goddamn it.

Mine.

CHAPTER 16

The last Saturday in July.

I woke up to golden sunlight streaming in through the windows. Another beautiful summer morning. I stretched slowly, then rolled over to snuggle in close to Brian. To watch his peaceful, sleeping face—a face that would be covered in the dark, early-morning whiskers that I loved so much. To run my fingers through the hair on his chest while I waited for him to open his eyes. Just like I did every Saturday morning. Then he'd smile and kiss me and we'd make love. Just like every Saturday morning.

Except that he wasn't there.

It was the first time I'd had to face the morning alone in over two months and I couldn't remember if we'd spent the night in my bed or his. I looked at the clock. **7:56**. Red. Brian's room.

I kicked off the covers, slipped on his favorite T-shirt—*Welcome to Maine–Now Go Home*—and staggered into the kitchen. He'd left a note propped against his coffee maker, right where I'd be sure to see it. Short and to the point.

Be back later.

So I drank my coffee, then spent the morning puttering in the garden. Running my fingers through the cool, dark soil, tossing aside errant weeds, removing spent blossoms from my marigolds and petunias. Summer had been kind to them, and they glowed their appreciation in hues of gold and fuschia, alongside spiky, red salvia and delicate, purple pansies. But behind them all stood a Highbush blueberry that hadn't fared so well. It was a gift from Laura's garden; supposedly old enough to produce fruit, but barely holding onto its leaves. I gave the thing a reproachful shake of my head, then stood up to brush the dirt off my hands.

And that, of course, was the moment Laura chose to show up for a visit. She gave the plant a thorough inspection and said, "I think it's your soil."

"My soil?"

"Blueberries need acidic soil."

She gave me a brief lesson about pH levels in soil that went right over my head, but I nodded along, just like I understood every word. When it was over I promised her that I'd visit the greenhouse in the fall to get sulfur and peat moss, even though I knew I probably wouldn't. Then there was silence, and it was my turn to fill it.

"Uh...if you came to see Brian, he's not home."

She nodded. "I know. He's at my house."

"He is?"

She didn't seem surprised that I hadn't known where he was. "Jeff is helping him fix his carburetor."

"I thought it was his alternator that was acting up."

"Everything on that truck is acting up."

"Ah."

That left us to stumble through the land of Small Talk. We exhausted the subjects of Zeke's walls, Brian's upcoming birthday—less than a month away—and the proper conditioner to use on color-treated hair before she finally worked up the nerve to bring up the real reason she'd come over to see me.

"Tess, I need to ask a really big favor."

I nodded. That was obvious.

"It's about Cassidy."

Long pause. "Uh huh."

"My mother's been watching her during the week for a while now…but we're going to stop that. She said some pretty rough things yesterday that…well, I don't want Cassidy exposed to some of my mother's opinions."

"I'll watch her for you. What days do you need me?"

She hesitated, so I gave her a smile. Because she needed to know.

This is no big deal. I don't even have to think it over.

She smiled back. "Tuesday and Thursday. I work nine till three-thirty."

"Perfect. All my Tuesday and Thursday jobs are in the evening." But she knew that. Either because she had a good memory or because she'd talked to Brian already.

"You're sure?"

"Yep. If Cassidy doesn't mind hanging out with me twice a week."

"She's actually looking forward to it."

There was no accounting for taste. "Then we're all set."

Almost. She wanted to pay, and of course I said no, so we decided on the barter system. The hair. She looked at it the way I always looked at Zeke's lilac wallpaper, and that's when I knew that when she'd brought up the subject of conditioner for color-treated hair it wasn't as random as I'd assumed. After we were done bargaining she lingered. Silent. Still upset. So I asked, "What happened with your mom?"

Another silence, one that was so long I thought she wasn't going to answer the question. But then she asked, "How old were you when you lost your virginity?"

It wasn't exactly the direction I'd expected the conversation to take. "Sixteen."

"I was seventeen." Then she told me her First Time story. Teenage Love. Visions of a thing that is full of Beauty and Fireworks and Romance. Instead, of course, she got Reality. Jeff, well meaning and kind, but with nervous, fumbling hands. There was a little bit of pain and then it was over. There was relief and guilt and then...Cassidy. But still there was Jeff and love, enough of it to keep them going; enough, even, to thrive on.

And, from her mother, a lifetime of If Only You Had Listened To Me. Judgment and condemnation. Lectures about Sin that Never Washes Clean, lectures that never ended, even after years and years. Even when what she'd done didn't feel like a sin anymore.

I knew what she meant about mothers who just couldn't let it go, but I didn't say so. I just said, "Laura, your mother is full of shit. You're a good person. And you're a good mother. That girl you've got...she's an awesome kid. So whatever it is you're doing, just keep right on doing it."

She actually burst into tears and collapsed on my shoulder. It was the first time anyone had ever done that and I just stood there, patting her head, trying not to get dirt in her hair, hoping it was what I was supposed to do. If it was enough. It must have been, because it didn't take her long to get control of herself. She thanked me, wiped her eyes on the back of her hands—carefully, so as not to smear her mascara—then looked at me, expectantly. I knew what it was she was waiting for. She'd opened up and that meant it was my turn. But it wasn't going to happen.

Fortunately Brian picked that moment to come home. Unfortunately he was in a rotten mood. He slammed his truck door, but managed to fake a smile as he walked over to us. He gave me a quick kiss and nodded a hello to Laura. She nodded back, then said:

"Your truck sounds a little better."

"Yeah, a little. The carburetor was running too rich. It was bogging down the engine."

I said, "Ah," just like I knew what that meant. Laura looked like she actually did, which surprised me. She lingered for a few more minutes, gave Brian a quick hug—which surprised me even more—then left.

He followed me upstairs to my apartment, stomping his feet all the way. He slammed the door behind him, then landed hard on the couch while I washed my hands. When I was done I sat down beside him, skipped over the *why did you take off without letting me know where the hell you were going?* lecture and went straight to:

"Bad day?" He only nodded and rubbed his hands on his jeans so furiously I thought he might catch on fire. "What's wrong?"

He sighed. "I didn't sleep good last night, and you were sound asleep this morning, so I thought I'd go see Rachel for a little while."

"How was she?"

"She's fucking insane. That's how she is." And he told me all about it. He'd caught her home with Fuckwad. And as I listened I nodded sympathetically and held his hand, just like a Supportive Girlfriend who had absolutely No Prior Knowledge of his sister sleeping with a drug dealer named Tim would do. Until he said:

"He's thirty-five, Tess. Thirty-five!"

My first thought was, *He looks older than that. Rough living sure takes a toll.*

Then, of course, there was the other thing.

"Wait a fucking minute. You say *thirty-five* like it's just this side of senility."

He amended his position. "She's still a teenager for Christ's sake! He's been married twice already and he's got a daughter who's fifteen. *Fifteen*. That's only four years younger than Rachel." He shuddered. "I told the pervert to keep his fucking hands off her and to stay the hell away. So he took off and Rachel got all pissed. She told me to get the hell out of her apartment and stay the hell out of her life and to leave her the fuck alone. I wanted to go out and find the sick bastard so I could kick his stupid pussy ass, but I went to Jeff's to cool down instead."

"Smart move."

"Maybe. But what the hell am I gonna do with her?"

"There's nothing you can do. Like it or not, she's not a little kid anymore. And if you keep coming down so hard on her about it you're just gonna push her away. She'll wise up eventually. Or this guy will move on to someone new."

"Wow. That's reassuring."

I shrugged, pulled a loose string from my shorts and tucked it away in my pocket. "I'm just being realistic. You can't live her life for her, Brian. She's got to make her own mistakes."

"No she doesn't. And...God, I don't wanna talk about this anymore." He stretched, suddenly restless, bounced fitfully up and down for a minute. Then he said, "I feel like dancing. Wanna dance?"

His sudden change surprised me. "Dance?"

"Yeah. I'm going fucking insane just sitting here."

"You know I can't dance."

He dropped to his knees on the floor in front of me and smiled. "Come on."

I shook my head. "I can't—"

"Yes you can." He lifted me up into his arms and spun me around. "I can see it in there, Tess. It's just bustin' to come out, so quit fighting it."

"No."

"Come on, it's easy. It's..." He stopped the spinning and grinned. "It's just like sex."

I wrapped my legs tightly around his waist. "Then let's have sex."

"Later."

I smiled and pulled off my shirt.

"That's not gonna work."

And my bra.

"Tess, you're not playing fair."

"I know." Then I kissed him. And the dance lesson was over before it had begun.

* * *

Later that evening we sat out on the lawn waiting for the sunset, Brian's arm around me, my head on his shoulder. The world was still and peaceful: crickets already chirping, the scent of pine needles heavy on the light evening breeze, the sky just beginning to glow.

And that's when an unfamiliar car crept up the driveway.

It was a big boat of a car. The paint was chipping and rusted and the color of the driver's side door didn't match the rest of the vehicle. It came to a stop almost directly in front of the porch steps. I could distinguish that the driver was a man, but he was looking down at something on the empty seat beside him so I couldn't see his face.

"Do you know who it is?"

Brian shook his head. "Nope." He stood up, stretched, then walked toward the car, and I followed close behind. Finally the door opened and a fairly tall man got out. He closed the door and turned to face us. Brian stopped in his tracks and I gasped out loud. Even with only the orangey light of the sunset for illumination I could tell who he was.

"Hello, Brian."

Brian said nothing. Just stood unsteadily, gaping at his father.

Mr. LaChance smiled at me, took a few steps forward and said, "You must be Tess. I've heard a lot about you."

I nodded. Wondered who it was who had told him a lot about me. And I tried not to stare, but I couldn't help it. Brian looked just like him, except for the eyes. His father's were some sort of hazel. Van Dyke Brown must have come from Wendy.

"I'm Rick LaChance."

The words roused Brian at last. He stepped between me and his father. "Don't you fucking go near her," he warned. "Tess, get in the house."

"But—"

He glared at me and I took a step back. I knew the anger was directed at his father, but it still scared the shit out of me.

"I didn't come to upset you, Brian. I just wanted to see you. To see how you're doing."

"I'm doing great. Never been better. Now get the fuck out of here."

Rick pressed on. "I just meant...I know it's probably been a rough day for you."

Brian folded his arms. "You think today's been rough? Why would you think that?"

"It's the day your mom died, and—"

"Oh my God. Brian," I murmured. Why hadn't he told me?

He ignored me and took a step toward his father, who didn't have the sense to back up. "You remembered? Holy shit, how'd you manage that?" He gave a bitter laugh. "Oh wait, I know! It's the day she made you a free man, so of course you remember. It must be like a birthday to you, right? If I knew you were coming I woulda got you a gift."

"Brian, I—"

"Fuck you. Just get outta here." He turned toward the house, and as he did he bumped into me. "Goddamn it, I told you to get in the house! I don't want you out here with him!"

Before I could say a word his father said, "Brian, wait. Don't walk away. Please."

Brian sighed and turned back around. His hand were clenched into two tight fists.

"I came here tonight...I want to tell you that I'm sorry. I know I let you down. I was a horrible father and a worse husband and I'm...I came here to..." He took a deep, shaky breath. "I want you to know that I've been making some changes. I quit drinking and—"

"Oh, sure. You quit drinking. Of course." He started back toward him, slowly. "You're taking it one day at a time. Doing those twelve steps. How many days has it been this time? *Dad?* Huh? How many steps?"

"Brian...you..."

"Oh yeah, I know all about it, all about that A.A. bullshit. You're powerless over the demon liquor, aren't ya? Yeah, I know." He shook his head in mock sympathy. "I know. You poor, poor man. It's not your fault, right? The booze made you do it."

His father finally backed away but Brian kept right on going.

"So what step are you on? Are you still trying to get in touch with your Higher Power? Didja find Jesus or something?" He laughed. "Oh yeah, you must've done that by now, because that's an easy one. Say a few 'hallelujahs' and 'praise the Lords' and you're all set. Ready to move onto the next step. You're good at the easy stuff, aren't ya? So why would you come here? Why would you wanna come and see me?" He pretended to mull it over. "You wouldn't do it on your own, because that's a hard one, and you're nothing but a fucking pussy, aren't ya? *Dad.*"

The mockery was starting to have an effect. His father looked surprised and hurt, which only encouraged Brian to keep at it.

"And that means you got yourself an idiot sponsor to tell you what to do and he must've made you come here. And why would he do that? He must've had a very good reason. Let me think. What step could it be?" He started counting on his fingers. "Moral inventory. Well, that wouldn't take long, would it?" He laughed again. "Jesus, do you even *have* any morals?"

I walked over and pulled on his arm. "Brian, come on…"

He shook off my hand. "No, Tess. This man has the balls to come to my house, on today of all days, and expects me to just welcome him back into my life with open fuck-ing arms? Just forgive and…"

He snorted, turned suddenly to face his father once more.

"Oh my God, are you here to make *amends?* You made it all the way to step nine? You actually hung in there that long this time? Holy shit, it's time to celebrate. Tess, quick! Run in the kitchen and get this man a drink!"

He laughed loudly, so loudly that it echoed all around us, through the trees and against the house and the shed. He kept at it for so long that he actually had to hold onto his stomach. It scared me and irritated his father, who finally broke.

"It's real easy for you to stand there judging me, isn't it, Son? I'm trying to start over. I'm trying to fix what I've done wrong. I left you, yes, and that was wrong and I'm sorry—"

Brian's laughter stopped.

"Sorry? What good does sorry do? Sorry does me no fucking good."

His father continued as though Brian hadn't interrupted. "—but I could've done worse by you. At least I left you with a home and a good business to run. You didn't have to start from scratch like I had to do, like I've got to do again. You never had to do that, Brian, so you don't have a fucking clue how hard that is. You had it all given to you."

"*Given to me?*" Brian's anger finally boiled over and I went suddenly cold. My legs shook, rooted to the ground. "You gave me nothing! Fuck you! I did better than start from scratch! I had to start from a fucking hole that *you* dug!" He wiped some spit from his mouth. "I had to start off in debt because you spent all our money on booze and whores. Drinking on the job and losing jobs because of it. Slacking off and doing fucking piss-poor work! Or not working at all, spending all your time screwing around. Fucking your friends' wives, fucking your workers' wives, fucking your clients' wives, just because you could!"

"Brian, please…"

"'Brian, please.' Fuck you! You know, Mom *knew* you'd leave us. She said you wouldn't stick around and she was right. You took off like a fucking coward and *that's* what *I* had to start with. That's what I had given to me, you fucking asshole."

Brian took another step, shoved his father, shoved him hard, but his father didn't back away.

"You know, I might not have much, but I worked for what I've got! I had to. I didn't have a choice. I have to work twice as hard as everyone else because most of 'em are still afraid I'm gonna end up just like you."

He shoved his father again, this time hard enough to send him stumbling back a few steps.

"What do you know about work? You don't know shit. I coulda run away, too, you know. I coulda run away and left Rach in a fucking foster home and had a life of my own, but I didn't. I did my job and *yours* too, raising your kid while you were out getting shit-faced and fucked. I had everything handed to me? Who the hell do you think you are, coming to my house and saying that shit to me? *Fuck you!*"

He had to pause to take a breath and his father took a turn, his voice shaking. "I know you did a good job with Rachel. I stopped in to see her tonight at Fran's and she said—"

He had finally done it, finally pushed the wrong button and even before Brian snapped I winced, knowing what was coming. He grabbed his father by the shirt, dragged him over to his car, threw him against it and punched him in the jaw.

"You stay the fuck away from Rachel!" He punched him again. "You've done *enough* to her!" He shook him hard a couple of times, then threw him back against the car. "You've done enough! You know what she's doing? Huh? She's out there fucking up her life, fucking guys who are old enough to…she's just looking for a…God *damn* you, you fucking bastard!"

He hit him again and again and again, wouldn't stop, no matter how loudly I screamed. I grabbed his shirt, pulled him back. "Jesus Christ, Brian! You're gonna kill him!"

He shook me loose, gave his dad another shove, punched him three more times, then backed off. Stumbled. Righted himself, then brushed his hands off on his pants.

His father stood up, too, stunned. He wiped his face with his hands, then his shirt, covering it so I couldn't see exactly how much damage Brian had done to him.

"I mean it." He pointed viciously at his father. "You fucking stay away from Rachel. Because I'll kill you if you ever go near her again." He grabbed my hand and marched into the house as his dad got into his car and drove away.

I sat down at the kitchen table, shaking violently, too horrified to think, let alone say anything, but wishing Brian would. Instead he walked to the sink and started washing his hands without a word. I gasped out loud as the water turned red.

"Oh my God! You're bleeding!"

He shook his head. "It's not my blood."

I looked down at my own hand, the one Brian had grabbed on the way into the house, and jumped out of the chair.

He turned around, annoyed. "What the hell is your problem?"

I had never been a witness to an actual fight before, not a real one with yelling and fists and blood. It had left me with a sick, hollow, fluttering in my stomach. Made me feel as powerless as a kid. But not so powerless that I was going to stand there and let him take his anger out on me.

"It's nothing," I said. "I'm going upstairs."

"Great. Go for it."

I shoved the chair under the table and marched toward the door, but before I got there he switched the faucet off and said, "Tess, wait." He wiped his hands gingerly on a towel. "Please don't leave."

He came over and put his arms around me. I was still shaking. He was too.

"I'm sorry I snapped at you and I'm sorry you had to be here for that." He kissed the top of my head, backed up and looked down at my face. "Are you okay? I mean, are you hurt or anything?"

I shook my head. "I'm not hurt. But I need to clean up." I showed him my bloody hand.

He shrank back from it. "Oh. Shit. I'm really sorry."

I walked around him to the sink without a word and he took the seat I had just vacated. I washed up, dried my hands on the same towel he'd used, and sat across from him. I really didn't know what to say, and I wanted, so badly, to say something that might help him, even if it was just a little.

I closed my eyes, tried to imagine what life must have been like for Brian after his mom died; how I would have felt if it had been me. Stuck, without any real guidance, to raise someone else's kid, to be suddenly responsible for her welfare and happiness. I tried to imagine it, tried to feel it, the injustice and unfairness of it all. Losing his mom, having his childhood ripped away, his life ripped away. So burdened with responsibility that he didn't take any time or pleasure for himself. Living in constant fear that he was going to screw up, hoping that every decision he made was the right one. So he didn't mess Rachel's life up the way his had been. And then having to watch, helpless, as she did it to herself.

I opened my eyes. He was sliding the salt shaker from one hand to the other, his eyes fixed on its movements. I cleared my throat. "I wish I knew what to say."

He blinked a few times, like he was waking up from a trance. "What?"

I felt stupid, but repeated, "I just wish I knew what to say. Something helpful. I—"

He pushed the salt shaker back to the middle of the table. "I gotta get out of here for a while."

I reached for his hand. It was swollen. "Where are we going?"

He shook his head. "No, I need to take a drive. I want— I need to clear my head." He stood up and got his keys from the peg on the wall. I walked over to him. He shook his head and said, "It's not you. It's not you, I swear. I love you and I'm sorry. I just…I just need to be alone right now. Just for a little while." He walked out and closed the door quietly behind him.

I stared out the window long after he drove away, waiting. Watching. As though he'd only left for a minute, like he'd gone to the store for milk and was coming right back. Listened to the clock on the wall. Ticking. Finally turned away, looked around the kitchen for something to do, something to clean. There was nothing. Even the supper dishes were done.

I walked into the living room, over to the small table in the corner. Sitting on top was a framed five-by-seven picture of Brian and Rachel. I'd seen it dozens of times but now I picked it up and really looked at it. The two of them at the lake. Brian had told me he'd been about seventeen, Rachel about eleven, and that Jeff had taken it at a party one of their friends was having. Laura was already pregnant with Cassidy and he'd said that it was the last real fun time they'd all had together as kids. But I saw something different.

It had been a party for a bunch of teenagers, but Brian wasn't there with a date. He was there with Rachel. She was wearing a pink bathing suit, holding a bright red beach ball, and the camera had caught her laughing. Brian was dressed in a tank top and shorts and had his arm around her. Stiff. Tired. Looking straight at the camera. It put a sad, clear face on what he had gone through for her, what he had given up.

I put the picture back on the table. He needed to pack it away. Rachel wasn't eleven anymore. But I knew, picture or no, that twenty years from now he'd probably still see her as the little girl in the pink bathing suit.

I walked into his room, quietly, like he was in there and sleeping and I might wake him up; fell onto his bed, buried my face deep in his pillow. His scent lingered there, and it released a thousand pieces of memory. Mischief and laughter and sex and love. I hugged the pillow hard, squeezed it, so tightly that my fingers cramped. Just like the scared, lonely ache in my heart.

I bolted upright, suddenly needing to feel completely wrapped up in him. I dropped to the floor on my belly, peeked under the bed and—sure enough—found one of his T-shirts and a pair of his old sweatpants. I stripped naked, threw my own clothes onto the bed, put his on. They still smelled like him, just like his pillow. I grabbed the extra blanket from his closet and headed outside. Spread it out on the lawn and lay down on my back.

The sky was twinkling with neon stars and the moon was just a thin, curvy sliver above me. Just like a smile, like the cat from *Alice in Wonderland*. I tried to concentrate on it instead of thinking about Brian, but it didn't work. He was out on the roads, driving too fast and not paying attention. Or he was out doing something stupid. Maybe drinking too much and taking out his frustration on some innocent, unsuspecting drunk in a bar. But being surrounded by the smell of him was vaguely comforting and I stared at the sky, at the moon, willing him to come back home to me.

Even at such a late hour our road, cut off from view by the thick growth of maples and pines, was a busy one. Mostly brainless, horny Lake Kids driving their parents' expensive cars. Leaving their expensive rubber behind on the back roads because they were bored with all their pretty toys. And why not? Mommy and Daddy could afford to fix the cars and replace the tires. And they probably figured it was better than having their Ivy League–bound dearies join the local teenagers in the old gravel pit on the other side of town, smoking, snorting, and injecting a wide variety of poisons into their bodies. They knew, of course, that some of those drugs were purchased with money made from selling items that had been stolen from their own precious camps. What they probably didn't know, however, was that most of the money came from their own precious little dearies who were more than willing to pay for blowjobs and more from those lowly local girls—and sometimes guys—who were desperate to escape from their own boredom and frustration. The kind that came from not having any pretty toys.

I lay silently, hoping to hear Brian's truck among the noise. It took another hour or so before I did, and even with everything weighing on my mind I was proud of the fact that I recognized it well over a mile away. I didn't move as he pulled into the driveway, or even as he climbed out of his truck and walked toward the house. He stopped when he noticed me, sprawled out on the lawn in his clothes, and asked, with no trace of amusement:

"What are you doing?"

"I'm staring at the sky. What's it look like?"

He shook his head and looked me over from head to toe. "You've got bare feet." He said it as though it was the oddest thing about my appearance.

"Yep."

He kicked his own shoes off and sat down beside me, crossed his legs and looked up at the sky. He sat like that for a few minutes and then pointed up. "Look at that. The moon looks like the Cheshire Cat."

"I know." I sat up and scooted over to him, and he put his arm around me.

"I'm sorry I acted like that. I'm sorry I took it out on you."

"It's okay."

He held me tighter. "No, it's not."

We sat quietly for a long time, looking at the sky, at the stars, at the grinning moon, and I finally worked up the nerve to ask. Because I wanted to know and because it's what Brian would have done. And that meant it was the right thing to do.

"What was she like?"

He was silent for a long time, and I thought I'd made a mistake. But at last he said, "She was a lot of fun. She was really strict about some things, but mostly she was fun. She loved the water. She was always taking us swimming at the lake, back when you could still get onto it. We used to pretend we were on a warm sandy beach, like we were in California or Australia."

"Really?"

"Oh yeah. And she loved music. She loved to sing. I mean, she sang all the time, all over the place. Around the house and even out in public, which is actually kind of embarrassing when you're a little kid." We both laughed. "But she was young, too. I mean she was only around my age, maybe a little older than me, when she got sick. She was only twenty-nine when she died. But before that, before she was sick, it was like...she was just so filled up with something, with...I don't know, life and love and just this...energy or excitement, or whatever, and she just had to let it out or else she'd burst."

He looked up at the Cheshire moon and squeezed my shoulder.

"My father didn't care about any of that. He probably never noticed. He didn't love her, you know. He only married her because he got her pregnant." He shook his head. "With me. She loved him, though, that useless, fucking asshole. But she always thought he was gonna change. She said he'd sober up someday and everything would be just fine. Someday. She kept saying that right up until she got sick, and he was never around. The son of a bitch was too busy screwing other women to bother with taking care of his wife. 'Cause that's all he does, Tess. It's all about him, all about what he wants. He doesn't give a shit about anyone else. He just hurts everyone. It's all he knows how to do."

He took in a sharp breath and I thought he was going to cry. I looked at his face but he was still dry-eyed, still staring up at the sky.

"You know...she never knew what it felt like to have someone who was in love with her. And she deserved that, Tess. She deserved someone better than him. She—"

His shoulders convulsed suddenly and I tried to put my arms around him, but he shook his head, held out one hand to keep me away and covered his face with the other. "Brian…"

I crawled in front of him, knelt above him and took his head in my hands. He finally stopped resisting and collapsed against me, threw his arms around my waist, buried his head in my chest, sobbing. Neither of us said a word, because we didn't have to. I held him close to me as he cried, didn't let go even long after he'd stopped crying. And still we said nothing. And finally we slumped down onto the blanket, still holding onto each other, and fell asleep under the stars.

CHAPTER 17

Brian's hand was so swollen on Monday morning that he couldn't go to work. He moped around, watching game shows and soap operas, calling me every half hour or so to see if I was done with work yet. I finally had to turn my cell phone off. Nobody wants to listen to their cleaning lady murmur words of love and comfort to her wounded boyfriend. And when I got home I pulled him into his living room, pushed him onto the couch, and fucked him. Not making love; fucking. Because I knew, of course, that it wasn't boredom or pain that was making him so restless, at least not the kind of pain we could see and pack in ice and wrap with an Ace bandage. It was the other kind, the kind that hurt even worse. Sex doesn't make it go away, at least not for long. But it's something. A distraction. And when we were done he kissed me, very gently. Told me he loved me. Then he fell asleep. And he was still in pain, even in his sleep. Both kinds of pain.

Tuesday wasn't quite as bad. He still couldn't work but it was my first day to watch Cassidy and that, at least, gave him something to do. The three of us played Monopoly and took turns squirting each other with the garden hose, then he and Cassidy made up poems about farting while I made lunch. She goaded him into eating his carrot sticks by calling him a chicken. Afterwards the two of them picked some Queen Anne's lace from the back field and I put the blossoms into three separate vases that were filled with food coloring and water while they watched *The Little Mermaid*. By the time Laura came to get Cass, the flowers were just starting to turn color. Blue and red and yellow.

Wednesday morning he still couldn't pick up a hammer but he went to work anyway, so frustrated with himself that he spent the morning yelling at his workers. Swearing at them, barking orders left and right, as if they hadn't done just fine without him for two days. That pissed him off even more, the knowledge that they hadn't *needed* him to be there, and he started in on them again, so badly that they all threatened to quit. So he apologized for acting like an asshole and then he came home, because he was afraid that they really would quit if he didn't. Even though there weren't many jobs available locally. Even though they really needed the work. They'd quit anyway. And it would be all his fault.

And then: Thursday. His hand was a little bit better, and so was his temper, and when he left for work he was actually smiling. At eight-forty Laura dropped Cassidy off, and they were both smiling, too. But at nine-thirty Rachel's car pulled in the driveway, and when she walked into my kitchen she wasn't smiling. Her eyes were flashing with the same desperation I'd seen in Brian's all week long. She slammed the door behind her and said, "Tess, I gotta talk to you about something."

And then she saw Cassidy, sitting across from me at the kitchen table, surrounded by construction paper and crayons. There were one hundred and twenty colors inside the crayon box now. Looking inside it was just like looking into heaven itself.

"Oh. Never mind. I'll see you later."

"No, Rach. Wait."

I jumped out of my chair and pulled on her arm. I couldn't let her leave. I knew where she'd go if she did. She'd run to Tim so she could lose herself in sex and in a haze. I knew. I'd been there. And even though the Something I'd been hiding from wasn't the same thing as hers, the distraction itself was. The only difference was that the sex had come from safer sources and so had the haze. It was the kind that dropped you into a beautiful world full of rainbows and music and gods. And it hadn't come from a needle.

Even if hers didn't either I knew that, if she wasn't careful, pretty soon it would. Tim was a shrewd business-man. He'd ruined the lives of a sixteen-year-old boy and his mother, just so he could rid himself of his only competi-tion. Had done it without even blinking. And, like a shrewd businessman, he wasn't going to be satisfied with letting the new clients he'd roped in settle for the cheapest haze available. Not even the clients he was fucking.

"Just stay here and hang out with us."

Cassidy nodded. "You can color with us."

"Yeah, right," Rachel said.

Cassidy sniffed. "What? It's wicked fun."

Rachel looked at Cassidy and then at the picture she was drawing. Blinked a few times. Then she smiled—it wasn't a real one, but at least it was something—and sat down beside her. I sat down, too, and she watched the two of us for a few minutes before grabbing a piece of dark blue paper for herself.

"So, Miss Dyer. What's the assignment for today?"

Cassidy explained the way it worked. "Tess doesn't give assignments. She says you should draw what you're feeling inside of you, because that's how you make the best kind of picture."

Rachel laughed. "What are you, Tess, a fucking psychiatrist?"

"Shut up."

"No, she's not," Cassidy said. She hadn't even flinched at Rachel's language. That irritated me just a little, because she was always very quick to correct even my slightest lapse. "Tess is a granola."

I dug out my old standby, Burnt Sienna. "Who told you I'm a granola?"

"It's what my dad told Grammy." Cassidy examined her landscape—a coastal scene complete with a lighthouse and a spouting whale—and added two more V-shaped birds to her sky. "Last night she told my parents that they shouldn't let you watch me anymore because you're a hippie."

Rachel snickered. I stopped coloring my tree trunk, folded my hands on the table, and tried to hide my own amusement. "Do you know what a hippie is?"

"Yep. Grammy said it's someone who hates America and smokes mar...mara..."

"Pot," Rachel offered. I kicked her under the table.

"Oh, thanks. She said hippies hate America and they smoke pot and they're very dirty and they have sex with lots of people."

"Ah."

"So," she continued, folding her hands together like mine, "I told her that you're *not* a hippie. You don't hate America because you sing "The Star Spangled Banner" with me every time we watch a Red Sox game together. Even though you have a really bad singing voice."

"Thanks."

"And you don't smoke pot—"

Rachel snickered again and I kicked her again. I wasn't about to be condemned, by her of all people, for something I hadn't done in a long time.

"—and you take a shower every day and your house is always clean, even cleaner than Grammy's house. *And* you only have sex with Brian."

"Oh my God."

"So that's when Daddy said, 'Tess isn't a hippie. She might be a granola, but she's not a hippie.' Then he told Grammy that she should mind her own damn business, and that I am *his* daughter and *he* could ask anyone to babysit me that *he* wanted to."

Rachel gave a brief nod of approval. "Go Jeff!"

It was fascinating, really, how much I had learned about the Burkes in the brief time I'd been watching Cassidy. In addition to Jeff's mother-in-law woes, I now knew that he didn't load the dishwasher properly, that Laura wasn't a natural redhead after all, and that she had recently caught him watching the "naked lady station" by using the channel callback on the remote control. I knew that Cassidy would report on my goings on just as faithfully, so instead of voicing my whole-hearted agreement with Rachel's sentiments, I merely smiled.

"So are you?"

"Am I what?"

"A granola, silly."

I laughed. "Sort of. I don't know. No, not really. They don't let you in the Granola Club if you dye your hair."

She nodded, taking my joke at face value, and I picked up Jungle Green to begin work on my leaves. She watched me for a few minutes. "How come your picture looks better than mine?"

"She's older than you, Cass," Rachel said. "That's why. Besides, yours is really good."

She smiled. "Do you like it?"

Rachel nodded.

"What about you, Tess? What do you think I'm feeling today?"

"I think you're feeling cheerful. Your sun is very happy."

"How do you know that? I didn't even put a smiley face on him."

"You didn't have to. Look at the way you mixed in the orange with your yellow...see? Those swirly lines?" She nodded. "They're all curving up, just like a smile."

She leaned in closer, gazed at her picture with new eyes. Looked at it for a long time. Then she said, "That's not orange. It's Atomic Tangerine."

It was the best crayon name I'd ever heard.

She put on a few finishing touches and surveyed her picture. Rachel gave it a brief once-over and said, "Don't forget to sign it. That's what all artists do."

Cassidy did so and slid it across the table to Rachel. "That's for your fridge."

"Thanks." She finished her own drawing—a minimalist effort: three stick figures with no faces, drawn in white crayon against the dark blue construction paper—signed it and gave it to Cassidy.

"Is this a picture of me and you and Tess?"

Rachel just nodded.

She spent the rest of the day with us. She admired the colored Queen Anne's lace that I'd hung up to dry, so Cassidy took her out into the back field and they picked some more together. I put the blossoms in three separate vases with food coloring and water. This time I mixed the colors together for purple and green and orange. When we sat down for lunch Rachel ate her celery sticks, but only after she ran downstairs to get Brian's ranch dressing to dip them in. I spent the rest of the afternoon weeding the garden while the two of them squirted each other with the hose. By the time Laura came to get Cassidy, Rachel's smiles were real. And so was her laugh.

Once Laura's car was safely away Rachel and I climbed the fourteen stairs to my apartment. I washed my hands while she traded her wet clothes for some of mine—a T-shirt that fit her and a pair of sweatpants that were about four inches too short—then we sat on the couch.

"So, Brian really beat the shit outta my dad," she started.

She sounded both angry and worried. I wasn't sure which of the emotions was directed at Brian and which was directed at her dad. "How bad is he?"

"Well, his nose is broken. He's got a lot of bruises and cuts, too. Really bad ones."

I nodded. At least Brian hadn't killed him.

"I warned him not to come over here but he didn't listen to me. Brian was already bitchy, 'cause he was at my place looking to start some shit earlier that day."

I smothered a grin. *Looking to start some shit.* She wanted to talk about Tim, too. But I could only tackle one thing at a time. "You've been in touch with your dad for a while, haven't you?"

That surprised her. "Well...yeah. He called me about a month ago. But Saturday was the first time I actually saw him. Well, since he left us, I mean. Then he came in to see me at work again Monday night."

"How's that going?"

She shrugged. "I dunno, Tess. Just 'cause he's not drinking anymore he thinks everything's just fine. Like he never walked out on me. Like he can fucking walk right back in and be The Dad. He wants to take me out to supper and see where I live and he wants to know what I'm doing and who I'm hanging out with. I mean, *he* didn't raise me. He didn't do shit. Even before he took off he wasn't around. And now he thinks he has the right to ask me about my life, give me advice about it? What the fuck does he know about anything? Why should that loser get to come back now and tell me what to do when Brian already did the hard part?"

Brian's words, all of them, even if they were coming out of Rachel's mouth. Not that it didn't make them true.

"What kind of advice is he trying to give you?"

"It doesn't matter. I know I'm fucked up but—"

"You're not fucked up, Rach."

"—I don't need *him* telling me what to do. If anyone has the right to tell me what to do it's Brian, and I don't even let him do it." She pulled down on the pant legs, trying to make them cover her ankles. It wasn't going to happen. She shook her head and continued. "He did the best he could, you know. 'Cause he was just a kid, too."

"I know."

"And he missed out on a lot of stuff because of me. A lot of good stuff."

"If he missed out it's not your fault. It's your father's."

"Well, whatever. He still missed out. He quit school and he broke up with his girlfriend and he stopped hanging out with his friends...except for Jeff, of course. And then when my dad took off Brian never did anything. The only time he ever left the house without me was go to work. He didn't get a chance to do all the normal things guys are supposed to do because he was stuck with me."

"He doesn't think he was *stuck* with you. He did it because he loves you, Rach."

She rolled her eyes and looked at her hands. Embarrassed. And it occurred to me that, quick as he always was to say it to me, I'd never heard Brian tell Rachel he loved her. Or vice versa. It probably didn't mean anything, though. I couldn't remember ever having said it to Dave.

"Besides, you missed out on a lot, too."

"I guess. But it's not the same thing."

"Yes it is. Your dad should've made your supper and tucked you in and helped you with algebra and...all the other stuff that dads are supposed to do for you. Brian had it rough. It sucks that he had to give up his childhood. He had to grow up way too early. But you did, too."

She hoisted her legs up onto the couch and hugged them tightly against her chest. "So you think I should tell my dad to get lost?"

"I can't tell you what to do, Rach. I mean...I wasn't here for all that, and I don't even know your father. I think you're right that he can't just waltz back into your life like nothing happened. But it seems to me like the easy thing for him to do right now would be to stay away, and he's not. If you want him to get lost and leave well enough alone, that's fine. But if you *do* want to get to know him, or whatever, it doesn't mean you're being disloyal to your brother."

She rested her chin on her knees, stared at the wall. At Kineo. I took a quick glance at my watch. I had to leave for work in a little while. But before I could I had to open up the other can of worms.

"So, what's up with Tim?"

"Not much. I'm just…hanging out with him. That's all."

I nodded. Cleared my throat. "Why?"

She shrugged. I wasn't sure how far to push it with her. I could probably get away with saying more than Brian would be able to, so I ventured:

"You're…not doing any—"

"Nothing I wasn't doing before."

"Yeah. That's comforting."

"If it makes you feel any better, I'm afraid of needles."

I looked at her closely, at her eyes. They weren't easy to read like Brian's were, but I had to know if she was telling me the truth and I did my best to find it there. Finally I gave it up and asked her outright, "You're not just bullshitting me, are you?"

"No, I'm not. I used to scream my head off whenever Dr. Stephens gave me a shot. You can ask Brian if you don't believe me."

And this is how that conversation would begin:

Hey, sweetie. Just wondering—and there's no reason for this question, other than mere curiosity. Your sister…is she afraid of needles?

She knew it, too. Knew I'd never actually ask. And so I had to take her word for it, which wasn't made of the stuff that inspired confidence. But, since we'd gone so far, I decided to push it a little farther by switching to another uncomfortable topic.

"You're using rubbers with this idiot, right?"

She blushed, then sputtered wordlessly for a few moments and even though I was honestly concerned about her it didn't stop me from making a mental tally.

Home: 1. Visitors: 2.

"I'm…I've been on the pill since I was fifteen."

Just like me. My birthday present from my mother that year was a trip into the doctor for the prescription because, *I know you're going to need these. Just a matter of time.* For once, she was right.

"So…Brian let you—"

"Of course not. Laura had that talk with me right after Cassidy was born. I was only, like, twelve or so and I probably knew more about sex than Brian did." She snorted, then, apparently remembering that she felt bad that he'd missed out on all the *normal* guy things, stopped. "Anyway, she told me that I should wait until after high school before I fuck anyone—"

I raised an eyebrow, so she amended her statement.

"She said I should wait until I was an adult to have sex—"

I nodded my approval. The idea that Laura would say *fuck* seemed almost sacrilegious.

"—but she also said that if it looked like I was gonna do it anyway, then I should go talk to her first and she'd take me to Family Planning. So that's what I did."

Fifteen. She'd lost her virginity a year earlier than I had. I wanted to go back in time to four years ago, back to the day before she'd let it happen. Take her aside and tell her not to do it. Tell her that Laura was right; tell her to wait. Tell her to wait for someone special, someone who loved her, at least a little. But then if I had that power I'd probably go back and tell me that, too.

"Okay. But you're fucking a guy who's probably fucking other girls, too, and God only knows what they're into. Don't you think a little more protection would be a wise thing?"

"Tess…"

"Rachel…"

But she was spared any more of my lecture by a sound the two of us would have recognized anywhere. The windows were open and we could hear Brian's truck long before he even pulled onto the road. I wanted to get a few more words of caution in. To tell her, again, to stay away from Tim. But I knew enough about the stupidity and stubbornness of nineteen-year-old girls when well-meaning adults tell them what to do, so I didn't. I just said:

"Rach. If you ever get into any trouble or…if you need anything—and I mean *anything*—then please come talk to me. Okay?"

"Whatever."

Brian burst through the door. Rachel looked up and hollered, "Hey, scumbag. How's it goin'?"

He cuffed her playfully on the head. "Show some respect to your elders, shithead." He gave me a kiss and said, "Hey, babe, it's hotter'n hell and I think I left my shorts up here."

"Check my middle drawer."

"Okay. Thanks."

He went into my room to change. As soon as the door closed behind him I whispered, "I meant it, Rachel. You—"

"Okay, okay. I get it."

When Brian emerged again he was holding Rachel's wet clothes. He tossed them at her. "You need to learn to take your stuff."

I looked past him, onto my bedroom floor. His dirty work clothes were lying in a heap in front of the bed. I grinned, but said nothing. Instead I asked Rachel if she wanted a plastic bag to bring her clothes home in so she wouldn't get her car all wet. She nodded and followed me to the living room closet.

"Holy shit, Tess. What's all this?"

The closet was filled with all the boxes I'd moved in with—broken down and stacked neatly on the floor—and almost five months' worth of plastic grocery bags, stashed inside a garbage bag that was hanging on a hook.

I shrugged. "You never know when you might need a box or a bag."

Rachel grabbed the bag of wet clothes then examined Brian's hand. It was still a little swollen, but the bruises were better; faded yellow instead of dark purple. Then she said, "You fucking idiot. At least you didn't break any fingers."

And that's when I smiled, because the worry had been for Brian, the anger for her father. Which is just how it should have been. And it meant that she was all right after all. Or at least that she would be. Just a matter of time.

CHAPTER 18

A warm front moved in on Friday, bringing what the weatherman called *stifling heat and oppressive humidity*. I spent the day working in air-conditioned comfort while Brian spent it fixing a roof. Carrying bundles of shingles up a ladder, thirty pounds at a time, for seven hours would have been difficult enough with a sore hand; the weather made it brutal. But he didn't leave until the job was done. He'd promised the guy it would be finished by three o'clock on Friday and, damn it, he meant it.

When I got home I found him sprawled out on his bed, naked underneath his ceiling fan, begging me for water. I called Dr. Stephens, who explained the differences between heat exhaustion and heat stroke, told me to keep a close eye on him and to call him if Brian got any worse. I spent a fitful night beside him, staring at his face and chest to make sure he was still breathing. Waking him periodically to force more water down his throat, holding my breath, willing the water to stay down. He finally opened his eyes on his own just before nine on Saturday morning. He looked up at me, ran his tongue over his dry lips, and croaked:

"It's fucking hot in here."

I nodded. "Stifling heat and oppressive humidity."

That got a small laugh and it made me feel a little better. Then he begged me to run down to the market to get him some ice cream. First I made him drink two more tall glasses of water. Told him to stand up, then to walk around the room, because *I can't leave you alone if you can't even hold yourself upright.* He rolled his eyes but obeyed. I got dressed and ready to go while he took a quick shower, then, finally convinced that he really would be all right if I left him alone for a whole fifteen minutes, drove to the market.

I nodded silent greetings to my fellow shoppers on my way to the frozen food aisle, tossed in three half-gallon containers of ice cream, then marched toward the checkout line. There were five registers in the store but only two of them were open, even though the place was packed, and it took me twenty-five minutes to reach the head of the line. Agnes explained why.

"Those damn teenagers," she grumbled. "You'd think they'd be grateful to even have a job. Three of them called in sick today, but I know they're really headed up to Bangor for the fair."

"Probably."

"Kids today. They get everything handed to them. They just don't know what it means to *work* for anything." She bagged the ice cream, then asked, "How does that boy stay so skinny eatin' like this? I bet he'll have one of those finished before noontime all by himself."

I only shrugged, because I didn't think Brian was skinny at all. He was rugged, solid; just like a tree trunk. But I knew what she meant. He should have been about three times his size.

She gave a wistful smile. "Seems like just yesterday his mom was in here buying diapers for him. Have I ever told you that I knew Wendy when she was just a little girl?"

She told me every time I came in. "Really?"

"Sure did. She was a spitfire, too, let me tell you."

And she did. She told me three stories in a row about Wild Little Wendy. She'd told them all to me before but I listened anyway. Then she handed me my receipt and smiled a little sadly.

"It's such a shame that the Lord called her home when she was still so young."

The idea that God had anything to do with killing young mothers—or anyone, for that matter—just so he could have extra company in heaven, especially when they were sorely needed right here on Earth, had always struck me as blasphemous. But I didn't say so.

"She surely hated the thought of leaving those kids behind. The last time I saw her was in here, after she started getting real bad. She was weak and in a lotta pain by then and she was having a hard time just pushing the cart around. When I asked her how the kids were holding up she said, 'It's gonna be hard, but I think they'll be okay. Brian's ready now.'"

My voice broke a little when I asked, "She said that?"

Agnes nodded. "And she was right. They turned out okay."

I nodded back, but didn't answer, and I drove home with a sad, heavy heart. I tried to imagine what those last few months must have been like for Wendy LaChance.

How many people had she reached out to before she died, knowing her husband couldn't be counted on? Had anyone understood the silent pleas behind the brave façade? Had they even tried to listen? I'd never met the woman. She had been dead for fourteen years. But I could hear her.

I don't want to leave them. They're so young and they'll be all alone. Please keep an eye on them. Please take care of them. Please don't let life get too hard for them. Please love them.

Please...

Why hadn't someone taken care of them? An absent, alcoholic father. A town full of people who knew it. Someone could've taken them into their home. How many people had Wendy begged, and how many of them, like Agnes, had paid attention to the wrong half of her prophecy? Forced her to put all that weight on the shoulders of a twelve-year-old boy.

I pulled into the driveway and, as I looked ahead, slammed both feet down on the brake, stupidly letting up on the clutch. My car sputtered, then tried to lurch forward before it finally stalled. Brian's truck was gone and in my usual spot was a familiar blue car—a car I never expected to see in New Mills, let alone sitting in my driveway. Waiting for me. The sunroof was open, windows rolled down. And for just a moment I could feel it. Again. The salty wind, blowing through my hair...

Not today, God. Please...

It was a stupid request, of course, because it was too late for it. So I did the only thing I could do. I restarted the engine, pulled ahead into Brian's spot, turned off the ignition, and took a deep breath. Then I looked toward the house.

And there he was. Jason Dyer. Sitting on the porch steps. Waiting for me.

He looked up, looked right at me. Or at least he probably did. I couldn't be sure because his eyes were obscured by a pair of dark sunglasses. I looked away, out toward where the orchard had once stood. There was nothing left of it, not even any stumps. And even though I tried, I couldn't remember what it had looked like before Brian had torn it down. Not the frozen orchard, not the imaginary springtime orchard. Nothing.

I grabbed my purse and the ice cream. Three double-bagged bundles and they made me wonder just where the hell Brian had gone. Why he'd left me here alone. Even though, really, I knew exactly why.

I opened the car door. I'd forgotten, because of the air conditioner, how hot it really was and it felt just like a slap in the face. I kicked the door shut. Gripped the bags. The purse.

Steady now, Tess. Deep breath. Deeper. Now, one foot in front of the other. Just like that.

I didn't look at his face as I walked toward the house. I couldn't. I concentrated instead on the sound of my sandals, flip-flopping against my sweaty bare feet. I took a quick peek at them, grateful that I'd painted my toenails in the middle of the night. Bright pink. I was even more grateful that I'd put on some makeup and a sundress before heading out to the store, instead of donning my usual T-shirt and jeans ensemble. Because the only thing worse than running into your ex-husband unexpectedly is doing it when you look like shit. And I almost smiled—almost, but caught myself in time—because Jason had always loved the way I looked in this dress. The skirt, he'd said, was nice and short and tight in all the right places.

Eat your fucking heart out.

He stood up without a word as I approached and opened the screen door for me. I climbed the four steps, tossed my purse and the bags onto the floor. Swallowed hard. And, finally, turned to face him.

He'd never looked better, damn him. He was tan and trim and healthy. There were faint traces of gray in his beard and in his hair which surprised me—even though it shouldn't have—and it looked good. He was dressed nicely, too, casual but neat in a cream polo shirt and green khaki shorts. I didn't give him any points for it, though. He'd been expecting to see me and had dressed appropriately, so it didn't really count.

He stood there, staring silently at me, his face completely unreadable behind his sunglass shield. I could never tell what he was thinking without seeing his eyes and he knew it. It was why he'd covered them up. Not that it mattered. I knew what to expect and braced myself for it. Clenched my stomach, my toes, my teeth as he finally took off his sunglasses...

And there they were. Cold, blue eyes. Cold, blue Jason.

He hates me. Still.

And so I did the only thing I could do. I folded my arms and glared right back at him. Shoved all the hurt away, shoved it into another crater, and packed it down tight. Because it didn't matter what he thought of me. Not really. Not anymore.

Except, of course, that it did. It mattered. Still.

What the hell happened to us?

He cleared his throat and opened the conversation, at last, with: "Blonde?"

The first word he'd spoken to me in nine months and it was a dig about my hair. I blew a piece of my bangs from my eyes. "It's not blonde."

Not technically, but it was getting gradually lighter with each visit to Laura. He shook his head, reached into the pocket of his shorts, and pulled out a pack of cigarettes.

"You're *smoking* again?"

He fished one out. "Observant as ever, I see."

"Well, you're not doing it on my porch." He gave me an irritated roll of his eyes and stuffed the cigarette back into the pack. "When the hell did you start that up again?"

"A couple of months ago, right after my mother died. I guess you and I have different ways of dealing with stress. Although, if you think about it, all we're really doing is reverting back to our old habits. I picked this up again," he patted the pack in his pocket, "and you started fucking a boy half your age."

He had baited me into the topic so expertly that I hadn't even seen it coming. I couldn't do anything except stare. And that made him smile.

"That's right. I heard all about your new boy toy. Congratulations."

I wasn't going to give him the satisfaction of asking who had told him about Brian. I didn't need to. "You came all the way down here just to give me shit about my love life? You're an even bigger dick than I gave you credit for."

"No, Tess, I didn't. Believe it or not, I've got more important ways to spend my time."

"Yeah. I remember."

He ignored the remark, reached inside his other pocket and pulled out a small white envelope. "I came down here because I need to give you this, for starters."

I snatched it out of his hand and gazed at my name. Bold block letters. **TESS**. I was almost afraid to open it, even though it was much too thin to contain anything dangerous. And the divorce had been final for five months—or at least it would be five months in three more days—so he couldn't be contesting anything, could he? After all this time? Wouldn't my lawyer have called? I took a slow, deep breath and pulled up the corner of the envelope.

"Your neighbor offered to give it to you," he said, and this time his voice was almost kind. "But I thought it would be better if I waited for you instead so I could—"

I stopped mid-rip. "He was home when you got here?"

He nodded. "You just missed him." He chuckled and added, "We had a nice little chat."

My stomach gave a violent, icy lurch that made me suddenly grateful I hadn't eaten any breakfast. "A nice chat. Really. What were you doing, Jase, pumping him for information about me? Or filling his head with bullshit?"

"Neither. I did ask him about the—boyfriend, though." He looked at Brian's apartment, then up toward mine. "Looks like he's got ringside seats."

Even without the sunglasses I couldn't tell if he knew he'd actually been speaking to *the boyfriend* and was just screwing with me, or if he really thought that Brian was just a neighbor who would give him the scoop on my sex life.

"*What* did you say to him?"

He gave a lazy shrug.

"God damn it, Jason, what the hell is the matter with you? My mother didn't give you enough juicy details? Now you have to come all the way down here and—"

"I haven't spoken to your mother in months."

"Well, why do you even care about what it is I'm doing or who I'm seeing?"

His eyes flashed at me and he lost the smug smile he'd been wearing. "I don't care, Tess. I don't give a shit about what you're doing with your life. You can fuck whoever you want to now. Isn't *that* what you wanted? You can spread those cute little legs for every guy you meet if that's what you want to do and it doesn't affect me at all. Not anymore."

How long had he been practicing that speech? He'd probably been itching to use it on me for months. A dull throbbing started in my left temple and I rubbed it with my free hand, tried to blink back the tears that stung my eyes at seeing the blatant disgust in his.

"What's this? You don't have some smartass come back all ready for me? Come on, Tess, isn't that what you do best?" Then he folded his arms. And glared at me again.

It was almost a hundred degrees outside, probably hotter than that on the porch. But I was shivering. Because he hated me. Still. He really did and even though I'd expected it, at least a little, even though I deserved it, more than a little...deep down I hadn't thought he still would. Not after all this time. Not so much.

I took another deep breath. Silent, in through the nostrils, took it in deep. Filled my lungs with heavy summer air, with stifling heat and oppressive humidity. Filled them to the bursting point and let it out.

"Well, Jase, you sure got me pegged. I'm just down here fucking everyone I meet. Spreading my legs for every guy I see. They've all helped themselves to a nice piece of this and I'm busy making the rounds again so they can each have a second helping." I rolled my eyes. "At least that's a new one. How many more of those zingers have you got for me?"

He didn't answer, only shoved his hands into his pockets. And he was still glaring.

"Oh come on, don't stop now. Let me have it. All those books you read, all those brilliant literary minds to help you out, and that's all you got? Tell you what, why don't I just help you out a little. I mean, really, if you're gonna come all the way down here to fuck with me you should at least do it right. I'd hate to see you waste your precious time. Let me think now..."

I tapped my chin, pretended to ponder. Just like I didn't remember every word. Just like I hadn't replayed the whole scene in my mind, over and over, all winter long.

"I dropped to my knees for the first fresh dick that came along. That was a pretty good one, actually. It conjures up a very vivid image with just a few short words. You should write that one down and have your students analyze it next year."

I gave him a tiny laugh and shook my head regretfully.

"It's too bad it wasn't true, though. Well, it *is* true that it was the first dick that...uh, came along after yours. But would you like to know how many fresh dicks I had the opportunity to play with all those years if I'd *really* wanted to? No? Fine, I'll just move on, because I seem to recall a particularly disgusting remark...something about my skanky cunt, wasn't that it? Now, I've been wondering all this time so I'm *really* glad you traveled all this way today to clear it up for me. Especially with your time being so fucking precious and all. Was that a Jason Dyer original, or did you borrow it from someone?"

"Tess, come on—"

"Maybe Shakespeare? Didn't Othello wax poetic about Desdemona's skanky cunt? Sure sounds like something your buddy Billy would come up with, that misogynistic prick."

His eyes snapped, but we'd gone round and round on that subject too many times for him to take the bait. I aimed lower.

"Not that it was too skanky for you to use one last time. I don't think I ever got a chance to thank you for that, by the way."

Bull's-eye. His face turned deep red with what was either embarrassment or rage. Probably both. Because it really was a low blow, the lowest. And, what was worse... it wasn't really true. It wasn't true at all, but it still hurt him. Because the truth was *I'd* used it. Tried to. I'd actually thrown myself at him, begged him to stay. Begged him to fuck me. I thought if he fucked me again it would make him stay.

Just once, Jason, please. Just one more time...

That's what I did. I begged him. To fuck me.

And he tried. He gave it a good shot, but he couldn't do it. He was too hurt and stunned. So he stood up, and I did, too. Both of us naked and sweaty. Both of us shaking. And he was disgusted. With both of us. Beyond disgusted, beyond hurt and stunned. Angry. Finally.

You fucked Chris. You fucked him *and now you want* me *?*

I didn't answer. Because I was too scared. And because, really, there was nothing to say. No way to explain, no words to make him understand, and I'd already begged him. So instead I gave him silence. Defiance. And I still wondered sometimes—still—if he'd already stopped loving me by that point or if that's what had killed it. Either way, that's when he let me have it. Hateful, hurtful, ugly words. And I couldn't blame him. Still. Because, really, all the words had boiled down to two questions; the two questions he'd never actually asked:

How could you do it? Why *him?*

I decided, finally, to give him an answer. And, at the same time, to rid myself of at least some of the venom that had been coursing through me for nearly a year.

"You know, it really is too bad you didn't listen to Coach all those years ago. He *tried* to warn you about me. The kind of person I am. The kind of *girl.* You remember, dontcha?"

He did. He went pale suddenly and I could see that he was dizzy. Queasy. And it seemed like as good a time as any to put him out of his misery. Or to add to it. At this point I didn't care—honestly didn't give a shit—which it was.

"'I'm not the girl you marry, Dyer. *I'm* the girl you fuck and toss aside.' Isn't that right?"

He shuddered. "Tess, no…"

"Just think of all the trouble you could have saved yourself, if *only* you'd listened to him. You could have found yourself a nice girl, a nice wife. The real kind. The kind that wants a house and a yard and dozen little Jason clones running around just so she could have the very distinct privilege of wiping their shitty little asses. Instead you married the town whore, didn't you? So now you've got nothing."

"He...Chris told you? What Coach Poulin said to us that day?"

"He told me all about it. And apparently Coach told you guys all about *me*. Jesus Christ, Jason, why didn't you listen to him? I mean, really, you had time to call it all off. Because if you go out and marry a girl who'd fuck her mother's boss, you gotta believe she wouldn't think twice about fucking your friend, too."

I'd done it. I'd shocked him. But it didn't last long, because then came the anger. He was filled with it, practically reeked of it. And for once I knew it wasn't directed at me.

"I always wondered what crowbar Chris used to pry your legs apart. Now I know."

I let go of all the air in my lungs, just like he'd punched me in the gut. It's what his words felt like, because they were true. It's exactly what Chris had done. He knew Jason and I were having problems. Must have known. Dave was Jason's best friend, but he couldn't talk to him about it. Not his wife's brother. So who else was there? The only other person he'd known long enough to trust. And Chris used it to get to me. I knew it even then, but I fell for it anyway.

Oh, I'm sorry, Tess. I thought Jason told you. It was such a long time ago...

Jason ran his hands through his hair, then stared at me for what seemed like an eternity. I felt myself withering under his gaze, so I folded my arms and squeezed them tight against my chest, then tighter still; so tight that my fingers started to go numb. But I didn't look away from him. I still needed to see his eyes, to feel connected to him somehow, even after everything that had happened. Still needed that...

Finally he shook his head and said, "It's true that Coach said that shit about you. He told me all about you and Mike, too—all of it—because he's an asshole. They're *both* assholes. I guess it runs in the family. And Chris is an even bigger asshole for telling *you* about it. But did you even bother to think about...did it ever occur to you, Tess, what that really meant? It meant that I knew everything...and I didn't care. It didn't matter to me. I married you anyway."

Of course it occurred to me. After Chris was all done with me. After he'd fucked me and tossed me aside. I shuddered, clenched my jaw, my stomach. Closed it all down, everything. Because, finally, I could feel it coming up, the tears and grief and vomit, and I couldn't give in. So I pulled it all back, pushed it in, shoved it down.

He reached out for me, touched my arm, and his hand was gentle and warm, just like it used to be; like it had been for all those years. And for a moment I remembered how much I used to love it when he touched me. Could almost remember—almost—how it had felt when I loved him. Almost.

Tess, I want you to know something. And don't ever forget...
I didn't forget.
I have loved you forever...
I didn't forget—but he did. He'd shut the door on all of that. Slammed it shut, locked it tight, and then tossed the key aside. Just like it was nothing. Just like love wasn't a thing that was precious and fragile. A thing that was easier to lose and to break than to find and to keep. All because

of his stupid, fucking, goddamn irrational obsession with babies and family. Just like *I* wasn't his family.

Just like I was nothing.

"Listen to me, Tess. I—"

I threw his hand off my arm. Just like it was nothing. "I don't want to listen to you. Don't you get that, Jason? Don't you understand? None of your words *mean* anything to me anymore, so just...stop saying them. It's too late for any of them. You're just...you're just too late."

He looked at his hand and then at me. Stunned. Like he couldn't quite comprehend what he was hearing. It took even me a moment to digest it all. Because it was true. There really was such a thing as Too Late.

Then he sighed. It was shaky and loud and seemed to come from some deep, horrible place inside of him. I looked into his eyes, stared hard, and I watched as it happened, as he let go of one burden and picked up another. He didn't hate me anymore. He'd moved on to the next step. Right in front of me. I'd actually seen it happen and the tears came, finally, too many of them to hold back. Silent tears. He saw them, of course, but said nothing. Did nothing. Because he couldn't. Not anymore.

He looked away from me, looked at the floor where the envelope had landed; picked it up. "Tess, I...I didn't mean to start in with you again. I really didn't. I thought I'd waited long enough...that I'd let enough time go by and... that we could...But when you came up the walk I..."

I kept my eyes down and wiped away the tears. I couldn't bring myself to look at his face. I didn't want to care, not about what he had said or done or thought, not about what he was thinking right now. I looked instead at the half-opened envelope in his hand. Straightened my shoulders, stood as tall as I could, and grabbed it from him again.

"What the hell is this anyway? I thought we were done with all the legal bullshit."

"No, it's...it doesn't have anything to do with the divorce. It's about my mom."

"Alice? What about her?"

"She left you something." He gave a short laugh that had no humor in it at all. "Well, she left it to us. I figured it belongs to you now. It's a painting, the one you did of her backyard, of my old swing set."

Another tear slipped out. I didn't bother to wipe it away.

"You did it when we were little kids. Although...well, it doesn't look like a little kid painted it." He cleared his throat. "You remember, don't you? The swing set with the broken slide."

I just nodded, because I couldn't speak. There were no words inside of me. None. Just images, flashes of memory. Of fun. Of a time, a place, when I was truly Happy. And of the day when it all ended.

Dave busted the slide one afternoon shortly after Alice took the three of us to see *The Empire Strikes Back*. We were acting it out in the back yard. Jason was Luke Skywalker, Dave was Darth Vader. I was Princess Leia, of course. I'd even braided my hair for the part. The idiots were using wooden bats as lightsabers. I had no reason to be there, because Princess Leia wasn't in that scene. But it was fun. They were fun and I wanted to see the lightsaber fight.

Jason was standing on top of the slide, Dave standing just below it. They were battling away, bats whacking and thudding together, when Jason lost his balance.

He grabbed hold of the top of the swing set with his free hand and tried to balance himself with the other. The bat flew from his hands and hit me on the side of the head.

Everything stopped for a few seconds. The earth, the universe, the three of us. Frozen. Jason, horrified; me, stunned, in pain; Dave, pissed. I thought—I really did, and Jason did, too—that Dave was going to pound the shit out of him with his bat. I held my breath. Waited. Waited for screaming and blood and death. Instead he took it out on the slide. Jason jumped off, landed right beside me, pulled me away where I'd be safe. And we watched together. Dave beat it, hit it, pounded on it, wood against hot, thin metal. Then he stopped for just a moment. Looked at it. Then he hit it two more times. It was all dented up and there was a huge crack right in the center.

I screamed and ran away from them, ran into the woods to hide. Not because I was hurt—although I was, but not bad; just a little bump that went away in a few days—and not because the slide was broken. But because it was supposed to be Jason's head and I knew that. And it scared me. I was scared because my big brother, who always seemed so calm and sensible, had reacted to something so violently. Scared that the two of them would hate each other forever. And that there'd be no more swing set races.

But when I emerged from the woods the two of them were gone. They'd taken off together down the road on their bikes. Without me. Without Tess the Pest. I sat in the sun staring at the slide until Alice found me and coaxed me into the house. She gave me an icepack for my head and a handful of Oreos. And when the boys came back they were full of apologies. Jason took the blame for the slide as well as my head. Alice wasn't fooled—because she had probably watched the whole scene from her workshop—but she didn't say anything. And she never bothered to replace the slide. Jason was ten years old and getting too big for it anyway.

And there were no more swing set races. Ever.

I blinked a few times, jolted out of my daydreaming. Jason was still talking, and I'd missed most of it.

"…thought that…maybe you'd want it. I had to sell her house, so it would be a nice reminder of—"

I didn't want it. Not the painting, and especially not the nice reminders that came with it.

"Jason, I…I'd…actually feel better if you kept it."

"Tess, no. I can't."

I swallowed hard, started shaking again. I had to make him keep it. I couldn't let him leave it here. I didn't even want to look at it. Couldn't even look at his car, knowing it was in there. But I couldn't tell him why. So I said:

"Jase, the painting is…it's yours. It was your mom's, and now it's yours. The swing set is you and Dave." I smiled but my heart was shrieking and I knew why. I wouldn't have to explain any further. He'd know exactly what I meant. He'd get it. Even though, of course, it wasn't true.

He smiled. It was a real one, the first I'd seen on him in forever. And it made me remember how I used to live to see him smile.

"Well…thank you. I don't know what Mom would have wanted, because she made her will years ago, right after we got married, and she never bothered to change it. Or maybe she just didn't want to. I can't really be sure."

There was nothing in his face now, nothing in his eyes, except for sadness. A sadness so deep it hurt to look at it. Like an open, infected wound. I didn't know if it was because of his mother or because he was remembering back to that time, right after we got married. When we really had been Happy. Together. I couldn't even remember what it felt like. Somewhere inside of him was the boy who'd been my friend forever, the man I'd once been hopelessly in love with. And now I could hardly stand to look at him.

What the hell happened to us?

I looked again at the envelope in my hand. "So, what is this? Do I need to sign something?"

"No." He stiffened up again. He was preparing for Round Two.

Oh. That again.

I held it out to him. "We've been over this before."

"Oh come on, Tess. Don't do this to me again. Not *again*."

I looked at the envelope again and ran my finger over my name. **TESS**. Just like it was all he could bring himself to write. And it made me wonder, for the first time, if he resented the fact that I'd kept his name.

I held it out to him. "Jason, you know I can't take this. There's no way I could spend it and live with myself. Especially not after…it's just not gonna happen."

"Why the hell not?"

"Because I'm not taking payment for services rendered."

I'd shocked him again, and this time it was even worse. "Tess, you are out of your goddamn mind if you think this is—"

"I don't need the fucking money. Okay? I don't need it and I don't want it." I looked at it the envelope again, felt suddenly weak with revulsion, knowing what was inside of it, and tried to give it back to him. To force it into his hand. I couldn't stand to have it in mine for even one more second. He wouldn't take it. I tried to stuff it into his pocket but he pushed it away, my hand, the money, me, so there was only one choice left, really. Ripping it to shreds. I was on the verge of doing it but stopped cold when I heard it.

Brian's truck, pulling into the driveway. I'd been so preoccupied that, for once, I hadn't heard it coming up the road. The noise startled Jason and I seized the opportunity to shove the envelope into his hand. Then I stepped back. He stared at it with new eyes, like it was something he didn't recognize anymore.

I looked past him and watched Brian stroll up the path to the house. I actually felt myself relax, could feel my heart beating again, thumping against my chest, almost as if it had stopped without him here. He was still dressed in the blue tank top and gym shorts he'd been wearing when I left. He never went out in public in those shorts, never. And he was barefoot.

I glared at Jason again. He'd said something. Something that pissed Brian off so badly that he'd taken off half-dressed in the god-awful heat, driven around town in an old, noisy truck that had no air conditioner, when he was already sick and wounded and completely exhausted.

He made his way up the steps, opened the door and Jason stepped aside to give him room to get onto the porch. Brian didn't look at either of us on his way through, tried to sneak right by me and into his apartment. I wasn't about to let him.

I wanted to find out if Jason had known who he'd been talking to; if he'd pissed him off on purpose or if he'd just run his mouth without realizing, just to get whatever it was he'd said off his chest. And there was something else, something even more important. A message. To both of them.

I grabbed Brian around the waist and forced him back. "Where do you think you're going?"

He turned toward me with a big grin and eyes that were filled with relief, but both faded as soon as he noticed my face. He touched my cheek, wiped the tears away with this thumb. I forgot that I'd been crying.

"What's going on? You okay, Tess?"

"Yeah. It's just..." I looked over at Jason. He was gaping at Brian, surprise clearly stamped on his face, and I almost laughed. It didn't seem possible that he hadn't known, or at least guessed it. Or that gossip had left out that very important detail.

He lives right downstairs...

It almost made the whole ordeal worth going through to see comprehension dawning on his face. I hid my smile and cleared my throat. "I'm okay, hon. It's just some old business we need to settle. Right, Jase?"

Jason nodded, still staring nervously at Brian. I turned back to look at him. He wasn't convinced that I was okay and was glowering at Jason, the same way he had at his father before he lost it. I squeezed his arm gently and he looked back at me again, studied my face, carefully. Studied my eyes. Then he gave me a smile, one I recognized immediately. I hadn't seen it on his face before, but I'd felt it, just a few short weeks ago, on my own. It was the same smile I'd hidden from him that night in the shower.

Mine...

He gave me a kiss—full on the mouth and longer than necessary—pointed to the grocery bags and asked, "Is that my ice cream in there?"

"Yeah. I hope it's not melted too badly." What would Agnes think if I had to go back to buy three more cartons so soon?

He grabbed the bags without a word. Headed upstairs to my apartment, even though it was hotter up there than it was in his. But it didn't take a genius to figure out why he'd chosen my door. He was sending a message, too.

When I turned back toward Jason he had recovered from his embarrassment and was ready to get back to business. "That's not what this money is about, Tess, and you know it. But it's too damn hot to fight about it today. I'll just hold onto it for you until you get over it and change your mind."

I cleared my throat. "Jason, I'm not gonna change my mind, so you might as well—"

"God *damn* it, Tess, would you—"

"Jason...stop it. Okay? I'm not gonna do this. I...I'm just so tired of it. Aren't you? I mean, I know too much has happened for us to be friends again, and I know that's my fault, but can't we at least be...pleasant to each other and...can't we just put it all behind us? Can't we just move on and...wish each other the best?"

And there it was again. Sadness, sorrow, something even deeper than sorrow and I knew what it was. Realization. The same one I'd had the morning Matthew was born. When I'd buried my head in my pillow. After I'd spent the night wishing it was Jason.

I hope you find someone soon. I really do. I hope she's beautiful and funny and kind and that she can give you the family you always wanted. And I hope it makes you happy. You deserve happiness, Jase. You really do...

He did. And I wanted it for him, wanted it more at that moment for him than I did even for myself, and the words were on the tip of my tongue. I wanted to say them and I almost did. But I couldn't. Because there are some things you really can't say.

"Well," he said at last. "I'd better get going."

I nodded. Because there were no words inside me except for one and I couldn't bring myself to say it. So he nodded back. Then he took a long look at me, at my face, my eyes. One more time. One last time. And his eyes were filled with something that was deeper than sorrow.

Then he turned away. Opened the screen door, walked down the four porch steps. And he left. Just like that. Leaving nothing behind. Just like he'd never been there at all.

I sent up a quick prayer:

God, please help him to be happy...

Because he deserved it.

And it wasn't until the sound of his car died away that I finally remembered what it had felt like when *we* were happy. When we were in love. I closed my eyes and it was almost real again. For just a moment I loved him again. And in that moment I was his. I was still Mrs. Dyer. Jason's wife.

My wife.

I used to love those words, especially the way he said them. Two little words and they sounded like a song, like a poem. Because they meant he loved me. It seemed like so long ago since I'd heard them, but it really wasn't. Just a year, and what was one year compared with all the years that had gone before? And yet here we were, months after the ink had dried on the divorce papers, and we were still bitter enough to resort to yelling. To playing mind games with each other.

I climbed the fourteen stairs to Brian so I could start the repair work. He was leaning back against the counter, drinking melted strawberry ice cream from a glass. I kissed him. Gently. Told him why Jason had come. Told him that the tears were about the painting. About Alice. And it wasn't a lie, because some of them had been. I told him about the money, too, and he shook his head. Told me that I was an idiot not to take it, that the money really was mine. It wasn't, of course, but I didn't say so. And I didn't tell him about any of the anger and bitterness between Jason and me, or about the sadness, because none of that mattered. I did tell him that I loved him and that I was over Jason, for real. Because I was. And because those were the things that did matter.

Then I waited. Waited for him to tell me what Jason had said to him. But he didn't. Not a word. And he looked exhausted. So we went downstairs to his bedroom and lay down on his bed, naked, underneath the fan. It was too hot for sex so we just lay there, silently immersed in our own thoughts. I didn't know exactly what his were, although I could guess. And as for me…I was trying to push away bleak images of what the future had in store for Brian and me.

Because even though I loved him, more than anything, it was going to happen. It was just a matter of time. There would be a day, there really would be, when there was no more Brian-and-Tess. There was nothing I could do to stop it either. But right now I couldn't think about it, couldn't bear to imagine what it would feel like when we moved onto the next step. The one that came after the love ran out.

Instead I reached over and grabbed hold of his hand, held onto it all afternoon. Concentrated hard on how it felt in mine so I'd always remember it. Rough, warm, calloused palm; long, thick fingers. I held it tight as he drifted off to sleep, as I drifted off, too. Even in my dreams I was holding his hand. And even there I knew.

I couldn't hold onto it forever.

CHAPTER 19

By Sunday morning the humidity had subsided, but not the cloud Jason left behind. We didn't talk about it because, really, there wasn't much we could say. Instead we found solace in the comfort of routine. There was sex and a shower together and breakfast. Brian rambled on about Foreign Policy and Fair Trade while we did the dishes, then I worked in the garden while he mowed the lawn. After that we ate lunch; and by then it was time to go to the Burkes' for Penny Poker and pizza. Just like every Sunday. Jeff won, just like he did every Sunday. When we got home Brian and I had sex again. And afterwards, lying in his arms, drifting off to sleep with his heart beating against my back, it felt—it really did—just like any other Sunday.

And then came the work week which kept us busy enough—for the most part—to forget that we'd ever had another unwelcome weekend visitor. And by the time Brian's birthday rolled around, the third Saturday of August, he was back to his old self once again. Even my own anxiety about The Future had faded. Exhaustion and heat and emotional turmoil can make a person paranoid, and it's not wise to dwell on those types of feelings. It's better to immerse yourself in cleaning and sex and work, to immerse yourself in how good it feels being in love *right now*. Because those are the things that are important, the things that matter. Not semi-conscious doubts about *Somedays* that follow you into your dreams.

And then, during the last week of August, Brian and I attended two funerals.

The first was for a local boy who was killed in the war. Twenty-three years old. Roadside bomb. The minister talked about heroism and patriotism and sacrifice and honor. We all nodded because no matter what we thought about the war we all knew that the soldier had been a hero. Then he talked about God's Will and about Keeping Faith. He said the soldier was now Residing In The House Of His Father and we all nodded again, even Brian who didn't really believe it. And after the funeral was over the soldier's mother talked about her son.

He liked to play the piano and work on cars. He had a big heart and a good sense of humor. He was intelligent. Focused. He wasn't going to waste his life. No sir. He had a goal and he knew how to achieve it. Computer engineering, and that meant college. No way to pay so he signed up. Experience and Army College Fund. Because times are hard and money is tight and you do what you have to do. But he was her only child. And now he was gone.

The second funeral was for one of Rachel's friends who died in the gravel pit on the far side of town. Nineteen years old. Heroin overdose. The same minister talked about Not Losing Faith and about Taking Comfort In The Lord During These Difficult Times instead of turning to drugs. This boy, too, was Residing In The House Of His

Father. It was all that the minister said, because what else can you say? And after the funeral the boy's mother talked about her son.

He was smart and funny, too, but not focused. He was tired and discouraged. Because times are hard and sometimes people deal with their problems and sometimes they hide away in a haze. He wasn't her only child, but he was the second one she'd buried. Same reason. And now both of her children were gone.

After the funeral Rachel came home with us and Brian started to give her a lecture, another one, about Having Focus and Using Your Fucking Brains, but she left before he could get too far. Once her car was out of sight he took off in his truck, and he was still gone when I got back from work three hours later. When he finally got home he walked quickly past me without a word and headed straight for the shower. He wouldn't tell me where he'd gone and I didn't push the issue until I was picking his clothes up off the bathroom floor. And saw the blood on his shirt. So he said:

"I kicked Tim's ass. Me and Jeff did. Now maybe he'll stay away from Rachel."

I just nodded and said, "Okay." And after he kicked the wall three times he grabbed a bottle of Jack Daniels from the cupboard. Because even when you have focus sometimes you still need the haze. So I grabbed the blanket from his closet and the pillows from his bed and set us up outside. We drank too much and laughed a lot and before he fell asleep he muttered something about the stars, but I was too drunk to understand it.

In the morning when we awoke we were both shivering and covered with dew. I was hung over but he wasn't, and that didn't seem fair. But neither is life sometimes and we both still had to make a living. Busy Friday. And I survived.

On Saturday morning Dave arrived bright and early. Labor Day weekend. Fishing. My father had begged off at the last minute claiming sickness. Dave's tone made it obvious that wasn't the real reason but he didn't let me in on what the real reason was. I knew him well enough to know that the matter was not open for discussion, so I let it go. I watched him silently while he transferred his gear into the back of Brian's truck. He had offered to take his, but the back roads were rough and Brian's truck was so old that a little extra damage wouldn't even be noticed.

"You be nice to him this weekend. He's had a rough time lately."

Dave seemed surprised. "Why wouldn't I be nice to him?"

I shrugged. He was right, of course. This time around it was easy. Brian was just the *guy my sister is seeing.* If it worked out with us, then great. If it didn't then he could say something like, *that's a shame, Tess, he was a nice guy but I'm sure you'll find someone new before you know it,* and that would be the end of it. Not like it had been when Jason and Tess became Jason-and-Tess.

He hadn't reacted well. He wouldn't have even if the news had been broken to him gently, but gentle is exactly what it wasn't. He'd come home unexpectedly from Boston College one fine Sunday morning in April because he'd broken up with a girlfriend. Made a beeline right for Jason's apartment to talk about it, or whatever it is men do after they've just broken up with a girlfriend. He walked in without knocking—because what's more natural than a guy having a key to his best friend's apartment?—and found us sitting on the couch eating breakfast.

Initially there was shock. All of us. Jason and I sat silently, cereal bowls shaking, waiting for Dave to speak. He stood in front of us for a horrible eternity, his mouth wide open, trying to process exactly what it was he was seeing. Because he'd just walked in on his little sister and his best friend. Sitting on his best friend's couch. Eating breakfast together. Early in the morning. And his sister was wearing nothing but his best friend's Def Leppard concert T-shirt.

And that's when the shock wore off. Next step: anger.

You and...Tess? You're fucking my sister? What the hell is wrong with you?

Jason set his bowl down and stood up to face him, tried to speak, to explain. But only got as far as *It's not what you...* before Dave took a swing. Jason ducked and before Dave could try again I ran over and stood between them. Dave tried to go around me, tried to move me out of the way, but I clung tightly to Jason, grabbed hold of his pajama bottoms. And Jason was trying to shake me loose, to get me out of the way. So I wouldn't get hurt.

Dave stopped struggling. Just stood there, breathing heavily, looking at us; first me, then Jason. Like he still didn't really believe it. And then he left without another word. He wouldn't talk to either of us for weeks after that, despite a constant barrage of phone calls. And when he finally did, he'd moved from anger to apprehension.

What's going to happen when it doesn't work out? Did you ever think of that?

By the time he came home for the summer he'd come to an acceptance of sorts.

Whatever makes you guys happy. Just leave me out of the mess.

We hadn't, of course, and it had been a huge nightmare for him when Jason-and-Tess began to unravel into Jason and Tess. A painful exercise in compartmentalization. Compartments with thick walls and no doors or windows. It had worked for a little while. But then, of course, came the affair and the separation and the divorce. And no walls were thick enough to contain the mess.

Brian came toward us, struggling with a giant cooler full of beer, and Dave trotted over to help him. After they loaded it into the truck he asked Brian, "Is that everything?"

"Now it is."

Dave nodded to me. "See you on Monday, Tess."

I nodded back.

Brian came over to me. "I feel guilty about leaving you alone all weekend."

"I'll be fine."

"You'll be able to carry on without me?"

"I'm sure I can manage for a few days."

He grinned. "And now I'll get to find out what a horrible kid you were."

"I doubt it. Dave doesn't run off at the mouth like some people I know."

"I bet if I funnel enough beer into him he'll tell me everything." His eyes gleamed with mischief. And I loved it. Passion and heat and...

Fire. This man is fire...

He gave me a kiss. And I watched them drive away.

I'd told him I could carry on without him for a few days and it was true. But it was boring as hell. Labor Day weekend, sunny and warm. And nothing to do. The garden was weeded, the house already clean, my place and his, and I'd read every book in the house. I tried scribbling in my sketch pad but the muses were still silent. There wasn't anyone for me to visit. Rachel and Zeke were working, the Burkes were out of town. And the lake was still swarming with Flatlanders. Only two more days until most of them went back home for the winter. I'd be happier about the prospect if they weren't going to be taking half my pay with them.

I settled for a Star Wars movie marathon on the good television, bored enough to include the prequels, wasting a perfectly beautiful day and evening and night indoors. By the time Darth Vader cut off Luke Skywalker's hand I'd polished off two bottles of wine, to ward off images of swing sets and bats and slides, but I still managed to stay awake until the second Death Star was destroyed. I fell asleep on the couch and spent the night dreaming of Alice's workshop...

Sunday morning dawned bright and sore. I couldn't face another day alone, so after breakfast I drove down to Rachel's apartment. I'd only been there once before. It was the smallest apartment I'd ever seen: a one-room studio above a gift shop that was only open from Memorial Day to Labor Day. It didn't open until noon on Sunday, so there were only two vehicles parked in the lot. Rachel's clunker and a freshly waxed red sports car. I knocked on her door anyway.

Tim answered. He was still bruised and battered, but not enough to keep him away. There was something creepy about him, something that went beyond the age difference between him and Rachel. Beyond the asshole drug dealer thing. *That* feeling. The one you sometimes get from a guy, that sort of spider-crawling-down-your-neck feeling that makes you want to squirm and wiggle and scrub yourself all over with a dozen Brillo pads.

He grinned. "What can I do for you, Tess?"

"Not a thing. I came to see if Rachel wants to go see a movie or something. You know," I added, "*girls'* day out."

A day without you, you stupid asshole.

Tim looked over his shoulder then back at me. "Rachel's in the bathroom right now. She's not feeling that good today."

"What's the matter? Is it a flu? Or a—"

He shrugged.

"Does she need anything? I can run to the drugstore or—"

"No. She's all set."

His grim eyes set off every alarm in my body. "You know, I think I'll stick around anyway. Just to make sure."

That's right. I'm not going away. I'll camp out here all fucking day.

He rolled his eyes, backed up a step and let me in. I looked around. Everything seemed okay. Normal. Nothing broken or out of place—no more than usual, anyway. Laundry in a heap in the corner. Dirty dishes and food still out on the counter and table. Sofa bed unmade, sheets and blankets draping off of it.

"Well," he said. "I'm gonna take off."

"Good."

He grabbed his keys from the counter. "Real nice, Tess."

After the door closed behind him I shuddered. I hated the way my name sounded in his voice.

I heard the shower start in the bathroom and looked around the apartment again. It was disgusting. I couldn't do the dishes, because it would probably cut off her water. There was no way I was going near the bed. So I settled for picking up the kitchen.

Dishes in the sink. Good food back in the fridge, spoiled food in the trash. Wiped up the counter and table.

A little better at least.

The shower was still running. I braved a trip into the living room area, avoided the bed, went through the mess on the coffee table. More dishes, pizza crust, beer bottles. Rolling papers and a lighter.

And a bag from the pharmacy.

I looked at it. Pondered. The shower was still running so I picked up the bag. There was no bottle or container of any kind inside it, but there was a paper, printed with instructions and warnings. I took a deep breath. Examined my conscience. Then slipped it out.

Doxycylcine.

It was an antibiotic. And I knew what it probably meant.

The shower stopped. I shoved the paper into the bag and tossed it back on the coffee table. Covered it up with the trash. Scooted back into the kitchen and waited for Rachel at the table. She got two steps into the living room before she saw me and stopped abruptly.

"What the hell are you doing here?"

"Hello to you, too."

She looked around. "Where's Tim?"

"He took off. Did you guys have plans?"

She looked at the coffee table. The sofa bed. Back at me. Shook her head.

"Wanna go see a movie?"

She thought it over. "Sure, I guess. Gimme a sec."

She headed back into the bathroom and shut the door. I drummed my fingers on the table. Tapped my foot against the chair leg. Traced the lines of my palm with my fingernail. Noticed, for the first time, that the line that went from the webbing between my thumb and pointer to the bottom of my hand was quite long and I wondered if that was normal. Wondered if it was my lifeline or something else.

Nearly twenty minutes passed before she came back out again and sat across from me. Hair and makeup just so. More makeup than usual. And I knew why.

"You know," I said, "concealer and foundation don't cover up bruises."

On her left cheek. Big and dark, even under the makeup. She shrugged.

"What the hell are you doing with him, Rachel?"

"What? Haven't you ever got a little rough in the sack before, Tess?"

"I'm not stupid enough to think that's what happened to you. He did that to you because of what Brian did to him."

She shrugged again. "What should I expect? I'm fucking a drug dealer."

"You need to stop doing that."

"Don't worry. He's done with me anyway. This morning was his last...whatever it was." She rolled her eyes. "He's bored with me and now he's moved on to another girl. She's *seventeen*. So I probably won't see him around here again."

Thank God. Little Miss Seventeen's family could worry about her. But.

"Does that mean he's gonna cut you off?"

"Tess, I told you. I'm not into that shit." She held out her arms.

"I'm a lot of things, Rachel, but I'm not an idiot. And there's other shit you can do that doesn't involve needles. So how about this. I promise not to give you any lectures if you promise to tell me the truth for a change."

She sighed. Scratched her arms vigorously for a few seconds and rolled her sleeves back down. Then she told me the truth.

She'd tried just about everything Tim had to offer that didn't need to be injected. But she'd been careful, she said, because she knew that he wasn't going to stick around forever. And once it was over the free ride was, too, and then where would she be? The same place half a dozen of his other throwaways were right now: selling themselves to the Lake Kids in the summer and to Tim and his sick friends in the winter.

The funeral had scared her, too, and that's when she decided to stop. Even before Brian's lecture, even before he beat Tim senseless. She missed it already, especially Oxycontin—she liked that more than anything because it made all the hurt go away, and she needed that—but it wasn't as bad as it might be. It was hard but she had it under control now. She had enough left to wean herself off and then she'd be all set. I nodded, just like I knew what she meant, even though I didn't. Because I'd never used it. But at least it wasn't heroin. I'd never done that, either, but I knew enough. Knew that once you get started on that, you just can't quit. And then she told me one more thing.

"Tim gave me the clap."

I tried to seem shocked. It wasn't too hard, because even though I'd figured it out, it was a different thing altogether to hear the words.

"Dr. Stephens gave me something for it. But I was stupid and let Tim fuck me again, so I probably oughtta go back and get checked out. Again."

I nodded. And I repeated, "Rach, you need to leave him alone."

"I already told you. He's done with me."

I ran my hand through my hair. Tapped my foot on the table leg. And I said it, even though I'd promised no lectures. "I don't give a shit. *You* need to be done with *him*."

She glanced over at the sofa bed again, and I recognized the look on her face. Because I knew the feeling. When the sex isn't about love or connection, when it isn't even about being horny or about having fun. When it's about hiding away. Burying and forgetting. When it's almost a compulsion.

I stood up. "Let's get this place cleaned up."

"What?"

"Seriously. It's a pig hole. And you're not a pig. You're too decent a person to live like this. And you especially don't need that," I nodded at the sofa bed, "staring at you all day."

She rolled her eyes, but stood up. And we cleaned. I made her change the sheets while I finished up the kitchen and we tackled the rest together. It took us almost two hours. And when we were finished she asked me about Having Focus.

"Did you start your cleaning business right out of high school?"

"Nope." I stretched, slowly, concentrated on each vertebrae as it snapped and popped. "I worked at a convenience store, a Qwik Stop, until right after I started living with Jason. I guess you could say he inspired me to start my business." She seemed interested, so I told her.

I'd moved in with him shortly after Dave found out about us. I hadn't even been there a week before he'd had enough of my constant cleaning. Toilet, carpet, sink, fridge, floor. Over and over, even when they didn't need it. Rewashed the dishes after he'd already done them, remade the bed after he'd already made it. Because it wasn't Quite Right. The final straw came one morning when I grabbed his coffee cup right out of his hand before he was actually done with it.

"Goddamn it, Tess, give that back. If you have to clean something, go clean my mom's house. Or your mom's house. Or anybody else's house. The superintendent is looking for someone to clean her house twice a week. Jesus, go do that and get it out of your system."

And so I did. Just to get it out of my system. That led to another job, and then another. After three months I was able to quit the Qwik Stop, but I didn't get the cleaning out of my system. Because nothing, ever, was going to be quite clean enough.

I didn't say that to Rachel. I told her instead that she could make some changes in her life if she put her mind to it. But she said she didn't have any skills. Not like me or Brian or Zeke. Laura had tried to talk her into going to *haircutting school* but that didn't interest her, either. And before I could say something that was encouraging and appropriate she changed the subject. I didn't push it, because, after all, I had all day. Longer, even. Rachel wasn't quite twenty, and that meant that I had plenty of time to help her. That she had plenty of time for making changes. For doing lots of things.

We went out to see a movie, a stupid chick flick that made us both cry, then we ate supper out at Friendly's. We even shared a huge hot fudge sundae with extra whipped cream and nuts, something I hadn't treated myself to in forever. And on the way home I talked to her some more about Focus. About going to school. Not a lecture, just something to think about. Because she had lots of options open to her. There was a big demand for nurses in the state, anything in the medical field for that matter. Or secretarial work. Or… whatever she wanted, really. The sky was the limit. Even if times were hard and money was tight. There were ways to get help for things like tuition and books.

She said she'd think about it, then she changed the subject again. Talked about her dad. She hadn't seen him or heard from him in weeks, even though she'd decided not to tell him to get lost. But it was okay, she said. Because it's what she'd expected. Brian was right about him after all. And so…it was okay. I knew that it wasn't okay. Not even close. But there wasn't anything either of us could do to change it. Then she said:

"You won't tell Brian about my little problem, will you?"

"I won't tell him about you getting the clap."

She sighed. "What about…the other thing."

I looked at her face, at the bruise that was visible even through the makeup, even with only the headlights of oncoming cars for illumination. I probably should tell him about it. But what if I did? He couldn't unbruise her.

Nothing he'd do would make it fade any quicker. And there would be Guilt. The kind that came from knowing that instead of protecting his sister, he'd pissed Tim off enough to take it out on her. And now that Tim had found a new Sweet Young Thing to corrupt he probably would leave Rachel alone, for real.

"I'll keep the rest to myself as long as you stay away from Tim."

She quickly agreed and promised that she'd start thinking about Making Changes. And by the time I dropped her off at her apartment she looked happy. Looked like she might be okay. And I knew she would be, someday.

Just a matter of time.

And then came Monday afternoon, Labor Day. I ate lunch at Zeke's because I knew the place would be almost empty and that meant we could talk. The ballgame was on, bottom of the eighth, but it wasn't holding the attention of the only two other customers in the place. They were too busy making out, hot and heavy, right there at their table, oblivious to the rest of the world. I lowered my voice anyway.

"Zeke, can you do me a favor?"

"Probably."

"I need you to help me keep an eye on Rachel."

I waited, watched him closely. He was usually pretty good at the poker face, unless he wanted to be discovered. This was one of those times. He knew something about Rachel and wanted me to know that he did. Still, I'd have to be careful. I started my digging this way:

"You know…when I was a kid I loved Oreos. If I was left on my own I would've eaten them for every meal and for dessert, too."

He nodded.

"But I started getting fat. So my mother put me on a diet. No more Oreos. And it worked because I lost the weight."

Another nod.

"And now that I'm older I get the fact that I can have an Oreo every so often as a nice treat, but that if I eat too many of them my ass is gonna get huge. And everything is fine."

He rubbed his nose. Cleared his throat.

"There are some people who love Oreos so much that they can't stop eating them. Even if it makes them fat. Even if it makes them sick. Sometimes they'll go on a diet and they'll do well for a while. But their friends have to keep an eye on them to make sure that they're not cheating on their diet."

It was my turn to nod. "You know, Zeke, Brian's been a little stressed out lately."

"He's been a little stressed out for a long time."

"Exactly. So the next time you see any crumbs around Rachel's mouth, can you call me first? Instead of him?"

"Sure thing."

I stuck around long enough to watch the Red Sox lose. On my way out I kicked Make Out Guy's chair. He and his girl jumped, and that made me smile. "Go get a fucking room."

Brian and Dave got home a few hours later. I helped them bring the gear into the kitchen and when we were done Dave said, "So I'll see you guys at the end of the month."

Brian nodded. I wracked my brain, but came up with nothing. "Why will we see you then?"

Dave just smiled. "Bye, Tess."

I watched through the window as he drove away, then turned to Brian. He was unloading what appeared to be a dozen foil-wrapped trout from a small lunchbox-sized cooler into the freezer. "We're going to Dave and Kim's at the end of the month?"

"Yeah."

"What for?"

"To spend the night."

"Why?" He was still concentrating on the fish. "Hello?"

"We're gonna watch Matthew so they can go away for a night."

"*What?*"

He closed the freezer door, turned, and smiled defiantly. "Yeah. They haven't had a night alone since he was born and they need one. It shouldn't be too difficult, Tess," he goaded. "You watch Cassidy, so what's the difference?"

I didn't want to talk about Cassidy. She was starting school on Wednesday, so tomorrow would be our last full day until her next school vacation in November. Only an hour or so twice a week until then, barely enough time for crayons. It sucked big time. But it wasn't the point, so I got back to it.

"There's a huge difference between watching an eight-year-old and a—*wait*."

His cooler was empty and he was getting ready to close it. "What?"

"Bleach that thing out first or you'll never get the fish smell out."

He shrugged and closed it up anyway. "So? The only thing that ever goes in here is fish."

I sighed and continued. "I don't know the first frigging thing about babies."

"Maybe not, but I do. That's why I said *we* are going to watch him. Besides, you should know about them."

"Just what the hell is that supposed to mean?"

"Jesus Christ, Tess, back off. I just think you should get to know your nephew before *he* gets to be eight years old and doesn't know who the hell you are. If you keep this up he won't even know your name by then. There's nothing to be afraid of, you know. He won't bite. Well, he might if he's teething. How old is he, again?"

"He's..." I did some quick backwards math. "He'll be six-and-a-half-months old at the end of the month. And I'm not afraid. I'm just..."

He waited for me to answer but I wasn't sure "just" what the problem was. And when he realized I wasn't going to finish my sentence after all he smiled, came over to me, and put his hands on my arms. His touch said, *I'm trying to reassure you* but his eyes told me he really was getting a kick out of my apprehension.

"You're not going to hurt him. Or break him. Babies are pretty easy. All you gotta do is feed him a bottle and probably some mashed carrots every so often and play with him a little. And change his diaper—"

"If anyone's changing a diaper it's you."

"Fine. I'll change the diapers. At least the shitty ones. You can deal with the rest."

"Wait a minute. I didn't even say I'd do it."

He laughed. "Then you can give Dave a call and tell him. 'Gee, I sure am sorry, but you can't get away with your wife because I'm afraid of your baby.'"

I flung off his arms and glared up at him. "You two set me up. That *sucks.*"

He smiled at me again. This time it wasn't a teasing one, so I let him put his arms around me. He smelled like campfire. It was nice. And he was right. The kid *was* my nephew and Dave and Kim really did need to get out. But he was wrong about them not having any time alone since Matthew was born; it had been even longer than that. They'd taken me into their home—mopey, lonely Tess—months before, made me stay with them so I could get over Jason by filling my face with Kim's snack cakes. Instead of filling my bed with a different kind of snack. I owed them at least one night to themselves.

"You change the shitty ones," I said to his chest.

"Yep."

"And you get up with him if he bawls in the middle of the night."

"Yep."

I was silent for a minute, trying to figure out what other irritating or disgusting things babies did that I wanted no part of. "I don't do boogers."

"*Fine.*"

"Okay then."

He laughed. "Cheer up. It'll be great."

CHAPTER 20

Dave had already packed their suitcase in the car and was ready to go, but Kim was dragging her feet, obviously nervous about leaving her son in my care. I certainly didn't blame her. I shared her apprehension and for three full minutes I held onto the hope that she was going to change her mind. But Dave intervened, literally pushing her toward the front door.

"It's just for one night. He'll be fine with Brian and Tess."

I knew Dave had invoked Brian's name first on purpose; it inspired much more confidence than mine. He was holding Matthew, blowing bubbles on his belly to distract him from his parents' departure.

I piped up with an almost convincing, "Don't worry, Kim. We've got everything under control."

She nodded. Almost convinced. And they left.

Brian set Matthew down on a blanket in the living room, on his belly, then lay down on his own directly in front of him, the beginning of some sort of male bonding ritual that involved squeaky animal toys. I watched them silently from the safety of the couch for a few minutes before turning my attention to Kim's collection of magazines. It was pretty impressive. I chose *Newsweek*, completely ignoring the stacks of parenting journals she'd left out in plain sight. I didn't need them. I had bought a book about baby development just the week before, and flipping through it had left me feeling prepared for whatever my nephew wanted to throw my way.

Until it was time to change my first diaper.

I plopped him down on the changing table. Everything I needed was within reach. Baby wipes. Powder. Lotion. Fresh diapers. I held my breath and unfastened the dirty diaper. Stared, mortified, for what seemed like an eternity, but could only have been a few seconds. Then I covered him right back up again.

"Brian! Quick! Get in here!"

He ran into the nursery, wide-eyed and out of breath. "What is it?"

I slipped the diaper open slowly and fixed Matthew with a guilty, sympathetic gaze. He blew a lipful of drool at me. Brian took a step closer. Nervous. He examined the contents for maybe five seconds.

"What's the problem?"

"What do you mean? Look at it!" I pointed at Matthew's little wiener. "I think I waited too long to change the diaper. Will it dry out and go back to normal? Or should we call his…"

I didn't finish the question. Brian was clutching the crib with one hand and his stomach with the other, laughing so hard that he actually started to snort. Matthew was apparently in on the joke and joined him, pealing merrily until he pissed again, a steady, curving stream that made it all the way to the crib. He sprayed the sheets and, I was happy to see, Brian, before I bothered to cover him up again.

"What the hell is so funny?"

He finally got control of himself. "Jesus, Tess. There's nothing wrong with his penis. He's just not circumcised."

I pulled the diaper down again and looked a little closer.

"That's what they're supposed to look like before parents let the hospital mutilate 'em. I guess Dave and Kim wanted to spare him."

"Oh."

I felt a little creepy staring at my nephew's penis, so I averted my gaze and got on with the business of cleaning him up. I gave him a liberal dose of baby powder, just in case. It smelled different, strange but familiar. I looked at the container. It had aloe in it. So did the lotion.

Brian dried his eyes, grabbed a baby wipe, and dabbed at his sleeve. "You've, uh, never seen a…"

"No."

"And your book didn't cover the subject?"

I figured it was better if I came clean. Because I'd actually only read the section in the middle, on five-to-eight-month-olds. It made me wonder what else I'd missed. I rarely read the directions for anything and when I did I usually just skimmed through. I'd only needed two sentences out of a twelve-page manual to get my new coffeepot to brew automatically at 6:00 every morning.

"Well," he said, still laughing, "I guess I know more about your ex-husband than I ever wanted to."

I kicked him, hard, then gave him the baby. Changed the crib sheets. Washed up. Slipped back to Matthew's room and rubbed some lotion into my hands. Then I joined them in the living room. They were lying on the floor again, still laughing. I ignored them and combed through the first part of my book. Sure enough. The Pros and Cons of Circumcision. More than I ever wanted to know. And it made me more grateful than ever for my own double-X chromosomes.

After almost an hour Brian looked up at me and said, "Would you put that fucking thing down and come play with your nephew?"

"No, I wanna finish this chapter. Then I'll be all caught up."

He scooped Matthew up off his blanket. Grabbed the book from my hands. Plopped the kid down in my lap. "There. Catch up that way."

"But...what am I supposed to do with him?"

He only shrugged and headed for the kitchen, taking my book with him. Matthew smiled and blew a spit bubble in my face. I wiped it off and we spent a few minutes staring at each other, sizing each other up. Finally I got up off the couch, deposited him on the blanket, on his back, and hovered over him, on my hands and knees.

"So, drool machine. What do you feel like doing?"

He smiled again, grabbed a fistful of my hair and shoved it into his mouth. I let him chew on it for a minute or so, until I remembered that I'd been to see Laura a few days earlier, and that hair dye wasn't a healthy snack for a baby. I disentangled it from his grasp and tied it back in a knot at my neck. He felt the loss of his new toy very keenly and started to cry.

"Oh, come on, kid."

I grabbed his squeaky turtle and waved it in front of his face. It didn't work. None of the squeaky toys did. Neither did his soft Teddy bear or Kim's old stuffed elephant.

"*Brian!*"

"Nope."

"God damn it!" Apparently Matthew didn't approve of me taking the Lord's name in vain, because it made him cry even harder. I tried to remember what my book had said about calming babies down. I drew a blank. Thought again. Looked at his face, all puckered up and red and miserable. I closed my eyes and tried to imagine myself in his place. Lonely, scared. My only means of comfort and fun ripped rudely away from me. It wasn't hard to imagine. I picked him up and held him closely. Whispered in his ear:

"Shhhh…it's all right. It's gonna be all right."

Whispered it again. Held him against me until he finally stopped crying. I waited until his grip on my shirt loosened up before I set him back down on his blanket, this time on his belly, like Brian had done. Then I lay down right in front of him. Like Brian had done. He smiled at me and I smiled right back. I gathered all his little squeaky toys together and picked up where he and Brian had left off. And when my grip on his blanket loosened up Brian joined us.

Matthew was an easy baby to keep entertained. We discovered that he liked Kim's elephant best out of all his toys, that his knees were extremely ticklish, and that his favorite thing in the world was for us to pretend to eat his fingers and toes. He took a quick nap right after lunch. Brian and I spent it hovering over his crib, watching him sleep. When he woke up Brian changed his diaper. We played a little

more and then I read aloud from Dr. Seuss's *Hop on Pop.* I
made sure all my p's popped because the sound made Matthew giggle.

Brian fed him rice cereal and peas for supper with
peaches for dessert then gave him a bath. I dried him
off, rubbed his arms and legs and belly with some of his
aloe lotion, then dressed him in cute, fuzzy blue pajamas,
the kind with feet. By then he was getting cranky, but
we couldn't get him to go to sleep. Probably, Brian said,
because he missed his parents. We took turns cuddling him
and rocking him, and Brian sang him lullabies, but it still
took well over an hour for him to settle down enough to
drift off to sleep.

I sat down in the rocking chair in his room, snuggled
him in close. Because, I said, I wanted to be sure he really
was asleep before I put him down. Brian said nothing, only
smiled and headed for the shower. After forty-five minutes
of rocking and humming and smelling his hair I figured it
was safe to put him in his crib. By that time Brian and I were
both too exhausted to do anything except crash in the spare
room—the room that had been my home the winter before.

Even so, I had a hard time drifting off. I thrashed
around, twisted the blankets into a huge, messy knot. I got
up three times to unravel them. Each time I did I checked
on Matthew. And each time I woke Brian up. Finally—at
quarter of three—he muttered, "Dammit Tess, either stay
in bed or go sleep in the baby's room." I grabbed a pillow, untangled the top blanket, scuffled over to Matthew's
room, and camped out in the rocker.

It was dark, but my eyes adjusted to it quickly and I
could see Matthew's form through the rails of his crib.

I rocked for a long time, just looking at him. It seemed strange that those were the same little feet that had kicked at me when I used to poke Kim's belly. Someday soon he'd use them to take his first steps. I thought about how his giggles and cries had sounded, just hours earlier, and wondered what his first word would be; tried to imagine how it would sound in his voice. I pictured him learning his ABC's. Reading *Hop on Pop* aloud to his parents. Waiting for the bus on his first day of school, holding Mommy's hand; little red backpack and lunchbox. Baseball games with Daddy. Help with homework. Prom. College. Wedding. Kids of his own...

I stood up, tiptoed over to him. Watched his chest rise and fall, each breath a light, precious sigh. I closed my eyes and saw his smile, his beautiful blue eyes shining up at me, and I was overcome by a strong, sudden yearning for him to wake up. Tried to will the sun to come up just a few hours early, anxious to hold him again, to play with him. Talk to him. Hear his laughter again.

In the next day or so I could probably come up with a hundred different reasons why I hadn't been able to sleep, and I might even succeed in fooling myself with some of them. By the time the week was out I'd believe that it was the uncomfortable bed that had kept me up. Or the fear that Matthew would wake up alone and scared, that I wouldn't hear his cries. But in the clarity that came with a kind of exhaustion I wasn't accustomed to I knew the real reason I was standing over my nephew in the middle of the night. And for a brief moment the image of him shifted in my mind, changed, and he was reborn. Smiling up at me with soft, dark eyes.

Van Dyke Brown.

* * *

His parents got home shortly before lunch.

"Are you guys hungry?" Dave asked. "We were thinking of going out to eat."

"Out?"

"Yes, that's right, Tess. Out. To a restaurant. One of those buildings where you sit down at a nice table and a waitress brings you your food."

"A server," Kim corrected.

"No," Dave said. "Coach only hires waitresses."

"You want to go to the café? Can't we just eat lunch here?"

Dave rolled his eyes and gave Kim an "I told you so" look.

Brian looked from me to Dave and then back again. "Why don't you wanna go out?"

"I don't feel like eating greasy, shitty food and...besides, I'm too tired to go out. Maybe we should just head home right now. We can grab something for you at a drive-thru once we get into—"

"Forget it, Tess," Dave said. "I'll just order something from Qwik Stop. What's the number there?"

"How the fuck should I know?"

"Didn't you work there?"

"Yeah, Dave. Back in my slacker days. Thanks for the fucking reminder."

Kim intervened. "Honey, the number is in the book by the phone." He didn't move. Just stood, staring at me.

I stared right back. Kim cleared her throat. "The phone in the *kitchen.*"

Dave stormed off to make the call with Brian on his heels. I picked up a decorating magazine from the coffee table and landed hard on the couch. The cover looked like the Burkes' kitchen: green, Country Chic. I pretended to read an article about faux finishing techniques while I watched Kim cuddle Matthew on the other side of the living room. He was looking intently at her face, almost as though he was trying to convince himself that it really was her. Then he smiled and filled her in on his weekend with little "wah bah wah" noises.

Don't leave me alone with those loonies ever again, Mommy. Okay?

I looked away and read through the article for real until Brian finally sat down beside me a few minutes later. I looked over at him, but his attention was focused on Matthew. Kim had put him on his blanket, on his stomach, and he was examining his fingers. They were apparently very fascinating, because he stared at them for quite a while and then began conversing with them in the same language he'd used with Kim. I laughed out loud and he looked up at me. Smiled. Then went back to his fingers.

I tossed the magazine back onto the coffee table and crawled over. Made silly noises at him, tried to mimic the sounds he was making, until he looked up at me. When he did I laughed again, because his expression said:

What the hell are you babbling about?

And he laughed right back. It sounded like little bells tinkling.

"Did you hear that, Kim?"

Dave piped up. "I thought you were used to that reaction."

I started slightly and glared up at him. I hadn't heard him come back into the room. "Fuck you, you stupid jackass." Hearing me telling his father off struck a cord in Matthew, because when I turned back to him he was laughing his little head off. I smiled again. "Is Daddy a jackass?" He laughed with even more gusto. "That's right, Sweetie. Daddy's a jackass."

"Tess!" Kim shouted. "Cut that out!"

I didn't, of course. "I wonder what's the matter with Mommy? Doesn't she know that I can say anything I want to you right now? Because you can't understand a word. Isn't that right, baby?" He was laughing so hard he'd started to hiccup. I added three or four more "jackasses" for good measure then picked him up, held him against my shoulder, and patted his back. Glared at Dave, daring him to say something.

He didn't. He just grabbed his jacket off the arm of the chair and said, "I think it's about time for me to go get lunch."

Brian stood up. "I'll go with you."

Dave nodded and followed him to the door. He shot me another dirty look before he left, slamming the door behind him.

I looked at Matthew. "Looks like your daddy's mad at me."

He hiccupped again then gave me another smile, put the full force of his eyes behind it. They were liquid blue, tranquil, like a summertime lake. I shivered and handed him quickly over to Kim, then took my place on the couch. Watched while she sat in the chair across from me.

Matthew lay his head on her shoulder, still hiccupping. But he was happy. Comfortable. Content.

"You know, Tess," she began, startling me. "You're going to have to face that man one of these days."

I crossed my legs and looked at my sock. Ten stripes, three colors. An extra green stripe. I'd never noticed that before.

"We heard about what he said to you. After your...after court that day."

I looked up. "Dave knows?"

"Yes."

"And the shithead wanted to take me there anyway."

"Tess, he only wants to help you—"

"Well, I don't want his *help*. And I'll tell you something else. I don't *have* to face that asshole. That's the beauty of moving away. I never have to deal with him or see him again. Not Coach and not any of them."

She shook her head, but didn't press the issue. She changed the subject instead.

"So, you survived the weekend."

"Yep. And, more importantly, Matthew survived." We both looked at him. He was already asleep. His face was squished against her shoulder, and it made his mouth looked like a little pink heart.

Kim laughed. "I know what's happening to you, Tess."

I groaned. "Nothing is happening to me."

"I don't believe that."

"I don't care. Just because I like my nephew doesn't mean I want one of...my own. I never have. You know that."

"I know you never did, and there was nothing wrong with that. Just like there's nothing wrong with the fact that you might have changed your mind."

"Well I haven't changed my mind. Besides, Brian and I have already talked about it."

She looked surprised. "You talked about having kids?"

"No. We talked about *not* having kids. Because he doesn't want any either."

I already raised one kid. I don't wanna do it all over again.

I cleared my throat. "It's actually a relief to know that this time I'm not with someone who's going to nag me about it constantly or try to talk me into something I don't want."

"Well, that's good, I guess. Brian was right that day, you know...what he said to your mother. Jason knew you didn't want kids before you got married. It's too bad he didn't deal with it then."

I let my gaze drop to Kim's belly. She still hadn't lost all her baby weight and, for a moment, I considered asking if it bothered her. Because if we were going to spend some time rubbing salt into open wounds, I might as well get my shaker out, too. Instead I countered with:

"Yeah well, we all know he wasn't thinking right at the time. He married me because I was different and quirky and fun, but that's only good for so long, isn't it? Pretty soon a man wants something a little more real. He wants a normal life. He wants a normal wife and kids and a huge house with a big, fat fucking yard with lots of green, green grass to mow and a dishwasher. Who knew it would take the idiot a whole fucking decade to figure that one out."

She smiled a little sadly. "Jason married you because he loved you, Tess. You know that. He just got a little antsy when he turned thirty-five because..." She sighed. "Well, I guess it doesn't matter now."

"I guess not. Besides, just look at him. He doesn't seem like he's in any rush to settle down again and start his little family. Last I heard he was still screwing everything in sight."

"Just listen to yourself, Tess. You get so indignant when everyone gossips about you, but you believe everything they say about Jason without question? After you there was just one woman, and that was…well, you know about her."

I sure did. The Ex; the woman he had dated before me. A few days after he walked out on me he went running right back to her. It lasted all of two days.

"He did just start seeing someone recently, but I don't think it's serious yet."

"Then I guess he's all set, isn't he? You know," I'd finally reached my breaking point, "that's the great thing about being a man. Here he is, thirty-six years old, hell he'll be thirty-seven in a few more months. If he was a woman, *right now* he'd be freaking out. He'd be thinking about hormone shots and in vitro fertilization and shit like that. But he can have his cake and eat it too. He got to screw around with lots of girls in high school and lots of women in college, then he wasted all those years with me. Now he can screw around again and he still has *plenty* of time to have kids. All he needs to do is find himself a fertile young chicky once he's through having his fun and he's good to go."

"Tess, that's not fair. Do you really think he *planned* for his life to turn out like…" She sighed. "Look, I don't want to get into any of that. Just…whatever issues you and Jason had about it, don't let that stop you from starting a family with Brian if that's what you want."

"I *don't* want that. And...even if I did, I'm too old now. It's my turn for thirty-five in November. Isn't that when everything starts shriveling up?"

"Not necessarily. I'm only a year younger than you. Dave and I plan on having one more."

"That's fine. For *you.*"

"All I'm saying is, you might want to figure out how you *really* feel about it. What if you wake up five years from now wishing you'd started a family when you had the chance? It probably will be too late by then."

"Maybe. But that's a hell of a lot better than waking up five years from now wishing I *hadn't.*"

She didn't have a reply for that one, and I rolled it around in my brain a few times. It sounded good, sounded right and I repeated it, out loud. Because Too Late really was better than If Only I Hadn't. I looked at Matthew again. Studied his sleeping face. He still looked just like Dave. Just like my dad. And then I thought about my own mother, who looked just like me, and I said it out loud one more time. And found myself actually believing it.

Nobody spoke all through lunch. Not even Brian. The only sounds at the table were made by chewing and crunching while they ate their pizza and I ate my veggie Italian. And by Dave clearing his throat. He did it five times. Each time he did I looked over at him only to find that he was already looking at me, and I'd wait for him to say something. Each time. But each time he looked away and went back to his lunch. Back to pepperoni and mushrooms.

And I was sick of it. Sick of being around grown men who were suffering from PMS, sick of the awkward silence. So I brought up a topic for conversation that would take advantage of the first problem and cure the second. Dave's work. He was defending a man accused of killing his wife. I only knew about it because I'd seen him on my television screen in his Lawyer Suit a few weeks earlier, talking to reporters about Fair Trials and Changes of Venue, because they had very kindly let the public know that the guy was guilty as sin. That he had a bad temper and that he'd beaten his wife for years and years. So I asked Dave if he had trouble sleeping at night. If he was haunted by the ghost of a Viciously Abused and Brutally Murdered woman.

It was a rotten thing to do to him, because he hadn't actually volunteered to handle the case. He was the court-appointed attorney, the kind that television cops told suspects they had the right to if they couldn't afford one on their own. But the question didn't even phase him. He just smiled and said, "No, Tess. I sleep just fine."

"Because of all that innocent-until-proven-guilty bullshit?"

The silence was over, but the awkwardness remained. We were all treated to a nice long lecture about Justice and Injustice. How the Presumption of Innocence is the foundation of any moral society. How the media influences prospective jurors' opinions even before the facts of the case have been gathered. And, especially, about how shameful it was that, even in a democracy, wealth—or a lack of it—still had such a bearing on whether or not a person gets a fair trial.

I listened intently to every word, held his gaze steadily throughout the entire lesson. I didn't look away when Brian interjected from time to time to ask a question or to give his opinion, or even when Kim—obviously irritated at me for irritating her husband—got up to get a crying Matthew from his crib. I nodded and shook my head and made appropriate replies, which pissed Dave off all the more. Because he thought, of course, that I was just being condescending.

The truth was, though, that I agreed wholeheartedly with every word he said. I really did think that the Presumption of Innocence was the foundation of every moral society. I thought that most reporters were inhuman bloodsuckers, more interested in money and ratings and notoriety than in the Truth. I agreed that the poor deserved competent legal representation. That they deserved a voice. And that, too often, they didn't get it.

The truth was that I was proud of my brother for being that voice. And even though I'd gotten him going on the subject partly for the fun of watching him rant, and partly to end the awkward silence, the truth was that I loved listening to him speak about the Evils of Injustice. It made me feel safe knowing that he was out there battling those evils. There was something about hearing those words in his voice that made me feel like I was home.

He ended his discourse with: "Believe it or not, Tess, juries usually get it right."

And I said the only thing I could say. "Good."

We stayed for a few more hours, long enough to watch the last Sox game of the season. There would be no players wearing red this October, at least not the Red that any of us cared about. But there's always next year. And then it was time to go. Hugs and kisses for Matthew, nods and brief goodbyes for Dave and Kim. And still Brian was silent. Even after I pulled out of the driveway.

I knew he wouldn't be for too long. His jaw and fists were clenched and his legs were bouncing up and down so fitfully that, if I was a mechanic, I could have rigged a wire from them to my engine and increased my fuel efficiency. He waited until I came to a stop at the end of the road before he finally spoke.

"Why didn't you want to go out for lunch?"

"You're pissed because we didn't go out to eat?"

He persisted. "*Why* didn't you want to go out?"

"I told you. I was too tired. You know I didn't sleep good last night."

"Bullshit."

"Excuse me?"

"You heard what I said. You're too tired to sit down in a restaurant but you're not too tired to drive home? That's bullshit."

I rolled my eyes, pulled the shifter into neutral and yanked on the emergency brake. I could tell this one was going to take a while. "You obviously think you know the reason, so why don't you just let me have it."

And he did. He took a deep, deep breath and the words shot out of him, flew out of him, because he'd been holding them back for a long time. He'd held them back on a catapult, just waiting for the right time to hurl them at me.

"I think you were too embarrassed to let your old friends see you with your little boy toy."

Sharper than an arrow, and they hit their target. Hurt twice as much in Brian's voice than they had in Jason's.

"God damn it, Brian, why the hell didn't you tell me he said that to you?"

"Gee, Tess, I don't know. Why didn't you ask me? You knew he said something, you were just too chickenshit to find out what it was."

"That's not fair."

"No, I suppose not. I guess it really isn't fair for me to expect you to actually talk about something, is it?"

I swallowed the *fuck you* that sprung to my lips. Gripped the steering wheel hard and focused on the real problem. "You know that Jason's full of shit, right? I mean…you don't actually *believe* I think that about you."

"Most of the time, Tess, no. I don't. Then something happens like today. Or I walk into Zeke's and have to put up with your little fan club there giving me shit about how much you like playing with dicks. Or—don't look at me like that. Did you really think I wouldn't hear about it?"

Of course the guys had told him. It was too juicy a thing to keep to themselves. No wonder they cheered me whenever I walked in. I kept the oven going day and night. They only had to hang around, waiting, plates licked clean, to see what I'd dish 'em up next.

"Those assholes are worse than a flock of old maids."

"Maybe. But it sure would've been nice if you were the one who told me about it instead of them, don't you think?"

"I didn't know there was anything to tell," I lied. "I ran into your ex-whatever-she-is. She was being a drunken bitch, and she covered my lucky shirt with beer. So I…told her off."

"Well, you sure did a great job of it. Do you have any idea of the shit I had to listen to from those guys? Huh?"

"It can't be any worse than what I have to put up with from them."

"Oh, really? 'Hey Brian, aren't you lucky,'" he mimicked. "'If she's been playin' with dicks for that long she must be real good at it by now.' Fuckin' Andy and his big, fucking mouth."

"Andy was just pissed because I didn't let him—"

"Yeah, I know why he was pissed and I know what you didn't let him do. Good for you, Tess. But the only reason I didn't beat the shit outta him is because Jeff was there with me, and Jeff's bigger'n I am."

He lifted his arm, like he was preparing to slam the door with his elbow, then thought better of it.

"God damn it, Tess, you should've told me what happened that night. And you should've told me what Ashley said to you. I would've told you all about it, and then you'd know that you've got nothing to worry about. But no, you come home and maul me in the shower instead, just like I'm a fucking piece of livestock you gotta brand."

I turned away from him and looked out the window, looked at the clear, pale blue sky. Just that morning it had been filled with fat gray clouds, wave after wave of them. They hadn't brought any rain, though; just a chill. For a moment the landscape turned gray, even though the clouds were long gone, and I had to close my eyes against it. To make it disappear. If I looked at it for even one more second I was either going to vomit or cry. But even behind closed eyes the whole world was gray.

"Look, Brian, I'm tired, okay? I'm fucking exhausted. And I *really* don't want to get into this." I opened my eyes, finally, and looked at him, but couldn't quite bring myself to focus on his face. "I don't want to talk about Jason or your sweet little Ashley, or any of the rest of them, either.

Not now, and not ever. Because…" I forced a smile. "Brian, none of that has anything to do with you and me. Anything that happened before we got together doesn't even count. So why go into it? We've got a clean slate here."

"That is the stupidest thing I've ever heard."

I twisted in my seat to face him, focused on his eyes this time, ready for battle. "Did you just call me *stupid*?"

"If you actually believed any of that bullshit about clean slates then I'd think you were, but I know you don't. If you did you wouldn't still be bothered about Ashley. You know, I'm not proud of being jealous of *your* ex, but at least I'll admit it. But whenever something comes up that you don't wanna deal with, you're happy just to close your eyes and pretend like it doesn't exist. Let me tell ya something, Tess," he pointed a finger at me, something I'd always hated, "it doesn't work that way. Sooner or later it's gonna come back to bite you in the ass. And it ends up hurting a hell of a lot worse than if you just deal with it as it comes at you."

"Is that so?"

"You're goddamn right it is."

"And you wanna know why I didn't want to go out with Dave today."

"Yes, I do."

"Fine." I released the brake, shoved the car into first gear, and peeled out onto the main road without really looking. I nearly hit an orange VW Beetle.

"What the hell are you doing?"

I didn't answer and instead looked straight ahead at the road, barely aware of the blurry trees whizzing by either side of the car, even less aware of whatever words were coming out of Brian's mouth as I sped along. It took less than three minutes to get to Hillside Café. It should've taken eight.

I turned the engine off. Shoved the keys into my purse. Opened the door. Turned to him.

"Well? Are you coming in with me or what?"

I slammed the door without waiting for an answer and walked over to the sign. It was an ancient roadside marquee, the kind that lights up so travelers can read it at night. It was just after four, so there was still well over two hours of daylight left. The sign, thank God, was lit up anyway. Bright, glowing yellow. The message on the sign never changed. Never.

Don't leave wit out visiting our bakery.

Brian finally joined me. He looked at the sign. It meant nothing more to him than the possibility of fresh-baked goods. I grabbed his hand, held it tight. Held it like it was all I had left. Then I pulled him inside.

The place was packed, just like I knew it would be, just like it was every weekend. Packed with staring people. Curious. Angry. Smug. Most of them didn't even bother to conceal it. My first instinct was to ignore them. Instead I gave them all a big smile and a friendly wave.

"Hey guys! How's it going?"

Fuck you and the horse you rode me outta town on.

Still nothing but stares, except from a small group of Jason's former freshmen students—seniors by now—who were sitting at a booth in the back corner. They returned my greeting with a hearty, "Hey, Mrs. Dyer!" I wasn't sure if it was honest affection that made them do it or the thrill of pissing off the older patrons, but I rewarded them with a real smile, as real as I could muster, and waved again. Then I turned to face Brian. He was through surveying the crowd and was waiting for an explanation.

"It's like this, Sweetie," I began in a low, bitter whisper, "Jason Dyer has a fan club, too. It's a little different from mine, though, because his is actually more like a cult."

I was only slightly exaggerating. Brookfield High School had a football team, like most schools, but nobody really cared. It was basketball that mattered here. The town ate and breathed and lived it. And Jason Dyer had ruled the courts. Led the school to the tournaments for four straight years. State champs each time. He was so popular in school that Dave—one of the neglected and ignored football players—had called him Jason, Patron Saint of the Basketball.

Our Jason, whose number's seven; hallowed be thy game...

And after college the hero returned so he could fill eager young minds with knowledge. Even more important to the townsfolk, he took over coaching the basketball team and led them to even further glory.

"In his defense," I conceded, "I have to add that Jason is a very reluctant idol."

He'd certainly enjoyed his status in high school, but it had worn thin by the time college was over. Even though he loved playing basketball he'd never actually sought glory on the courts. It was a means to an end for him. It paid for college so he could teach, just like he'd always wanted to do. Like his dad had done.

Brian nudged me. "Tess, maybe we should just get out of here."

"Oh, no. We can't leave yet. You haven't met their fear-less leader."

I strode over to the counter, trying to look braver than I felt—which was not at all. Brian stood close beside me, tense and alert. I whispered, "Promise me something."

"What is it?"

"Whatever this guy says you let *me* handle it."

He nodded, even though he had no real idea of what he was agreeing to. Then I turned toward the counter once again. And saw him.

Coach Poulin.

He probably had a first name but nobody knew it. He had coached Brookfield's basketball team for twenty-two years. After his third heart attack he handed the reigns of command over to Jason—he would have done so for nobody else—but even his own children still called him Coach. He was in his early sixties. Nearly as tall as Brian, but hard and tough. Quick temper. Vietnam vet. He smelled of fry grease and Old Spice. He hated me more than the rest of them did, but for different reasons. To him I was the worst kind of enemy. Insidious. Deceptive. Domestic.

I smiled up at him sweetly. He hated that. Then I began the introductions.

"Brian, this is Coach Poulin. Coach," I pointed beside me, "this is my boyfriend, Brian LaChance." *Boyfriend*. It really was the stupidest word in the English language. "I'm sure my mother's told you all about him."

He nodded without even looking at Brian. He kept his steely eyes fixed right on mine.

I chuckled lightly. "Well, don't you believe a word of it. You know how my mother is."

That got him. I knew it would. But he said only, "Is there something you want, Bellows?"

"Well, there's a lot of things I want, Coach. Like world peace and lower gas prices and a woman president." I considered for a moment. "On second thought, I think I'd like to see Bill Lee in the White House first, 'cause his first act as president would be to outlaw the designated hitter rule. After *that* we can elect a chick. But I think for now I'll have to settle for a cup of coffee and maybe a snack. I can't leave wit out visiting the bakery now, can I?"

I rested my hands on top of the glass counter. Smudged fingerprints on glass bugged him even worse than they bugged me. He narrowed his gaze, leaned in close, ground his teeth. For a moment I honestly thought he was going to growl at me. I leaned in closer, too—so close I could smell his sour breath—and rubbed my fingertips along the glass until they squeaked. Then I smiled again, still looking him squarely in the eye.

Say it, you asshole, you fucking bastard. Say it again. What am I? Say the word. Say it.

I wrapped my brain around the words, tried to wrap them in some sort of electrical, cosmic energy field so I could fling them at him. I wanted him to say it. Wanted to hear him call me a whore. Again. He wouldn't have done it if I'd come in here earlier with Dave, because Coach was actually scared of him. Dave knew it, too. Probably it was the reason he'd wanted to bring me here. So he could feel like The Man. The Big Brother. The Protector. But Coach just might say it in front of Brian and I wanted him to. He needed to know:

I'm not ashamed of you. I'm ashamed of me.

Even if it meant he'd know other things, all the things I was afraid of him knowing. All the things Coach had told Jason, the stuff that most people didn't know about; not even Dave. But I didn't care anymore, didn't care if Brian knew, if everyone knew. I had a slingshot of my own waiting to snap.

My experiment with telepathy worked. Coach took in a sudden sharp breath, like he was ready to go, and I braced myself for it. Waited for it. Smiled. He noticed the smile and closed his mouth. Looked over instead at Brian. Sized him up.

Brian's whole body clenched like a fist and he was ready for battle. He thought Coach was looking to start some shit, and he was right. But it wasn't the kind of shit he thought. And that's when I knew. He deserved to know the truth. He really did. And if Coach wanted to give it to him, the same way he'd given it to Jason and Chris all those years ago, then he was welcome to do it. Get it over with. It was bound to happen. Sooner or later.

He finally looked back at me again, that cold, silver man, and I could see it in his eyes. Even before he said it. His voice was so low that it was barely audible. But the words echoed in my brain just like he'd shouted them inside an empty gymnasium.

"I don't know this kid, Bellows, and you're not worth the trouble or the energy. You're just not worth it."

It was a slap in the face, another one. He'd chosen the words on purpose. Not. Worth. It. He watched my face as it fell, then he grinned, because he'd won again and he knew it. I could actually see him tallying up the score.

Coach: 3. Tess: 0.

"I'll just send Deb over to help you two." Then he walked away without another word.

I knew Brian was looking at me, wondering what had actually just happened, but I stared straight ahead. Stared at blueberry muffins and chocolate donuts and lemon pie and fancy pastries with pretty pink frosting. I relaxed my eye muscles and let them all swirl together into a colorful sugary haze. Then I brought them into focus once again, gazed up at the menu, and actually smiled. The code hadn't changed since I'd first used it, right after high school, and that was good. The prices hadn't changed as much as I'd anticipated. And that was even better.

Deb Poulin walked out from her kitchen to help us. She was in her early forties and quite tall for a woman. Her figure testified to her profession of baker, but she was better known in town for her remarkable gardening abilities and the excellent crop that resulted. Her dislike of me wasn't as strong as her father's, but she wasn't my warmest admirer either. She managed a smile, though, and even made her "Hi, Tess," sound almost chipper. Her gaze fell on Brian and I got the introductions over with so we could finally get down to business.

"You'd better get his order first. I'm still deciding." It was a lie, of course. I knew exactly what I wanted. She looked at me a little closer and her eyes gleamed. Because she knew, too.

It had been so long since Brian had actually spoken above a whisper that his voice cracked and he had to clear his throat. He finally managed, "Um, coffee—extra cream, extra sugar—and…a double chocolate donut."

She dispatched his order then turned her attention to me.

"The Usual."

She nodded. "Dozen?"

"Half."

"You sure just half will do ya?"

"Yep. I'm sure." It had been a long time. Best not to overdo it.

She reached underneath the counter and pulled out a box.

"I need some rainbow sprinkles with that, Deb. If you've still got 'em." Because it had been an even longer time since I'd had that.

"Yep. Those are still real popular."

"Good." I saw, out of the corner of my eye, Brian's head turn to me with what was probably confusion, because none of the donuts or pastries had any sprinkles on them. But I didn't look back at him. "Oh, and Deb. Can you throw in some extra…tissue papers in for me? I, uh, don't want the donuts sticking to the box."

She nodded and went to work. Half a dozen glazed donuts. And before she closed the box she looked outside, then back at me and asked, "Getting chilly out there. Are you guys all set for firewood this winter?"

"You know," I said, "we're not." Brian had apparently caught on by now, and didn't bother to tell her our house had an oil furnace.

She nodded again, reached down underneath the counter, and slipped the donut box into a large paper bag. "Anything else?"

"Actually, yes." I glanced behind her, at the door that lead into the kitchen. "Does your dad have any of his coffee going back there?"

She laughed—it was the first time I'd ever heard her do it—and considered for a moment. "Let me see what I can do."

She wandered out back and I finally braved a look at Brian. He looked toward the kitchen a little suspiciously, then back at me, so I said, "Coach was a Navy man. He makes his coffee good and strong."

"Ah."

Deb snuck back with a large, steaming Styrofoam cup. She looked a little guilty, probably the first time that particular emotion had crept into her bosom in years. She appeared to be enjoying it. "Black?"

"Better give me some cream and sugar. Even I'm not that brave."

"Anything else?"

I shook my head. Brian reached for his wallet but I waved him off. "I've got it." I reached in behind my driver's license and pulled out my emergency fund, then slid the folded bills across the counter as she punched the price of the coffee and donuts into the register. I told her to keep the change, even though she'd already slipped it into the pocket of her apron.

"Good to see you again, Tess. I hope you make it back into town again soon."

I took one last look toward the kitchen. Coach was in the doorway, glaring out at me. I raised my cup at him and then said to Deb, "I wouldn't count on it."

CHAPTER 21

I set my coffee cup on top of the car, popped my bag of treats in the trunk, covered it with my sweatshirt and closed the trunk again. Then I turned to Brian. "Do you mind driving?"

"I don't mind."

I tossed him the keys and took my first sip of coffee. Coach was a first-rate asshole, but he did know how to make a decent brew. Brian finished eating his donut just as we reached the interstate. He waited until my coffee was gone before he spoke again. It took me fourteen miles.

"Poulin. Was that shithead back there your mom's boss?"

I shuddered. His memory was too good. "Nope. Her boss is *Mike* Poulin. Coach Poulin is his older brother."

He nodded. "And *Coach* Poulin hates you."

"Yep."

"All those other people in there do, too?"

"Yep."

"Because your ex is their sports god and you divorced him."

"Because I had the nerve to marry their sports god in the first place. And then I cheated on him."

I'd said it. It was out there and there was no taking it back. All I could do now was close my eyes and wait for the reaction. Because I knew how he felt about that particular sin. He rarely referred to his father as anything other than That Cheating Bastard, and he always put and extra dose of venom in the *Cheating*.

"Oh."

That was all he said. *Oh*. And after a few more minutes he cleared his throat.

"That can't be the reason that coach asshole hates you, though. Seems to me like it went a little deeper than that."

It was my turn for the Great Debate: An easy lie or the difficult truth. Because there was only one way for that story to begin:

When I was sixteen, I fucked my mother's boss...

And it would end with *that* word. The one I'd dared Coach to say. Less than half an hour ago I was too tired and too defeated to care if Brian knew the truth, if he knew everything. Now I was even more tired and more defeated than I'd ever been in my life. And that's why I had to keep it from him. And so I lied.

"That's the only reason."

Then there was more silence. Three miles of it. Three miles and a half.

"I don't know what you want me to do, Tess."

Let me help you. Let me fix it. Fix, fix, fix. Like it was a hole in the wall or a leaky roof. "There's nothing for you to *do*. You asked me a question and I answered it for you. That's *all* that happened back there."

"That's all."

You're not worth it.

"That's. All."

He was silent again, but not for too long. Just two more miles. Because he couldn't just leave it at that. "You know what? Just fucking forget them. People like that, they've nothing to do so they stick their noses in other people's shit just so they can tell them how bad it stinks. Believe me, Tess. I know those kind of people."

I nodded. I knew he did. Small towns were all the same. Filled with small people who spent their time waiting for leftover bits of other people's misery. A scrap of truth here, a dollop of assumption there. Stir it together in a mixing bowl, stuff it inside a flaky crust, bake until golden brown, and you've got yourself a tasty gossip pie. Serve it hot and fresh and you'll be the star of next Sunday's potluck supper.

Eight more miles of silence. I wanted to know what he was thinking, but I didn't dare to ask. I looked at the radio and almost turned it on, but we had a rule. The driver chose the station. So I looked ahead at the black tar, tried to count the white lines coming at us, but they were too fast, so fast that they looked like dots. I tried counting anyway and got to fifteen before nausea forced me to give it up. I looked out the window and saw a big sign.

Rest Area Ahead. 2 Miles.

One-point-seven miles later Brian hit the blinker and clicked off the cruise control. Drove up the long ramp, parked in a spot far away from the restrooms, turned off the engine and pocketed the keys. We were the only car there. I still couldn't look at him. I was afraid he'd know the truth, that he'd be able to see it in my eyes. That I was a big fat ugly liar. That I really was a whore. But I was more afraid of what I'd see in his. What I wouldn't see there anymore.

"Do you, uh…need to use the bathroom?"

I nodded, still looking straight ahead. "Yeah. But you go first." We couldn't go at the same time. I didn't want to leave the trunk unguarded. He left without a word, came back a few minutes later, still silent. I opened the door. Hesitated for a few moments. I wanted to say something to him. Something. But I didn't know what to say. So I left. Without a word.

The bathroom was filled with cold, white tile. Ceilings, walls, floors, counter. I did my business, washed up, fixed my makeup, and turned to leave just as another woman walked in. She was probably my age. She had big hair that was stiff with spray and a warm smiling face. It was the friendliest face I'd seen in a long time, so I nodded a greeting.

She shook her head. Confused, indignant, almost hurt. "Y'all don't do much talkin' up here," she said.

Southern accent. And that's when I knew why she seemed so upset with us all up here. Dave's roommate in college was from Georgia. He'd always talked a blue streak whenever I called, whether Dave was there or not. Not to flirt. He just liked to talk. Open, chatty, warm. Apparently Southerners were all like that. I envied them.

I couldn't say that to this strange woman, of course, but I managed a smile and tried to reassure her. "Nothing personal. Just New England reticence."

She heaved a sigh and headed for a stall.

There was a green minivan with North Carolina plates parked directly in front of the restroom. Kids wrestling inside, husband standing outside the closed driver's door. Smoking. Ignoring the commotion. Accustomed to it. I made a point of walking through the smoke that blew toward me on the breeze...

Brian was leaning against the passenger door, apparently tired of driving already. I held out my hand for the keys but he shook his head. He closed his eyes for a moment and inhaled deeply through his nostrils. I stifled a groan and braced myself for a long'un. He opened his eyes and began it this way:

"Here's the deal, Tess. I hooked up with a lotta girls after Rachel moved out. A lot. I was horny and tired of being alone and...mostly I did it just because I could. It was actually pretty easy. I know how that sounds, but it's true. I'm not gonna bother you about most of that because most of those girls *don't* have anything to do with us. But the whole thing with Ashley is different. I should've told you about her a long time ago, because I knew she was bugging you. I knew it all along, and I was just waiting for you to—"

"I told you already, Brian. I don't *want* to hear about her."

"Well, I'm gonna tell you anyway. Because you seem to think it was this big deal and it wasn't. Not the way you think anyway. I was at a stupid party I had no business being at and I saw her there. She was cute and I knew she had a crush on me so I went home with her. And the sex was horrible. It was just...really quick and really bad."

I almost laughed, even though it wasn't funny. Of course the sex was bad. She hadn't know what the hell she was doing. He'd helped himself to the poor girl's virginity...and he didn't even know it.

"I woke up the next morning in bed with a girl I barely know who's a fucking dingbat to boot. And then I had to tell her that I used her, 'cause she thought...well, you know what she thought. I felt like shit about it. I still feel like shit about it and I wish it had never happened. Whenever I see her now, I'm not thinking about the sex or about how cute she is or anything like that. I think about how she got hurt because I acted like a stupid, selfish asshole. And I think about Rachel, about how she's been treated just like that. And it makes me remember that nobody deserves to be treated that way. Nobody. Okay? See, that's what I would've told you if you'd ever asked me about her. But you never did."

North Carolina finally started to pull away and I looked over. Friendly Lady stared at Brian in obvious confusion as they rolled past. She was probably making herself a mental note to double-check the definition of "reticence" when she got back home to the land of cotton.

I turned back to him and let him continue.

"See here's the thing, Tess. I believed in clean slates once. But it's bullshit. You know it, too. We bring our old shit with us. Okay? All of it. Whatever it is. Whether it's an ex-girlfriend or an ex-husband or a dead mother or...whatever. It's all there, Tess, all of it. And I'll tell you, I didn't give it a thought until your ex showed up at my door looking for you. Up until that moment I thought just like you did. That whatever happened to us before we got together didn't really matter that much. That it was just ancient history and didn't have anything to do with what's going on now. But I've been thinking about it ever since and you know what? I think he was always there. He was always right outside, just waiting to knock on my door. Since the day you moved in. Just like Ashley was waiting there to corner you. And I'm not bringing all this up because I want you to...I don't give a shit about..."

He stopped and seemed to consider his words. Whatever it was, it was ripe.

"I don't *care* about how many dicks you played with before you met me. That's not it. It's just that...It's *him*, Tess. It's him. You loved him once. You loved him enough to put on a white dress and stand in front of your family and friends and a priest and God and promise that you'd spend forever with him. I'm not saying that I'm ready to run out and get married tomorrow. Or in a month or..." He shook his head. "Hell, that's not true. I'd do it right now, right this second, if I thought you were up to it. And I'm not saying that you have to feel that way right now, too. I just need to know that what we've got here is...real. That it's not just about you using me to get over him. And—"

"Brian, please—"

"No, Tess. Let me finish. And as far as what happened with you and your ex, about you cheating on him? With whoever the guy was? I don't really need to know anything about it unless you want to tell me. But there's one other thing I *do* need to know, Tess. Just one and it's this. What else have you got out there that's waiting to knock on my door? Is it that other guy? Because...I don't know who it is or what it is, but there's something there. That much I know."

He wasn't angry. Just a man gathering intelligence. Preparing for a possible frontal assault. And, of course, he was right. And he really did deserve the truth. After all, I'd brought him into that place. He didn't ask to go. I'd grabbed him by the hand and pulled him inside, expecting someone else to do my dirty work for me. But I still couldn't bring myself to tell him. Not everything. So I took a deep breath and told him what I could.

"His name was Chris. He was one of Dave and Jason's friends. They were all buddies in high school. Last fall I was lonely and scared because my marriage was going to hell and Chris was...there. He was convenient I guess and it just happened. Just once. And it was my fault because I made the first move."

I actually couldn't remember if I'd made the first move. I couldn't remember if I'd planned my seduction before or after he spilled the beans about what Coach had said to him and Jason. Or if I'd planned anything at all. All I could remember was reaching for him. A sudden, desperate, nameless Need. Like when you're working outside in the heat and you realize—all of a sudden—that you're thirsty as hell; that aching, light-headed thirst that borders on dehydration. So you run to the garden hose and just start sucking the water right out of it. And even though it's lukewarm, and tastes dirty and metallic, it's exactly what you need so you don't notice the taste. It was just like that.

"Chris left Brookfield too, just like me. I don't know where he is right now and I don't care. But he's not gonna show up at your door. Or my door. Not literally or figuratively. Because it was nothing. I ruined his friendship with

Jason. And with Dave. That's all I am to him, okay? I'm nothing to him but a fuck. A stupid, worthless fuck."

She's the girl you fuck and toss aside.

"Just like I was to all the rest of them. Everyone except for you."

He didn't take the bait, didn't even blink. He only said, "And except for Jason."

It was the first time he'd ever said the name and it sounded like it hurt him to do it. Hurt him because, of course, he was right. Even after Jason finally noticed me, once he wanted me, he didn't do anything about it. I would have let him make a night of it, or even two or three if he'd wanted to, because it was the only way I could think of to get him. And he knew it. But he had waited, just like Brian had waited. Even if it was for a different reason.

He waited partly because of Dave, because he was afraid of him. But mostly he waited because of Us; the three of us. Because of summer vacations we spent running through the grass in his backyard and rolling down hills and fishing for trout in the brook. Eating Alice's special tuna sandwiches with the pickles cut up so, so tiny and Fritos on the side. Swing set races, pumping our legs furiously, higher and higher until one of us said, *NOW! let go!* Then flying through the air, the best feeling in the world, the best feeling ever. Pushing the air aside like it was water, trying to use it to push ourselves farther forward, just a little bit more, to stay in the air just another moment longer. Then landing hard on the ground.

An entire lifetime of friendship and love. And I was content to lump him in with the rest of the nobodies and nothings who all thought of me as a nobody and a nothing.

As just another worthless fuck. I had to. Because I couldn't bear it otherwise.

Tess, I want you to know something...

The evening before we got married. Standing alone outside the restaurant after the rehearsal dinner, standing there under the stars. He kissed me, so gently, with his beard tickling my lips. My cheek. The way I loved it.

...and don't ever forget...

Held me, so closely, with strong arms, stronger than they had ever been. And he said it, the most beautiful words in the world, the most beautiful words that he'd ever spoken.

I have loved you forever.

He said it because he knew. Because Coach had told him about Mike.

...and I didn't care. It didn't matter to me. I married you anyway.

And I wondered, not for the first time, what would have happened if he'd told me he knew. Right then, at that moment.

Flying. Falling. Landing hard.

But it didn't matter. Because now there was Brian, and it was just as real to me with him as it had been with Jason. That feeling of being Almost There. And he really was right there, waiting for me to talk again.

"Jason is...nothing now. Not anymore. And you're not my boy toy. Okay? I don't give a shit what he said to you. If all I wanted from you was sex I would've just grabbed you that night in my apartment and made you stay with me. Maybe for a night or maybe for a little longer. We would've had a good time, and...that would've been it. But, Brian, that's *not* all you are to me. You...you're..." I sighed. "Listen to me, Brian. I *love* you."

I put as much feeling and power behind the word as I could, but it still didn't seem like enough. Because what I meant, of course, was that he was fire and music and life. That he was everything that was good and decent and strong. That his heart was so big and full that I couldn't understand how his body could possibly contain it; why it didn't just burst open and spill out all over the place, all that passion and wonder and heat.

Because love is a weak word. Just four little letters. But it was the only word I had. So I said it again, because I really did love him. Even though what I meant was all those words I couldn't bring myself to say, all the emotions I didn't even know the names for. The ones that meant even more.

"I love you. And I know you want more from me and you deserve it, all of that. And I'm trying, Brian, I'm trying so *hard* not to be scared of it. So...please just be patient with me. I'm trying."

It was all I could say to him, because I couldn't promise him the white dress. Couldn't even wrap it up in a Someday. Even though I wanted to. Even though the worst thing I could imagine was being without him. Living without him. I couldn't actually bring myself to imagine it, even though I knew that I would be. Someday. Because I knew something that Brian didn't. There really is no such thing as forever.

"I know you are, Tess."

"And that whole thing back there was...I'm sorry I made you go in there and see that. I just didn't want you to keep thinking I was ashamed of you. Because it had nothing to do with you. It was something I should've taken care

303

of months ago, before I moved away and I couldn't. But I just did, so now I'm fine. I'm…better. It's all better now."

"Really. All better now. You're just feeling so happy and in love with life and the universe." He gestured toward the trunk. "So your little snack in there is for…what? For kicks?"

"No, that's just…"

He waited. "Just?"

Just a cloud, Brian. A cloud and a rainbow. One Something to help me float away and another Something to bring back the colors. Because they're all gone and I need them back. Even if it's just for one night. Even if it's for just a few hours. At least enough to help me get through the rest of the day and night and make it into tomorrow…

"I just need to unwind. It's been a fucking long weekend. Hell, it's been a long summer. And I worked hard to squirrel away enough money to get me through the winter and…I just needed to use some of it to unwind a little."

"Unwind."

"Yeah. And it's been a long time since I've had either of those…snacks. Let alone both. And I've got sugar in there, too. Real sugar and deep fried fatty dough and—"

He laughed at that, so I did too.

"One night won't kill me." I put my arms around his waist and pulled him close. "Or you. If you want."

He waited before he answered and I knew what he was thinking. Rachel. Because I was, too. Thinking about all the advice I'd given her and what a hypocrite it made me to be going down this road. But even though it was almost the same thing, it wasn't really.

He gave me a big sigh and a little smile. Then a nod. "All right. It's been a while for me, too. But I don't want you to think that we're done talking about this."

"I know." I said it even though I knew I'd do my best to see that we really were done talking about it.

When we got home it was already dark. There was no moon, only a sky full of stars. Brian grabbed the donut bag from the trunk and met me on the lawn. I didn't bother to go inside for a blanket, even though it really was chilly. We unpacked our little picnic right on the grass, which made both of us laugh, even before we'd begun. And when our snacks were finally ready he had a warning for me.

"This shit makes me...well, I'm gonna talk your frigging ear off."

"And that's different how?"

It didn't take me long to find out. He became the Philosopher of Everything. Great and small. It seemed unreal to him that love, a thing that was so chaotic and irrational, could even exist in a universe that was, at its very core, so orderly and precise, let alone keep that universe in motion. He heard music in the gently swishing pines and it was the same music he remembered hearing once in the ocean's white, frothy waves as they crashed on glittery, stony shores during a childhood trip to the coast. I could actually hear the musical waves as he spoke, just as if I'd been there with him, and it washed away the lonely, empty ache inside me, better than the trippy haze alone ever could have done. Because his voice was deep and sweet and rich and slow and the words that poured out of him sounded just like poetry and honey.

I begged him to keep talking, to just talk and talk and never, never stop, so he told me all about the stars. He loved them, had always loved them. They were winking at us, he said, because they knew something that we didn't. It was a secret they were forced to hide, a secret so great and wondrous that they wanted to shout it out so the whole world would know, but they had to keep it buried deep inside. Even so he knew what it was, because someone had told him a long time ago. The stars, he said, were actually souls, all the souls that were too restless to be locked up in heaven. They were so restless that God let them stay outside at night to play.

It was the most beautiful thing I had ever heard him say, that I'd ever heard anyone say, and I forgot for a moment that he didn't even believe in God. And when I did remember I still believed his words and I was thankful that He had chosen tonight to let so many restless souls out to play. I smiled up at them and they smiled right back. Giant prism smiles that shattered the white light into a thousand colors I'd never even seen before. They dripped everywhere, spilled all over the sky, slowly, just like hot candle wax. And then they froze. Stood still for a beautiful brief eternity and I tried to whisper to them. Wanted to tell them that I knew their secret, but no words would form. I could tell that they heard me though, or that they'd at least heard my thoughts, because they came in a little closer. They were so close that I knew I could touch them. I reached up, way up, stretched as far as I could stretch while still lying on my back...and I swept my fingers across the cold, wet, colorful sky.

Brian reached up, too, but not for the stars. He grabbed my hand, brought it back down to Earth and I think he knew, even though I didn't tell him. I think he felt it, felt it all, in my fingertips. Because he kissed them, each one, so gently, with precious, tender lips. And when he kissed my mouth I could taste the night on his lips and his tongue. Sweet honey words and neon stardust, and we made love, in slow motion, naked underneath the mischievous stars.

The night was chilly and the ground was cold, like I was lying on January's carpet. But it soon melted away—the cold, the grass, the ground itself. It all evaporated and we were enveloped in its steam. Because Brian was burning with a heat more intense and pure than the sun. He *was* heat, the source of everything warm and in that night of mist and haze and waxy skies his body was the only thing that was real. Our love the only thing that was solid, the only solid thing in the world, in the vast expanse of the universe. For a brief moment lucidity flickered, and I begged the starry, restless souls that it was true. That it would still be true even after the mists were gone and the haze wore off and the ground returned.

That it would always be true.

CHAPTER 22

October always begins with a promise. Color and flavor and fragrance. Movement and beauty. Change. A crisp lovely chill. And so I dug inside my closet for my lime-green sweater bin and was surprised to find, packed in behind it, a box that held three bottles of bleach. All summer long I'd been buying it for home and for work when there were three perfectly good bottles right there. In my closet. Behind my sweater bin.

I closed the door, unpacked the sweaters, and refilled the bin with my summer clothes. Swim suit and tank tops and shorts, all neatly folded and layered with dryer sheets. I opened the door and set the summer clothes bin on the floor. In front of the box that held three bottles of bleach. And closed the door.

Because it's not like bleach goes bad if it's stored in a closet behind a bin of summer clothes. Not like if I wanted to store a box of crackers or Slim Fast bars or even a case of Brian's Chef Boyardee in there. After about thirty years or so even canned ravioli goes bad, regardless of how many chemicals and preservatives they stuff inside the pasta. But bleach? That would keep forever. It would certainly be fine until summer, until I unpacked my swim suit and tank tops and shorts. Summer. That's when I'd need that bleach anyway. Work picks up in the summer, so that's when I use more of it.

Summer sounded great.

But all night long I heard it. Very faint. But I heard it.

Tess, wait...

I snuggled in closer to Brian, my head against his chest; hoped his snoring would block out the sound. But it didn't. I hid my head under the blanket. Underneath my pillow. But still it was there. I squeezed my—

...this will change everything.

—eyes shut. Tightly. Tried self-hypnosis. Imagined Hawaii, white sand and foamy white waves; pictured fluffy white clouds, soft and billowy; counted sheep and they were white, too, all white, all of it. Just like it had all been scrubbed with bleach...

The next day I cleaned. All day long. Cleaned my apartment, scrubbed every inch of it, from ceiling to floor. Then Brian's. I called Laura at work, begged her to let me watch Cassidy at her house after school instead of mine so I could *please* clean something there, even if I only had time to do the bathroom. She was confused but readily agreed. And afterwards, of course, there was work. And when I was done I burst through Brian's door and pulled him into his bedroom.

"But, Tess...supper is—"

Threw him onto his bed.

"Here's your supper."

And we fucked forever. Rough, wild, loud, in every position I could think of and a few we made up, and I came three times, came so hard that I could barely move. He fell into a deep, sound sleep, even though it wasn't quite seven forty-five. Even though his supper was cold and untouched on the table, and I lay down beside him. Waited for sleep to claim me, too. Because I knew it would. Surely I'd sleep. I was fucking exhausted, completely worn out from a night awake and a day of work and an evening of back-breaking sex. So I waited. Waited. Spent hours. Just waiting…

…he was there, the whole time, just waiting to knock on my door…

The evening after that I got home before Brian did, walked through his door, and when he walked in half an hour later I snapped at him.

"I clean all day long, I clean other people's messes, and I sure as fuck don't need to clean up after you, all the time, and it's always the same. Breakfast dishes still on the table and the toothpaste cap in the sink and the shaving cream cap on the floor and your dirty goddamn underwear in front of the hamper instead of inside it and—"

He walked right back out without a word and I knew where he was going. He was going to Zeke's, which is where he always went when I was being a complete raving psycho bitch.

I had the nerve to stay downstairs in his apartment, because I was afraid of mine. I lay down on his couch and watched his television, watched old movies because black and white always put me to sleep. When he came through the door two movies later, my eyes were closed but I was only pretending to be asleep. And I watched old movies all night long. Black and white. All night long.

Tess, wait. This will change everything…

310

When the sun came up I took a shower and made him breakfast, a big breakfast, with toast and eggs and bacon even though the smell made me want to puke. I said I was sorry I snapped at him and he said it was okay, even though it wasn't. He ate and then put his dishes in the sink; he brushed his teeth and shaved, and he twisted the caps on tight; he showered and all his dirty clothes were inside the hamper and not in front of it, and the wet towel was hanging on the towel rack. Then he kissed me and he went off to work.

I ran up the stairs, opened the closet, dug behind the summer bin. Pulled out the box that didn't really contain three bottles of bleach. Carried it out into the living room, opened it up, and started sorting the pictures. And I discovered that I wasn't the only one who had closed it up without really looking. Jason couldn't possibly have gone through them before he'd packed them. There were too many that were his; Jason's life before Jason-and-Tess. And there were mine, too. The Me before Him. And so there was only one thing to do. I started three piles. His. Mine. Ours.

The Our pile grew quickly. Bar Harbor Anniversary. Our apartment, the Love Shack. Holidays and birthdays. Everyday life, and all of it Happy. I was close to tears again, and just about ready to give it up until next summer, when I began to find lots of Him. Young Jason. Childhood: His parents, a family barbeque, Cub Scouts. High school: Him in his basketball uniform, a dozen of those at least. Candid shots of perky cheerleaders whose faces I barely recognized from a million years ago. Jase and Dave and their buddies on their way to a rock concert. There was a picture of Chris in the group and I crumpled it up, chucked it into the kitchen.

But lots of them were of just Jason and Dave, the two of them, and I came across one that I'd never seen before. They were standing in Alice's living room, and she had probably taken the picture. They looked about seventeen or so. Cocky, flexing their muscles for the camera. Handsome. Smiling. I smiled back, then focused on Jason, wondered why I hadn't had a thing for him back in high school. I was probably the only girl who hadn't. He really was a good-looking guy, even back then. Blonde, fresh-faced, confident. But, of course, the answer was obvious.

"He can throw a ball into a hoop. Why the hell is that a big deal? It's just...Jason."

Because after Dave busted the slide, Jason became the boy I hated. The boy who took away swing set races. The tall, stupid dork with the goofy-looking grin who packed ice in the snowballs then aimed for my head. The big-shot basketball hero who strutted the hallways like he owned them. Alice's son who was so busy with girls and his buddies that he frequently forgot to spend time with his mom.

And then he was gone, away at college, and I never gave him a thought. There were too many other things to think about. Worry about. Deal with. Avoid dealing with. Bury.

Until a cold, February morning.

He walked into the Qwik Stop and gave me a brief nod as he headed toward the coffee. He looked more like an absentminded professor that morning than anything else, with his crooked tie and scuffed shoes, groping clumsily for the Styrofoam cups. And when he stumbled to the counter a few minutes later with his coffee and a greasy breakfast sandwich that should have been marked Hazardous Waste, I asked:

"Rough night?"

He pulled out his wallet and mumbled, "Mmm hmm." Then he finally looked at me. There was a vague spark of recognition on his face, a momentary uneasiness.

Don't I know her?

I did some quick backwards math. I was probably only ten or eleven years old the last time he'd noticed my existence. Tess the Pest.

"I...overslept. I was up late grading term papers." And it was there again:

I know her.

His discomfort amused me. He could tell and it irritated him, so I switched gears. "You teach high school here in Brookfield?"

He nodded. "This is my first year."

"Brave man. In that case, the coffee's on me."

He examined my face even more closely, still trying to place me. Probably wondered if I was one of the many nameless girls who had obliged him back in high school. I thought about letting him suffer for a little while longer, but decided instead to let him off the hook. Off of one and onto another.

"Did Dave ever tell you that I beat your Space Invaders score on our Atari?"

He smiled, obviously relieved. "The hell you did, Pest."

Then there was a flicker of guilt. I saw it, even then, but didn't understand it. He told me later—much later— that he'd noticed my tits in my tight uniform the second he'd walked through the door and that he'd been trying to imagine me naked. Until my mention of Dave wiped all that away and replaced it with a very different image, a memory of a long-forgotten summer afternoon. Jason and Dave, both age eight, and Tess, age six. Jason was sitting on my back, holding me down, so Dave could give me a noogie.

I didn't know that at the time, naturally. I only knew that the arrogant boy who had aggravated me for so much of my life was gone and that I wanted the handsome, intelligent man who had taken his place. I didn't want him in the way I'd wanted and taken so many other boys and men. Not just as something fun to put between my legs for a little while—although he certainly seemed like something that would be great fun to put between my legs. There was something else, a Something I couldn't quite put my finger on. The only words I could form in my mind that fit the need—the Something—inside me were:

I want him.

And I only had about a minute to get him.

I had no clear plan. So I continued on, praying for inspiration. "It's true. It was three in the morning, January seventeenth, nineteen eighty—"

"Wait a minute. You remember the *date?*"

I gave him a wink. "No. I made that part up. I did beat your score though."

He shook his head, handed me a five and did a remarkable impression of Jason, Age Twelve. "I don't believe you. You can't prove it."

"Proof? I don't need no stinking proof."

He laughed. Laughed. That was all. It was the sweetest sound I'd ever heard. And the moment I knew what the Something was. There were no bells or lightning bolts or fireworks, no angelic chorus from heaven singing

Hallelujah. I just knew, in the same way I knew that I had to pee. It was that primal and that obvious. I wanted him, yes. It was **Want**. But a want of all of him. His mind and heart and body and laughter; his words and smile and soul and life. His life.

I wanted the rest of his life.

I didn't believe in love at first sight. Hell, I didn't believe in love. Not really. But in that moment I fell in love with Jason Adam Dyer. Love. A glimmer of Forever, the first I'd ever known. And of something else. Elusive, familiar, a whisper of childhood...

Motion. Momentum. Letting go. Flying through the air, suspended in time, floating in air.

Landing hard on the ground.

Panic. Shaking hands. Too many coins to choose from...

I know how to make change; I'm not an idiot. Count backwards, back up to five dollars. Three pennies, a dime, two quarters, two Georges. But he's a teacher. Math? Maybe. No, there are no term papers in math, everyone knows that, just like there's no crying in baseball. But still. What if I counted wrong? What if he thinks I'm an idiot?

I glanced up. He didn't even notice my discomfort. He was too busy with his coffee.

It's change. It's no big deal. It's only change.

Then I smiled.

Motion.

I slid the bills across the counter and he looked up at me again. He was smiling. Hand out. Waiting for his change.

Momentum.

I had the change in my fingers. Put it in his hand.

Letting go.

I let my fingers slide over his open palm. Slowly. Softly. Let them linger on his for a few hot seconds of eternity before finally pulling them away.

Flying through the air...

His head snapped up.

Did you just...?

I gazed steadily into his eyes and raised my right eyebrow just slightly.

Yes. I did.

He swallowed hard and his face flushed, deep red, from the top of his forehead all the way down to his collar. He shoved the change in his front pocket, the bills in his wallet, the wallet in his back pocket. Took a shaky breath. Grabbed his breakfast. Muttered a stunned goodbye. Couldn't get out the door fast enough.

Landing hard on the ground.

But he was back the next morning.

Coffee and cigarettes. I slid the pack of Camels across the counter.

"You really should quit. Those things'll kill you."

I said it to him because I was honestly concerned about the state of his lungs. I honestly thought he should quit, honestly wished he would. But—honestly—I loved the way they made him smell.

"I know. I'll quit one of these days."

"They'll make your face all wrinkly too, which is even worse."

"Getting wrinkles is worse than death?"

"Definitely."

He laughed. And my heart started beating again.

"What's the matter, Tess? Don't you have any bad habits?"

"Nope. Not me. I'm perfect."

"Naturally."

He stopped in every morning after that, even throughout February vacation when he had no real reason to be anywhere near the store. We'd talk a little, about school or books or politics or movies, any topic that didn't make us think of Dave. Then I'd flirt with him. And he'd flirt right back. It was all very light. Casual. He made it perfectly clear that he understood it was all just friendly, all in fun. All the while letting his eyes linger on my lips or breasts. Or, best of all, he would stare directly into my eyes.

Then he'd leave.

And then came the first Thursday of March. Rainy and cold. He strolled to the counter like he always did and I slid his pack of cigarettes across the counter. Just like I always did. Except for one thing.

"What's this? No lecture from the surgeon general this morning about the evils of smoking?"

I was hoping he'd notice, and hoping even more that he'd ask. I cleared my throat and quoted, from my recent research: "'I haven't a particle of confidence in a man who has no redeeming petty vices.'"

And then my smile faded. Because his reaction wasn't what I'd been hoping for. Not even close. He wasn't mildly surprised or impressed, or even touched that I'd been reading a book about a man whose words I knew he loved. He was shocked. Open-mouthed, wide-eyed shock. And I thought I knew why.

"What? Just because I didn't go to college you think I'm some sort of fucking idiot? You think just because I work in this shithole that I can't pick up a book and *read* it?"

"I...no, Tess. Jesus, no. I just—you..."

And that's when I knew. I'd blown it. For real.

Because I was wrong. It wasn't shock I'd seen on his face, not amazement that the slacker standing before him had a brain. It was realization. I'd gone out and bought a book about a man whose words I knew he loved. Read it. And then I let him know it. I'd punched a hole right through the We're Just Friends Having A Few Laughs Every Morning façade and forced him to face what was really going on.

I'd acted like A Girl.

He blinked rapidly, then closed his eyes, trying to piece together what he should say. Not that it mattered. Whatever the words were going to be they'd boil down to the same thing, even if he wrapped them up in a Sorry.

It's not going to happen, Tess.

I waited for them anyway.

"I'm sorry, Tess." Then he opened his eyes. They were bright blue and perfect, like a clear summertime sky. "I don't think you're an idiot. You're *not* an idiot. I'm just not used to hearing *anyone* quote Mark Twain at seven in the morning. Not just at a convenience store. Anywhere. Not even at school."

I nodded but didn't say anything. I just took his money, his grubby ten-dollar bill, and slid his change—bills and coins—across the counter. Watched him put it all away. Watched him walk out the door. Neither of us said *goodbye.*

And when I got home from work I lay down on my couch and cried. All afternoon. Because even though he hadn't said it—not yet—I knew that he would. All he'd done was buy himself some time to think of the right words. Kind words. Let-her-down-easy words. Then, after the tears were all gone, I made a phone call to a girl from work, the one who worked the overnight shift. Gave her a bullshit story about an important appointment I had in the morning, and could she trade shifts with me, just for one night? Of course she said yes. Because no one really wants to work from ten at night until six in the morning if they can work from six in the morning until two in the afternoon.

No one except for the idiot woman who doesn't want to face the mess she's made. Who doesn't want to face having to hear the man she loves—more than anything—tell her: *It's not going to happen, Tess.* Because if he went into the store on Friday at seven in the morning and I wasn't there, then he'd know: *Don't worry, Jason. I get it.* He'd have the weekend to recover and on Monday he'd start going somewhere else for his coffee and cigarettes. Or he'd go back to wherever it was he used to go before I'd given him his Change. That way I'd never have to see him again. And then I could forget that I loved him. More than anything. I could just go back to doing what I'd always done. I could hide away in a haze and fuck guys I didn't care about.

And so I went to work, went in to face middle-of-the-night customers. Rowdy men who bought liquor and stared too long at things they shouldn't. Truck drivers who needed twenty ounces of coffee to keep them going until their next stop. Teenagers who snuck out of the house to hang out in the parking lot, because there was nowhere else to hang out in Brookfield in the middle of the night. And finally six o'clock came. Early morning, but no sun. Just dark, gray clouds and pouring rain. And so I went back home and slept.

It was still raining when I woke up at noon. A cold and windy rain that let me know that I'd never be warm again. Not after a hot twenty-minute shower or underneath a heavy, red sweater and itchy wool socks. Not even lying down on the couch, wrapped inside a thick log cabin quilt. I shivered through every layer. I shivered for hours.

Until I heard the knock at my door. Because I knew it was him.

He was breathless, wet, nervous. Still in his teacher's clothes. It took me a moment to process it all, but once I did I smiled. Because I knew what it meant. All of it. He hadn't gone home to change; he'd come to see me directly from work. I'd never told him where my apartment was, not even the street name. He'd actually asked someone where I lived. But most of all, best of all, was the look on his face. It wasn't telling me, *It's not going to happen...*

"Tess..." Then he shivered.

"Oh. Shit. Come in here, Jase. Get out of the rain."

He nodded, walked in and shut the door behind him. Stood there, looking at me with no words. Just hot breath in my face, breath that smelled like smoke. I looked at his dripping coat and then at his tie. Touched it. Slid my fingers along the soft red silk. And still he said nothing. I looked back up at his face, right into his eyes, and slipped my hands underneath his coat, where it was warm. It was an intimate gesture, probably too intimate, but it felt natural, touching him like that. He was supposed to be there, to be with me. It felt right. He felt right.

He felt like home.

And still he said nothing. He didn't make a move. So I smiled, pushed his coat off his shoulders, let it drop to the floor. Pulled on his tie, gently, pulled him down to me and kissed him. He tasted hot and smoky and his beard was rough, but his lips were tender and his eyes were open and they were so, so blue. It was all perfection and beauty and big exploding heartbeats, because it was the first time I'd ever kissed someone I was in love with.

He finally gave in, kissed me back, his hands in my hair, on my face, my body. They were everywhere, touching everything I'd waited so long for him to touch, and so gentle that I almost cried, just like it was the first time I'd ever been touched. Because, really, it was.

He pulled off my sweater and kissed me again, urgent this time. Hands and lips, his and mine, everywhere. Everywhere. I struggled with his tie while he unbuttoned his shirt, because the clothes couldn't come off quickly enough. And finally we were naked, finally and his body was pressed against mine so close and *please*, Jason, kiss me again, just never stop kissing me. Then walking back, back toward the bed, stepping over clothes, toward the bed, finally at the bed.

And then he let go of me, uneasy again. Shaking. Breathing heavily. "Tess, wait."

"No."

I pushed him onto my bed, climbed on top of him, straddled him, but didn't take him inside me. Because he was looking up at me, into my eyes. Into my eyes. Even though I was naked, even though my breasts were naked for him. Even though they were…right…there. His.

Into my eyes. And I looked right back. Into his. They were glowing.

So. That's what it looks like.

I was twenty-one years old. And I'd never seen that look before. Never.

Letting go.

"Tess. Wait. This will change everything."

And that's when I smiled. "Jason, this won't change anything."

"But—"

Not inside me. Not yet. But I knew. And so did he.

"Everything has already changed."

I have loved you forever.

And I had loved him that long, too. Somewhere down below the hard, packed ground. Even before I knew what it was.

I looked at the picture again, smiled again at Jason and Dave. Put it in My pile, right on top of Golden-Haired Jason. It took the rest of the morning but I looked at every one of the pictures, every single, painful memory. Separated them, sorted them out. Remembered. Cried.

And when I was finished I put the piles into three large manila envelopes. I put Mine on my bookshelf. Ours went into the trash with Chris. Then I wrote a brief note. Read through it. It was dispassionate, but nice. Read it again. Slipped it inside Jason's envelope along with Windy-Haired

Tess. Sealed it, addressed it in bold, block letters and drove to the post office. Watched silently as the young brunette stamped the package, dropped it in the Out Of Town bin. And wheeled it away.

CHAPTER 23

I checked my hair in the bathroom mirror then headed downstairs to say goodbye to Brian. He was making himself some lunch and I watched, nauseated, as he took a bowl of ravioli out of the microwave, poured on Tabasco sauce, salt, and Parmesan cheese. Then he leaned back against the counter and actually took a bite.

"Want some?"

"Uh…no thanks."

He shrugged. "Suit yourself."

"When's the last time you had your blood pressure checked? Or your cholesterol?" He shrugged again. "And how the hell do you not weigh five hundred pounds?"

He took a huge gulp from a glass of milk—whole, not skim—and smiled. "Would you still love me if I weighed five hundred pounds?"

"Nope."

He laughed. "You're an evil woman."

"That seems to be the general consensus."

He wiped his mouth on a paper towel. "What time are you meeting your dad?"

"I'm supposed to be there at twelve-thirty." I checked my watch then fiddled around in my purse and pulled out a tube of lipstick.

"You've already got some on."

I shoved it back in, walked over to him, and kissed him firmly on the cheek. It left pink lips behind. "Whaddya know. You're right."

He touched his cheek, but didn't wipe it off. "What's up with your dad?"

I sighed. "Beats me."

"What do you *think* it is?"

Bad news. It had to be. My father had never invited me out to lunch just the two of us. Never. Probably he was sick. Cancer, or something else just as bad, but what was worse than cancer? I didn't want to think about it or worry about it until I had to and if I didn't say it out loud then it wouldn't be true. He'd be just fine, and the reason he'd invited me to lunch would be that he missed his daughter. It's perfectly natural to miss your daughter. Especially when she lives so far away and you only see her once every few months. That's when you miss her.

"I think he misses his daughter. Isn't it perfectly natural that he'd miss his daughter when she lives so far away? And when he only sees her once every few months?"

"Yep. Perfectly natural."

I gave him another kiss—lighter, on the lips this time—and said, "I'd better go."

He nodded and kissed me back. He tasted awful, but it was still a good kiss. "I love you."

"Love you, too."

Dad was waiting for me inside the restaurant. He looked fine, better than fine, actually. He looked like he'd been sleeping well for a change. Our waitress—a pretty woman who looked to be in her late forties—must have picked up on the father-daughter vibe, because she flirted brazenly with him while she handed us our menus and rattled off the specials. He was too distracted to even notice it.

I had never thought to wonder whether my father was attractive to other women. Hell, I'd never even wondered if my mother thought he was attractive. I studied his features while he studied his menu and decided that he was. He was very distinguished with his silver hair, had a rather worn, outdoorsy look about him and, away from my mother, actually seemed relaxed and confident. It's what Dave would look like eventually.

He set his menu down, and I looked at mine so he wouldn't know I'd been staring at him. Then he cleared his throat and dropped the bomb:

"Tess, there's no easy way to say this. Your mother and I are getting divorced."

"*Divorced?*"

I had nearly shouted the word and several lunchers stopped their conversations to look our way, probably in the hopes of witnessing a pleasant family drama. I scanned the crowd, mortified that I had put my shy father at the center of such a scene, and singled out a pucker-faced elderly woman. Her hair was a reddish mahogany color, so inexpertly dyed that it looked almost purple. It was butt-ugly and irritated me even more than her blatant curiosity. I shot her a dirty look—one that the rest of the crowd correctly interpreted as being directed at them as a whole—then turned my attention back to my father.

"I'm sorry," I whispered.

"It's not your fault. I shouldn't have broken the news to you in public." He lined up his silverware so that the bottoms were all touching and even. The redness in his face eased a little and he continued. "I've already told Dave."

It occurred to me that he would have had no problem breaking the news to my brother in a crowded restaurant. Dave probably would have blinked a couple times, nodded, then asked Dad to please pass the salt.

"Um...when? When did all this happen?"

"It's been coming for a while. But I left last week. It was my decision," he said, taking, as usual, all the blame, "so your mother is keeping the house. I'm renting an apartment in town until...well, until everything is settled."

He reached beside him, into his jacket pocket, and pulled out a small piece of white lined paper. He looked it over before sliding it across the table toward me. I stared at his new address and phone number for quite a while, long enough for the numbers and letters to blur and mingle together. Then I slipped it into my purse.

"Why the hell should she get the house? It's your home, too."

He shook his head. "It's not a home, Tess. It hasn't been for a very long time."

I nodded. Because he was right, of course. It had never been a *home.*

I wasn't sure what to do next, what to say, so I watched his fingers drumming silently on the table. The waitress returned to rescue him, asked if we were ready to order, but

I hadn't really looked at the menu. My appetite was gone anyway and all I really needed was half a dozen strong, stiff drinks. It wouldn't be particularly kind to make my dad eat his meal in front of his fasting, inebriated daughter so I opted for the soup of the day—without bothering to find out what that was—and a diet soda. Dad smiled nervously as the waitress wiggled away. It would be up to me to get the conversation going again but I couldn't do it. He surprised me by taking over.

"There is something I want you to know, Tess."

He paused to take a sip of water and I had the feeling I knew what the "something" was. Another woman. It had to be. He'd found someone normal and loving who wasn't a manipulative psycho bitch from hell. Finally. But he seemed so nervous, probably expected me to freak out. Holler out accusations, play the part of the stunned, betrayed daughter.

He didn't know I'd been praying for him to leave my mother since I was seven years old, when a girl in my class moved away to Nebraska with her mom while her dad stayed behind in Brookfield. It was the first time I'd ever heard of parents who lived apart and it opened up a whole new world of possibility for me. A world of freedom and beauty and blue skies. It was a world I escaped into each night as I drifted off to sleep, in which Dad would divorce my mother, move away to lovely, exotic Nebraska...and take me and Dave with him.

His bracing sip took longer than I expected. He finished his entire glass of water then said, "I want you to know that there was a time when I did love your mother. Very much. And that I did try to make our marriage work."

I clenched my toes inside my boots, held back the laughter that was threatening to explode. I had to take my own minute-long sip of water to do it. It was the speech he would have given seven-year-old Tess. And even she would have had a hard time keeping a straight face.

I set down my empty glass. Looked him in the eye, made him hold my gaze. "No, you didn't. You didn't love her and you didn't try to make it work. Neither of you did. So what the hell took you so long to leave?"

He gave me a weak smile. He was cornered. No escape. And so he told me about a summer of abandon, of meeting the most beautiful woman in the world. A woman who was smart and focused and ambitious. And foolish. Both of them were. It only takes once, and nine months later her ambitions for Money and Greatness were washed away by Real Life. What little feeling had once existed there at all was gone long before then and they were stuck. First with each other and then with a family that neither of them had planned on. At least he could take solace in that family. At least it was something. But not for his wife. She longed for more.

"I don't know why she chose to take it all out on you, Tess. I wish I did. But I knew if I left then it would be even worse. I couldn't do that to you. And after you and Dave moved out, after you had lives of your own…I guess I just stayed out of habit."

I knew it wasn't just habit. It was more than that. He didn't want to rock the boat. He'd always been that way. Left for work early, stayed gone all day long. Came home from work and ate supper with us. Asked Dave and me about our day. Need help with your homework? At least it was something, certainly more than we ever got from Her. Then he went off into his den. Stamps and coins and base-ball cards. All night long. Slept on the sofa bed. A good hiding place. Hide away from the wicked witch. Close the door. And she doesn't exist. When he opened it up again and peeked outside…almost thirty-eight years had gone by. He'd spent most of his life hiding behind four little walls.

I knew all about it.

"Are you leaving her for someone else?"

He seemed surprised at the question. "No. There's no one else."

"Dad, it's okay. I'm not upset, you know. I'm glad you found someone. You deserve to be happy. You really do."

"Tess, no. There's no one."

He was telling the truth. And it was the saddest thing I'd ever heard. So I said the only thing I could say:

"Oh."

And then I looked at him more closely. John David Bellows. Half of me was this man, but what we really know about each other? I flipped back through my book of Dad Memories and tried to come up with something that might mean that he knew me. Even a little. And I found it.

My fifth birthday. It was a day of rainbows, because that was the day my dad gave me my first big box of crayons. Seventy-two of them. Just the number seemed too big to believe. I remember taking a moment to imagine what Seventy-Two Crayons might actually look like. And when I opened up the box…that was when my life changed. Forever. Because I didn't realize until that moment— that really was The Moment—that there were so many colors in the world. And it was the moment I realized that sometimes you cry even when you're happy. That there is a Happiness that is so big and round and full that there aren't any real words to put to the feeling. Instead there are tears. I looked into that box of crayons with eyes that were full of happy tears and they swirled together through the mist. All of those colors—Periwinkle and Mulberry and Copper, and especially the eight neon colors that had Ultra in their names. They glowed at me, winked at me. Just like Christmas lights.

Beauty and Light. That's what Daddy had given me.
I'd wanted to thank him, but there were no words inside of me. None. And after the happy tears have faded what else is there to do to let your daddy know what a wonderful, precious thing he has given to you? And I had known, even then, that his vocabulary was just as small as mine. So I'd looked up at him and nodded my appreciation. And he nodded right back.

But right now, almost thirty years later, I knew he needed more than just a nod. I reached across the table, squeezed his hand, and said, "Dad...I just want you to be happy. I know it's been a long time since you've had that and God knows you've earned it. Just—please be happy."

His eyes moistened slightly, but he blinked the tears before they could escape. Then he squeezed my hand right back.

After we ate I watched him drive away, then sat in my car for a long time, so long that my teeth started chattering. Even though it was only the last weekend in October and not really all that cold. I started the engine, turned the heater up on high, and just sat there. Still. Waiting. Summoning up every ounce, every drop of courage in my body. Then I dug out my phone from my purse. Adjusted the rearview mirror so I could see my own face, just to keep myself steady. And dialed my mother's number.

She seemed brisk and bright. She even said that she was thrilled about my father moving out and I believed her. She continued on about it for several minutes before she confirmed what I'd suspected when Dad told me he was letting her keep the house.

She'd already sold it.

"Really?" My heart raced, pounded so hard and so fast so suddenly that I was afraid I was going to pass out. "Sold it?"

"That's right."

I squeezed my eyes shut. Swallowed. Took a deep breath. Opened them up again. "That was quick. It's only been a few days. Does your realtor walk on water, too? Turn water into wine?"

There was a long pause. "I sold it myself."

Of course she did. "Mike bought it. Right?"

"Well?" she snapped. "What if he did?"

"How much?" Another long pause. "How *much* did he give you for it?"

She told me. I looked again at my reflection. Frightened. Pale. I glared at myself.

Suck it up, Tess, you weak, stupid shit. Just fucking suck it up.

And it worked. I was still pale, but cold and unforgiving. Just like my mother, which was just what I needed to be.

"So, Mrs. Rockefeller, what are you going to do with that much money?"

"I'm moving away."

I raised my eyes heavenward, thanking God for his many miracles and wonders before asking, "Where to?" I knew Nebraska probably wasn't on her itinerary.

"Europe." I could actually feel the word dripping from her mouth.

"Your dream's coming true, then?"

"I think I've waited long enough. Don't you?"

"Haven't we all." I'd had it with the bullshit and cut to the chase. "You're giving Daddy half of that money."

She actually snickered. "I'll give him half of what the house is actually worth. That's fair enough."

"I don't think we have time to go into what is fair about any of this. But you're giving him half of what Mike gave you. Or else I'm going to tell Dad exactly how *much* Mike gave you. And then I'm going to tell him why."

The mirror told me I wasn't bluffing and I believed it.

"That's not going to happen, young lady."

"Don't bet on it. Because…" I actually caught myself smiling. "You know, I realized something recently. I don't give a shit who knows. Not anymore. The only person in the world who would get hurt at this point is you." I gave a mirthless chuckle. "Mike's retired from business, retired from politics—if you can call being selectman in a hick town 'politics'—he's got more money than God, and his wife is dead. So the only thing he's got to lose anymore is his precious reputation. And in this day and age it's really not going to be a big shocker. Especially not after all this time. I'm surprised you actually got him to cough up the money for the house."

"Well…what about you? Everyone will know—"

"They all hate me anyway, so what's one more strike? But *you* on the other hand—"

"You won't tell your father. You won't tell anyone. I know you."

"You don't know a fucking thing about me."

"Theresa—"

Her tone was almost, but not quite, pleading. It was the first time I'd ever heard that. I liked the way it sounded.

"—don't be ridiculous. You know your father. He won't take any money at all from the house, not even the actual value, let alone—"

"That's because he thinks you've been fucking Mike all these years. Didn't you know that? He thinks you've been whoring yourself out to him all this time and he thinks that's how you got all those...raises you're so fucking proud of. He thinks it's how you paid for Dave's college tuition. Isn't that funny?"

Funny. Wasn't it funny? Jesus, God, Mary, and Joseph. It was just the funniest thing ever. Funny, funny, so fucking funny.

"I'm calling him in a few days, so you'd better fork over the money. Tell him whatever you need to so he'll take it. You're pretty good at that. Just...make him take it. Because he's *earned* it. He's put up with you all these years, hasn't he? And he's worked his fucking ass off at a job he hates even more than he hates you. Hell, probably more than you hate me. You really think he *likes* doing other people's taxes? Are you a fucking idiot? Or do you not even care?"

There was nothing but dead space in my ear, dead space and the sound of her workout video cheering her on in the background.

Keep it up! That's right, kick it higher! You can do it!

You're goddamn right I can.

Finally she said, "And just how much money are you hoping for?"

"I don't want a fucking penny of it. *Mom.*"

I could almost hear her nerves snap. "You don't have the right to call me that, Theresa. Not after this. Not—"

I didn't even blink. "And you never had the right to hear it from me, you cold, ugly, money-hungry bitch."

I hung up without waiting for a response and tossed my phone onto the seat. I sat without shaking. Still staring at my reflection. Waiting. Waiting for my face to relax. To change back. Waiting to look like me again. Even if I had looked like a frightened girl before I picked up the phone. It would be better than the cold, determined, unfeeling, ruthless woman staring back at me now. I glanced away for a moment, watched the purple-haired lady walk out of the restaurant. She was wearing a tacky faux-fur coat. She sauntered into the parking lot, got into a black Lincoln Towncar, and pulled regally away. I looked at my reflection once again.

I still wasn't there.

I felt the tears burning, pulling, stinging. Not just my eyes but my brain, my ears, my throat, felt a sharp, hollow knot in my gut and my heart. But I knew.

There are some things you just can't cry about. Some things you just can't let out.

Two years too late.

At all.

You're just not worth it...

Because once you do it's like an eruption. Once it starts it doesn't stop, won't stop, not ever. I held it back, held it in, pulled it back down deep, deeper than I'd ever had to. Shoved it away into another crater, and it stayed put, once again. And it was so far inside and packed so tightly that I knew I'd packed away the last bit of anger, of fear, of shame...of anything my body would carry. And the tears went away, somewhere, to the place they always fled to. Hidden inside some secret pocket, and it was deeper still. So deep I knew they'd never find their way out.

But no pit is truly bottomless and I knew I was only safe for a little while. It would find a different means of escape. There would be an eruption, the kind I could deal with, and so I started my car quickly and left the restaurant behind. Because it was only thoughtful to have the kind of breakdown I was due for in private. Away from paying customers and their children, far away from hardworking waitresses and waiters who were struggling to live off their tips.

There was a convenience store across the street and so I pulled in there. Turned off the car. Took several deep, deep, deep cleansing breaths, just like Kim had taught me. It bought me enough time to walk into the store with a smile, nod to the clerk—a young guy who only looked seventeen or so but was probably older—and make my way calmly into the bathroom. I locked the door and waited. Waited. Avoided looking at my reflection, avoided looking into the toilet, wondered when it had been cleaned last. The bathroom stank, which gave me the answer, but I didn't have much of a choice.

I pulled down viciously on the dispenser, grabbed two thick wads of brown paper towel, wrapped them around my hands. Closed my eyes. Kneeled carefully over the toilet, and vomited quietly. Vomited forever.

I stood up as soon as it was safe, without opening my eyes, shut the lid, and flushed. I didn't want to see my former lunch or the condition of the bowl that had just been so close to my face. I chucked the towels, scrubbed my hands and my face, swished a couple handfuls of gross city water around my mouth, and spit. Waited again. Waited to make sure it was all over.

Fluffed out my hair. Smoothed it back down.

Powder compact. Mascara. Pink lipstick. Just so.

Then I walked back out into the store. Bought a bottle of water and a pack of mint gum for myself and a bag of mini chocolate candy bars for Brian. Waved a friendly goodbye to the clerk and drove back home. Just like nothing had happened. Because nothing really had.

CHAPTER 24

It was the Tuesday before Thanksgiving, the end of November. The worst time of year. When the calendar says it's still autumn, but there are no colorful leaves to make summer's passing bearable. When the sun and wind are bitter and cold, but there isn't any snow to show for it. When all of the trees are naked and ugly and gray.

But inside my apartment I tried to make it feel just like summer. It was easy to do, at least for a little while, because Cassidy had the week off from school, and that meant that I had her for a full day. We played Rummy and watched cartoons and ate pasta salad for lunch, just like we'd done back in July and August, when the sun and wind were golden and hot. But after she helped me with the dishes we dug out the crayons and spent the rest of the afternoon making placemats for Thursday's big meal at her house. Turkeys and Pilgrims and harvest vegetables. And that was a stark reminder that summer had long since passed.

After Laura picked her up I headed off to work. I passed by the lake on my way into town. It was cold and barren, too. I tried to picture how it had looked a month earlier, surrounded by full, gorgeous maples and lovely, delicate birches, when the leaves were vibrant and alive with yellow and orange and red. I couldn't do it, though, couldn't remember it. And I wasn't sure if I'd seen it and forgotten, or if I'd spent October in such a fog that I'd just driven by it every day for a whole month…and never noticed it at all.

I was nearly done with my last job when my cell phone rang. It was Zeke. And that, of course, could only mean one thing. Rachel.

"Cookie crumbs?"

"Not exactly. But…can you head over here when you're done with work?"

He didn't have to ask twice. When I got to the diner he led me through the kitchen—past staring employees, including a smiling and oblivious Donny—and into the employee break room. Rachel was sitting at a table by herself, staring at the floor. She didn't even look up as we came in.

"I'm through talking to you so now you're going to listen to Tess."

She glared up at him. "I told you I didn't want you to call her."

"And I told you I don't give a shit. You're lucky I didn't try getting ahold of Brian. Now, are you going to show her or am I going to lift your shirt up myself?"

She glared at Zeke, then at me. I glared right back at her. Because she'd promised. No needles. Not *that*. She had *promised*…

She stood up, kicked her chair behind her as she did, then yanked up her shirt. Not her sleeves, though, not needle marks; it was her back. She turned around and then, more gingerly, slid her pants down a few inches, revealing a huge, ugly purple bruise. It covered part of her lower back, her hip, and at least halfway down her ass.

"Tim hit her," Zeke said, "and she fell onto the coffee table. She won't call the cops. The only reason I even know about it is because I noticed she was moving a little slow tonight, so I followed her in here and caught her checking it out in the mirror."

"Oh my…God."

It was my fault. Because I'd left her there. I knew he'd hit her, should have known he'd do it again. And I'd left her there anyway.

I did that to her…

She covered herself back up. Still wouldn't look either of us in the eye.

"When I was there with you that day…that wasn't the first time he hit you. Was it?"

Zeke pointed at her. "Rachel, you just said he hadn't done anything like this before."

She still said nothing, only stared down at her shoes.

I rubbed my head. I had to figure out what to do. But I couldn't think. I kept seeing her face the way it had been that day. Bruised cheek. Hopeless eyes.

Abandoned.

I took a deep breath, looked over at Zeke. "Can you give Brian a call and have him come down here?"

I didn't want to. He had enough to worry about and sure as hell didn't need this. But I'd failed her. Left her alone. And I'd held too much back from him as it was.

Rachel sprung at me and grabbed my arm. "No!"

I ignored her. "He's home by now. Just…give him a call."

Zeke nodded and started for the door. Rachel let go of me and ran over to him. "Wait, Zeke, don't go." He wriggled out of her grasp and she grabbed his shirt. "God damn it, Zeke, just...please wait! Don't call him yet."

She'd said the magic word—yet—and he came back into the room. "Well?"

She turned to me. Pleading. "You *promised* you wouldn't say anything to Brian."

"Yeah. I did."

Just like an idiot. You left her there, Tess. You left her all alone.

"But only *if* you stayed away from Tim."

"I wasn't...this...he wasn't at my place so I could score or to..." She glanced at Zeke. Embarrassed. "I needed some money and I thought he'd give it to me."

"Money? What the hell for?"

"I...for an abortion."

I blinked. Did it again. Because she'd said some words, but they didn't make any sense. I looked over at Zeke. He didn't seem surprised. I rolled the word around in my brain. Because I hadn't heard wrong. She really had said it. She had skipped right over the *guess what, I'm pregnant* and went right to...

"Abortion."

"Yes."

I saw her every week, at least once a week. Usually more than that. She hadn't said anything and I hadn't noticed anything. I glanced at her stomach. Big shirt. Loose pants. She was far enough along that she had a belly to hide. How could I not know?

"I thought you were...the pill. Aren't you on the pill?"

She gave Zeke another sideways glance, then she charged right ahead. "Remember that day, Tess? When we went to the movies? And I was…with him that morning?"

I nodded. Hit the rewind button. Tim left. I cleaned up the apartment while she was in the shower. Kitchen. Living room. Coffee table.

Pharmacy bag.

"Antibiotics…"

…make birth control pills ineffective.

She nodded. Red-faced. Miserable.

"Oh, shit, Rachel, didn't you *know*?"

It was a stupid, hypocritical question, because I knew better, too. I'd seen them, and hadn't thought to say anything to her. With everything else going on that day I just never thought about it.

Okay then. Step two.

"You…you're *sure* you want an abortion?"

"Yes."

"Tim's not putting you up to this is he? Is that what the bruise is about?"

"No, Tess. It's my decision. I made an appointment already. It's in Portland on Friday."

"Friday."

She nodded. Of course. Friday. The day after Thanksgiving. And why not? It was just as good a day as any other. God really did have a sense of humor.

Step three. I did the backwards math. Counted back to Labor Day. Eleven weeks…

"Jesus, Rach. You're cutting it pretty close."

"I know, Tess. I just…" She kicked her chair again and took a deep breath. "MaineCare won't pay for it unless it's rape or if I've got something wrong with me, so I have to come up with the money myself, but it's almost five *hundred* bucks and I don't have that kind of fucking money, so I figured I'd see if Tim would give me the rest, because he's got it coming outta his ass, and if I have to wait another week I'll have to go all the way to fucking Boston, and it costs even more and…"

I'd never, since I'd known her, heard her say so many words in a row, let alone so quickly. She had to stop to take another breath. And when she let it out it was shaky. Just like her hands.

"So, I called him this morning, but I didn't tell him why till he got to my place. He probably thought I wanted—"

"Yeah. I know what he probably thought, Rach." But I didn't, exactly.

Gonna wean myself off of it…

Couldn't be *that*. How hard could that be?

"Well, when I told him what it was about…he fucking flipped. He pushed me into the coffee table and…anyway, he said he wasn't gonna let me kill his baby, even if he had to…"

But she couldn't say it. And it was just as well, really, because I didn't want to hear it. Didn't want to know what he'd threatened her with. What I'd let happen to her by leaving her there. Alone. And she was so lost, looking at me—looking to me—like I had something to offer her. Like I knew what to do. Like I could just magically make everything all right. So I said it:

"Don't worry, Rach. It's all right."

How the fuck is it all right, you idiot?

"I mean, it's gonna be all right."

343

Even though, of course, I had no way of knowing whether it was going to be all right or not. I didn't have the vaguest idea of what to do. I glanced at my watch. Brian was waiting for me, right now. Probably worried, wondering where I was. How the hell was I going to tell him? He had too much on his shoulders already, too much burden. All of it was stamped in bold, block letters: **RACHEL**. And here was one more thing. More than one. And I didn't know if he could take it.

I sighed. It was time to sort it out. Because there were some things I could keep from him, protect him from. And some things I couldn't. It was time to separate those things.

Drugs.

"Are you using anything? Right now?"

"No."

"*Nothing?*"

"Nothing."

I gave her a careful up and down. Her arms were folded but she wasn't fidgeting. Her eyes were tired—exhausted, actually—but they weren't bloodshot. And other than that…I wasn't an expert. I didn't know what the hell to look for. I only knew that I didn't believe her. But I knew if we got Tim out of the picture then the rest would be easy.

"We've gotta call the cops, Rachel. We need to make him go away."

"No cops." She was adamant.

"Rachel—"

"You call the cops and I'm fucking dead. You know what he's into, Tess."

Yeah I do. So did you. And I tried to tell you. I tried to warn you, God damn it, Rachel, why the hell didn't you listen to me?

"It won't do any good anyway, you know. His ex-wife's got a restraining order against him and he still bugs her all the time."

Zeke nodded. "It's true, Tess. You know how it is."

I did. The closest State Police barracks was in Westville, a half-hour drive on a good day. And they were up to their asses in drug enforcement and domestic violence there. They had little time to worry about what was going on in the boonies.

I cleared my throat.

"Brian can take care of him, then. I'll—"

She shook her head. "No. Tess, you can't. Brian won't just kick his ass this time. He'll kill him. You *know* that."

"Well...yeah. Then we won't have to worry about him anymore, will we? The whole fucking planet will be a bright and beautiful place."

"Sure. That's a perfect idea. He's such a fucking idiot when he's pissed off that he'll go off on Tim without even thinking to cover his tracks and he'll get caught. Hell, he'll probably drag Jeff into it again. You want them spend the rest of their stupid, fucking lives in jail? You want Cassidy to—"

"All right, all right. Just...shut up for a second. Let me figure this out. You said you've got an appointment?"

Rachel nodded. "Friday."

Friday.

"But I don't have the money."

"Just...don't worry about the money."

Zeke touched my sleeve. "Tess, I can help out if—"

I shook my head. "Thanks. But I've got it."

I did, in my savings. It was for the winter, for rent and heat and food. Because I'd saved up just like a squirrel. But I'd have to worry about that later.

Rachel sat back down. "Tess, I can pay you back."

"I said don't worry about it." Because there was something more important to worry about. A Something I didn't want to think about.

Two years too late...

But it was there anyway.

I looked at Rachel. She was scared. Sad. Alone. And that was more important than anything else. More important than any*one* else. Even a tiny, helpless Anyone. So I made the offer. "Do you want me to take you?"

She gave me a weak, relieved smile. "Could you?"

I nodded, already rearranging my schedule. I could do my office jobs early in the morning. Busy Friday wasn't as busy as it was during the summer because most of my house jobs had moved away for the winter. Except for Zeke.

He said, just like he'd read my mind, "Don't worry about it, Tess. Just get to my place whenever you can."

I nodded and moved onto the next thing. Then I shook my head. Because what was next was Brian. It all came back to Brian. What to tell him. What to keep from him.

"Zeke, can you give us a minute?"

He looked at his watch. "Yeah. I gotta get back out there anyway."

I waited until he was gone before I said, "So. You don't want to tell Brian...anything?"

She shook her head. "I can't."

I stuffed my hands in my coat pocket and shivered. Because she was right. He wouldn't just freak out.

He wouldn't just knock the asshole around a little and then call it a day. He'd go crazy. He would go out and find Tim. And he would kill him. It wouldn't be any great loss to have that bastard out of the way, but it would mean that Brian's life would be over. And Tim sure as hell wasn't worth that.

"I'll cover for you, Rach. On one condition."

She groaned.

"You know what? I don't think you're in the position to give me any shit. The condition is that you have to stay with us."

"Oh, fuck that."

"Fuck *you*, Rach. There's no way I'm letting you live by yourself right now. That would be like painting a big fat target on your ass. And I'll tell you something else, even though you already know it. Brian already worries enough about you right now. If anything happened to you, for real…what do you think *that* would do to him?"

She rolled her eyes.

"Well, you're staying with us, and that's all there is to it. At least for a little while. You can stay upstairs in my apartment."

I said it like it was a done deal. Like Brian wouldn't have any problem with me moving in with him. Because I knew that he wouldn't. If it was up to him we would have done it months ago. And he was right, of course. We'd been living together, really, since the first time I'd slept in his bed.

"This isn't negotiable. You either stay upstairs or I tell Brian everything. Period. You *have* to be safe. And I don't think Tim will try anything while you're living with us."

She sighed. She was cornered and she knew it. "I know he won't. He's afraid of Brian."

"He should be." I walked over to the mirror that had caused all the commotion, surveyed my own reflection, and rubbed under my eyes. "Jesus Christ. I look like a fucking raccoon."

She rolled her eyes again. "Who gives a shit? What are we gonna tell Brian?"

And there it was: Lies. Not the *yes, I'm fine* lie when I really wasn't fine. Not the kind where I told him only half of the truth about something, or just didn't bother with telling him the something at all. Those were bad enough. These would be the kind where I'd look him right in the eye and form words with my mouth and lips and tongue and teeth that weren't true. And say them out loud to him.

He'd want to know why she was so hot to move in, when she'd always refused his help in the past. He'd wonder about drugs. And he'd probably even ask outright if Tim had ever hurt her. It's what he'd been afraid of all along. He'd ask her, and she'd lie, and then he'd ask me, just to make sure. And then I'd have to lie.

Tess, are you sure he never laid a hand on her?

No, Brian. He never touched her.

I looked at my reflection. Not just the smudged makeup, but Me. And I didn't like it.

I sighed. "Are you trying to straighten out your life here, Rach?"

"Well...yeah. I guess."

"Getting rid of all the shit in it. You're gonna just say no to drugs and all that?"

She shrugged. Still confused.

"How about that idea I had that day? About you saving for school? Have you actually given that any thought?"

348

"I can't afford that."

I cleared my throat. Started concocting the lie that I hoped would turn out to be true. "What if...you woke up this morning and decided you wanted to make a change. What if you decided that you were sick of living the way that you have been and you came to me asking for help, because you were too proud to ask your brother. Because you were afraid of getting another lecture from him. And what if I offered to let you stay at my apartment. And I offered to still pay the rent, like I've been doing, and maybe even the heat and lights. And that way all you'd have to worry about is the phone and your food and that sort of thing. Then you could save up all winter and spring and summer and start school next fall. I think it would be a relief to Brian if he thought you were trying to make something of yourself. Don't you?"

This was it. Her moment. It could either be a bullshit story to appease her big brother or it could be something more. Something real. Change.

She smiled. "Actually, I did read up about nursing."

"Really?"

"Yeah, 'cause..." She shook her head and considered something. Then plunged in. "I remember being at the hospital with Brian the day my mother died. They let him in to see her, but he wouldn't let me go in. Probably because she was so sick and she looked like shit by then. She smelled real bad, too. But one of the nurses stayed with me in the waiting room all day long. We watched cartoons and colored and she read Little Golden Books to me. I'll never forget that, because it helped a little. Even though it was the worst day of my whole life, that nurse staying with me made it a little bit better. And…maybe I could do something like that."

I wanted to believe her, so badly. And I almost did. "If I paid the rent for you, you'd really save the money for that? For school?"

She smiled again and it made me believe her. But then the smile faded, because there were lots of little steps to take before she got anywhere near that goal. So we talked it over, made the plans. Outlined the steps. Then she went back to work while I went into the bar to convince Zeke. He promised to keep his mouth shut if Rachel really did make some changes. Because he was tired of watching her fuck up her life. And he was tired of seeing Brian have to watch it, too.

"Zeke, I think she's serious this time."

He nodded. But he didn't look too optimistic.

"No, really. I think she'll be okay. If we just keep an eye on her, if both of us do, then she'll be just fine. It'll just take her a little while to get her head screwed on straight, but…you'll see. She'll be safe with me and Brian, and she'll be away from Tim and…after Friday she'll be fine. Really."

And I believed it. I really did.

A few hours later Brian was sitting beside me on his couch, holding my hand. My heart was racing faster than it ever had. Even though this was the right thing to do. Even though it wasn't lying. I was just protecting him. Even while I protected Rachel. She was standing in front us. Performing. Convincingly sheepish.

Tired of wasting my life, Brian. I need to make something of myself. You didn't give up half your life just to watch me flush mine down the toilet.

She'd struck the right chord. He nodded emphatically and waited for the rest. So she took a deep breath and told him the plan.

He looked at me, surprised. "Really?"

"Well...if it's okay with you."

Of course it was, except for the money. He didn't want me paying the rent on an apartment I wasn't living in, and that was that. There were plenty of people who worked and paid rent and still managed to pay for school, and *there's no reason why Rachel can't do that, too.* So I told him about Dave and Kim, how they'd taken me in when I was down and out. I couldn't pay them back; there was just no way. But I could help Rachel and it would be almost the same thing.

"Fine, Tess. If that's what you want to do."

But there was a question in his eyes, the one I'd known would be there. He wouldn't ask it in front of Rachel, though. Instead he looked back at her, folded his arms, and said:

"So. Just how far along *are* you?"

She wasn't prepared for that. She stuttered a bit, then denied it.

"I'm not an idiot. Excuse me for noticing it, but you've got a bit of a belly there. And..."

Rachel and I followed his embarrassed gaze. Boobs. I hadn't noticed in her work shirt. So she gave it up and told him about our Friday plans.

"Um...I don't think Tess is up to taking you, Rach."

"Why wouldn't she be up to that?"

I intervened. "I'm okay with it, Brian. We're all set."

He said nothing, only stared. I stared right back and saw it there. He knew.

Two years too late…

Goddamn that brother of mine and their fucking fishing trip. How much beer had it taken for Brian to get that out of him? Still I persisted. "I'm taking her."

He let it go, but I knew the subject wasn't really closed. And he moved onto his next objection.

"I'm paying for it, Tess, not you. I've got the money and….it's *my* job to take care of her, not yours."

I nodded and tried not to show my relief. It would have been a very long winter.

And so it was settled. Brian stood up and looked at his sister, stared closely at her face. Something else was wrong and he knew it. It was in his eyes. Those eyes that never let him hide what he was feeling. They absorbed every emotion inside of him, just like a sponge, and held them there— right there—on display for the world to see. He was hurting because she was. She'd learned a lesson he'd wanted to shield her from, lots of them, really. Some that he knew about and others that he didn't, but suspected. He still wanted to protect her, to keep her safe, to keep her away from the Big Bad World just as long as he could. Keep her far away from any more Learning the Hard Way. For once she was letting him and that made him suspicious. Because it wasn't like her to give in. He didn't say anything, though. He only stared at her, pleading with her silently. The unspoken question hovered in the air, hovered for a long time.

What aren't you telling me?

Her confidence faltered slightly under his gaze, but she quickly recovered and, for the first time in his life, the first time in hers, he didn't push her. He just sighed, and headed for the shower.

So it was time for me to put *my* foot down. Because it wasn't just his eyes that had told me everything he'd been feeling. It was experience, however slight. I'd only had a small piece of the burden, a tiny bit of **RACHEL**, and only for a couple of months. But I was already buckling underneath the weight, underneath the fear and helplessness and suspicion. He'd had to carry all of that, for so long, and he needed some help. So I began the work of easing him of that load.

"You're staying *here* tonight. Upstairs. Got it?"

She nodded.

"Do you need to borrow some pajamas? Or anything like that?"

"Nope. I packed a suitcase."

"Good. And no bullshit. Not while you're home, and not while you're out. Not while you're living here. Because if I get even a whiff of any, then—I swear to God—I'm telling him everything."

"Yes, Mommy."

"Goddamn it, Rachel, I'm serious."

"I'm sorry, Tess. I promise I won't fuck this up."

"You'd better not."

And she headed up the fourteen stairs. To the apartment that wasn't really mine anymore.

I waited for Brian in the bedroom. Sat on the bed, cross-legged, trying to ignore the guilt that gnawed me from all the lies I'd told him, the lies I'd let Rachel tell him. I didn't have the energy to deal with the guilt right now. It had been a long fucking day, a day of too much planning and trying to think ahead. Of trying to shield and help and protect. And I knew my day wasn't over.

It didn't take him long in the shower. He sat down beside me and got right to the point.

"You're not going with her on Friday."

"It doesn't bother me, Brian. Really."

"Yes, it does."

I shrugged. "Well. I'm going. She can't go alone. She won't go with you. And who else is there?" No one. Just her druggie friends and a psychotic drug dealer who'd kill her if he knew what she was doing. And what was I going to do about Tim, anyway?

"Tess…"

"I'm going. And that's that. So let's just not talk about it anymore."

Because Friday would get here soon enough and then there'd be more guilt, a different kind. But I'd have to deal with it then. Because right now there was something more important to worry about. I brought it up first, before he could.

"I was ready for this. Moving down here with you, I mean. Even before she—"

"I know you were, Tess."

But he didn't know. I thought about the bleach box that had been filled with pictures, thought about the three piles. Things that you keep and things you discard and things that you give away. About saying goodbye and moving on. But I didn't know if he'd understand. And I was too tired to explain it to him.

I stood up to change into my nightshirt. Once I was naked he gave me an apologetic smile and said, "I'm not up to doing anything tonight, Tess. I'm just too tired."

"Well…yeah. I know."

"I'm just...I'm real tired. Maybe in the morning or—"

"I *know*. It's okay."

We crawled into bed, but didn't sleep. He tossed and flailed all over the bed, his body contorting wildly underneath the blankets. He tangled up the sheets and finally pulled them right off of me and onto the floor.

I sat up and snapped the nightstand lamp on. "Brian, what the hell is the matter with you?"

"I've got a itch on my back and I can't reach it."

"I'll get it." I reached underneath his shirt and found the itch.

"Okay, good. But left now. A little more. No, up...up... oh, you got it. Now, back to the center..."

I sighed. "Take off your shirt and I'll get the whole thing."

I didn't have to ask twice. I scooted him over to the middle of the bed and sat on his ass; straddled it. It felt like the sexiest thing I'd ever done to him and I just sat like that for a long moment, enjoying the way he felt underneath me. It made him smile. Then I began.

I scratched his back all over, lightly at first, then a little harder, and he groaned his appreciation. Murmured something about sheetrock dust and how he always felt like he was covered in it. Even when he wasn't. I didn't stop scratching until his shoulders relaxed. And even when they did they still looked tight. Tense.

They were always tight. Always tense.

I leaned over and grabbed a bottle from the nightstand. It was lotion, but not the kind we sometimes used in this room. Not one of those oils that have a hot, sexy name and an arousing fragrance. It was just plain lotion in a plain green bottle. Just plain aloe. I rubbed some together in my hands to warm it up and looked down at his naked back. It was the first time I'd ever really looked at it like this. I was usually too interested in the other side. His chest. In hair that was Van Dyke Brown.

But his back was beautiful. It really was.

His shoulders were broad and strong, tender and powerful all at once. I put a hand on each of them. Leaned down, kissed him gently between his shoulder blades. It was my favorite spot to touch when he was lying on top of me, inside me; the softest spot on his whole body. I kissed it again, gently, without any passion. Because I knew what he'd meant by *I'm too tired tonight*; knew why he'd said it. And I needed him to know:

That's not all you are to me.

He didn't say a word, didn't make a sound. Just lay there, breathing silently. I sat up again, caressed him lightly, barely touching him. Just enough to let the lotion soak into his shoulders and neck and back. I loved his skin, all of it. Loved the way it was tan, all over, and not from the sun. The way it was always so warm, always, even on a cold night like tonight. Loved the way it smelled, the way he smelled. All of him. Not just his soap or his cologne, although I loved that smell, too. But him.

I looked at his profile against the stark, white pillowcase. His eyes were closed but he wasn't really at rest. His jaw was still tense, his whole face drawn and worried. And a single tear slid slowly down his cheek.

There were no words I could think of to say to him, nothing that might even begin to get rid of the ache in his heart. So instead I rubbed his aching body. Slowly.

Massaging, kneading, gently with probing fingers, then harder with the heels of my hands. He opened his eyes, just barely, and gave a feeble, muffled protest.

"Tess, cut it out. You need to get some sleep, too."

"Shhhh...don't worry about me." It was a stupid thing to say, because he always worried about me. Almost as much as he worried about Rachel.

My first job on Friday morning would be Dr. Stephens's office. If I waited long enough, waited until he walked in the door at seven-thirty, I could ask him how many muscles were in the human body. He would probably laugh, but he would rattle off the exact number without even having to think about it. He could tell me each of their names, tell me all about how they were each connected to tendons and bone, how they were all connected to each other. But it wouldn't matter, because I already knew the names of each tight spot on Brian's shoulders and back and neck, each hard knot. And I knew exactly what each one was really connected to.

Like the tightness in the muscles right below his neck. Tight and hard from holding it in for so long, holding it back. Holding onto it forever. Sometimes he sat hunched over at night, his shoulders bowed down, like it was finally just too much. Like his soul was finally, completely crushed by all the pain and fear and rage from his father leaving him and Rachel and his mom. Because Rick had left them, in all the ways that were important, long before Wendy passed away.

And the spot between his shoulder blades, the spot I loved...that was a tender spot. A hollow sort of ache. Sad. Empty. He missed his mom. He missed hearing her voice and laughter and music. Her beauty and encouragement. She'd been stern, too, and he missed that, missed her guidance. Her love. Even now that he was a man he still missed all of that, wanted her there so she could see him. As a man. Wanted to know that she was proud of him, to hear her say that he'd done a good job. He wanted her to see him happy and in love.

Some of the tenderness and tightness was me, I knew. Small pains, here and there. Twinges, mostly, but sometimes they flared up for real, sometimes so badly that I could almost hear it. Why won't she open up, why won't she tell me anything? *Tell me something real, Tess. Something real.* I know she loves me, she says it, so I have to believe it. I have to believe her. *You loved him enough to promise that you'd spend forever with him.* It's real, everything love is supposed to be. I know it. Because she says it. And it is…right?

I know, Brian. I know and I'm sorry. It is real, I swear. And I'm trying to believe in forever again. I really am…

And, of course, Rachel.

Rachel was everywhere, in every knot. Every single one. I wouldn't be able to rub away that burden, that ache, that tightness, not if I let him lie here underneath me forever. Because she was all alone and hungry and scared while I was out having fun and screwing around. Even after I promised to take care of her, I still let her down. But now I'm here and she needs me to protect her but she won't let me. She won't listen. She won't do her homework, won't buckle down, and that means she's gonna be stuck in a dead-end job. Stuck and she doesn't get it. And now she's fifteen, she's only fifteen, and I think she's having sex. She's too young, that's too young, and I can't make her stop it. How can I get her to stop? And now she wants to leave, and I can't stop that either because she's old enough, at least the law says she can leave and there's nothing I can do about it, but she's not ready. Not really, because can she afford her own place? Will she pay her bills? Get enough to eat? How can she be safe on her own if I'm not there? And now there are guys, lots of them, too many, and she doesn't even bother to hide it. And drugs, I know it. I can see that in her eyes, she's been trying it all. Shit, I didn't do it right. I messed it all up, screwed it all up, did it all wrong because she's looking for a daddy. She's looking for anything, she's doing everything, doing everyone, just trying to fill up that hole in her heart, that lonely, awful ache. And now there's Tim and it's even worse, worse than I ever imagined because he's not like the rest of them, not just there for fun. And now she's back, she's safe, but she's not. She's not safe because she'll never be safe. She's hurting, hurting, and I can't stop it. She needs me to protect her again. Still. Always.

Forever.

His breathing slowed. Light and steady. Drifting. Until, finally, he was asleep. But still I didn't stop.

My own tears came, light and steady and silent, and I let them drip onto his back. Rubbed them into what little lotion remained, and they made it slick again. I worked at it, worked on him, until I couldn't do it anymore, until my arms and hands and fingers were too stiff and sore. Until my tears stopped.

And still. His shoulders and back and neck were tight. Tense. Hard. Even in his sleep.

CHAPTER 25

Thanksgiving Day. And there was lots to give thanks for.

My mother was gone. *Europe.* It was a big continent and I wasn't sure exactly where she had landed, and I didn't care. Because it didn't matter. What mattered was that there was an entire ocean between us at last. And what mattered even more was that she'd probably never cross it again. Sometimes I said those words out loud, just so I could hear them. *Never. Cross it. Again.* And every time I did they tasted just like honey.

Dave and Kim had taken my dad to her family's house for the holiday weekend, and I was thankful for that, too. It's not that I didn't want to be with my dad; in fact I actually missed him. But space was a good thing, too, at least until everything settled down. Until lawyers had spoken and papers were signed and a judge's gavel ended things once and for all.

And most of all: I was thankful that Rachel was safe.

She came with us to the Burkes' for the holiday meal. We all ate ourselves sick then watched football. Two teams we didn't care about, but there's no messing with

Thanksgiving Tradition. Then we ate some more. Cassidy ate so much that her stomach hurt, so Laura gave her some Pepto Bismol and made her lie down in the living room with a movie while we played Penny Poker in the dining room. Just like the Pilgrims did.

Rachel was in a bubbly mood, which seemed odd to me considering what tomorrow was going to bring. But everyone has their own ways of dealing with life and stress and it was better than being stuck with bitchy, mopey Rachel. She rambled on and on about everything and nothing, to the point where even Brian had a hard time getting a word in. Finally she stumbled across a subject that was of interest to all of us.

"Hey, did you hear Zeke's got a boyfriend?"

I studied my cards very carefully. As usual they sucked. Almost as much as my poker face. Rachel laughed.

"Oh. So *you* know, Tess."

I shrugged. "Not really."

And I didn't. Not really. I only knew that there were finally more than seven cups and spoons and bowls in the sink every Friday. An extra toothbrush and razor. And the mess at his house wasn't a lonely mess anymore.

Jeff said, "It's about time."

I threw in my hand. "What's he like?"

"He's blonde and buff and...he's fucking *hot* is what he is. His name is Dean...something. Zeke doesn't talk a whole lot about him, but I think it must be going pretty good."

"What makes you think that?" Brian asked.

"Well, he hasn't been cranky in a while so I figure he's getting laid pretty regular."

That got big laughs all around. Except from Brian. Rachel noticed.

"Hey, *Brian*...do you have a problem with gay people getting laid?"

"Don't be stupid, Rach. Of course not."

"Because it looks to me like you have a problem with it."

"Well, I don't."

Jeff scooped in the pile of pennies, victorious yet again. "I think he's got a problem with his little sister talking so cheerfully about people getting laid." He was kind and didn't add what we were all thinking: *Especially not when she's knocked up.*

Cassidy picked that moment to wander in. She took a seat beside her mother and we all turned to her eagerly, determined to hang on her every word. She talked about winter. She couldn't wait. Snow forts and snow angels and snowmen. Then she rubbed her still-aching tummy.

"Mommy, I think God is punishing me for being a glutton."

"God doesn't do that. Your stomach is just teaching you a lesson."

She knew that, she said, because it's just what Sister Charlotte had told her. God doesn't punish us, but He lets us suffer the consequences of what we've done. But she still had to remember her gluttony because she was due for her First Communion in the spring which meant, of course, making her First Confession. She was keeping a list of all her sins so she'd be ready. Rachel muttered something about brainwashing and pagan rituals and I gave her a kick underneath the table. She kicked me back, hard, then said:

"Hey, Tess. Aren't *you* Catholic?"

I groaned silently. I knew where this was headed.

"How come *you* don't go to Confession." She gave me a big, shit-eating grin and added, "I bet you've got a big, fat list of old sins just piling up. Dontcha?"

"I'm not a practicing Catholic, Rachel. That's why I don't go."

It was Cassidy's turn. "You should go to Confession, Tess. If you do then we can take Communion together."

I tossed a handful of pennies into the pot. I had a full house, my first one ever. "I don't think so, hon. It's just not my thing."

"But—"

"Cassidy," Jeff warned. "Drop it."

She did, but she folded her arms moodily.

"Come on," I said. "Don't give me the pouty face."

She stuck her lip out even further.

Brian, safely ensconced in his atheism, nudged my elbow with his and asked, "What's the problem, Tess? Just go and tell the priest all your sins and you're good to go, right? Then you can splash holy water on your face and go eat the bread with her."

Rachel laughed. "You'd better give him the *Reader's Digest* version, or you won't be done in time to watch the kiddies march down the aisle."

Cassidy and I furrowed our brows at them.

We are not amused.

Laura called. I lay down my cards in a big, beautiful fan and gave Jeff a huge smile. It faded quickly enough. "A four of a kind? Jesus Christ! Don't you ever lose?"

"There you go," Rachel said. "Taking the Lord's name in vain."

"Dammit, Rach, would you just drop it?"

She seemed surprised by my irritation. "Shit, Tess, don't get all bitchy at me. What's the big deal, anyway?"

All five sets of eyes turned to focus on me. I tossed my useless full house over to Laura. Watched as she added it into the stack of cards. Waited until she was finished shuffling.

"Because it would be hypocritical to go now, at this stage of my life." I hoped *hypocritical* wasn't in Cassidy's vocabulary. "I'm not gonna start up with all that again. I haven't even been to church since...shit, I can't remember the last time I went to church."

Brian started: "What about..."

I waited for him to continue, but he looked away. "What about what?"

The eyes that had been staring at me turned toward him. He sighed and finished his question. "What about when you got married?"

I had the spotlight once again. "I didn't get married in the church."

"How come?"

I looked at my fingernails and flipped through the long list of reasons. I found only one that was appropriate to say in front of Cassidy. "Jason's not Catholic."

"Then...where did you get married?"

"We rented a hall."

"Oh."

And then it was back to poker. I took one look at my cards and folded. So did Brian and, for once, Jeff. I couldn't tell from his expression if he'd actually had a bad hand or if he was tired of everyone giving him a hard time about winning. Rachel's flush beat Laura's three of a kind. She scooped up her pennies while Jeff shuffled and dealt. When he was finished Cassidy said:

"Well that's something you can confess."

I glanced up to see who she was talking to. It was me. "What is?"

"If you're Catholic you're not supposed to marry someone who isn't." Laura gave her a warning look, but Cassidy persisted. "Well, you're not."

"Cassidy, I told you already. That's enough." Jeff came down hard on each syllable and sealed it with, "That's your last warning."

She looked at me again, and this time her pouty face was real.

"Cass...please don't. Okay? Look, in the spring I'll go to your First Communion and I'll be really happy, because it's a good thing you're doing. It's a big step and I'll be very proud of you. But I can't do it myself. Okay?"

She sighed deeply and said nothing.

Two more hands. I lost seventy-three cents and Jeff finally lost his patience with Cassidy's pouting. Bedtime because, *You were warned.* Laura stood to go upstairs with her.

"Wait," I said. "Can I tuck her in?"

She nodded and sat back down. Cassidy said goodnight to everyone and gave her parents their kisses and hugs. Even Jeff. I followed her up the stairs and waited in the hallway while she changed into her jammies. When she was ready I opened the door to a Little Mermaid room, complete with matching curtains and bedspread. I'd asked for a Wonder Woman bedroom when I was her age, but never got it. I listened to her prayers and tucked the covers over her shoulder. Then I said:

"Cass, I need to tell you something and I think you're old enough to hear it. I think you're smart enough."

She gave me a big smile. A big girl smile.

"I'll go to Confession if you really want me to. But here's the thing, and it's something I think you already know. I'd only be going because of you, because *you* want me to do it. It wouldn't be real. I'd know it and you'd know it. Even if I wasn't telling you right now, you'd know it. And God would, too."

She nodded.

"I wouldn't be doing it so I could show God I'm sorry for…stuff I've done, or to get forgiveness for it. I'd be doing it so I could take Communion with you and to make you happy. That's almost a good enough reason for me to do it and if I thought I could fool you—if I *really* thought you wouldn't know that's the only reason I was going—I'd do it. Because I love you, Cass, and I'd probably do just about anything if it would make you happy. But if I did that, it wouldn't *really* make you happy."

"Because I'd know."

"That's right. I know you don't understand all of it, but…I just can't do it right now. One day I'll confess my sins to someone, because we all get around to it sooner or later. And when I do it'll be real. And you'll know that, too, because you'll be able to see the difference."

And I got another smile. Not a big one, but it was a smile.

"So, are we okay?"

"Yes."

She fluffed her pillow and snuggled in with her Teddy. All covered and cozy. I gave her a kiss on the cheek and asked, "Cass, have you ever heard the Parable of the Sower?"

She nodded. "The Sower is God. He plants seeds in the soil. And the soil is your soul."

Soul. Heart. It was the same thing.

"Yep. He plants seeds there so love can grow. And there's something I wanna tell you about that."

And then I took a deep breath. I had to be ready for it.

Because this is it. One of those moments, Tess. She'll remember what you say right now for the rest of her life. Your words. It's not arrogance to think that. Just a fact. One of those moments. So don't screw it up.

"You have a very beautiful soul, Cass. You're honest and curious and colorful and...whenever I look at you I can see God's love. When I see you it reminds me that He's real. Your soil is just right."

I wanted to tell her to never let anyone make her think otherwise. I wanted to tell her to never change, to never let her heart get trampled down and hard. But she'd remember that too. And right now—right now—she didn't know that there was any other way to be. That she could ever be anything other than soft and lovely and fertile. And she needed to stay that way as long as she could.

So I gave her another kiss on the cheek and told her I loved her. And she said she loved me right back. Then

I joined the grown-ups downstairs. And tried not to think about paths through the field or souls or hearts. Especially hearts. Because that would make me think of what tomorrow would bring.

Then it was home. Brian and I lay in bed, naked in the darkness, talking about the day. His arm was around me, my head on his shoulder. And when his voice finally trailed off I reached over with gentle fingers and played with the hair on his chest. I waited for him to roll over, waited for him to kiss me. Instead his arm tensed up underneath me, hard as stone, and he didn't move. Didn't even breathe for quite some time. He was listening to the television going upstairs. Listening for Rachel.

So I rolled over on top of him and kissed him, a hot, sweet, deep kiss. I needed it tonight, needed him, needed the distraction. Because of what tomorrow would bring. He kissed me back but he wasn't into it. And even in the darkness I could see his eyes, open wide and looking up. At the ceiling. Listening to her footsteps. Trotting into the kitchen for a glass of water. Then into the bathroom. I kissed him anyway, even as she padded her way into her bedroom and hopped into my bed. It let out a series of squeals and squeaks as she did. Brian cringed at the sound and that's when I knew.

It wasn't going to happen.

Still, I knew enough to give him a way out. I gave a yawn that wasn't fake and said, with perfect truth, "I'm exhausted."

He nodded, relieved. "Rain check?"

"Yep." I gave him another kiss before I rolled off of him and glanced quickly at the glaring red numbers. Almost one in the morning. I watched the clock while he drifted off to sleep. Watched it, still, until I heard him snoring. Waited a few more minutes. Just in case. And then I gave in.

There was no guilt, because it was Brian in my mind. Wet and naked in the rain, his voice whispering in my ear, hot and sweet and deep. And when I was done I rolled over, looked at the clock. It was just after two. So I closed my eyes and finally slept.

CHAPTER 26

The alarm buzzed me awake at five, an hour earlier than usual, and at first I didn't know why. Until I remembered that it was Friday.

I drove into town to do my two office jobs. Bathrooms to clean and desks to dust and carpets to vacuum and trash cans to empty. I examined the garbage bags closely before I tossed them into the dumpster behind the insurance company. They were thick and sturdy, and it seemed like such a shame to waste them on flimsy items like paper, pencil shavings, and Styrofoam coffee cups. And I noticed, for the first time, how my fingerprints stood out against the black plastic surface.

Brian was eating bacon and eggs when I got back home. I held my breath to block out the smell and headed straight for the bathroom. I scrubbed the bleach from my hands, then examined my hair in the mirror, pulled it back, wound it into a tight bun, and secured it with extra pins. Gave it a liberal dose of hair spray so no strands could escape. I gave my cosmetics bag a quick glance, but decided against putting on any makeup. I'd have to look at my reflection too closely for that; I'd have to look at my eyes.

Rachel was downstairs and ready to go by the time I staggered back into the kitchen. She took one look at me and actually shuddered. "You look like hell, Tess."

"Thanks."

"Why'd you put your hair up like that? You look like a fucking schoolmarm."

I sighed. "Do you want me to take you or not?"

Before she could answer, Brian stood up and announced, "I'm taking you, Rach."

"Uh, no, you're not."

"Tess isn't up to this. I didn't schedule any work for today so I could—"

"I told you... *no.*"

"I'm fine, Brian," I said.

"Tess—"

"It's all right. I don't mind. Really."

He didn't believe me. Neither did I. But there wasn't anything we could do about it. I grabbed my purse from the counter, looked inside to make sure I'd remembered to pack a book for the waiting room. Then I gave him a kiss, pushed Rachel out the door, and we drove away.

It took twenty minutes to get from the house to the interstate and we still had an hour to go until we'd reach Portland. It was only quarter after eight, and the end of the day was nowhere in sight.

"So," Rachel said, finally breaking the silence, "how come you don't go to church anymore? I mean, you believe in God. Right?"

A thousand and one other possible topics for conversation, and she wanted to talk about God. While I was driving her to get an abortion.

"Yes, I believe in God. I just...I don't feel close to Him in church."

"Really? Why's that?"

I shrugged, even though I knew exactly why. I knew because I'd felt that way since I was a little girl, sitting in my church clothes, listening to the Mass. Trying to feel His presence. Struggling to feel His love. But there was nothing there. Nothing but words I didn't completely understand and scary statues. And then, one beautiful Sunday spring morning when I was nine years old, something occurred to me. Something I never told anyone else.

He's not really in here. God doesn't live inside a building, and that's all a church is—just a building filled with lots of words. A beautiful building, except for the scary statues, and beautiful words, some of them; but there isn't anything real *in here.*

And from that moment on, every Sunday I would imagine that He was waiting for me outside the church. That He was peeking in the windows, a little impatiently, waiting for the priest to finish saying the words. Waiting until I could come home and change into my play clothes. And in my mind He was with me as I played in the meadows and the forest near my house. Running with me through the wildflowers and climbing the tall, tall trees and rolling down the steep hill in the thick, green grass. And when I read *Anne of Green Gables* a year later I knew I'd been right all along. Because Anne said that if she *really* wanted to talk to God, a real, true prayer, then she'd have to go outside to do it. She'd need to surround herself with God's creation, with His beauty. Drink it in and let it fill her up. And then she could look heavenward and just *feel* a prayer.

I couldn't say that to Rachel, of course, so I turned the tables on her. "Didn't your parents ever take you guys to church?"

"Nope. Brian said once that everyone in my father's family was all too busy worshiping at the alter of Jack Daniels to worry about God." Neither of us laughed, because it wasn't funny. "My mom's parents went to the church that gave Zeke such a hard time. But my mom never went and she never made us go."

"Do your grandparents live around here?" Brian had never mentioned them before.

"Not anymore. They're dead."

"Oh. I'm sorry."

"Don't be. I never met 'em. Brian either."

"Did they die before you guys were born?"

"Nope, they just didn't wanna have anything to do with my mother. She was a sinner, so they cast her out."

"A sinner?"

"Yeah. You know. Fornication. That's a sin."

"Ah."

She gave me a fake smile and changed the subject. She'd tried watching *Gone With the Wind* after we got home from the Burkes', but had to turn it off about halfway through. Because any movie where a woman took more than two hours to figure out if she wanted to be with a whining, sniveling wimp or a dark, dangerous renegade wasn't worth bothering with. When I told her that Scarlett had chosen the renegade, but that by then it was Too Late, Rachel smiled and said, *Good for him.* I told her that I hated most movies that were made from books, because they usually screwed up the story. And she said that it was probably because studios know that most people need the Hollywood Version of things, because it makes them feel better.

And on it went. Harmless, meaningless, inane chatter that was supposed to take our minds off of where we were headed and what was going to happen when we got there. But we got there, of course, and were both forced to think about it, forced to deal with it. I helped her fill out paperwork and sat in the waiting room while she had her counseling. While she debated for the final time whether or not she really wanted to go through with it. There were other women waiting, too, and some men who were there for support, but I didn't look at any of them. I just read the book I'd brought with me. It was a crime thriller. All about vengeance and punishment. Retribution.

And then it was time.

The Room was white. Stark white. And it made me long for the Pepto Bismol Pink that had offended me months earlier in Kim's maternity ward. I turned away while Rachel changed into her thin, chilly robe. Looked out the window at Portland Maine. It was Black Friday. Early-bird specials for early Christmas shoppers. Streets and parking lots that were packed with cars. Stores that were packed with angry customers in crowded aisles, fighting over the latest Must-Have Toy. This year, like most years, it was some stupid stuffed animal that, when properly stuffed with too many batteries-not-included, spit out three different phrases. It was outrageously priced and in high demand because supplies were short. Supplies were short because the manufacturer had kept production low. That way they could create a high demand and charge outrageous prices.

Ho ho ho.

Rachel cleared her throat and let me know she was done changing. She was sitting on the padded table with the white paper sheet. Waiting. Determined. Nervous. I wanted to ask, *Are you sure? Are you really sure?* But a doctor or nurse or both had already asked her that and she had said *yep* or *yes* or maybe even *hell yeah.* Because there we were. Waiting.

Finally, the nurse. Friendly. Smiling. She was wearing scrubs that were Dusty Rose. She asked kindly about our Thanksgiving as she took Rachel's blood pressure and pulse and did all the other preliminary garbage. Then the door opened, and in walked The Doctor.

She was friendly, too. Motherly. Earth mother, actually. A true Granola with proudly graying brown hair and no makeup. She told us her name but I didn't pay attention to it. In my mind she'd always just be The Doctor. She looked at Rachel's chart, scribbled something down and nodded to herself. Then she looked up. Asked Rachel if she had any questions. She did. Just one and it surprised me. Because although The Doctor misunderstood her at first, I knew, right away, exactly what it was she meant.

"Is it gonna hurt?"

"I'll be giving you a few injections, to numb your cervix. That will sting just a little, almost like a pinch. But it will help with the—"

Injections. Needles. She winced. And it was a relief for me to see that she really did hate them. "I know. They told me that already. I mean…is this gonna hurt the baby?"

For a few moments there was nothing but silence, except in my mind. Because what I heard there was a scared, lonely voice that said:

It's not a baby, Rachel. Not a baby. It's an embryo. A fetus. A mass of cells. A mass of something. But not. A baby...

The doctor cleared her throat and said, "No. Not at all."

And then she told us about nerve centers and weeks of gestation. Explained that there was *no fetal pain before twenty-six weeks.* That was a fact. And I looked at her, looked to her. Because she was The Doctor. The One Who Knows. And I searched her eyes, suddenly panicked. Because there was something that *I* needed to know.

Is this bullshit? Something you tell women to make them feel better? To ease their conscience? To ease yours? Because how is that possible? How the fuck, how the bloody goddamn hell can you even know that? What tests can you run to figure that out? What kind of scientific proof could you possibly have that could possibly fucking tell you that Rachel's baby, or fetus, or embryo—that the mass of cells inside of her—won't feel a thing?

But she wasn't looking at me. She was looking at Rachel. Calm. Confident. Competent. Which is exactly what she should have been doing. What I should be doing. So I did it. I held Rachel's hand and she looked at me. Determined, still, but scared. I looked right back at her, looked her right in the eyes. And I said it.

"She's right, Rach. They've done tests and stuff. So they know."

She gave me a weak smile. Nodded. And lay down on the table. She looked up at the ceiling so I did, too. It was a drop ceiling, a grid. Big white squares with yellowish water stains here and there that looked just like piss. The Doctor and Dusty Pink Nurse talked to each other in low voices, about whatever it is that doctors and nurses talk about. And then it was time.

Stirrups. Ultrasound. The screen was pointed merci-fully away from Rachel. Even if it hadn't been she wouldn't have seen it. Because she didn't shift her gaze, not once. Still looked straight up and I wondered if she was counting tiles. Or maybe counting the tiny little holes in the tiles. What were those holes? Were they there just for looks? Ven-tilation? Air bubbles that formed when the factory cooked the tiles? What the hell were those tiles made from, any-way? Styrofoam? Plastic?

It didn't matter, and now I had to listen to The Doctor again. She was saying something about sedation. Demerol for pain and Valium to help her relax. Rachel nodded. She was all for that. Until The Doctor mentioned the dangers of giving it to her if she'd consumed any drugs or alcohol in the past twenty-four hours. And that's when she had to tell us.

She'd taken Something last night. Right before she'd hopped into my bed.

"Just so I could sleep, Tess. Just so I—"

I put my hand up. "It's all right, Rach."

I said it even though it wasn't all right. It was as far away from all right as we could get. But it was a done thing and right now I couldn't do anything about it. Right now she needed to settle down and not worry about Condemnation and Judgment and Consequences. There would be enough of that later. But when it came it wouldn't be from me, and it wouldn't be about the Something that had helped her drift off to sleep. It would be even worse. It would be Rachel judging Rachel. I knew it. I could see it in her eyes. Already.

So I gave her a small smile that I hoped looked reassur-ing and we listened to The Doctor once again. Because she wanted to explain each step as it was happening. There was the speculum, and that's never fun, and antiseptic, which is one of the foulest stenches known to man. Then Rachel clamped her eyes shut, asked, begged, *please, please, please don't tell me about the needle. Just do it.* And she squeezed my hand tightly, tighter and tighter still, until I thought my fingers might just fall off from a lack of circulation. Finally she relaxed her grip a little, letting me know the evil needle was gone. But she didn't let go of my hand.

Dilators. I didn't know what those were, what they did, what they meant. I didn't want to know. Didn't look. I looked right at Rachel and, now, she was looking right at me. Wide eyes. Van Dyke Brown. And that's when I wondered, even though I didn't want to wonder:

Did the baby get those eyes?

It didn't matter. Because The Doctor was doing it. A vacuum. It sounded—almost—like mine. The one I used every day. And that's when I wondered…even though I… couldn't wonder…

Does it hurt? Is it hurting right now? What's it like, inside there? Right now?

Oh…my God.

But I couldn't think about that, even if I wanted to, which I didn't, because right now—right now—Rachel was hurting. For real. In every single, horrible, godawful way a person could hurt. A hurt I could actually see and feel and smell. And that's the pain I had to think about, to worry about. So I gave her another smile and squeezed her hand. She was crying. Silently. Looking at me while the tears streamed down her cheeks and I had to do something. But I couldn't. What could I do? Nothing. Except…

I leaned forward. Closer to her. Didn't let go of her hand. Whispered in her ear.

"It's all right. You're doing the right thing."

I said it even though it wasn't all right. Not yet. But it would be Someday. I'd make sure of it. And I said it because it *was* the right thing. For her.

It felt like the vacuum had been sucking and whining and hissing forever, but it had only been four minutes. Only four and The Doctor had said it would probably take ten. Six more minutes. And I didn't know if I could take it. If Rachel could. Because her eyes were pleading with me to do something. To make it all go away.

Then I remembered Kim. Lamaze. Focal point. But it was too late for that, really. Nothing to focus on except the ceiling, and who wants to stare at tiny white holes and piss? And if there was no focal point, then what else could I do?

"Tess..." Weak, begging. "Please talk to me. Say something. Anything..."

Anything. Anything that wasn't about what was actually going on. I searched for a topic but there was nothing inside me. Nothing except the whine and hiss and screech of the vacuum. It was everywhere. It echoed inside my brain and heart and gut and what was left of my soul.

I took a peek around the room, hoping for inspiration, which was stupid. Nothing but stark white walls and white tiled floor with ugly light gray specks and white ceiling tiles that were stained with piss. I searched anyway and inspiration finally came to me from an odd place. The nurse. She had on a ring. It looked like a ruby.

So I told Rachel about my broken pin with the missing stone that was probably a fake ruby. Told her about beaux and true love and gifts. Separation and sacrifice. But in my version that separation was only temporary. In my version the pin broke because it fell from the sad girl's hands as she watched her beau drive away toward New York. Toward work and success and riches. And in my version the lovers were reunited. And they lived happily ever after.

The Hollywood Version. Because sometimes that's what we need.

She listened but didn't smile, grateful through her clenched teeth, and I finished right before The Doctor did. It was quiet once again. Except inside of me. Because that's where the vacuum was still shrieking. It probably always would be.

We had to wait another hour before they let me take her home. Gave her three prescriptions to be filled which we did, before we left town. Because she didn't want to get them at the drug store in New Mills. Not where the pharmacist knew her. Had known her mother.

By the time we were back on the interstate Rachel was floating on a Vicodin cloud. I expected her to drift off to sleep, but she talked instead. She kept her eyes closed as she did, and what she told me made me want to close my eyes, too. Cover my ears. Crash the car into a guardrail. Anything to make the story stop. Because this time she was too worn out to make idle chatter, too gloomy for Hollywood endings. Instead she told me about Tim.

He hadn't just knocked her around. Not just a smack now and then. Not out of anger or revenge because of Brian beating him senseless. Violence and humiliation. That was his thing. It's what turned him on, and it was the real reason he sold drugs, not just the money. That mattered, of course, and he had it, but it only mattered a little. It was the power of it he loved. Getting young girls hooked, and then taking it away. Leaving them hurting and begging and willing to do anything for just…one more…hit. *Please…*

He'd tried it with Rachel, tried to get her hooked, but she really was afraid. She'd lied to me, though, when she said she'd never done smack. *Just once, Tess. I swear.* She let Tim shoot her up with her eyes closed tight and she'd loved it. It was the best feeling in the world, the best she'd ever felt in her whole, miserable fucking life. Ever. And that scared her even more than the needle. Because she knew—*knew* at that moment—that she really would do anything in the world, anything, to feel like that again. And so she never used it again. Even though he wanted her to. Even though *she* wanted to. She stuck with what was safe. With her Oxycontin.

That was fine for him at first, because for a while it was enough for him just to fuck a young girl. But after a while the novelty wore off and he needed more. And that's when it started. He had to hurt her. To get it up. To get it off. And he was smart, of course, because he never left a mark where anyone could see it. Never did anything that anyone else could know about. Except for him.

And except. For her…

Once she understood how it worked she'd scream and screech and pretend that it was worse than it actually was, just so he'd stop. Or so he'd stop sooner. But it just got worse. She wanted to tell him *no* but she knew he'd do it anyway. Wanted to run away and ask for help but she was embarrassed. Ashamed. And because she was afraid that he'd leave her. All alone. And it went on and on and on…

Until Brian and Jeff got to him. Because once Tim recovered that was the worst ever. Not just for kicks; it was retribution. He tied her up. Beat her. Cut her. And raped her. And that's when I knocked at her door. I'd saved her from...something. She'd known something was coming but she hadn't known what. And by that time she didn't care. She'd just given up. She was just going to let him do whatever it was. She was just too tired to fight...

I drove along as she told me her story. Colder and colder, my heart and gut and soul, as each mile ticked by. But I didn't speak. She didn't seem to want me to say any-thing. Seemed to want to just get it all out. And by the time she was done we were a mile from home.

The lake.

The leaves were bare and the water was gray and ugly. Cold. I stopped anyway, pulled over, so I could say some-thing. Because once we got home, once Brian heard my car, he'd come running right out. And I wouldn't be able to say a word.

"I'm so sorry I didn't get you out of there."

"Tess, it's not your fault."

"I should have—"

"Should have what? I lied to you. What can I say? I'm good at it."

Maybe. But I still should have known something was going on. Done something. I should have made her leave him, whether she wanted to or not. I was the grown-up, not her, and I should have protected her.

I cleared my throat. "You really need to stay with us, Rach. For a long time. I know you don't want to, but you need to anyway."

She nodded. Tired. Ready to agree to anything.

"And don't tell anyone else what happened today. Not because you should be ashamed. Because you shouldn't be. But because you don't want it getting back to Tim."

She shook her head. "You don't think he's gonna figure it out when he sees me not getting fatter?"

"You let me take care of that. Just…don't say anything."

"I won't. It's not like I want the world to know anyway."

"I know. And…one more thing, Rach."

She rolled her eyes. Beyond tired.

"Rach, don't ever think you have to put up with any of that shit again. Okay? Because you deserve better than that. You really do. You're a great person and you're beautiful and you deserve someone who treats you that way."

She was smiling. "Okay."

"And don't ever lie to me again."

She nodded.

"Especially about Tim. If he shows up or calls or anything like that…you tell me." I didn't bother to threaten her with Brian. I didn't have to say it. Because she knew. "I mean it. You tell me right away. Do you understand?"

"Yes, Mommy."

"Shut up."

Brian was waiting on the porch steps when we got home.

3:47 p.m.

He jogged to the car to help Rachel out and she accepted the help without an argument. Then up the stairs and into my apartment, the one that wasn't really mine anymore. Even though most of my stuff was still there.

She surprised Brian by giving him a quick hug before she stumbled off to bed. It's where I wanted to go, too, because I was beyond exhausted. Even beyond fucking exhausted. I was hovering in a land of stark white fog, fog that was stained with piss and blood.

Brian pulled me to him and kissed me on the forehead. Held me gently. Close. He was warm and beautiful and strong, even through the fog.

"Are you okay?"

I nodded into his chest. Smelled his shirt. Listened to his heartbeat. It was trying telling me that everything really was all right. Or at least that it would be.

He stroked my hair, held me even tighter. "Let's go downstairs. You need some sleep."

I shook my head. "I can't. I have to go clean Zeke's place. And then I gotta do the Kendalls'. And then I've got a couple errands I gotta run."

"But…Tess, you can do those jobs tomorrow. Zeke doesn't mind, and the Kendalls aren't even in the state."

"I know. But if I don't do them I won't be able to sleep. I'll keep thinking about the dishes and the toilets and the dust. This way I can sleep in late tomorrow."

He sighed, because he knew better than to try and keep me away from neglected dishes and toilets and dust. "Well, fine. But at least wait till tomorrow to do your errands."

"I can't. Christmas shopping. I missed the early-bird specials, but there are still some good deals going on until midnight."

"Oh come on, Tess. Don't be stupid."

I pulled away from him. Looked into his eyes. Tried to make mine believable. "I just need to get away, Brian.

I need to get out by myself for a little while. You know what that's like, don't you?"

"Yeah, but…" He sighed again. "Yeah. Just…be careful. You look a little fuzzy or something. And call me if you're too tired to keep driving so I can come get you. And…"

He went on and on, and I listened to every word. Each *don't* and *please* and *try not to*. Because I knew that the words meant *I love you*. And then he said it, even though he really didn't have to. He said it anyway.

"I love you, Tess."

And I said it right back. "I love you too, Brian."

Because I did. More than anything. Even in the fog.

CHAPTER 27

I drove to Zeke's house as quickly as I could. Dean's bowls and cups were in the sink, his razor and toothbrush sitting alongside Zeke's in the bathroom, but I couldn't even smile. They were trying to tell me that Zeke was happy and content at last, but all it meant to me on this day was extra work. Double the dishes, double the shaving cream and toothpaste stuck to the sink, double the time spent cleaning the apartment...when I had more important things to do.

I finished up, then headed for the bar. My fan club hollered something and I waved in their direction without even hearing what it was. I nodded to Zeke, turned down a beer, and got right to the point.

"I need a huge favor."

"Okay."

"Rachel's schedule. It would be good if she could be home when Brian and I are. As much as possible. If you can work it out."

He hesitated for a moment, then pulled out the schedule from underneath the bar and looked it over.

"I'll still need her to close on Fridays and Saturdays. She can have Tuesdays and Sundays off, and the rest of the week I can give her the eight-to-four shift. She's been here longer than the others, anyway, so she has seniority, for what it's worth. Will that do it?"

"Close enough. I really appreciate it, Zeke."

"She might bitch a little, because the tips are bigger at night."

"Let me worry about that."

He nodded and put the schedule away. Scratched his chin. "You know, Tess. Even with all this, you still can't watch her all the time. She's a big girl and if she's gonna get in trouble, she's gonna do it no matter what you do."

I rubbed my eyes. I had never been so tired in my entire life. "I know. But at least this way she'll be safe from him."

"Maybe, but—"

"I gotta go, Zeke."

I really did. I still had lots to do.

5:11.

I sat in my car, thinking it all over. Zeke was right. I couldn't protect her; not this way. If she wanted to go back to doing her thing, that's just what she'd do. And now, with no rent to pay, she'd have extra money to do it with. Because there was no guarantee that she'd save it for school. And even if she was serious about making changes, even if she really did want to straighten out her life, there was still Tim. There would always be Tim. And there couldn't be. Not anymore.

I ran through the mental list I'd started the minute I'd crawled out of bed. I'd been adding to it, bit by bit, all day long. Because even though I'd never committed a crime, I'd spent the past seven months watching cop shows with Brian. And even though those were only fictional, they were at least somewhat steeped in fact. So I had a good idea of how to do what it was that needed to be done without incriminating myself…or anyone else.

First step: Walmart in Westville. It was Black Friday, the busiest shopping day of the year. I wouldn't be noticed or remembered in the crowd of people. And it wouldn't look odd, buying the things I'd need.

Next step: Kendalls' camp. They wouldn't be back in town until January, when snowmobiling and ice fishing would beckon. And until then, *Mrs. Dyer, can you give the camp a quick cleaning every week?* I had the key to the front door on my key chain, next to half a dozen others. A key… and knowledge of what was inside the camp.

There was a gun in the den closet. Locked up in a box. The bullets were locked in the desk drawer. And the extra key to those locks was in the bathroom medicine cabinet.

Tiffany, darling, don't be scared. It's for protection.

Because there was a rampant teenage drug problem in New Mills. And sometimes those teenagers got desperate enough to break into houses. Desperate enough, sometimes, to kill. And sometimes rich people bought guns to protect themselves from those desperate teenagers. And, sometimes, they talked about things in front of their cleaning ladies. As if their cleaning ladies didn't have eyes and ears and a brain. As if they weren't there at all.

The parking lot was packed. I adjusted my mittens, pulled my big, knitted hat over my schoolmarm bun, and did a quick check in the rearview mirror. Pulled the hat down even lower to cover my eyebrows. Just like lots of other women on this cold, November night. I stared at my feet as I walked in the door, away from the cameras, and that wasn't odd, either. Lots of women hated looking at their big asses on the security screen.

I nodded to the greeter without looking at her and wheeled a cart toward Men's Shoes. Grabbed a pair of size ten boots. My feet were size seven. Brian's were size twelve. Then the winter clothes department. Big, thick, manly gloves, for fingerprints and gun shot residue. A scarf to cover my face, a brand new coat, and a pair of big, bulky jeans. Because there would be lots of blood splattering, everywhere, and maybe even some brain. Then I stopped for a moment in the electronics section to get a gift for Brian. It was the action flick we'd gone to see on our first date—the one that wasn't really our first date. And, finally, I tossed in a package of wrapping paper. Cheerful and red. Santa and his reindeer.

Ho ho ho.

The checkout lines were all long, which was no surprise. It took me twenty minutes to reach the cashier. I paid with cash. Then I drove to the Kendalls' camp.

Front door. Alarm code. Lights. The grandfather clock in the living room read:

6:45.

I was over three hours late and now the alarm company knew it. But that's natural on a day when you've taken your friend to a doctor's appointment and then done some Christmas shopping. Especially when your client is in

Connecticut. That's when you don't have to worry so much about being on time.

I did a quick cleaning. Just so. Then I slipped on the new gloves, snatched the keys from the medicine cabinet, and ran into the den. I flipped on the light, sped over to the closet, and opened the door. It was the first time I had, so I wasn't sure what it normally held. But right now it was empty.

Except for a metal box on the top shelf.

And here was a moment of truth. Because there was nothing in this closet, nothing on that top shelf—and there never had been—that a cleaning lady would ever need. No way to explain it away if an errant hair—slicked carefully back, plastered in place with hairspray, and covered with a knitted winter hat—or a drop of spit or sweat was found inside of this closet by a hardworking detective or crime scene investigator. No excuse, no alibi. Only one reason.

Less than a minute later the gun was in my hand. It was old, but in good condition, and it was butt ugly. Black rubber grip. There was something stamped on the short, silver nose.

Undercover. 38 SPL.

I had never held a gun before. Ever. It wasn't as heavy as I'd expected. Would it kick when I pulled the trigger? Would it make me fall backwards, or at least throw me off balance?

Think about that, Tess. Prepare for that.

I sat down at the desk. The same key that opened the gun box opened the bottom drawer.

Bullets.

I loaded the gun. It was easy, really. Push the catch, like so. Cylinder thing swings right out. Bullets slip right in.

Five bullets. Just. Like. That.

I stood up. Straighter. Did the math.

He's taller than Rachel. But just a little. Maybe...five ten? Or so?

I imagined his head. Lifted the gun, my finger well away from the trigger. Right about...there. Because it had to be in the head. Had to be. I had to make sure he'd die, right away. As much as I would have loved to make him suffer first.

I ran to the kitchen and checked under the counter. Found what I was looking for. A box of big, black trash bags. I grabbed three. None of them had my fingerprints on them because Mrs. Pelletier never let me near her cupboards.

Then it was back to the living room. I entered the code. Locked the door. Ran to the car. Chucked the gun onto the front seat. Changed into my new clothes and boots. New coat. Scarf. Laid one of the trash bags over the seat. Started the car.

7:18.

I drove to the far side of town, beyond the gravel pit, onto a back road. Because if you're a drug dealer then you want to live in the woods where you're hidden. I drove slowly. Got closer. Could see his mailbox coming toward me. Dangling from a chain. On a thick wooden post.

And that's when I had to think about it. To be prepared. So I thought about all the violent movies I'd ever seen, the really bad ones. Blood and wounds and gore and splattering.

I tried to imagine the smell and the sound. Couldn't do it. But I knew it would be bad.

Remember that. And be prepared for it. Be prepared for all of it. Because it's gonna be loud and bloody and sticky and gross.

And that's when I started to feel something stirring underneath the hard, frozen soil. Finally. Fear. Nausea. Guilt.

Guilt? Why? You helped Rachel kill his son. Or his daughter. You did that, Tess, you did it to protect her. From him. From herself. And that's why you're doing this. So what's the difference? None. There's no difference at all. And this isn't even as bad, because this way you're protecting other people, too. Ex-wife and daughter with an ineffective restraining order. Little Miss Seventeen—whoever she is. And the next one in line after he gets tired of her. And the next one and the one after that. And don't forget about Brian. You're doing this so he doesn't have to do. Because he will. He will if he ever finds out what Tim did to her. And he'd probably get caught because he'd go out without thinking. Just blow Tim away or beat the shit out of him without taking any precautions at all. Not like me. Not like this.

Tim's house was at the end of a long, graveled driveway. I killed my headlights. Pulled in slowly.

And saw that there were three cars. Sitting there. Right beside his.

Thank you, God. Thank you. Even though I don't deserve it...

Time for Plan B. Because, of course, I had one.

I backed up, slowly. Parked the car in the middle of the driveway, where it couldn't be seen from the house or the road. Just in case. Stuffed the gun into my new coat pocket.

Just in case.

I knocked on the door. Took a big, fat, deep breath. Held it. The door opened.

And there he was. Asshole. Coward. Rapist. Killer.

I didn't even flinch.

He smiled when he saw me standing in his doorway. "Well, this is a real surprise."

I said nothing. Just clenched my jaw. Because I couldn't remember what it was I had planned to say.

He laughed lightly, raised his eyebrows, gave me one of his sick stares. "I'll be honest, Tess, normally I'd send you away, because you're way too old for me. But I've *always* wondered what it'd be like to do you. I bet you're fucking wild."

I gripped the gun inside my pocket. Tight. My finger was nowhere near the trigger.

He was getting impatient. "So...what brings you here? Looking to score? I can give you a senior citizen's discount."

And still I said nothing. Just stood there in front of him, trying not to shake.

He gave me a greasy smile. "Or is it something else? Is Brian finally all done with you? Did he realize he doesn't need his mommy around anymore now that his little sister's back home to take care of him?"

That was the moment when I knew. That face. Those words. Mingling with Rachel's words, the ones that had told me all the things he'd done to her. I knew, even through the fog. I would have done it. For real. If not for the other three cars and the people they'd brought here. The witnesses.

Oh...my God. I would have done it.

I clenched my toes inside my great, big boots and cleared my throat. Because I finally remembered my Plan B. "I just came here to tell you that Rachel lost her baby."

Because he'd see her, not pregnant. And I had to make sure she was safe. She wouldn't do it herself. She didn't care, one way or the other. She'd given up months ago and she was still too tired to fight it. To fight him. I knew it, and it was something to work on. But for now...she needed protection.

His smile fell. "She lost it?"

"Yeah. Well, *you* know. Some asshole shoved her and she fell back against her coffee table. It did something to her...I don't really know what. But it made her lose the baby."

He stared at me, blankly at first. And then there was anger. At who? Me? Rachel? Himself? I couldn't tell. But what I didn't see there was concern. Or remorse.

None.

You fucking bastard.

I tightened my grip around the gun. It was still in my pocket but it wouldn't be for long. My finger was on the trigger now, and I could do it. Right now. Blow his stupid, disgusting, fucking head off before he even knew it was coming. Watch the bullet pierce through it, maybe right through his eye, and wouldn't that be great? Even if his blood and brains and bone got on me, even it covered me, all of it, I didn't care. Not even a little. It made me smile and I kept right on smiling, even though it meant getting something in my mouth, blood or brain or bone, and I didn't care. Couldn't care. Because I was ready. I was prepared. Whoever was partying inside was probably too stoned and drunk to think or move quickly enough to catch up with me. Whip the scarf over my face to cover it. Big, big boots would leave big, big footprints. My car was far away enough not to be seen and there were lots of tire tracks on this road. Mine would blend right in. Get in the car, sit on the black trash bag, drive away, stop somewhere safe, change the clothes, bloody clothes in the black trash bags, ditch the bloody trash bags. Bleach my hands and face and anything else. Bleach makes everything glow in luminol, just like blood does. And what could be more natural than for a cleaning lady to be covered in bleach?

Premeditated. All of it. From the second you woke up this morning. All of it was planned, every single step. And even Dave can't save you from that. Because you wouldn't be innocent-until-proven-guilty. You're just guilty.

I looked over Tim's shoulder. Someone was there. We made eye contact.

Little Miss Seventeen. She almost looked like Rachel. Probably the ex-wife did, too.

It was too late now, so I let go of the trigger. I held onto the gun, though, just in case; but my chest felt hollow and I had to force myself to breath. Almost like my heart and lungs had stopped working until she'd come into view. I waited a few more seconds, looked her right in the eye and said:

"Do your parents know where you are?"

She put her cigarette to her lips. Inhaled deeply. Exhaled with: "Fuck you, bitch."

I rolled my eyes and turned my attention back to Fuck-wad. Almost felt normal again. Which meant, of course, that I felt nothing.

"Anyway, Brian's pissed. Worse than he was last time. So you'd better stay away from Rachel."

"Why the sudden concern for my well-being?"

"I'm not the slightest bit concerned about your sorry, ugly ass. But if Brian kills you—which he could do, very easily, and wouldn't *that* be awesome—then he'd spend the rest of his life in jail. And...you're just not worth it."

I clomped back to the car without waiting for his reply. Brushed the dirt off the boots. Got back inside. I changed the clothes, then folded the new ones, just so, and put them back in the bag with the boots. After all, there was no blood or brain or bone on anything. And I had a receipt. I put the new coat in the other bag, the one with Brian's movie. Because it would fit Rachel.

Ho ho ho.

The new gloves could stay in the car. Because you never know when a nice, warm extra pair of gloves will come in handy. Then I drove to the end of the road and called Brian.

"I'm running a bit late. Have you eaten?"

He chuckled. "Yeah. But I'm still hungry."

"I can pick something up at Fran's."

"Sounds good. But don't bother getting anything for Rach. That pain pill put her right out."

Vicodin. Two doses already. I'd need to keep an eye on that.

Then it was back to the Kendalls'. Front door. Alarm code. Got the key from the medicine cabinet. Placed the gun and bullets back in their homes. Put the key back in its home. Just so. Then I grabbed my bucket of cleaning supplies from where I'd left it in the hallway.

Yes, Mr. Kendall, that was me. Twice in one day. Pretty careless of me to leave my bucket behind. It won't happen again…

I trudged out to the car. Looked at it. Shivered. It was cold out and I'd left my coat—my real coat—in the back seat. I stood outside anyway and looked up at the sky. It was dark. Spooky. No moon and no stars. Nothing but tall, naked trees.

I whipped off my sweater, let the frigid wind bite at my bare skin. My stomach, my arms, my chest, my back. I needed to feel something and I didn't care what it was. Sharp, bitter, cold wind. And that was better than nothingness. I stood there forever, half undressed. Shivering. Thought, for just a moment, about praying, but my heart was empty and I didn't know what to pray for. Help? Forgiveness? Punishment?

God doesn't punish us. He lets us suffer the consequences.

That was bullshit. I'd sinned. Worse than Rachel, for much longer, too. And what consequences had I ever suffered? A mother who hated me. A broken marriage. Exile. Those weren't consequences. God had taken away family and love and home, but he'd given me back all those things—all the things I didn't deserve—and he'd never given me the things I did. I'd never been beaten by a boyfriend. Or raped. Never got knocked up. I'd never got the clap or crabs or AIDS. Not so much as a yeast infection. No punishment. No consequences. Nothing. But Rachel had. And it wasn't fair.

"It's not fucking fair!"

The words came from somewhere deeper than my heart, from somewhere even deeper than my gut. They bounced off the trees and the camp and my car, and the echoes told me again and again how un-fucking-fair it really was. God had taken away Rachel's mom. Taken her away so early that Rachel could barely remember her. All she had was an image of a sick, dying woman, surrounded by nice nurses. And Brian's memories.

Once upon a time, in a faraway land, there lived a Mom. She was beautiful and loved to sing and her eyes were Van Dyke Brown...

But He had done worse than that. He'd given her a useless father. He'd given her nothing to protect her from all the evils of the world except a well-meaning brother who was in over his head. Then He'd heaped Consequences on her. A whole shitload of them. He'd given her heartbreak and emptiness and loneliness and guilt. And she didn't deserve them. Or if she did then I deserved them, too.

"Tell You what. How about a deal? You leave *her* alone and You come after *me*. Doesn't that sound fair?"

And there was nothing. No lightning bolt. No booming, threatening thunder. The cold breeze didn't get any colder. It didn't turn into sudden, fiery gusts from hell. It didn't stop and it didn't pick up any speed.

Nothing.

I threw my sweater to the ground, climbed on top of the hood of my car, then onto the roof. As close to heaven as I could get.

"I said come after me! Come on! Can't You fucking hear me?"

Echoes, all around me. Loud. Insistent. A challenge.

And still there was nothing. Except for the wind, which still hadn't changed. I closed my eyes and listened. Very carefully. Because sometimes there's something there.

Sometimes you can hear it on the wind. A whisper. A message. And after a few minutes I did. Through my shivering. Through my chattering teeth. Even through the fog.

I heard it. A message from God.

You're just not worth it.

And so I hopped down. Dusted off my sweater. Because a person looks odd walking into a diner with a dirt-covered sweater. And she looks even odder to the all-seeing eyes of her boyfriend. Then I got into the car and drove back into town.

Donny was standing behind the counter in Rachel's absence. Was that a promotion? Better than a greasy kitchen. Because out here he could do a little flirting with a curly, blonde-haired girl. Ashley saw me first. She gave me a quick, embarrassed glance, our first eye-to-eye since her drunken outburst, then looked away. Donny gave me a big, friendly smile. Two LaChance throwaways, together. Was it a rebound or something real?

It didn't matter.

"Hey, Tess. Here for your usual?"

I had to laugh. It didn't mean the same thing in New Mills as it did in Brookfield. And that was funny. "Yep. To go." And then I considered. "On second thought, Donny, make mine...a meatball sandwich."

He raised his eyebrows. "Red meat?"

"I'm feeling a little carnivorous today."

"Then I'm glad I've got this counter to protect me."

Cute. Nice. Funny. Where would Rachel be, right now, if she'd kept him?

When I got home Brian was reading the newspaper, and he rambled on all through supper about The Economy.

Blah blah blah, stock market, blah blah, too much money in the hands of the powerful, another few blahs, recession's coming—mark my words—blah-ty blah blah blah.

I nodded and muttered a few appropriate remarks, but it was hard to pay attention. Especially through the fog. Even though I wanted to. I wanted to be interested in the things he was passionate about. Because I loved him. Loved everything about him. I especially loved that he was so passionate about the things that interested him. But economics was not my thing, and it wouldn't have been even if I'd had a normal day. A day in which I hadn't driven a twenty-year-old girl to have her insides and an embryo vacuumed out. Or seriously contemplated and almost executed a brutal murder in New Mills. Or been soundly defeated in a futile pissing match against the Almighty. Even then I would've had a hard time following the drift of the conversation. Because, honestly, even on a good day, I didn't really care about the U.S. economy. As long as I could afford rent and music and beer and food and jeans then the economy could sink into a shithole. And I wouldn't care.

After supper we snuggled on the couch and settled in to watch the television. Another cop show, because they were everywhere. Before this week's episode began the writers let us know that it was based on actual events by claiming not to be. Fortune 500 company executive murdered. Embezzlement and blackmail. Rich and powerful people with powerful, sleazy lawyers. A surprise ending with a last-minute confession. The real murderer is caught…but was justice really served? Cue dramatic music. Roll credits.

Brian stretched and said, "I saw that coming."

"Everyone saw that coming."

He nodded and looked at me. He had to look down because my head was resting on his lap. His face was sideways. And still he was beautiful. "I know you're not okay, so I'm not gonna ask."

"No. I'm not. But I don't think I'm up to talking about it right now."

He gave me a kiss and said that he loved me. I said it right back. Then I said:

"I should go check on Rachel. Then I need a shower."

Up the stairs. Fourteen of them. Rachel was snoring in my bed, covered up with my winter quilt. Alice had made it for me, years ago, even before there was a Jason-and-Tess. It was a log cabin pattern with brightly colored calicos. At least they'd been brightly colored at one time. Now they were faded and worn. It was still a lovely quilt and seeing Rachel wrapped up in it made me feel safer about leaving her upstairs. Almost like I'd be with her. Like Alice would be, too.

Then I peeked at the pill containers on the kitchen counter. Opened up the Vicodin and counted them. Only two doses missing. Just right.

Down the stairs. Fourteen of them...

I stayed in the shower much longer than usual. Long after the sweat and shampoo and soap were gone. I still didn't feel clean. Brian hadn't asked me any questions like I had expected. Like I'd been waiting for. Three full days now and nothing direct at all. But I had still lied to him. I had stood by and let Rachel lie to him. And he didn't suspect anything. Why should he?

I know you're not okay...

No, Brian, I'm not. I'm a terrible person, a liar, the gullible idiot who left your sister with an abusive asshole, even after I knew better. I just closed my eyes so I could pretend it didn't exist. And it wasn't me who got bit in the ass this time. Then I chickened out when I could have done something real to help. To make sure he wouldn't hurt her again. Ever.

But she's hurting still, Brian, more than you know. She's still hurting even though she's safe now. And she's still gonna be hurting a year from now. Ten years from now. Maybe forever. I know it, Brian. I know it. I can feel it.

Please God, help her. Please? I'm not worth it, I know. But she is....

And the other thing. That was there, too, and I didn't push it away this time. I let myself wonder if there had been pain for the baby who wasn't really a baby. The mass of cells that hadn't had yet formed any nerve centers that registered pain, and so couldn't possibly have felt anything. Even though—probably—it had felt everything. So I made myself imagine how it had been. Inside there. Forced myself to think about it; about how close I'd come, once, to finding out. Back when it wouldn't have mattered. When I didn't really exist. When I really wasn't worth it.

I reached down, turned the cold water off, let the hot water burn me, scald me, my shoulders and back. I gritted my teeth and didn't cry out. Not even a whimper. Rachel had cried out when Tim hurt her, hurt her just like this, hurt her even worse. But not for help. She couldn't. And even if she had, no one would have heard her. Just like no one heard her baby scream. I stood up straighter, breasts and stomach and it hurt, fucking burned like hell, like hell would certainly burn me someday, and I took it, I let it hurt, let it burn, because I deserved it, I really did. And even though it hurt, that was better than not feeling anything at all.

Finally I couldn't take it another second. I reached down, adjusted it again, this time icy cold. Then I dropped to my knees and covered my face with the washcloth, bit it hard, tasted cotton and water and leftover soap. I clenched my teeth even harder to stop the chattering. Fought it back, everything that wanted to come up. The tears and the shouting and the shrieking and it stayed down. Even though I had thought I couldn't hold down anything else. Even though I thought I'd reached my limit a month ago. A year ago. Twenty years ago…

I turned off the shower, dried off, and waited for the rest. The eruption. The one that would surely come and it did. Ground beef and tomato sauce and beer. Then I brushed my teeth. And when I slipped into bed beside Brian he asked me—this time—if I was okay. And I told him *no, but that will teach me for eating red meat.* And he said *yep, I guess it will.* Then I fucked him. Even though I'd just taken a painful shower and vomited out what was left of my soul; even though I was so completely exhausted that I couldn't think of any profanity that was harsh enough to qualify it; even though I wasn't horny at all, and neither was he. I fucked him anyway. I even managed to come. A vague reflex, a purely physical reaction; the same way your stomach will begin to digest your supper once you've eaten it. Even when you're not hungry.

And when he was finished, too, he pulled me to him. Put his arms around me. Snuggled in close, so close that I could feel his heart beating on my back. And I knew that it was trying to tell me that it was all gonna be all right.

Someday.

CHAPTER 28

The Doctor had warned Rachel that, in addition to having to endure the twin joys of bleeding and cramping as her body returned to its normal state, she might be a little moody. A pregnant body becoming suddenly unpregnant equals hormones run amok.

"Expect something along the lines of a very bad period."

As soon as she'd said the words I'd known what was really coming. Everyday Rachel was moody. PMS Rachel was crabby. Hormonally Imbalanced Rachel was like a demon let loose from hell. And poor Brian was her favorite punching bag.

She screamed obscenities at him one minute:

"Do you think you could get off your lazy goddamn ass and do something about those drafty fucking windows upstairs?"

And sobbed her apologies to him the next:

"I'm sorry, Brian. I'm sorry I'm such a stupid bitch…"

"You're not stupid, Rach."

Brian wasn't her only target, though. She let Zeke have it, too. She was pissed about her new schedule and told him so. Frequently and loudly. He didn't back down and, fortunately, he didn't tell her it had been my idea. This earned him my undying gratitude, because she was already irritated enough with me.

"I'm fucking sick of you checking on me every god-damn day! Just stay downstairs where you belong and leave me the fuck alone!"

I tried to be patient with her, and mostly succeeded. It was obvious the girl was not well. Because on top of everything else she came down with a stomach flu a few days after her appointment. Chills and vomiting and diarrhea. The whole works. And, of course, more wonderful mood swings. A few days after that I got my period—bringing with it the worst case of PMS I'd ever had in my life—and Brian made the decision to spend his evenings with Jeff until the worst was over at home.

Not that he had much room to talk. The stress of dealing with Hurricane Rachel, combined with a lack of sex, made him almost as cranky as me. Because despite my best efforts, he still couldn't perform while his sister was home and awake. Between her flu, her new schedule and her apparent insomnia, that left us with Friday and Saturday evenings while she was at work. It embarrassed him, so he wouldn't talk about it, and that meant that there was nothing to be done. Except to count the hours until the weekend. And hope that he'd get over it. Soon.

After a few weeks Rachel's hormones seemed to settle down. She was still moody, but she kept mostly to herself instead of taking it out on Brian and me, so that, at least, was something. And on the Saturday before Christmas I was brave enough to venture upstairs to invite her to the upcoming Bellows' Family Christmas Gathering. It would be our first one since the Wicked Witch had flown away—France, as it turned out—and for once I was looking forward to hosting it.

Rachel let me in. It was spooky being in my old apartment, seeing all of my stuff still there. Rachel's stuff was all packed away in Jeff's garage. It would stay there until she moved out again or until I got around to bringing mine downstairs to Brian's apartment. And the place wasn't a mess like I'd expected. My log cabin quilt was lying in a heap on the couch, the television tuned to *Tom & Jerry*. Except for that and some dust, the apartment looked oddly unlived in.

I turned my attention back to Rachel. She was groggy-eyed, swaying a bit. Her hair was matted down on one side and the cording from my couch pillow was imprinted onto her cheek. She grabbed hold of a kitchen chair to steady herself. "What time is it?"

"Eleven-thirty."

She squeezed her eyes shut tightly for a few seconds, shook her head then finally managed to focus on me. "I musta fell asleep watching TV."

"Maybe if you went to bed at night you wouldn't sleep all morning."

And maybe I could get laid.

"How am I supposed to sleep at night? My schedule's all fucked up. Days one day, nights the next. Fuckin' Zeke—"

"Zeke loves you, which is the only reason you still have a job at all. I would've fired your ass if you'd gone off on me the way you did to him."

"Yeah, yeah…whatever. I already got that lecture from Brian. I don't need it from you."

Something that was almost guilt colored her face as she said it, though, so I dropped the subject and plunged straight ahead with the invitation. She nodded absently and said she'd be there, as long as she didn't have to dress up for the occasion.

"It's not formal. But," I gave her a quick up and down that wasn't subtle at all, "it might be nice if you wash your hair at least once between now and then."

"Well, get your ass downstairs, then, and let me take a shower."

I clomped down the fourteen steps and back into the kitchen. The sugar cookies I'd baked were cool enough to frost. Green and red icing with little silver candies. I was nearly halfway done when Rachel came in and sat down beside me at the table. She smelled nice, like jasmine. She watched me frost four of the cookies with green then picked up a knife and went to work with the red.

"Where's Brian?"

"He's doing some last-minute shopping. Although I'm pretty sure that means he's doing *all* of his shopping."

She laughed heartily for some time—as though it was the funniest thing I'd ever said—and told me I was probably right. Then she became Chatty Rachel. Told me funny stories about dimwitted customers. Chubby women who ordered greasy cheeseburgers and then a diet soda; fathers who looked longingly at the double doors, wishing they were watching football and drinking beer at Zeke's instead of watching their kids gobble pizza and play video games;

idiot teenagers who paid for snacks with loose change, then were impatient when it took her a while to count it out.

She laughed at all of them and I laughed right along with her. It had been a long time since I'd seen her so chipper, since Thanksgiving Day, and I asked her if the holidays always did that to her. She only shrugged. She ended up eating more frosting than she spread, but I was too relieved that her moodiness had finally subsided, not to mention that her appetite had returned, to let it irritate me. After the last cookie was frosted and I was up to my elbows in dirty dishes, she said she had something important to tell me. I grew concerned.

"Okay," I said, bracing myself.

"Tess, I've decided I'm gonna be a lesbian."

It was my turn to laugh heartily, because it had been a while since I'd heard a really good joke, but I stopped when the cup hit my head. Fortunately it was plastic.

"Quit laughing at me."

"You're serious?"

"Yes. I am."

"You've decided you're gonna be a lesbian."

"That's right."

"*Decided.*"

"Yeah."

"Ah. So…you're attracted to women?"

"Well…"

"I think you'd better figure that one out, Rach. Because if you're not attracted to women, I'm pretty sure they're not gonna let you in the lesbian club."

"Tess…"

"What? Isn't that sort of the number-one rule?"

"You're making fun of me."

"No I'm not. Well, maybe a little. But I just don't think you're a lesbian."

"Why not?"

"Because. If you were, and I asked if you were attracted to women, you would've said *Hell yes* or at least *sometimes* or maybe even *a little*. Not *well*...in the same voice Brian uses when he's about to try a new vegetable."

I waited for her to say something, but she didn't, so I turned my attention once more to my dishes. Rinsed the bowls, put them in the dish rack, pulled the plug, and let the water drain out of the sink. I had to replace it. The remnants of red and green frosting had turned it a color that reminded me of blood. Then I filled the sink up again and started on the silverware.

"What if I'm a lesbian and I just don't know it 'cause I haven't tried it?"

I dried my hands on a paper towel and turned to look at her again. I knew why she was asking, knew exactly what this entire conversation was really about. And I knew I had to deal with it, for real. Not just stand in front of her making lame jokes and avoiding the issue, hoping it would just get magically better on its own. Or just go away. So I leaned back against the counter and tried to figure out how to say what it was I wanted to tell her without sounding preachy.

"Look, Rach. I don't know how it works. Okay? I don't know why we're...attracted to certain people. Or what makes it so some people are gay and some people aren't. But if you like men...well, you can't flip a switch and change just because you think you want to. Or because you're afraid. Any more than Zeke could change just to shut those assholes up."

She stood up, wandered over to the window, and looked outside. It was cold, but there was still no snow to show for it. It made it seem even colder.

"Listen to me," I said. "Most men aren't like Tim."

Or like your father.

I wanted to say it. Probably I should have. But I didn't know how many worms she could handle at a time. Or how many cans of them I could juggle.

"I know." She was still looking out the window.

"No. You don't. But believe me, most of them are nice. Some of them are even better than nice. And, I swear, Rachel, if you just give it time you'll find one of those guys. Because you're a good person and that's what you deserve."

"You said that already. You've said it a million times."

"Well, I'm saying it again. And I'll keep saying it until you believe it."

She sighed heavily and finally looked at me. Her eyes were so dark. Dark and gloomy, just like the sky behind her. "Tess...I couldn't have that baby."

"I know, Rach."

She shook her head. "No, Tess. You don't."

"Well...I know you were afraid of Tim. And that you didn't want to be tied to him for the rest of your life."

What would that have been like for her? Kim and Laura each saw their husbands when they looked into their children's eyes. They saw love. What would Rachel have seen? What would she have remembered? Every time she saw those eyes...

She didn't say anything, just yawned and rubbed her own eyes with the heels of her hands. I didn't bother to warn her about smudged mascara, because she wasn't wearing any. She hadn't worn any makeup since her appointment. Or done anything more to her hair than pull it back into a half-hearted ponytail. She hardly bothered to take care of herself at all. She looked like shit, and if she hadn't already missed so much work I would have suggested she call in sick.

"What's your schedule today?" I asked.

"Three to midnight. But I think I'll head out now."

"Why? It's not even twelve-thirty."

"Yeah, but if I get there early Zeke might let me punch in early." She yawned again, scratched her arms vigorously and said, "Oh, Tess...I just remembered...I mean, I really hate to ask it, but...is there any way I could borrow twenty bucks or so for gas? Just till Friday."

"Oh, sure. Hang on."

I walked into the bedroom and grabbed my purse from the top of Brian's dresser. Dug through my wallet, sighed, then headed back out to the kitchen. Rachel was standing in front of the food cupboard with her hands in her pockets.

"Well, I've only got five in cash, but..."

I was about to offer her the use of my debit card. *Fill 'er up, Rach. Early Christmas present.* It was on the tip of my tongue. But—

What is she hiding in her pockets?

—it meant giving her my PIN number. Access to my checking account. Savings account.

What the hell could she have in there, you idiot? Do you think she's stealing cans of Brian's Chef Boyardee?

All of my money. Everything.

I cleared my throat and finished the sentence this way: "...I can follow you into town. I gotta get some groceries anyway, and we can stop at the gas station."

"No. Actually...never mind. I'll fill up on the way home with my tips."

"Come on, Rachel. It's no big deal. Besides, you're getting pretty low on food up there. You need to use your tips to buy groceries."

I knew, even before I finished the sentence, that I'd blown it. I couldn't tell if it was fear or anger that clouded her face. Probably it was both.

"Have you been goin' through my shit upstairs?"

"*No.*" She didn't believe me and I didn't blame her. After all, I had seriously considered doing just that on more than one occasion. "Rachel, I mean it. I haven't been. It's just that...I've hardly seen you bring home any groceries. That's all."

"So you've been *watching* me? What the fuck is this, a prison?"

"Excuse me for being concerned about you."

"Well, don't be. I eat at work and sometimes I bring stuff home from there. That must be why you haven't seen me bringing home groceries. And...anyway, just cut it out."

I nodded. Looked at the table. At the red and green cookies.

"Well, I'm gonna get goin'."

I nodded again. Told her to have a good day at work. Even though I knew she wouldn't. She liked Zeke—she loved him—but she hated working there. I didn't blame her. And before she left I made her take the five. It made me feel like an idiot, because it was barely worth a gallon and a half of gas. She hesitated for a moment, looked at Abe—who stared up at her with a quizzical eye—then tucked it away in her pocket. She threw back a quick *thanks* without looking at me. Then she went upstairs. A few minutes later she got into her car and pulled away.

I checked the cookies. The icing was hard, so I placed half a dozen of them on a plate for Brian. I put the rest in a Tupperware container and hid them under the counter, in the back, behind the pots and pans. Then I sat at the table and stared at the phone. I wanted to call Zeke. I almost did. But that's when I heard it. Brian's truck.

So I pasted on a smile and met him at the door. He was empty-handed, but I tried to peek over his shoulder so I could see into his truck, to get a glimpse of what he'd bought. Futile, of course. Even if none of the gifts in there were for me—and, of course some of them were—it was That time. Rachel was gone and so it was time to have sex.

He lifted me up, into his strong, strong arms, and kissed me, full of passion and fire and tongue, just how I loved it. Then he carried me into the bedroom and tossed me onto the bed. And I tried to enjoy it; I tried really hard. Because Saturday Sex was better than Friday Sex, always. Friday was quick and frantic, just pent up horniness and frustration from a week of going without exploding onto the sheets. Saturday was always slow and hot and beautiful.

But as I was lying underneath him I wasn't thinking about his gorgeous body or his breathy, warm whispers. Not about his rugged hands or hot lips and tongue or even about how much I loved him. I was thinking about Rachel.

Because even though Zeke was a good guy, he was a businessman. And even though he liked Rachel—even though he loved her—I couldn't imagine him giving her any overtime. I knew that business was slow. Because when there's a choice of either paying the oil bill and buying Christmas presents or taking your family out to eat, the diner is going to lose. *Oh, yes, Brian...right...there.* Every time. But Zeke might be taking pity on her, because she'd missed so much work. Due, of course, from having to recuperate from a medical procedure. And then coming down with a very nasty stomach flu shortly afterwards. That's tough for anyone who works for minimum wage, especially around the holidays. *Oh, Brian, I really do love it when you kiss the inside of my thigh. Just like...oh, just like that.* And besides, she barely had enough money for gas, let alone for any recreational haze. But of course, I knew. There are other ways of paying for haze. Lots of ways that boiled down to one. And now that the Lake Kids were gone there was only one place, really, for her to go for that. One person...

That's when I knew that Brian must be getting tired, and it just wasn't going to happen; not if he stayed down there all day long. So there was only one thing to do and I'd never done it with him before. Ever. I grabbed his head gently, just like I always did, and I gave him a show. Tried to think of how it was—exactly—I sounded when it was happening for real, all the groans and grunts and quick, light breaths. But it wasn't something I'd ever paid attention to. I did my best, and must have been convincing, because before long his body was on mine again and his breath was warm and tangy on my face. And by then I really was thinking about how very much I loved him. I really was. Even as I was still worrying about Rachel.

When he was done he flopped back down on his pillow, and I snuggled in close beside him. Told him how good it had been. Because, really, it would have been if I'd been able to get into it. And once he caught his breath he rolled over onto his side and said:

"I gotta ask you a question."

I nodded. I was ready for it, had been expecting it for weeks. I even had my answer prepared:

No, Brian. Of course it's not weird. It's probably just leftover guilt from that night when your dad left her alone and you were out getting laid. It's okay. Really. You'll get over it soon. Everything will get back to normal. Soon. I understand. It really is okay…

"Was Rachel right? Are the windows really drafty upstairs?"

"Uh…oh. Um, I don't know. Yeah I guess they are, actually. Most of the time I was up there it was warm weather, but…it was a little chilly last spring."

"That's what I thought." He grabbed a wad of the blanket and wiped some sweat off of my stomach. "This house is wicked old, you know. It's kinda falling apart. It needs new insulation, the pipes are rusty…the water pressure sucks, too."

"Yep."

"And I've been thinking that…maybe we should start saving some of our money together. So we can build a house of our own."

"Uh…"

Saving. Together. House?

I blinked. Then blinked again. "Oh. Well…I…that sounds…"

"A little out of left field, huh?"

"No. I mean, yeah. But."

I looked at him. Looked right into his eyes. He wasn't scared and I knew why. He didn't know that *together* and *we* and *our* are scary fucking words. Not yet. And I hoped—really—that he never found that out. Because it was a lesson he could only learn from one place. One person.

It was a big step. Huge. But he thought we were strong enough and I believed him. Because there was something besides the eyes. There was his heartbeat. And it told me something even more important:

Safe. You're safe with me. I'm strong, I can do it...

So I said:

"That sounds perfect."

Because it did. Sounded like exactly what I needed. He kissed me again, gently, and said that he loved me. And when I said it back I meant it.

I stayed in the bedroom while he wrapped presents in the living room. And while he struggled with paper and tape and ribbon I struggled with *Zen and the Art of Motorcycle Maintenance.* Because I'd never really given the thing a fair shot. If Tiffany Kendall could read it, then I sure as hell could too. And when he was done with the presents he burst through the door, tossed my book aside and we made love again. Beautiful and hot, and this time I didn't have to fake it. Because I knew.

Rachel was all right. Really. She was doing fine and would only get better. Stronger. It was almost Christmas, and today she'd actually smiled. She'd even laughed. And after Christmas was the New Year. A fresh start. That's what she really needed, what everyone needs. And then would come spring and summer. And someday—someday soon—she'd be educated. Making Something Of Herself. Happy. Someday soon.

CHAPTER 29

Christmas Day.

It was the first time Brian and Rachel had celebrated a real Christmas since long before Wendy died, so we'd gone a little overboard with decorating the tree. Brian had brought in a blue spruce from the back woods that took up nearly half the living room and we had covered it with so much tinsel and lights and popcorn and cranberries that you could hardly tell it was a tree at all.

Rachel shocked us by crying when she opened Brian's gift and shocked us even more by telling me that she loved me when she opened mine. And as I watched her try on the jacket I tried not to remember the real reason I'd bought it. Then we spent the rest of the morning preparing Christmas Dinner. I kneaded the dough for rolls, Brian stuck cloves into the ham in lopsided rows, and Rachel cried some more while she peeled the potatoes. She said it was because the three of us together felt so much like a family. And she'd never really had that before.

My family arrived just in time for dinner. There were no awkward pauses or desperate glances across the table for rescue—just normal, pleasant conversation. My dad, for once, did most of the talking. He told us about his new computer, and said that he'd recently started playing chess online with people from all around the country. It made him think about doing some traveling after the divorce was final, because he'd never been outside of Maine. It wouldn't be long because my mother had agreed to split everything with him, fifty-fifty. It surprised him, he said, because he hadn't expected kindness. Hadn't expected Going Down Without A Fight. Not that my dad would have fought her. He would have taken whatever crumbs she'd given him and that would have been that.

When everyone was finished eating I piled the dishes in the sink. They could wait until later, because there was no reason to hide behind a wall of soap and suds. And for a moment I had a glimmer of what my childhood might have been like if She hadn't been there. If every holiday had been just like this one. Even so I wondered—for just a moment—what Christmas was like in Europe. If there was snow in France. If there were spruce trees and tinsel and smiles. Or if she was eating her Christmas dinner all alone.

Brian brought his chess board out from the bedroom closet and waited for my dad to finish "getting a breath of fresh air" so they could play while Kim and Rachel sat on the porch to talk about nursing school. There were programs Kim knew about where students could trade the hospital *this* many years of work for *that* many years of school. They were having their discussion on the porch because I'd asked Kim, privately, to keep Rachel away from Matthew. Because even if not having a baby really is the right decision for a woman—whether by taking a pill to prevent it or by driving to Portland to stop it—sometimes there's still regret.

But right now regret was gone for me, so I joined my brother and my nephew in the living room. Dave was reading aloud from a new ABC book, a gift. And the card had read:

To Matthew. From Aunt Tess and Uncle Brian.

Matthew smiled and held out his little arms to me, tried to wriggle away from his father so his Aunt Tess could hold him. I balanced him on one leg and took over the reading.

L. I looked right at Matthew and said the letter slowly. He watched my tongue slide against my teeth as it made the sound. So I said it again. "L…lollipop."

I made the "pop" pop for real and he rewarded me with a big laugh.

"M…monkey."

It was my turn to laugh, because the picture showed a monkey who was so giddy that I had to wonder if it was one of those hippie chimps from the Congo, the kind that are always getting laid.

"N…nest. O…ostrich."

Ostrich. A funny-looking bird with a fat, feathery body and long, long legs and an even longer neck. But no head. It was buried in the sand. And for a moment I wondered why the author had chosen an ostrich. I thought about how much better, how much easier, life would be right now— right this moment—if he had chosen an Octopus instead. Or an Oboe. Or maybe even Osteoporosis. I kept right on reading the alphabet to my nephew, didn't even miss a beat. But even as I told him about Peas and Queens and

Raccoons I was thinking about Signs. The ones I had been ignoring for weeks. Ever since Rachel first moved in.

Because you can spend a few weeks telling yourself that the only thing responsible for your friend's moodiness is hormones. That when a friend has had an abortion, moodiness—sometimes even insane, psycho bitchiness—is normal. Expected. And when, at the same time, that friend begins to vomit and have diarrhea and chills, it's perfectly natural to believe that she has caught a stomach flu. Even when you live in the same house and you haven't caught it. Even when no one else you know—and no one else your friend works with—has caught it, either.

And when, a week or so later, that same friend's moodiness and stomach flu vanishes nearly overnight that makes perfect sense, too. Time goes by and hormones start to go back to normal and viruses die or move on. And if that friend starts sleeping more than usual, well there's a logical reason for that too. The reason is probably that the friend's work schedule has recently been changed. Days one day, nights the next. That explains your friend napping and nodding off during the middle of the day. Even when, a few minutes earlier, she was jumpy and restless and irritable.

There are lots of explanations for all of the things we don't want to see. And that's one way to live. That's just fine. As long as you don't mind getting sand in your eyes.

And so I read to my nephew and visited with my family. But the whole time I was blinking and rubbing. The sand from my eyes. And while everyone else was eating leftovers for supper, I pulled Kim into the living room to ask her a question. Because when you're a nurse there are certain things you know. I wasn't quite sure how to broach the subject, so I started this way:

"So...what did Rachel have to say about nursing school?"

"Well...she didn't have much to say about anything. Mostly she nodded and grunted and tried not to fall asleep."

"Oh. Well, she's been working nights a lot lately and—"

And.

And, and, and...

How many "ands" are there, Tess? How many excuses? Are you still trying to convince yourself she's all right? Just how the hell are you supposed to help her this way?

Kim shook her head. "Tess, just look at her. You know what's going on as well as I do."

I looked over my shoulder, into the kitchen. The guys were talking and laughing and stuffing their faces. Rachel was staring at her mashed potatoes, chewing on a thumbnail. Her legs were crossed underneath the table and both feet were bouncing up and down, just like my dad's had done earlier when he was getting antsy for a smoke. She looked up at the clock, then back at her plate. She was waiting. Counting the minutes, probably the seconds, until my family went home. Until she could make her escape upstairs. Until she could escape from everything...

I faced Kim once more and this time I asked her the question I'd wanted to ask before.

"What do you think it is, Kim? What is she on?"

* * *

When the last goodbye had been said and the red tail-lights from Dave's minivan had faded away, Rachel said, "See ya later," and bolted upstairs.

It was seven o'clock. On the dot.

Brian and I sat at the kitchen table. We talked for a few minutes about what a good time we'd had and how much we looked forward to the next time we could spend the day with my family. And it felt good to say those things and really mean them. But the whole time we were talking I was listening to Rachel. Waiting for the right time. Her foot-steps had brought her into the bedroom. Then into the kitchen where she had turned on the faucet. Then into the bathroom. After the toilet flushed she wandered into the living room and plopped down on my couch. And—right now—she was spacing out. Nodding off. Looking at noth-ing. Feeling nothing.

And that meant it was time.

I cleared my throat. "Rachel left her gifts down here. I think I'll bring 'em up."

"Just stay down here and relax, Tess. It can wait till tomorrow. You've had a busy day."

"I'd better do it now. It's chilly tonight and she might want those slippers."

He shrugged and stretched noisily. "Okay. I guess I'll start the dishes."

I grabbed the gifts and climbed the fourteen stairs. It took her a while to stumble to the door and let me in. I dropped her stuff onto the table, took a deep breath and turned to her.

"I need you to sit down."

She gave me a drowsy smile. "What?"

"You heard me. Sit. Down."

She didn't even hesitate. Grabbed the closest chair and parked her ass.

I ran my fingers through my hair. I needed a moment to settle down. Because facial expressions and body language are important. Sometimes fear and nervousness can be perceived as anger. And Rachel needed to know.

I'm not angry with you. Not at all.

So I knelt down on the floor, looking up at her instead of hovering over her. It made her giggle. I sent up a quick prayer—

Please help her, God…she really does deserve it…

—took another deep breath, and asked:

"What exactly are you on?"

She giggled again. "I'm on the chair."

"Stop it, Rachel. What are you taking?"

"Nothing. Well, I was taking a nap until you knocked on the door, but—"

I wasn't going to get anywhere like this, so I grabbed her arm and yanked up her sleeve. Then the other one. There were no needle marks or bruises or blown veins, and that was good. But it wasn't good enough. Because there were long, red, raw scratches all over her arms. And Kim had asked me:

Does she scratch herself a lot? Because there's an almost constant itch…

I'd noticed the scratching before, but never thought anything about it. Why not? A person doesn't just itch like that for no good reason. Why hadn't I at least asked her about it?

But it wasn't the time to ask *what if* or *why*, so I examined her eyes, and saw what Kim had noticed right away. Pinpoint pupils. It's hard to see that sometimes when someone has dark, dark eyes, like Van Dyke Brown. Especially when your own eyes are filled with sand.

"Oxycontin. Right?"

She pulled her arms away from me and nearly fell out of the chair. I caught her in time and helped her lean back. Then I held her hands and looked into her eyes again, made her look into mine. Because I loved her. I really did. I loved her so goddamn much.

"Rachel, you need to get some help."

She looked away, stared at my hands. Holding hers.

"Listen to me. I'm not mad. I swear. I swear to God I'm not mad. I *know* you don't want to be like this. I know you tried to quit on your own after you moved in here. That's why you were sick. Right?"

She still wouldn't speak. Still wouldn't look at me.

"But you're gonna kill yourself like this. Either with the drugs or else Tim's gonna get at you again and—"

That got a rise out of her.

"I'm not getting it from Tim. I'm getting it...from some friends."

"I know that. But tell me, Rach, where are your friends getting it from?" There was only once place. One-stop shopping. "So they're buying it for you and you think that's not gonna get back to him?"

She sighed. She was having a hard time sitting upright and her head rolled slightly to the left. I stood up, hoisted her out of the chair, and helped her over to the couch, where she could slump more comfortably. Then I knelt in front of her once more.

"Listen to me. He's gonna find out. Hell, he probably knows already. And what's gonna happen when you run out of money? When your friends can't buy it for you anymore? What's gonna happen to you when the only thing you've got left to do is to go to him yourself?"

Tess, there's no such thing as weaning yourself off of it. It's too strong, even if they don't inject it. They crush it up and swallow it and it's just like heroin. It's that kind of drug.

Just like heroin.

You know, I'd do fucking anything to feel like that again...

"Rachel please say something. Please tell me that you'll let us get you some help."

She smiled an almost-smile. An I-don't-give-a-shit smile. Because she probably didn't. "I don't want any help."

"Rach..."

"It doesn't matter anyway, Tess, so why don't you just go on back downstairs. Go back to Brian. I know I'm a fuck-up and I know where this is goin' because I ran out of money already. I don't make enough to do it on my own and I took the last shit I had right before you came up here and I got nothin' to sell anymore. Nothin'." She chuckled. "Well, except that iPod Brian just got me. But I won't get much for that, so I'm fucked. And I know it. And I don't need you tellin' me about it."

It took me a moment to absorb everything she'd said. "Sell? What the hell are you talking about? What did you ever have that you could sell?"

She let go of my hands and scratched the insides of her wrists, then her fingers, before she said, "Your rings."

"What rings?"

"You had a ring in your jewelry box in the bedroom. I sold it to a guy at a pawn shop in Westville."

I opened my mouth, but there were no words. None in my brain or my heart or on my tongue. Nothing.

"I'm sorry, Tess. I really am."

And she probably was. The real Rachel was probably dying deep inside there, somewhere. Ashamed and guilty. But not this Rachel. Not the one I was looking at right now. She said it again anyway.

"I'm sorry, but I was out of money and I had fuckin' nothin' left and I had to have some. I couldn't...I was out. And I know you don't wear expensive jewelry, but I thought maybe you still had an engagement ring hiding in your jewelry box, 'cause some women hang onto 'em. But you didn't, so I took the only thing you had that looked like it might be—"

She was still talking, still saying lots of words, but I didn't hear any of them. Because my heart was shrieking, shrieking, fucking shrieking, so loudly that the only thing I could hear was Jason's voice:

Any woman can wear a diamond ring, Tess. But not you. You're too beautiful for just a diamond.

Until I heard the words:

"—and the guy at the store thought he could sell it to this jewelry store in—"

"Rachel...wait. When did you sell it?"

"Friday, after you left for work. I didn't want to, but I used up the last of my tip money, and it wasn't a pay week so I—"

Friday. She'd stolen my ring and sold it. To buy drugs. And then she'd frosted sugar cookies with me on Saturday.

427

She'd even asked to borrow more money. Just like it was nothing. And she was still talking. Still. Even though the room was spinning and cold. It was frozen, frigid. Because winter was here. For real.

"—but I'll pay you back, Tess. I swear. The guy gave me fifty dollars, but I know it's probably worth more than that, right? So I'll—"

"*Fifty. Dollars?*"

That did it. She finally stopped talking, because even through the haze she knew.

She was in some deep shit.

"He gave you...fifty fucking dollars for that ring?"

...I have loved you forever...

"Rachel, that *was* my engagement ring."

Watermelon tourmaline, emerald cut. Pale, pale pink and the palest spring green, swirled together into one beautiful gem. It was surrounded by tiny, delicate diamonds and set on a thin, gold band. The clasps that held the gemstone in place had always reminded me of Jason's hands. So that when I was wearing it, it felt like he was right there with me. Even when he wasn't.

"Jason had that ring made for *me*. He...because... Rachel, that was a custom. Made. Ring."

"Oh."

"*Oh?*"

"Don't worry, Tess, I'll pay you back. I can—"

"Rachel, I don't give a fuck about the money. I don't care about money at all."

I had, honestly, no idea how much the ring was worth. How much Jason had paid for it or what kind of money it might bring now. As far as engagement rings go it was probably a bargain. But it didn't matter. I didn't care. Not then and especially not now, because it wasn't the money. It hadn't been for Jason, either. He would have paid whatever it cost to get me any ring in the world he thought I'd like.

It's why I couldn't wear it anymore, why it had been sitting in my jewelry box for over a year. Because it was the ring that meant I Love You, More Than Anything. But I had saved it anyway because there was always Someday. When the hurt and sadness were gone for real and it might just be a beautiful ring. And I might be able to wear it. But even if I could never put it on again there was always Passing It Onto Someone Special. It might have been Cassidy. Or even Rachel.

Right now—right now—someone else was wearing my ring. It had probably been a Christmas present. And that Someone would never know the story behind it. The story about a man who had loved a woman so much that he thought she was too beautiful to wear just a diamond. So he searched for a stone that was as colorful and lovely as he thought she was. Then he took her on a summer picnic in a field of wildflowers and gave her that ring. And when he asked her to marry him it sounded like this:

"There was never any color in my world, Tess. Not until I fell in love with you."

And they made love in the wildflowers, in a fragrant breeze of pastel petals. They loved each other for a very long time and they were very happy. Until the love went away. But even after the love was gone she still had the ring. A whisper of summer. Because that's what Jason was. Summer. Just like Brian was Fire.

How many hits had it bought Rachel? A day's worth? Maybe? She'd traded my ring for a day of haze and now it was gone. The ring and her drugs, too. And she'd need more. Once the haze wore off and the ground returned, along with the shaking and puking and chills and diarrhea. She'd stolen my ring and it wasn't enough. It would never be enough.

So I took a deep breath and let it out with a loud, clear, ringing cry. Not a cry for revenge; a cry for help. Because she needed more help than I could give her. More help, even, than the name I called out could give her.

"Brian!"

But at least he'd make her get it.

CHAPTER 30

Christmas night. Hospital emergency department. I sat in the same waiting room where Dave and Jason had sat seven months earlier, while Alice's weak heart had stopped beating in one of the cold, white-tiled rooms down the hall. It might even have been the same room where Brian and Rachel were waiting—right now—to see the doctor who would send Rachel to detox. And then to rehab.

If she agreed to go.

I looked around me. The place was buzzing with people. Car wrecks and suicide attempts and, probably, other addicts waiting for detox and rehab. And there were other injuries, of course, other sicknesses. Mundane things. A kid with a broken arm who cried on his father's sleeve; an old lady with a bad cold who coughed her germs into the air instead of onto a tissue or a handkerchief; a sad, worried girl who was holding a tiny bundled baby closely against her chest.

She was only about sixteen. Her diaper bag was clean, but old and worn out—even though her baby couldn't have even been a month old—and her coat looked even worse. She looked exhausted and scared and she was all alone.

With a sick baby. No parents or boyfriend or husband. On Christmas night.

I wanted to ask her if she was all right, ask what was wrong with her baby. An ear infection, maybe, or a cold like the gross old woman, or possibly a bad reaction from a vaccination shot. I didn't get the chance to ask, though, because a tired-looking woman, who I recognized as Registration Lady from the nurses' desk, trudged in and called her name. Or it might have been her baby's name. The girl tucked the kid in a little closer, grabbed the diaper bag, and followed Registration Lady into the corridor. She disappeared from sight, off toward a room where she would wait for another eternity to see a doctor.

I flipped through a magazine and read an article about an actress—*a very brave actress*—who had gained twenty whole pounds for a movie role. Critics had hailed it as her Best Performance Yet. The article mentioned that, with the help of a gang of personal trainers, a yoga instructor, her very own chef, and months of Sacrifice, she had been able to take off the offensive baggage in time for the premiere of the movie. And on Oscar Night she would stroll down the red carpet wearing a gorgeous, one-of-a-kind, haute couture gown with shoes that matched and a million-dollar diamond necklace.

She wouldn't pay for them, naturally, because movie stars don't pay for anything. Plastic-faced women on the television would say *ooh* and *ah* and gush about how fabulous and elegant she looked and how proud they were because she was *so brave* for having *ballooned to one hundred and thirty-five pounds* and how much of a Sacrifice she had made in order to slim down in time for Awards Season.

Then they'd ask *who are you wearing* and she'd tell them with pride and everyone would be happy. Dress designers and jewelry designers who would delight to hear their names broadcast to a billion viewers worldwide. Television executives who would crow about big ratings and big, big money. And, of course, the actress would be happy. Because she got Attention. And even if her portrayal as a fat-ass trailer park mother wasn't rewarded with a heavy gold statue, she could always comfort herself with knowing she was the Best Dressed Actress at the Academy Awards.

I tossed the magazine onto a table, leaned my head back against the wall, and closed my eyes. Thought about Bravery and Sacrifice. Thought about Brian, who was sitting with Rachel inside a cold, white tiled room. He'd been sitting with her like that for years. And the lonely girl with the sick baby in another room—a room that was just as white and just as cold. Parents who were whispering comforting words to bruised and broken children. Old ladies who had probably raised families and yet were sitting alone in a hospital, suffering from bad colds. Waiting. All of them. Waiting for doctors and nurses and registration ladies who'd been here all day, on Christmas day. Filling out insurance forms and making phone calls to pharmacies; setting broken bones and giving shots; looking down infected throats and up runny noses; diagnosing sick infants and giving guidance to teenaged mothers. Referring depressed people to the psych ward and drug addicts to detox and rehab. And somewhere, in homes nearby, there were husbands and wives and children whose wives and husbands and parents had been away from them all day. On Christmas day.

I fell asleep and didn't know it. Not until Brian shook me, gently, and whispered my name. I blinked myself awake and looked around the room. Sick Old Woman and Broken Arm Kid were gone, replaced by a different kid with a towel pressed to her ear, sitting beside her mother. Then I looked at Brian. His eyes were red and wet and exhausted and that's when the guilt came. Guilt. Because I'd fallen asleep while Brian was awake and worried and crying and tired. Because I hadn't admitted to myself sooner that I knew Rachel was addicted to drugs and now it was going to be that much harder for her to stop. And guilt, still, about leaving her alone. So she could get beaten and raped and knocked up by a sadistic asshole.

Leaving her alone is what was bugging Brian, too. Because Rachel had agreed to detox and rehab. And while I was asleep Brian had followed a doctor who had wheeled her away to another wing of the hospital. She was shaking again, shaking already, even though there was still Oxycontin in her system. Shaking, he said, because she was afraid. Afraid of the shaking and chills and puking and diarrhea that were yet to come. The aching in her body and brain because every cell inside of her would be calling out for her to give it what it wanted, what it needed. *Just. One more. Please?* Afraid of Judgment and Condemnation. Mostly, though, she was afraid of being left alone. But Brian had left her anyway. And his guilt was worse than mine.

I held his hand. "You're not leaving her alone. You're making her get help."

He nodded, but I didn't know if he believed me.

"Why don't you let me drive home. You look like shit."

"No, I'd better do it. The clutch in my truck is really sensitive."

It was, but I'd driven it before. I didn't argue, though, because I knew what he meant was that he needed to drive. Needed to be in control. Of something.

Before we left the hospital I stopped by the Registration Desk and asked about the girl with the baby. Asked if they were okay. And, of course, Registration Lady couldn't tell me anything. I looked over her head I saw that they were still in a room, talking to a doctor. So I reached inside my purse and pulled something out.

My dad's Christmas gift to me had been a card. It read:
Tess, use this to pay a bill so you can spend your own hard earned money on more important things. Like crayons.

So I did.

I asked for an envelope, put Benjamin Franklin inside and wrote down the name I'd heard in the waiting room. Handed it to Registration Lady.

"That girl dropped this in the waiting room earlier. Could you see that she gets it?"

She smiled, but said nothing, which was a relief. I waited until I saw that she'd really gone into the girl's room before I grabbed Brian's hand and led him out the door.

We rode toward home in silence, even though there were a million things to talk about. Questions for him to ask and answers for me to give. And, of course, Condemnation and Judgment and Anger. All I could hope for was that it wasn't too much. That after it was done there would still be an Us.

When we reached the sign that read, *Welcome To New Mills,* he turned left instead of right and I didn't ask him why. I just sat beside him, still silent, and waited. It was a three-mile drive down the roughest road in town, but he didn't slow down. Because at the end of the road was the cemetery.

It was cold outside. Cruel, frigid winter, but there was still no snow. And it made it feel even colder. I stuffed my hands inside my coat pockets, because I'd forgotten my gloves, and followed him to the headstone. Her name stood out clearly, illuminated by the headlights of Brian's truck.

Wendy Jane LaChance

The dates underneath her name told us that she really had been much too young to die. And that reminded us that life wasn't fair. He stared silently at the stone for a long time, so close to me that I could feel him shivering. That's when I started to breathe again, when I knew that we were going to be all right. Because even though his conversation with his mother was a silent one, and even though I would never know what it was he was saying to her...I was still standing beside him while he was saying it.

When he was done he looked up at the sky, up toward heaven, and I followed his gaze. But there were no stars. They were covered by clouds that refused to give us snow. So he turned to me and asked a question. It wasn't the one I was expecting.

"Tess...how old are you?"

It was the first time he'd asked since that night on the couch.

"Thirty-five."

He nodded. "It's been almost a year since I first met you. It will be in March, anyway. So, have you had a birthday already and just didn't tell me? Or is it coming up?"

I cleared my throat. "It was the day after Thanksgiving."

He was silent. Doing the backwards math. It took him even less time than I thought it would. "You brought her *there*...on your birthday?"

"It doesn't matter. It would have been just as hard if it was any other day."

He shook his head. "I shouldn't have let you take her at all. It should have been me."

"She needed me there with her. And she wasn't going to let you do it anyway, because..."

I took my hand out of my coat pocket and gripped his as tightly as I could. Thought again about the three piles of pictures, and how I could explain them to him.

"Brian, there are some things that Rachel's gonna need you for. And some things that she needs to do on her own. And then there will be things that she's gonna need help with...but not from you."

He looked again at Wendy's grave, at the place where his mother wasn't. And then he asked me the question I'd been expecting before.

"Did you know she was taking that shit, Tess? Did you know and just not tell me?"

"No. I asked her and she said no. And I thought..."

But I couldn't lie. Not to him and not to Wendy. So I took a deep breath and I told them the truth.

"I knew. But I didn't want to know."

He squeezed my hand so hard that it almost hurt. "Me too."

Then I waited for him to ask me about the rest, about Tim. Because if he asked I would tell him. And if he didn't I wouldn't. Because I need to keep his burdens as light as I could for as long as I could.

If Brian knew what had Tim had done to her, for all those months and especially after he and Jeff had beaten him senseless, he would kill him. And it wouldn't change anything. Rachel would still be shaking, just like she was now. And tomorrow and the next day and for a week—and maybe even longer—she'd be hurting and sick and dead inside. Praying to God to kill her for real. To put her out of her misery. But after that there would be Pain and Heartache and Guilt. And some time after that there would be Healing. Home and Love and Safety.

That's when Brian would probably have to know about Tim. That would be the time for protecting his sister. Because Tim knew everything. He must know. To Rachel, Haze was a time and place for confession. And if she had told me about stealing my ring while she was in that haze then she must have told her druggie friends about the abortion. And somehow, if it hadn't already, it would get back to Tim. And he would try to get to Rachel. Power. It's what he needed. And what she'd need to be protected from. Someday soon.

But right now Brian was the one who needed protection, so I said nothing. And when we were home and in bed I held him in my arms and waited for him cry. Because he needed that even more. But there were no tears. Even though he was awake and shaking. Even though he was thinking about Rachel and about his mother. And that's when I knew. When I knew for real.

It was winter. Cold, cruel, frigid winter.

CHAPTER 31

Day after Christmas.

Buzzing alarm clock. Bright red numbers. Because there's always Work. Even the day after Christmas. Even the day after you've abandoned your sister in a cold, white hospital. Even when you know that—right now—she's in hell and there's nothing you can do about it. So after Brian clicked the button that made the buzzing go away, and after he rubbed his eyes against the dim morning sun, he did the only thing he could do to make everything else go away.

He fucked me.

Rough and noisy and sweaty and desperate. His eyes were open and he was looking at me, but he wasn't really seeing me. Wasn't really seeing anything. Fucking, not making love—even though I knew he loved me. A distraction. Something soft and wet and hot that *feels good, feels so good, feels so fucking good.* Fucking just to drown it out, wash it all away. All the words in all the voices that had never let him just live, guilt and burden and exhaustion that had been crushing him forever.

And so he fucked me forever, trying to make it go away. And even though I understood, even though it was all right—because I'd been there before myself—I knew that it wasn't really all right. Not for him.

I'd been there before myself.

He wasn't all right after he was done and he wouldn't be all day long. Because he'd swing his hammer and listen to its pounding, listen carefully to each strike against the wood, every thump-bang-knock-tap-smack. Then the power tools, because that was even better. Saws and drills and compressors, whining and hissing and whirring, and that was loud, too, but not loud enough. Because none of it would drown out the voices or wash away the burden.

And after he was done working he pulled his truck into the driveway and burst through the front door. He looked at me without really seeing me, and his eyes were shrieking. I knew before I even saw them what he wanted, what he needed, but I couldn't help him. Because Cassidy was there. She'd been there all day because of Christmas vacation. And when he saw her sitting at the table, eating the second to the last of the Christmas tree cookies that Rachel and I had frosted only a few days earlier, he stumbled. Because he'd forgotten it was Tuesday.

He made a recovery of sorts, the kind where you slip on a mask and smile, and he sat down beside her. Ate the last cookie. And I knew it was one that Rachel had frosted because it was red. Laura knocked on the door a little while later and when I let her in she asked about Rachel. Brian made a brief reply and stayed in the house while I walked

Laura and Cassidy to their car. She asked if she should send Jeff over and I said, *wait till tomorrow.* Because today Brian needed something different. So I watched them drive away then I walked back into the house and gave him the Something that he needed.

He fucked me again, right in the kitchen. Right against the counter; the same place he'd threatened to do it our first night. His mouth tasted like sugar and he smelled like sweat and dirt and sawdust. And right before he came, which was right after I did, I felt his tears on my cheek. Then I cleaned myself up and drove into town. Because there's always Work. Even when it's the day after Christmas. Even when your boyfriend—even when the man you love— is being crushed under the weight of lives and responsibilities and problems that aren't his. Even when you know that—right now—he's in hell and there's nothing you can do about it.

And so I went to work. Bleach and brushes and dust rags and other chemicals that burned, always burned, my nose and eyes. Then the vacuum. The noise that used to drown out all the words in all the voices inside my head. But now it added another voice instead. Two of them and they were both shrieking. So I looked at the carpet, at the dirt that disappeared and at the lovely lined pattern that took its place. And still there were the voices. And the ticking clock. The clock that said:

5:47.

And that meant that it had been twenty-two hours and forty-seven minutes since Rachel had last swallowed the Something that made all the words in all the voices inside her head go away. And—right now—she was in hell. Because the voices were back, along with the shaking and aching and nausea and soon it would get even worse. Right now she hated me and Brian and she loved us, too. Mostly, probably, it was hate. And I wondered, not for the first time, if Wendy really was looking down on her. On Brian. On me. If her heart was shrieking, too. If she hated me for leaving her daughter alone. For letting my eyes get filled with sand.

Then there was home. The front door. And I wasn't sure what to expect when I opened it. Because he'd been alone, listening to the ticking clock, the sound that's hard enough to bear when there are hammers and saws and flushing toilets and vacuums on top of it. But when all you can hear is the ticking…that's when it's just too fucking much.

I opened it up and walked inside and he was pacing. All around. Like a wild thing caged. When he heard me he turned, looked into my eyes, and this time he saw me. I took a deep breath and held it. Waited. To see what the words were going to sound like.

"She stole your ring."

I swallowed. Let out the breath with: "I know."

"No. You don't."

And that's when I did. Even though I'd already known. *…I sold your rings…*

Rings. Plural. Because he'd had *that* piece of jewelry, the one that was really a question. But before he could ask it there was another one he had to ask, a question about saving and building and The Future. Our future. And when he had asked it I'd said yes. But I'd hesitated.

He kicked the wall. Kicked it again. Kicked it until his foot went right through. He yanked it out, left behind a huge, gaping hole, and when he did he fell back against the table. His empty supper plate fell onto the floor and broke into three pieces. He looked at them, at the pieces of blue and white plate, for just a moment.

"God *damn* it! God damn it all to fucking hell!"

He stepped on them, hard. Then again and again. Crushed the three pieces until they were in dozens. Of pieces. Just like he was.

He kicked aside some of the plate rubble and looked at me with deep, hurt eyes.

"It was my mom's ring, Tess. It was her grandmother's, Memé Rose. And it belonged to *her* mother first. She gave it to my mom because my grandparents were fucking assholes and they kicked her out when she got knocked up. Because my father was such a goddamn loser that he couldn't afford to buy her one."

Not a loser. A broke teenaged boy who'd gotten his girl-friend pregnant. And he had no one to turn to because his family was too busy worshipping at the altar of Jack Daniels to have the time or the money—or the inclination—to help him out.

"It's not like it was a huge diamond or anything. Probably not as good as the one Saint Jason got for you—"

"Brian, please. Let's not go there..."

"—but it was a nice enough ring. It was pretty. It was silver and it had this...it had a..." He struggled to think of the words to describe whatever it was. "I don't know. Some sort of scroll or something. I don't know what the fuck it's called."

I knew what it was called. I cleared my throat. "Filigree?"
He took a step back. Blinked. "Yeah. I think so. Maybe."

I could almost see it, or at least I had a general idea.
Quick backwards math. Memé Rose's mother; Brian's great-
great-grandmother's ring. That would have been in the
early 1900s, probably. I knew a little bit about the Edward-
ian Era because of Jason. He had always loved going to the
antique shops on the coast, even though we rarely bought
anything, certainly never any jewelry. But I'd seen enough
of it to know that Brian's ring was probably platinum, not
silver. And he had no idea what he'd had in his possession.
Depending on how intricate the filigree, how big the diamond—depending on a lot of things—that "nice enough
ring" was probably worth a couple thousand dollars at least.
And it didn't matter. The money wasn't the point. Neither
was the diamond or the platinum or the filigree, although
it was probably a beautiful ring. Probably the most beautiful ring in the world.

It was the History. Family. Memé Rose. She had loved
her granddaughter and wanted her to have something
that was beautiful. Even though she was a teenager and
pregnant. Even though the boy she was marrying was
broke and came from a bad family. Maybe that's why she'd
given it to Wendy. Because she was beautiful and wild and
deserved so much more than what life was about to give
her. At least she could have that one lovely, rare, expensive thing...

And Rachel's pawn shop guy must have known how
much the ring was worth. Knew exactly what it was he'd had
in front of him. How much had he given her for it? The
druggie loser girl who was back with her second stolen ring

in as many days. Shaking. Desperate. He'd given her fifty for mine, so he may have gone as high as a hundred. But probably not. And it was long gone by now. Sold to an out-of-state antique dealer. Or maybe it was up for bid on Ebay. And soon someone else would be wearing it. Instead of me.

But Brian had already moved on, back to Rachel, which is where my mind needed to be. And he was still pissed. Pacing again, all over the kitchen. And ranting. She didn't have to steal it. He'd asked her if she wanted it. *Asked* her. Because it was her family, too, and she should have it if she wanted it. But she'd said, *No, what would I do with the fucking thing?* Then, less than a week later she'd looked where she knew he must have hidden it, the only place in the world that was safe from my eyes and my ever-present dust rag. In the food cupboard, behind the Chef Boyardee. She'd stolen it. And sold it. For a couple days of haze.

He wanted to call the cops. Call them about his mom's ring—the one he'd called mine only a few minutes earlier—and about *the other one*, too. Because that's what Rachel really needed. Consequences. If she didn't learn sometime then she'd end up a fuck-up for real, just like their father. Maybe, he said, she already was and he'd just been fooling himself. Because she'd acted just like Rick already, and even worse. Stealing and lying. Fucking lies. Every word from her fucking mouth. Ungrateful and self-ish. She had *no idea* of what he'd done for her, didn't give a shit about what he'd given up. Family and Love and Sticking Together. Those things had meant something to her, once. What had happened to *that* girl? Where the fuck had *she* gone?

And then he remembered. He picked up a chair and hurled it at the wall. The two front legs busted off and it landed on the floor in a loud heap. But it wasn't enough. He picked up his glass and just before he hurled it to the floor I noticed the white ring of milk clinging to the bottom. It shattered as it hit, but neither of us flinched. And he stood there for a long time, surveying the destruction. First the chair, then the pieces of broken glass and broken plate. They mingled together in a spiky, warped mosaic on the linoleum. He swore again and kicked it out of his way. Most of it went under the stove. Then he grabbed his coat and his keys.

"I'm gonna kill that fucking bastard."

"No! Brian—stop—"

But I knew it was a futile mission. Even if he wasn't nearly a foot taller. And ten times as strong. I followed him out to the truck anyway, pleading and begging and pulling at his sleeve. For a brief moment I debated whether or not I should stand in front of the truck, try to block his way out. But even in that moment I knew.

It wouldn't stop him.

I ran back into the house, even before he was out of the driveway, and grabbed the phone. Dialed the number of the only person in the world who might be able to stop him from killing Tim. And when I hung up the phone and I knew it would be all right. Jeff could do it. He'd either talk some sense into Brian or he'd beat him senseless. But either way it was gonna be all right.

And while I waited I swept the floor. The glass made a clink-crash-smash sound as it slid across the floor that almost—if I concentrated on it hard enough—sounded like bells. And when I moved the stove away from the wall it made a louder sound, almost like a car horn. Then more bells, because of the glass underneath the stove, and more honking as I shoved the stove back against the wall. Dumped all the glass into the trash can and it still sounded, in my mind, like bells...

I knew I should clean, because it's what I did. What I did best. But there was nothing, really, to clean. Not downstairs. So I went upstairs to the apartment that wasn't mine anymore, because I knew that there'd be something to clean up there. Something. And when Rachel got home, once she was better—which wouldn't be *too* long a time, after all—then she'd want a clean apartment.

Up the stairs, fourteen of them, and I counted them all out loud. Because the sound of my voice was easier to take than the sound of hers in my mind.

Just so I could sleep, Tess...

And I had believed her.

No you didn't, you chickenshit liar. You knew.

I did. I knew. I just didn't want to know.

I started in the bathroom. Toilet-shower-sink. But before I mopped the floor I checked the medicine cabinet. There was nothing in there. And after I mopped I checked the kitchen cupboards. I made the bed, then the nightstand drawer. I found nothing until I looked through the dresser, in the underwear drawer. But it wasn't what I thought I'd find. It was a wire-bound notebook, a journal. A pretty pink cover with tiny white flowers.

Tess, please talk to me. Say something. Anything...

But now I needed to listen, to hear Rachel's voice. The real Rachel. Not the girl who stole and lied to keep the demons away, but the one who had lived behind all that. Hiding. Scared. Alone. And I found her in the words she'd written.

Some of it was just mundane, daily routine. Observations on life and people. Customers who'd been rude and guys who were cute. But most of it was deeper, almost like poetry. Lovely and heartbreaking words. Donny was there and I discovered she'd really liked him after all.

I love his eyes. They smile even when he doesn't. Even when he's tired and sweaty and greasy.

A few days later she fucked him. And then she let him go. Even though he was nice and good in bed and even though she thought she could fall in love with him.

It was easier for me to say goodbye to him than it would be if I had to hear him say it to me later. Because he would have.

Her father was there, too.

Brian was right. He's just a fucking loser. But I wish he'd call again anyway. Even if it's just to say hello. I wonder why he doesn't love me?

And, of course, Brian. She'd written about him a lot. And he was wrong, because she knew too well what he'd given up for her. Education and money, girls and fun. Freedom. Careless youth. Having a life, a real one. And it was more than she could bear.

I wonder if it would be easier for him if I just disappeared?

After she started up with Tim most of the words didn't make any sense, because she'd written them in the haze. Not words about beauty and rainbows and stars. They were dark and menacing. Vermin and rodents that bit and sucked and lived off of blood. Branches that came to life after the sun went down and scratched and scraped on the windows, trying to get inside. Buildings that were locked from the outside, leaving helpless children inside to suffocate alone.

And then there were passages she'd written after she'd moved into my apartment. It was a history of her summer with Tim. Drugs and sex. Violence and humiliation. Lucid confession. A message. To me? Brian? God? Whatever the case, it was painful to read.

When Tim was with her she got it for free...at first. Until she was hooked. And then he made her beg. So she did. She begged him for it, please, please, Daddy, please, and that was good enough for a little while. Then the pain started. But always, after the pain, was the haze and that meant the pain didn't matter. It didn't exist. And when that got old he made her *take it in the ass* because he knew she hated that. But even that wasn't enough and it got worse, so bad I had to skip part of it, three full pages. And then, two times, he'd whored her out. The first time to some guy she didn't know, to pay off a bet. The second time was one of his buddies. He made her fuck him just so he could watch. Just to get his kicks. And she did. Because if she didn't it meant there was no more haze.

And then came the kid who died of an overdose. The funeral had brought her a glimpse into her future, and that brought the Great Debate to her door: Die in the haze or live in the cold, scary world? And before she'd even made her decision, Brian and Jeff made it for her, the day they gave Tim a taste of violence and humiliation. Then he'd taken it out on her. I skipped over that part, too, because hearing it once was enough.

And that's when she wanted Change. Wanted it badly, and she tried to stop. But she couldn't. She used her rent money and food money and bill money. Everything she could scrounge up. Stole from the tip jar, other people's tips, then the cash register. Little bits, here and there, covered over with cash out receipts. But it was just a matter of time, she knew, before Zeke figured it out.

And then the day she discovered she was pregnant. By the time she noticed she'd missed her period—two of them—she was already nine weeks along. And no money. She'd tried to save, but she needed it for the haze. And if Zeke hadn't found her, if he hadn't called me, if I hadn't taken her to Portland, taken her into our home…

I probably would have just killed myself. Maybe I should have anyway.

And that's when I knew what the journal was for after all. Because that's where she'd scribbled a note to herself:

Read this. Read it every day. And don't fucking do this again. You don't deserve it. You deserve better than this.

It was the last thing she'd written. And then she'd hidden it away in her underwear drawer. And sometime later—maybe even the next day—she'd gone out. And she fucking did it again.

That was her summer. For Brian and me it had been the birth of everything beautiful. Love and joy and sex and fun. For her it was months and months that were worse than hell. And she'd gone back for more anyway.

I should have known. She was right upstairs, right here. Right above me while she was suffering. She was angry, too, so it was easy for me to keep my distance. But I should have known. Should have done more, said more. Even if she'd used my words to comfort herself during that time of withdrawal it wasn't enough. She should have heard those words in my voice, for real, every day. Ten times a day, a hundred. Every time I saw her. Or maybe if I'd told her about the soil, told her the same thing I'd told Cassidy...maybe then she'd be all right. Maybe she would have opened up. Let me have a glimpse of all of these powerful and vulnerable feelings that had been inside her. Underneath the tough, angry, irreverent mask. Underneath the hard ground.

And that's when I began to pray, for the first time since the night I'd screamed at Him in the woods. And even as I did I knew God wouldn't hear. Because this is what it sounded like when I prayed:

Please, God, please let Brian get to Tim. Let Tim die. But first let him suffer. Because he deserves it. Just, please, please, please don't let Brian get caught...

As soon as I finished I knew my prayer hadn't been answered. Because that's when I heard it. Brian's truck. I looked out the window. Jeff's car was right behind it. I tossed the journal underneath the couch, ran down the stairs without counting them, and met Brian and Jeff on the porch. There had been a fight. They were both bruised and bloody but Jeff had won. Because Brian looked worse. And because he was home.

Brian gave me a quick kiss and said, "I gotta take a shower." Then he turned back toward Jeff. "See you tomorrow."

Jeff only nodded. He waited for the front door to close behind Brian before he said, "He's gonna get drunk tonight."

"I know." Because sometimes you really do need the haze. "Are *you* okay?"

He grinned and touched a deep cut on his forehead. "Oh yeah. This is nothing."

"You should clean up before you go home. You'll scare the shit out of Laura and Cass."

He washed his cuts in the kitchen sink—the same sink that Brian had used just a few months earlier to wash his father's blood off his hands. Then I gave him a quick, tired hug and thanked him for kicking Brian's ass. And after I watched his tail lights fade away, I looked at the clock. Again. Because I still heard the ticking.

8:24.

Twenty-five hours and twenty-four minutes. And Rachel was still in hell. So was Brian. When he was done with his shower he opened his liquor cabinet and pulled out a bottle of Jim Beam. We drank it together in bed, because it was much too cold to sit on the lawn outside. And there were no stars out anyway. I let him drink most of it and before he got too drunk I told him I was sorry I'd hesitated when he'd asked about building our future. Told him I loved him, more than anything. He said it was okay. And that he knew I loved him.

And as he got drunker he talked about Rachel. How she'd always been angry and sad, ever since he could remember. He should have done more, he said, to help her. Should have told her he loved her because he didn't think he had ever said it. So I told him that next week, next Tuesday, he could say it. Because that would be the first day we could go see her. Our first visiting day. And he said I was right. And that he loved me.

"You're so smart," he said. "You're wicked fucking smart."

Except that he really said *smucking fart.* And so we laughed. Like drunk people laugh. Laughed for a long, long time. Just like it was the last time.

CHAPTER 32

It snowed overnight, but just a little. Just enough to coat the ground in a light, white dust. It was gone—melted—by seven-thirty. And it made it feel even colder.

Brian woke up stiff and sore and bruised from his fight with Jeff, and with a hangover. But, of course, there's still work. And the banging and whining and hissing and whirring that hadn't blocked everything out on Tuesday still didn't block it out on Wednesday. Neither did the headache and the nausea of his hangover, because it only reminded him that the hell Rachel was in was worse than his. When, after an hour and a half, he finally gave up and came home, he was still in hell. The kind where you lie in bed and moan, and then dash to the bathroom and lean over the toilet and puke. Then you lie on the bathroom floor and watch the ceiling spin and pray to die. But, even through all that, there are still the voices and the burden.

I was in a hell of my own, but not the same kind. Tuesday's hell had been easier. Cassidy had been with me, which forced me to wear the mask. The kind where you smile and pretend that life is fine, that everything is going to be all right. And, after a while, you start to think that maybe it is.

But with a light work day and no Cassidy and no mask, all I had were voices—the ones that came from having read Rachel's journal. They mingled with the voices from my own life, two radio stations struggling to broadcast over the same frequency. And it made me wish for Brian's hangover. Because then I'd have Pain and Nausea to distract me.

After a supper we didn't eat, the Burkes came over for Penny Poker, even though it wasn't Sunday. Brian won five hands in a row. It pissed him off because he knew that Jeff was letting him win. Jeff just shrugged and rubbed the cut on his forehead and the bruise on his cheek. Then he looked at Brian's black eye and the cut on his lip and let him win some more. And when they got ready to leave Brian's eyes were a little panicked. Because once they left there would be no more distraction. So I said:

"Why don't you let Cass spend the night? That way you don't have to come back here in the morning to drop her off."

All five heads nodded and smiled at that. Cassidy would have Novelty. Brian and I, Distraction. Jeff and Laura would have the house to themselves which meant Sex with Noise, as much as they wanted. It was a concept I'd taken for granted until Rachel had moved in.

So our Wednesday Night became Disney Channel Night. Brian gave Cass an old T-shirt for a nightgown and we told her that she could stay up as late as she wanted. She fell asleep on Brian's lap at 10:25. And that meant it had been fifty-one hours and twenty-five minutes for Rachel. I wondered how bad it was getting for her. If she still hated Brian and me.

With Cassidy snoring on the couch and Brian's hangover mostly gone there was only one thing left to distract us.

And so we had sex in the bedroom with the door closed. It was quiet but good and it made us both tired enough to finally fall asleep. Still there were voices, even in my dreams.

And then Thursday, exactly the same as Tuesday. After Laura picked up Cassidy we had sex. Again. And it was all right. Maybe even a little better than all right. But not much.

Then it was Busy Friday. Real estate office and Dr. Stephens's office and then, of course, Zeke's house. I spent my lunch break watching stupid game shows and even stupider soap operas and trying not to listen to the ticking clock. Then, finally, it was time to clean the Kendalls' camp.

I'd been back every week since I'd stolen and returned their gun, and every week it beckoned from the top of the den closet. The beautiful silvery nose and the sturdy black grip and the lovely engraving that said *Undercover 38 SPL*. And on this day, a day when Distraction was a necessity, I tried to imagine what a freshly fired revolver smelled like. In my mind it was like woodstove smoke, only metallic. It made me wish for my too-big boots and extra clothes; made me grateful for the heavy, thick gloves in my glove compartment and the big black trash bags that waited for me in the Kendalls' kitchen. If I wanted them. If I was strong enough.

But then: reality. The reality that comes when you pull into a driveway and—once again—find cars that you aren't expecting to see. Two cars this time. Mr. Kendall was back in town early. And he'd brought company.

3:30. On the dot.

I walked to the kitchen door and found it locked. The cleaning lady can't go through the front door, not when her

Client is home. Not even when she has a key and a code. So I knocked. Then again. Knocked a third time and, finally, it opened. But it wasn't the cook and it wasn't George or Tiffany Kendall. It was a man who looked about my age. He had a sour, snobby face and wore a light-blue sweater, probably cashmere. It reminded me of Baby Powder Fresh deodorant. He gave me a look that made me think he knew I'd recently stolen and returned the Kendalls' gun for the purpose of committing a brutal murder, then he asked, "What can I do for you?"

He was looking at a shabbily-dressed woman with a bucket of cleaning supplies in one hand and a canister vacuum in the other, the hose coiled loosely around her shoulder. And he had to ask what he could do for her.

I cleared my throat. "It's Friday. I'm here to clean."

He gave me a quick up and down and, apparently satisfied that I was telling him the truth, let me in. He gave my vacuum cleaner a quizzical eye and said, "I'd like you to leave the vacuuming for next week. We arrived from Connecticut only an hour ago and my father is asleep."

I gave a brief nod and waited for him to move his soft, useless ass out of my way so I could start dusting the dining room. He didn't. He just stood, rooted to the spot. Staring.

I hate that.

Finally he spoke again. "I don't suppose you're a cook as well?"

"No, sir. Just a cleaning lady."

He gave me a faint smile. An amused air of superiority. I *really* hate that.

"Do you *know* how to cook?"

The Great Debate, the one that wasn't really a debate at all. He was a first-rate asshole, obviously. There were lots of words bouncing around in my mind, and some that I could actually taste. But there were two jobs at stake, and a very long winter ahead. So I said:

"Yes, sir. I know how to cook."

"My father decided to come up here rather hastily. Apparently his cook is out of town visiting family, so we're a little short-staffed here."

His tone made it obvious that he didn't approve of an old woman leaving town during the holidays to visit her family. Naturally, she should stay locked inside her home, waiting breathlessly, whisk in hand, on the off chance her employer might gallop into town a month early with his spoiled shithead son.

And he waited. For me to drop my cleaning supplies and my canister vacuum, don a frilly apron and prepare him a feast. I smiled sweetly and said, in the thickest, most dim-witted accent I could manage:

"Sir, Mrs. Pelletiah didn't leave no food in the cub-bahds, 'cause it'd just rot right away. If Mrs. Kendall makes up a list I kin run down t'market aftah I'm done cleanin' and fix you guys up somethin' wicked good f'suppah."

He scoffed and rolled his eyes, but not because of me or my accent. "*Mrs. Kendall* isn't here. In fact, you won't be seeing her again."

Did she find herself another sugar daddy? Or did she get caught with the pool boy? I tried to smother my grin, but it was too late. He noticed.

"Excuse me, Miss…"

I cleared my throat. "Mrs. Dyer."

He glanced at my empty ring finger. Still didn't notice the heavy bucket of cleaning supplies that it was helping four other fingers to hold. Then he scoffed again.

"*Mrs.* Dyer, my father is in a very vulnerable state at the moment. He came up here to recuperate, not to shop for a new wife."

I dropped my bucket. Bit my lip, hard, so I wouldn't laugh. Even though it really was the funniest thing I'd heard in a long time. But he wasn't amused.

"I can imagine that for someone like you this might seem like a perfect opportunity to improve your lot in life."

I un-bit my lip.

Someone. Like. Me?

Two jobs, Tess. Not just yours. Brian's, too. And not just this job. All the jobs you've got in all the camps over here. Year-round jobs and summer jobs. All over the lake. His jobs, too...

So I picked up my bucket. Swallowed. Took a deep, deep silent breath. In through the nostrils. "If you'll excuse me, sir, I've got work to do."

But he didn't move. He just looked at me. The look that was really a word. The look—the word—that I knew all too well. Then he cleared his throat and said, "Before Tiffany became my father's third wife she was a waitress. And his second wife was once our cook. So I know all about the kind of *work* women like you...do."

Women. Like me.

I closed my eyes briefly and when I opened them again I thought the room would be spinning; but it wasn't. It was blurry, though. In fact the only thing in the room—the only thing in the world—that was in focus was this man's ugly face and the expression on it. I took another deep breath, the kind that wasn't silent, and I let it out with:

"Fuck you. *Sir.*"

I turned around. Dropped the bucket again, this time on purpose. Grabbed the doorknob with my free hand, the one with no ring, and opened the door. Then I picked up my bucket and walked out on the job that paid well and on time. I shoved the bucket and the canister vacuum into the back seat and started the car.

3:41.

And that meant it had been ninety-two hours and forty-one minutes. For Rachel.

I drove home quickly and hopped in the shower. It was Friday so Brian and I were going to Zeke's. Not just because there's distraction in Routine, although there is, but because we didn't want Zeke to think we were pissed at him. He'd had to give Rachel's job to someone else. Just temporary, he'd said. Just till she gets back. Till she gets better. But we knew the truth. And we couldn't blame him.

The phone rang while I was getting dressed. Mr. Kendall, Senior, full of apologies for his son's behavior. It was a relief, of course, because I really couldn't afford to let the job go. And Brian couldn't afford to let the job go, or any of the others, because of me. So I smiled, even though Mr. Kendall couldn't see the smile, and when he begged me to reconsider quitting I opened my mouth to tell him I'd stay on.

And then he said it.

"I'll double what I'm already paying you."

I grabbed hold of the chair that was leaning against the wall, waiting for Brian to fix it, because the room was spinning and nothing was in focus. And through the fog I searched for words that were Polite. "I'm sorry, Mr. Kendall. Unfortunately my schedule is just too full right now."

There was a long pause. Then he said, "Excuse me, Miss Dyer?" He sounded irritated, almost angry. I didn't know he was capable of it. "Are you saying you won't come back to work for me?"

Of course I couldn't say that. Not to this man. Not to his money. Because I really did need it. And because there was still Brian's job to consider. So I closed my eyes, took a deep breath, and said, "No, sir. I'm sorry. I only meant…I only meant that a raise won't be necessary, sir. I'll be back next week."

"Very well, Miss Dyer."

I hung up the phone without another word, then opened my eyes—

You fucking whore.

—and let go of the chair. Grabbed my coat and my purse. Even through the fog and the spinning room I could hear the ticking clock. The ticking that told me just how bad Rachel was feeling. Right now. I looked at my hand and wondered if hers was shaking, too.

Brian wasn't at the bar when I got there, and that was good. I hadn't had a chance to really talk to Zeke since before we brought Rachel in and there was something I had to know.

"Do you mind if I ask you a question?"

"Go for it."

"It's kind of rude, so feel free to tell me to fuck off."

"I always feel free to tell you that."

"I'm glad to hear it." I took a couple strengthening swallows from my beer then plunged ahead. "When did you know you were gay? For sure?"

"I was ten years old. The Dukes of Hazzard gave me a hard-on."

"Bo Duke?"

"Yep."

I nodded, because I'd had a crush on him at that age, too. Outlaw with a heart of gold. Blonde and blue and hunky. Fast car, exotic accent. What's not to love?

"Are you asking because you're curious, or is there something you're trying to tell me?"

I shook my head and didn't smile, even though his joke was a funny one. "It's not me. I just," I sighed. "It's something you *know*. Right? The same way you know you like Oreos or—"

"It's just the same as *you* knowing that *you* like men. It's just like *that*."

"Yeah, but what if—"

"Rachel isn't gay. She's scared of men right now, but that doesn't make her gay. If that's what you told her, then you got it right."

I smiled weakly. "She talked to you, too."

"Yeah, she did. And I told her pretty much what you did. But that doesn't matter right now. What matters is that you know that Rachel is where she is because of what *she's* done. Choices that *she* made. Not because of anything you said or did, or didn't say or didn't do."

I shook my head, because I knew that wasn't true. "Zeke...the first time I met her was right behind that counter out there, behind those doors. Right *there*. She was stoned out of her fucking mind. And I thought it was funny. I thought it was *funny*. And even after I knew better I still didn't—"

"Listen to me. You tried to help her. Okay? The rest was up to her. You did what you could. And that's all any of us can do."

I wanted to tell him that it wasn't enough. Because if it had been enough then she'd be okay. Right now she'd be standing behind that counter, rolling her eyes at customers. Hollering back orders and giving people their change. Bored and restless and hurting...but healthy. Nearly healthy, anyway. But I couldn't say that, or anything like it, because that's when Brian sat down beside me. He cleared his throat and, without even a *hi, how was your day*, said:

"George Kendall called me."

I just nodded and stared at my beer.

"I'm supposed to talk you into going back to work for him."

"I—"

"It's not his fault his son is an asshole. And he thinks you do good work."

I took a sip of my beer and glanced at Zeke. He set our supper plates in front of us then walked to the far end of the bar, pretending not to eavesdrop. Not that it mattered. He was going to hear the story from both of us at some point anyway. "I talked to him already. I'm going back."

"Oh." He sounded surprised, but relieved. "Good."

Good. Of course it was. His job had been at stake, too. But I said nothing, just looked at my watch. Six o'clock on the dot.

He waited until we were both nearly finished with supper before he spoke again. "Did you know that Tiffany signed a pre-nup?"

I shrugged. "Don't they all?"

"Probably. But she left him, even though it means she doesn't get a penny."

"Really? How do you know that?"

He laughed. His first real one since he'd climbed the stairs to save Rachel. "The lady in the camp next door to the Kendalls. I was doing an estimate there this morning and she was talking on the phone to someone she knows in Connecticut."

I knew which lady he meant. One of my Wednesday house jobs, a year-round lake family. And I chuckled. Because sometimes rich people talk about things in front of their carpenters. As if their carpenters don't have eyes and ears and a brain. As if they're not there at all.

"I guess all Tiffany gets to keep are any gifts he got her."

I nodded and filled my fork with celery while Brian finished his steak sandwich. And while I chewed I wondered how much money a Connecticut pawn shop would give her for all of those diamonds. Then, just like he'd read my mind, he said:

"She left all that jewelry behind, though. She said she didn't want it."

"What?"

He nodded and wiped the mayonnaise off the corner of his mouth. Then he winked. "The only thing she kept was some painting he got for her birthday last summer."

I gave him a smile, and it was my first real one since I'd noticed the sand in my eyes. Because Tiffany had seen it.

Not just a nice, pretty green that matched her wallpaper. She'd seen something that had made her strong enough to leave the cold comfort of a wealthy old man and grab hold of life. Before it was Too Late. And I wondered if it was Hope that she'd seen there or if it was Fear. Maybe, if I'd done it right, it was a little bit of both.

It made me wonder, too, why I hadn't been able to paint anything since then. Just sketches since the orchard. Sketches of the lake that was really Brian and me. I wondered until later that night, just a little later, when I followed Brian's truck home. The moon was out, two-thirds full, so I could see the lake clearly through the naked trees. It was cold. Gray. Frozen. I shivered and looked away.

And then it was home again. Home to the ticking clock.

CHAPTER 33

It snowed over the weekend. Real snow. All Saturday morning and afternoon and into the night. And so Brian spent the weekend plowing out driveways and parking lots, each one at least twice, and I rode beside him. We started late Saturday afternoon and didn't finish until very early Sunday morning. It was noisy and cold and beautiful, the most fun I'd had in forever. And when we got home we drank hot cocoa and then crashed on the bed in our clothes. I didn't think about checking the time until I was drifting off; fading away. But by then I was already asleep...

Until the phone rang. At first it scared the shit out of me, because I thought it was the middle of the night, and the only calls that wake you up are the kind that bring bad news. But just after it rang the second time I glanced at the clock and saw that it was 10:45 a.m. And I couldn't, for the moment, remember how many hours that meant it had been for Rachel. It turned out not to matter, because that's when Brian said into the phone:

"What do you mean she *left*?"

That's when a different counting began.

Rachel had checked herself out of detox at 10:32. And that meant, when the hospital called, it had been thirteen minutes since she went missing. At least, that's what it meant to us. Because to the cops—whom Brian called as soon as he hung up on the lady from the hospital—she wasn't missing at all. She was an adult who had checked herself into detox on Monday night and then checked herself out on Sunday morning. Another druggie loser girl who'd taken a shot at getting clean. And failed. So I said:

"Brian. Give me the phone."

"Shhhh…wait Tess, I'm—"

I grabbed the phone out of his hands, took a deep breath, and told the officer about Rachel's summer. About violence and humiliation. About the abortion and Tim's threats. And before I was done talking, Brian grabbed his coat and his keys and I knew where he was going. Because with no money and nothing to sell for a day of haze—except for herself—Rachel had only one person to turn to.

When I was done with the phone I ran up the stairs and reached under the couch, to where I'd hidden the only proof of Rachel's summer. Then I sped away, too. My cell phone rang before I was off of our road. It was Brian. Panicked. Breathless.

"He wasn't…Tess, he wasn't home."

I cleared my throat. It wasn't a time for explanation. Not yet. That time would come. Condemnation and judgment and anger. And all of it would be deserved. But right now was the time for something different.

"The cops are gonna look for her, Brian. They believed me and it was enough for them to start a search. And right now I'm on my way to make a statement."

"Okay."

But the State Police barracks was a half-hour drive in good weather.

"Are you gonna meet me there?" I asked. "Or do you want me to meet you somewhere so we can drive up together?"

"I...I don't know. I don't know what to do."

I thought for a moment, tried to figure it all out. Because I didn't know what to do either. There was no way to know where she was. She must have called Tim from the hospital before she'd checked out, begged him to meet her there. Promised him something, God only knew what. And that meant they could be anywhere. He could be doing anything to her—right now. Right now she was probably in pain and hell, whether or not he gave her the haze. Right now she might even be...

But right now I couldn't do anything about it. And there was Brian, who was in hell, too. "Meet me at Zeke's," I said. "We'll ride to Westville together and then—"

"*No.*"

I swallowed and tried to stop shaking. Sometime between the five seconds or so that had separated *I don't know what to do* and *Meet me at Zeke's* his panic had fled. Just like that. Next step: anger.

"Brian, please listen to me..."

But there was nothing. Just dead air. And when I tried to call him back I got nothing, too. So I headed for

Westville to do what I could, which wasn't much. I drove carefully because the roads really were bad. And even though I didn't give a shit if I slipped off the road and died in a bloody, painful wreck it might mean that Rachel's voice would be silenced forever. The voice from her journal and her real voice, too.

It took me forty minutes to get there and when I did I showed the officers the journal. Let them hear her voice for themselves. Pointed them toward what was the most important, the most coherent. Then I told them about the bruises I'd seen. Gave them Zeke's name and phone number, because he'd seen them, too. And when they said she should have reported the abuse and the threats I told them about her fear of Retribution. About Tim's ex-wife, about restraining orders that did no fucking good when you live in a town with no god-damn police station and when the nearest State Police Barracks is half a fucking hour away on a good day. The officer in charge smiled sympathetically and told me they'd do what they could, that I was free to go home. Which meant, of course, *get the hell out of here because we've heard all we need to hear from you.*

So I did. And when I got home it was 3:14. And that meant it was four hours and forty-two minutes since Rachel had gone missing. I checked the messages. There were lots of them from Zeke and Laura, but none from Brian and none from the cops. I called Laura first and she told me what I'd already figured out. Brian had picked up Jeff and they were looking for Rachel. Or for Tim. And I knew what that meant. So before I called Zeke—and turned down his invitation to hang out with him at the bar—I called Dave. Because he's a lawyer. And before the dust settled I knew that, unless the cops got to Tim first, Brian would need one. And I called him because he's my brother. And I needed to hear a voice that loved me and would tell me that everything would be all right. And he did; he said it.

"It's going to be all right, Tess."

I nodded and tried to believe the words, even though Dave had no way of knowing whether or not it was going to be all right, Tess. If Rachel was going to be all right. No way of knowing if she was in pain and hell, right now. Or if she was dead. Right now. Right now while I was breathing and blinking and talking to my brother who loved me. Even though he'd never said it.

And then I sat on the couch and waited. For a knock at the door. For the phone to ring. For anyone to call. Brian especially. I listened to the ticking clock. Looked out the window at the snow bank Brian had made just a few hours earlier. It was glowing in the moonlight and it made it feel even colder. Finally I lay down on the couch and listened to the ticking clock. I looked at my hand and hoped that Rachel's was shaking, too.

At 11:07 the phone rang. Twelve hours and thirty-five minutes since Rachel had gone missing. It was Jeff.

"The cops found Tim."

"Where is Brian?"

"He's on his way home. He should be there any minute."

"What about Rachel?"

"They...she wasn't with Tim. Brian will tell you when he gets home."

That's when I heard it. Brian's truck. So I hung up the phone. Walked into the kitchen. Leaned back against the counter. And waited. Because this was it.

He slammed both doors on his way in, the one on the porch and the one in the kitchen. Stood still and silent. Glaring at me. For a very long time. And all I could do was grip the counter behind me. And wait. And even as I did I knew—I *knew*—that whatever happened it would never, could never, be as bad as what Tim had done to Rachel. Ever. That I would never know that kind of fear or be in that kind of danger with Brian. Even though he was angry and scared, more than he'd ever been or ever could be. Even though I really did deserve it.

Finally, he spoke.

"The cops found Tim. But he didn't have Rachel. They still don't know where she is because he says he hasn't seen her in weeks." He took a step toward me and I didn't flinch. "He said she called him this morning but he didn't go to meet her. He said he left his house right after that and that he's been with some friends. All day."

I nodded. Even though it was bullshit. Even though we both knew it was. Even though it meant she was probably dead by now.

He took another step forward. Kicked a chair that was in his way. Kicked it again. Bent over, picked it up, threw it against the wall. It was still in one piece. And he wasn't.

Here it comes.

And so did he. Right at me, right in my face.

"You knew. You *knew*! How could you know what he was doing to her? How could you know, all that time, and never tell me?"

"I...she..."

"You let her lie to me. And *you* lied to me. You fuck-ing *lied* to me! I was supposed to protect her, Tess. I was supposed to keep her safe. And I coulda done that. But you kept me in the dark, like some sort of stupid fucking animal—"

"She didn't want you to know, Brian. She...she was ashamed and she wouldn't let me tell you. She wouldn't let me do anything."

"*Let you?* Fuck you! You're smarter than that! I thought you were, anyway, but I guess I was wrong. So why don't you tell me, Tess. Might as well tell me now. Tell me *everything* you know. And, goddamn it, don't you leave out a fucking thing."

And so I told him everything, all the way from the beginning. From seeing Tim and Rachel together at Fran's to seeing him at Rachel's apartment the weekend Brian was fishing with Dave. Then what she'd told me on the way home from Portland. And I didn't stop talking until he knew about how I'd almost killed Tim. How I would have, if it hadn't been for Little Miss Seventeen.

"So I told him she had a miscarriage. I thought he'd leave her alone, Brian. I thought she'd be safe here with us. I thought—"

He backed away, finally, and gave me a bitter laugh.

"You thought. You *thought?* That's fucking hilarious, Tess. When the hell have you ever *thought?* About anything? All you did was close your stupid, fucking eyes just hoping it would all go away. Because that's all you *ever* do."

"No...not this time. I tried, Brian. Jesus, I tried. I love her so much and I wanted to—"

"That's bullshit, Tess. And all of this is your fault. It really is. You know, that, right? Do you know...do you know where she'd be right now if you'd told me all of this when it mattered? When I coulda done something about it? If you'd just let me kill that fucking bastard when I had the chance? Do you? I'll fucking tell you, Tess. She'd be..."

She'd be...where? Doing what? He couldn't answer it and neither could I. There was no way for either of us to know. Maybe she'd be safe. Upstairs. Watching television or writing in her journal. Lying in a haze, staring at nothing. Or in rehab or at work. Or out scrounging around looking for someone to fuck or something to steal or looking for someone, anyone, who could give her the Something that she needed. Doing anything for it. With whoever would have her. Maybe she'd be dead. Maybe she was dead already. Anyway. Right now. Either way. There was no way to know.

And because we couldn't know, there was nothing we could do. Nothing that he could do. Except look at me with cold hard eyes. And say:

"Just get the fuck out of my sight. I don't want to even fucking look at you. I don't give a shit where you go or if you ever come back. Just...leave."

He kicked the chair again on his way toward the bedroom. Kicked it twice. It was still in one piece and he wasn't.

Neither was I.

So I grabbed my coat and my purse and I left. Not upstairs. I couldn't go up there. I couldn't be where Rachel was supposed to be, but wasn't. And Brian didn't need to hear me up there. Not my footsteps or the television or the springs on the bed. So I got into my car and drove away. And I wasn't sure where to go.

I drove past the lake without looking at it. I didn't need to. It was frozen and it always would be. Instead I looked at the clock. It was 11:39. And that meant that Rachel had been...

It didn't matter. I knew. From now on there wouldn't be anymore counting hours. It would be days and weeks and months. And then years. I knew it. Already.

So I pulled into Zeke's, into the back parking lot, because Fran's was closed this late at night. The lot was packed, though, and that surprised me. Sunday nights were usually dead. I went inside anyway because I needed to talk to Zeke. Needed to talk to someone. Or maybe I needed to get drunk. Or find someone to fuck. Something. Anything. To make the ticking stop. To make all the voices that were shrieking inside of me just shut the fuck up.

When I opened the door it was noisy and more crowded then I'd expected it would be. Not just people sitting at the bar and at the tables. People standing and laughing and drinking. So many people that I couldn't see Zeke. Couldn't see anyone, really. Just People.

I clawed my way through, in between too many bodies that smelled like sweat and beer and liquor, until finally, through a small break in the crowd, I could see the television. And that's when I knew why Zeke's was so crowded. Another countdown. A different kind. Because I'd forgotten.

It was 11:51. It was only nine minutes until the New Year began. I knew it would be the worst year I'd ever have to live through.

I turned around and headed back toward the door. Because on this night I wouldn't be able to talk to Zeke. Or to anyone. They were too busy drinking and counting. And I was fucking tired of counting.

I clomped back toward my car, concentrated hard on the sound of the salt crunching underneath my boots. Jingled the keys in my hands, listened to that sound, too. But it didn't work. I could still hear—

Just so I could sleep, Tess...

—everything. The words she'd said—

...give fucking anything to feel like that again...

—and the words she hadn't—

I wonder why he doesn't love me?

—the ones I should have heard anyway. They mingled, still—

...not...

—with the words of my—

...worth it...

—own life. And I tried to push them away, all of them—

...I married you anyway...

—but I couldn't. Not this way. I needed something else, needed the other thing. My hand was on my car door handle, but I could turn back around and go back into the bar. There were lots of people in there, so many, who were lonely and—

...close your stupid, fucking eyes...

—scared just like me and I could do it, find someone. It didn't matter who, didn't—

...get the fuck out of my sight...

—matter at all—

...I don't even give a shit where you go...

—nothing mattered anymore.

I wonder if it would be easier for him if I just disappeared?

Except. For Rachel.

Rachel. My poor Rachel, my beautiful girl. And she's dead. Right now. I know it. No more laughing and breathing and eating red frosting. No more profanity in front of eight-year-olds who shouldn't hear it. No more loud footsteps and louder squeaky bed. No more haze. Unless being dead is just like the haze. Where are you sleeping, right now? Cold and dead in the snow somewhere? Oh God, oh Rachel...my beautiful, beautiful girl...

I was shaking so badly that I dropped my keys. I bent down to pick them up, still shaking. Trying to stop the shaking. Zeke's door opened and I heard, even above the ticking and voices and shrieking in my head, a loud, joyful cry; a cheer:

Happy New Year!

Even though it wasn't. Even though it wouldn't be.

And then a second sound came from down the road a little way, the sound I would have recognized above anything. The sound that meant I had to stop shaking, had to block out the ticking and the voices and the shrieking. I closed my eyes and clenched my jaw, my stomach, my fists...clenched everything. Swallowed hard. And pushed it all down. As far as I could. Because I had to be strong, or at least pretend that I was. At least long enough, maybe, to help Brian. To help Rachel. Because please, God, *please* don't let her die. Take me instead. Please...don't let her...

I waited. Waited. And it stayed. Down.

I took a deep breath and turned to watch Brian's truck as it pulled into the parking lot. He parked a few spaces past mine, because the lot really was packed. I walked over and watched him get out of his truck. And waited.

He'd been crying, but his eyes were dry now. He grabbed my hand and held it tight and I felt my heart start beating again. Because he didn't come here to fight some more. Or to break up or kick me out for real. He could have waited at home for that. I'd known the second I'd heard his truck why it was he'd driven outside in the cold while his whole world was falling apart.

But I said it first.

"I'm sorry. I didn't tell you and I should've told you."

He shook his head. "I think...I knew. I knew she was lying about something. And I knew you were covering for her. And I figured that Tim was...that she moved in with us because of him. But I didn't *want* to know and...Oh Jesus, Tess. She can't be dead. Please tell me she's not dead..."

I held him tight and let him cry on my shoulder. And while he cried I told him that Rachel wasn't dead. Told him that she was out somewhere, out there, lost in the haze. She'd found a way, somehow, to get some and eventually she'd come home. And we could help her again, this time for real. And I told him that—someday—she'd be all right.

I said all of it even though I didn't believe it. Even though I knew I was lying. Because as I was telling him that Rachel was fine, just fine—even as I was saying those very words to him—his world fell apart for real, even though he didn't know it yet. Because over his shoulder and through his truck window I saw them. Two State Trooper patrol cars. Their lights were flashing but their sirens weren't on. And, thankfully, Brian's eyes were closed so tightly that he couldn't see the blue lights that were headed away from the main road and off toward the lake. To our road. Our house. To tell us the truth.

But right now Brian needed Hope, even if was just a few more minutes of it. Right now he could spend those last few minutes believing that his sister was alive. Somewhere. And believing that—someday—she'd be all right. Because as soon as we got home he'd see Blue Lights and he'd know the truth. And from that moment on he'd start counting again. For the rest of his life. And so would I. Days and weeks and months and years.

Since Rachel died.

CHAPTER 34

Tomorrow it will be two months since Rachel died. And this is what we know:

At 10:19 p.m. on New Years Eve a seventeen-year-old girl named Emily Smart was brought by ambulance into an emergency room. She was severely injured in a car accident that she herself had caused while driving under the influence of alcohol and Oxycontin. For reasons unknown, her Chevy Nova swerved into the opposite lane, right into the path of an oncoming Jetta. The impact sent her car spinning on the icy roads, where it finally came to rest against a snow bank. Although she was wearing a seatbelt it wasn't buckled properly. As a result her liver and spleen were lacerated and she began to bleed internally.

The Jetta was being driven by thirty-three-year-old Lisa Atwood, who was bringing her six-year-old daughter, Samantha, home early from a slumber party. Samantha thought she was brave enough to stay away from home all night on New Year's Eve. But once the realities of the darkness set in, combined with too many ghost stories and a belly that ached from eating too many brownies, she thought it best to call her mommy. She wanted to go home so she could sleep in her own bed. Where she'd be safe.

When the Nova hit the Atwoods' car, it went spinning, too, from one lane to the next and then back again on the icy roads. It was hit again by an SUV that had already managed to miss it twice. Lisa Atwood wasn't wearing a seatbelt and was ejected from the car during its impact with the SUV. She was subsequently run over by the minivan that had been trailing the SUV a little too closely and was killed. By that time Samantha was already dead. She was sitting in the front seat, just like she shouldn't have been, and her neck was broken when the airbag deployed during the first impact. The one with Emily Smart's Nova.

So in the ambulance, when Emily Smart said, over and over, *I killed her, I killed her,* none of the paramedics thought too much about it. Neither did the doctors and nurses in the emergency room. Not until one of the nurses stroked her cheek gently and murmured something comforting in order to settle her down. That's when Emily Smart looked the kind nurse right in the eyes and said:

"He told me to kill her and I did. He gave me a gun and I blew out her brains. They're all over the snow."

Sure enough. There was blood on Emily Smart's jacket. Some of it was hers and some of it wasn't. And there were other stains. Stains that, like some of the blood, didn't come from Emily Smart. And right before she was wheeled into the elevator that would take her into surgery, and right after she prayed out loud for God to strike her dead, Emily Smart told a State Trooper where she had killed Rachel LaChance.

They found her less than twenty minutes later. Crumpled up, face down in the snow. Cold and dead. Alone in the woods, less than two miles away from the hospital. Because Emily Smart had been taken to the same emergency room in the same hospital where Brian and I had brought Rachel less than a week before she died. The same hospital where Rachel had signed the papers that admitted her into detox. The same hospital where she spent almost a week aching and shaking and puking. Trying to be strong. Trying to get clean. The same hospital where she had given up. Signed another paper. And made a phone call. The one that got her killed.

And even though several skilled doctors worked on Emily Smart inside of a cold, white operating room, she died, too. And when, at 12:45 a.m. on New Years Day, a very tall State Trooper sat beside me at Brian's kitchen table and showed me a school photo of Emily Smart, a photo her grieving mother had given him just an hour earlier, I recognized her right away. Only, in my mind, she would always be Little Miss Seventeen.

And now that she was dead there was no way to prove that the "He" she'd told the kind nurse and the overworked State Trooper about was Tim. No way to prove that the stolen gun she'd used to kill Rachel had come from him, either. No witnesses who had heard him tell her to kill Rachel. No proof, even, that the drugs she had taken, the drugs that had caused the car accident that had killed her and two innocent people, had come from him. No witnesses to anything at all. Nothing except for the half-conscious ramblings of one druggie loser girl and the semi-coherent journal entries of another. Even the fact that I'd seen Little Miss Seventeen at Tim's house one evening meant nothing, since he freely admitted to having been involved with her. She'd been over the legal age of consent, so even that wasn't a crime. And when he was asked about the call Rachel had made to him the morning she was killed, Tim said, with his lawyer sitting beside him:

"She called for Emily, not for me. I don't know what they talked about, and I have no knowledge of what happened after Em left my house."

So he was free, for now. And he was gone. Hiding somewhere. We knew the truth and so did the police. But what we know and what they know doesn't matter. All that matters is what they can prove.

And for a day and a half after Rachel was murdered, Brian did nothing but cry. Loud howls that came from a deep pit somewhere inside what was left of his soul. Anguish and fury and grief that ravaged through him, his heart and his brain and his gut, and it was so bad that I finally had to call Dr. Stephens. Because when a person cries for so long that there aren't any more tears and they keep on crying, crying until they puke, until there's nothing left to puke and even water won't stay down, then something needs to be done. And so Dr. Stephens came. Made a house call just like doctors used to do. He gave Brian something that made him sleep, and he slept for another day and a half. And he was still crying. Even in his sleep.

When he woke up he stopped his crying, picked up the phone and made arrangements for Rachel. Because that's what he had to do. There was a memorial service at the Grange Hall and everybody came and almost everybody cried. It was Zeke who talked to all of us about Rachel, not a priest or a minister, because we all knew that Rachel hated religion and churches. That she didn't believe in God. Except I think she did.

But listening to Zeke, who loved her more than he loved almost anything in the world, was better than it would have been if we'd had to listen to a priest or a minister. They would have told us about God's Will and about Not Losing Faith. Because, they would say, She's In A Better Place. And they may have even told us that we should Rejoice to know that she was in The House of Her Father.

Her father's house.

Instead Zeke spoke about a beautiful girl who was filled with joy and love and sorrow, with humor and pain and wonder. And hurt. He talked about friendship and family and love. How we should remember her and love her for-ever. Remember to love each other with hearts that were full and open. To love each other just like it was our last day.

And after he was done, people who were kind spoke comforting words to Brian and me. To Zeke and the Burkes. Even Rachel's druggie friends were shown a little bit of sympathy. But nobody spoke comforting words to Rick LaChance, who had come to listen and to mourn his daughter with the rest of us.

So I walked over to where he was sitting alone and cry-ing, without any idea of what to say. He looked up at me and managed a weak smile. His nose was slightly bent, a souvenir from his fight with Brian, and his hands were shaking. When he finally spoke, his voice was shaking too.

"I fucked up bad with those two."

I wanted to say something appropriate, something com-forting, but I couldn't. There was nothing I could say and he probably didn't expect me to. Because he *had* fucked up. Badly. He wiped his eyes with the back of his hand, but the tears were still coming down. And when he spoke again it wasn't about Rachel or Brian. It was about their mother.

"Wendy hated winter, you know. She hated everything about it. She hated the cold and the snow and..." He shook his head. "I was supposed to take her away from it. We were gonna graduate and pack everything in my car and head on out to California. She wanted to live on a beach some-where and swim all day in an ocean that wasn't freezing."

Then he laughed. Even though he was still crying.

"Everyone else I knew was listening to disco and punk rock, but not her. She was obsessed with the Beach Boys. The girl had never been out of Maine, never even seen a surfboard, but, God, she loved that music. She was even gonna dye her hair blonde so she could look like a Califor-nia girl, but I told her not to." He gave a sad smile. "She was so beautiful and I didn't want her to ever change."

I smiled back at him, wishing Brian would come over so he could see that he'd been wrong. So he'd know. Because even if I told him the words Rick had just said I couldn't tell him, with any accuracy, the expression on his father's face when he spoke about Wendy. And I wanted Brian to see that his mother really had known what it was like to be with a man who was in love with her. She had seen it—seen love—looking at her in this man's eyes. Like she deserved.

"Is that where Brian got his name from? Brian Wilson?"

"Yeah." He seemed surprised I made the connection.

"What...about Rachel?" I wanted to fill myself up with everything about her, all of the things I didn't know. Even though it hurt so badly to think about her. To see her face in my mind. Even to say her name.

He shrugged and said quietly, "I have no idea where Wendy got that name from."

And that's how quickly it had faded. By the time Rachel came around, Rick's wife was a stranger to him, and probably he'd been one to her. Just six years of marriage. And by the time Wendy died, six years after that, things were so bad that she knew enough to tell Brian that his father wouldn't stick around. Made him promise to take care of his sister. She had to make him promise. Because she knew this man wouldn't.

He had loved her once. Once. But not enough.

And Wendy had loved him. She had trusted him with her dreams, with her future. He'd held it all, that fragile treasure, in his hands. And then he let it go. Because of the haze, the one that the bottle brought him. And he'd never given his kids the chance to even have those kinds of dreams. They'd been too busy trying to live. To survive. Carrying burdens that weren't theirs, burdens that were too heavy. He'd left them alone and scared. Searching for a haven. Any haven. Anything.

I knew I should hate him for what he'd done to them, to all three of them. That I shouldn't even be talking to him or listening to him. But I couldn't find any room in my heart to hate anyone, except for Tim. I did say goodbye, though, and walked away. Left Rick to fend for himself. Not because of hate, but because I was drained. Of everything. It was all fading—strength and hope and energy.

And I knew that I'd need to save my energy for Brian. I knew it already.

* * *

The day after the memorial service is when the drinking started. And the blaming.

Brian brought home a half-gallon bottle of Jack Daniels and we drank it together, fully clothed, in his bed. And, because he needed someone to blame, he picked the easiest target. His father.

"He left her alone, Tess. He left her alone and she spent the rest of her life looking for a daddy. And she found one, right? She found one and fucked him and he fucked her up good."

He said other things, just like that, and when he woke up the next morning he'd forgotten he'd said them. He brought home a lot of Jack the rest of that week. He woke up one afternoon, the third Saturday in January, hung over again, and that's when he started thinking it was his fault.

He didn't do enough to protect her. Or maybe he pushed her away because he was over protective. He should've moved her out of New Mills. Away from the drugs, away from the losers, away, away, far away where she would've been safe. So it was all his fault. And nothing I said made him think that it wasn't. Not, *she knew you loved her.* Or *you did the best you could.*

"It wasn't good enough, Tess."

By the time we looked at the calendar and noted that Rachel had been gone for one month he'd had a new revelation, this one courtesy of Jose Cuervo. It was everyone's fault. Mine and his and Rick's. It was Rachel's fault. Zeke, too. It was everyone's fault who looked at her, knowing she was in pain, and said to themselves, *oh, she'll be all right.* Or *she's just going through a rebellious stage.* Or *she's too smart to do anything really stupid.* And in a way he was right. But the worst really started a week later when he realized, like the rest of us had done already, whose fault it really was. It was Tim's fault.

Yes, Rachel was in pain. Hurting inside. A hurt that was deep and obvious to everyone. And even though we tried we could have done more to help her; all of us. But that's not what killed her. Because there are lots of people who are in pain like she was. People who try to hide from it in a haze, to float away on a cloud and pretend it's not there. Just like she did. But most of them don't die. Sometimes they do, of course, because sometimes shit like that just happens. Usually it's nobody's fault but their own. This time it was. There was nothing the police could do about it. Nothing Brian could do about it. Because Tim was gone, hiding from Brian.

Brian took it out on his workers, because they were the easiest targets. He shouted and swore, tore apart work they'd already done and made them do it over again, to *do it until it's fucking right, goddamn it.* What else could they do? It was the middle of winter and there was no work anywhere else. And even if there was, they knew the real reason Brian was being such an asshole. And even though it pissed them off, they said nothing. Waited for the storm to pass. And that pissed Brian off even more.

And one evening—one month, one week, and four days since Rachel died—I got home from work to a note on the table that said only, *Don't wait up.* I tried to anyway, of course, but after only one black-and-white movie I felt myself fading. I gave into it and went to bed, even though it wasn't quite nine-thirty, because there had been so many sleepless nights. And after a timeless eternity asleep, I began to dream.

Rachel and I were lying side by side in the front yard, making snow angels. Everything was peaceful and silent. The whole world was beautiful, even though it was covered in white. White snow, blowing, freezing, more and more of it. So much that I couldn't see Rachel anymore. So much that I couldn't see anything. Couldn't feel anything. So much that I couldn't breath. I tried to, tried to take in a deep, silent breath through my nostrils, but I couldn't find any air. Because we weren't making snow angels anymore. We were just lying there. Face down in the snow...

And when I jumped up out of bed I was shivering, even worse than usual, and still a little groggy. That land in between awake and asleep. A land where I knew there was too much noise coming from a place that was close by, but I wasn't sure exactly what the noise meant or who was making it. Until I heard Brian's voice, loud and deep and obviously drunk:

"Well if you had kept your dick in your pants back in high school you wouldn't have to worry about that, would you? You could stay here with me and drink all fucking night."

And then there was Jeff's voice. It was too low for me to hear what he was saying, but I could tell that, whatever it was, it was something kind, instead of the crack over the head Brian's remark had actually deserved. So I ran out to the kitchen, to where the voices were coming from, to see what was going on.

Jeff was standing over Brian, who was sprawled out on the kitchen floor, leaning back against a table leg.

"Do you need any help?"

"Nope," Jeff said. "I've got it." He pulled Brian to his feet, held him firmly around the waist and started off toward the bedroom. Brian caught sight of me at that moment and grinned.

"Holy shit, Tess. You look good enough to fuck." Then he reached out with an unsteady hand and grabbed my breast.

I backed away, out of his grasp, and folded my arms over my chest. It hadn't occurred to me until that moment that I was standing there, in front of Jeff, wearing nothing but Brian's T-shirt. It was emblazoned with the logo of a local radio station and quite long on me; but it was white and not very thick. And I wasn't wearing anything underneath it.

"Oh, come on, Tess. Don't be like that. Look, I got a hard-on now so you can go for a ride. I know you've been waiting for it."

I backed up another step and hugged myself even tighter. Jeff gave him a hard sideways kick and said, "Shut up, you stupid shit."

"No, Jeff, you don't get it."

They stumbled forward a few more steps.

"I haven't been able to fuck her for a *really* long time and if I don't do it soon she'll—"

Jeff stopped cold and slapped his hand over Brian's mouth. "I told you to shut your fucking mouth." He said it slowly and forcefully, came down hard on each syllable. Brian looked at him dumbly and nodded. And when Jeff dragged him into the bedroom he did it with his hand still over Brian's mouth.

489

I grabbed my bulky winter coat off its peg, threw it on, and waited for Jeff to return. He was full of apologies, even though, of course, he hadn't done anything wrong. Then he told me about Brian's night.

He'd walked into Zeke's with the stated purpose of getting shitfaced. Zeke let him, because Brian was usually pretty easy-going under the influence and because he figured he could use a temporary escape. And because he knew that it wouldn't be difficult finding him a ride home. Everyone in the bar, everyone in town, was just looking for a chance to do something for Brian. Something kind. Until several hours—and several double shots of Jack Daniels—later.

It began harmlessly enough. He and a few of the guys started ribbing each other. Good natured. Just guys being guys. Until Brian caught sight of an apparently familiar face and said, "Hey, didn't my dad fuck your mom once? Doesn't that make us brothers?"

And it went downhill from there. Zeke's was filled nearly to capacity, and Brian discovered that many of his "brothers" were in the crowd. And he made a point of letting everyone know about it. Loudly. Zeke cut him off at that point and tried to shut him up. When that didn't work he hopped over the bar and tried to pull him into the break room, much like Jeff had pulled him into our bedroom. But Brian pushed him to the floor and said, "Sorry, Zeke, I don't go that way. Why don't you give Andy a try instead. He's so desperate he'll fuck anything."

Of course Andy leapt at Brian, wanted to beat the shit out of him, and that's just what Brian had been hoping for. Because he hadn't gone into Zeke's to get drunk—at least it wasn't the main reason he'd gone in. He'd gone in to bait, to badger, to instigate. He didn't care who, just as long as he could get someone to take a swing. Anyone. Just so he could swing back, so he could really mess someone up. Anyone. And even though he'd managed to insult almost everyone in the bar, and even though they were all honestly pissed at him, no one there let Andy get anywhere near Brian. And they didn't let Brian take a swing, either. They just held him back, held both of them back, kept them far away from each other. And called Jeff to take Brian home.

"He's...you might want to..." Jeff took off his glasses and rubbed his eyes. It was the first time I'd ever seen him without them, and I was struck, more than ever, at his daughter's resemblance to him. It almost made me smile. He put the glasses back on and said, "Why don't you let me call Laura. You can stay at our house and I'll stay here with Brian."

"No, Jeff. I mean...thanks. I appreciate it. But I'll be fine."

"Tess, he's really messed up right now. There's no telling what's gonna come out of that mouth if he wakes up before morning."

"I'm sure I can handle it."

He sighed. "Well...just don't take anything he says to heart. Okay?"

"Okay."

I watched him drive away and waited until I couldn't see his taillights through the trees before I turned off the kitchen light. I went into the bathroom and got my mop bucket, brought it into the bedroom and set it in front of

Brian's nightstand. Then I crawled back into bed. He was lying on his back, fully clothed, and his jeans felt rough against my legs. He rolled over onto his side, facing me in the darkness, threw his arm clumsily around me under the blanket and muttered, "It's gone now."

"What's gone?"

He yawned, a long, noisy one, then said, "I can't fuck you tonight, Tess, and I'm sorry, because I know how much you like it."

"Stop it, Brian."

"But I don't think I can do it tonight. I don't think I'll be able to do it again. So if you need to find someone else to fuck you, then you go right ahead 'cause I'll understand. And I promise I won't get mad."

"Brian, just shut up and go to sleep."

"Okay." He rolled away from me and fell off the bed. There was a moment or two of silence, followed by a hollow thump. "What's this? A bucket?"

"Yes."

"What for?"

"For you to puke in. Just in case you don't make it to the bathroom."

He sat on the floor laughing for some time, then finally let me in on the joke. "What's the matter, Tess? You had someone puke on you in bed once or something?" And he laughed again.

"As a matter of fact, Brian, yes I did. I was twenty and I met this wicked hot guy at a party and brought him home. And right after we fucked he—"

"Tess?"

"Yeah?"

"Shut the fuck up."

I helped him back into bed, even though I really didn't want him anywhere near me. And when I made my way back underneath the blankets again he said, "Tess, I lied. Before. I really don't want you to fuck anyone else. I don't think I could deal with that. Can you please promise me that you won't? Maybe you can just keep on doin' it yourself for a while. I'll try and get better soon so I can take care of you again."

I didn't answer him. I just rolled over, facing away from him. Facing the wall. Facing the window. Looked out at the cold, white moon. I knew I should be insulted by what he'd said, that I should be pissed at him. Knew that I should be embarrassed because he knew how I got myself to sleep most nights. Knew it should hurt that he was afraid I'd jump into bed with someone else; that I'd actually spread my legs and let the someone else inside of me while he was drowning in grief. I knew what it meant he really thought. And maybe that meant it was true. I knew it should hurt, but it didn't. I didn't feel hurt or embarrassed or angry or insulted.

I didn't feel anything.

And when Brian woke up the next morning he didn't remember anything. Not what he'd said to me or to Jeff or to any of the guys at Zeke's. He only vaguely remembered having gone to the bar at all. When he asked me if I knew anything about his night I reluctantly filled him in on what had happened. And once his hangover subsided he spent the weekend calling everyone he'd insulted during his drunken tirade, groveling and apologizing. Of course, they all forgave him. Even Andy. I forgave him, too, even though he never apologized for what he'd said to me. Because, of course, I never bothered to tell him.

Then came Monday. The work week. Rachel had been gone one month, two weeks, and one day. That's when Brian started staying away from home. He left for work in the morning and didn't come home until long after I was asleep. I did my best to stay awake for him, to wait for him, just so I could see his face. Because I missed seeing it. Missed him.

I wasn't sure what he was doing. Where he went. Maybe he was out looking for Tim. Maybe he drove around in his truck, wandering aimlessly, thinking. Or trying not to think. Maybe he went to the cemetery and stared at that headstone. And wondered what it would be like in the spring, when Rachel's headstone would be there, too. Maybe he just parked his truck somewhere and looked up at the stars, trying to see Them up there. Restless and beautiful...

It's what I tried to imagine he did, even though I had no way to know. All I knew was where he didn't go. He was too embarrassed to go to Zeke's or to Jeff and Laura's house, even though nobody was harboring any hard feelings. And I knew he wasn't out fucking anyone. He even told me that he wasn't.

I'm not screwing around on you, Tess. I swear...

And I knew he was telling the truth. Because he couldn't. Not with me or with anyone. Not at all.

But I'm not sure where he goes, really. Because he doesn't talk too much even when he's home. And when he does talk it's just to say things like, *I miss her* or start sentences with *If I had only*. And when that happens I hold him and tell him that I miss her too and that it's not his fault. And I always say *I love you* and he always says it back. And we both mean it, we really do. But I still can't feel it. It's still buried under the hard ground and the ice. Still. Even though, tomorrow, it will be two months since Rachel died.

CHAPTER 35

Two months, three weeks, three days since Rachel died. Middle of March. And not much has changed. Even though—really—everything has.

We both go to work every day. Swinging the hammer, scrubbing the toilets. Brian still stays out most nights, but not as late as he used to. And while he's gone I don't do much. Not anything, really. I clean a lot, everything, every day, even though it's already clean. Downstairs, of course, because we don't go upstairs. I still pay Charlie the rent for the apartment, the same way I did when Rachel lived there, the same way I did before Rachel lived there. But we can't go up there.

I stare at the walls sometimes and wish I could paint them. I would like to have lots of color around me right now. Colors like Radish and Marigold and Violet. But there's just white and it will have to do. I look at my easel and my palate and my paints, but I don't hold the brushes in my hand. Because there's nothing inside of me that wants to come out. Not sadness or fear or love or hate. Just Titanium White.

I babysit Cassidy still, two days a week, and those are the days I'm forced to smile and put on the mask. Because she is still crying. And I can't cry. I want to, but I can't. We read and talk and I watch her do her homework, because she's so smart and doesn't need me to help her with it. But we don't color with crayons. Not right now. Maybe soon.

I cook some and eat a little and I always make sure there's something for Brian to eat whenever he gets home. And I watch black-and-white movies when he's out and cop shows when he's home. But that's not often. And I miss him. I miss his dark, glowing eyes and sweet, deep voice, his strong arms and his heart beating against my back. I miss it all. Even when he's home.

One night when Brian was out, the night that was two months, one week, and four days since Rachel died, there was a knock on the door and it was Rick. He didn't say anything for a few moments, just stood there on the porch, staring at me; and looking so much like Brian that it almost made me cry. But I held it back and managed to say, "Brian isn't home."

"I know. That's why I came. I need to talk to you."

"Talk to me? Why?"

He took a deep breath and said, "Something needs to be done about the drug problem here in town."

I nodded. Because I'd heard rumors, that weren't much louder than a whisper, about Someone being back in town. Heard that even though he was still hiding somewhere he was close by. And something did need to be done. Should've been done months ago. Except that someone chickened out because she was weak. And now Rachel was dead, along with a little girl who had just wanted her mommy on a cold, dark night.

"And if something ever is done about it," he continued, "I hope it happens at a time when Brian has someone can vouch for him. Someone besides his girlfriend."

I nodded again and thought for just a moment. Then I cleared my throat and made pleasant chitchat. I told him about my brother in Brookfield who liked to go ice fishing. About my father who had an icehouse on a lake in a town about an hour north of there. Far enough away that, if my brother invited Brian to go ice fishing over the weekend, to get his mind off of things, he'd most likely have to spend the night at his house in Brookfield. And Rick said that sounded good. Sounded just like what Brian needed. Then he gave me a piece of paper with his address and his phone number and made me promise to call him if, for some reason, the fishing trip didn't work out. And I promised that I would.

And then I talked some more. I told him about cops shows that Brian liked to watch. Because it's only natural that a man would be interested in what sort of television programs interested his son. Especially when he didn't know anything about him. So I spoke to him about shows that had plots that revolved around forensic evidence. Talked about tire tracks and luminol and bleach. About black plastic bags. And when I was done with that I told him about bargains I'd seen at Walmart. About boots that were too big and clothes that were affordable enough to throw away after one use. Fibers that could be traced to hundreds of different people. Because when you live in a poor area, everyone you know shops at Walmart.

He nodded again and thanked me for talking to him. He asked that I not tell Brian he'd been there and I told him that I wouldn't. Then I watched him drive away in his big boat of a car. Not unlike dozens of other cars in the area, all with the same brand of cheap tires.

And when I didn't see his taillights anymore I called Dave. He thought that an ice fishing trip was just what Brian needed. And when he called back the next morning, early enough to catch Brian before he left for work, Dave didn't tell him it was my idea. Just like I hadn't told Dave it was really Rick's.

We went up together, because a visit with my nephew seemed like just what I needed to get my mind off of things. Brian spent Saturday freezing his ass off, drinking beer and Jack Daniels and catching fish on a frozen lake, while I spent it watching Matthew walk around the house without anyone holding his hands. I sang him the Happy Birthday song, because he was going to turn a year old in just four more days. After Kim put him down for his nap she and I talked about Rachel. She said it wasn't my fault. Said that I'd tried to help her. And I said *I know*. Even though what I really knew was that I hadn't done enough. Then I asked her about Jason and she told me he was doing good. She told me about the woman he was seeing, the same one he'd started seeing back in the fall, and she said it was getting serious. I nodded and said, *That's good*, because he deserved to be happy. And I tried not to remember that it had been a year and three days since a judge had banged the gavel that had killed Forever.

Brian and Dave got back late that evening, too late for us to travel back home. Brian was tired, and a little drunk, so he marched off to bed and fell asleep right away. I joined him shortly afterwards and stayed awake for another hour, imagining Tim as a little boy. Wondering about what his family might have been like, what had happened to him that had turned him into a monster. And for about ten minutes I shook. Cold and nauseous and guilty. Made myself imagine what might be happening to him—right now— as I was lying beside Brian, warm and safe in my brother's house. What might already have happened. While I'd been watching my little nephew try out his new legs.

But then I thought about Rachel, lying cold and dead in the snow, wearing the jacket I'd given her for Christmas. The jacket that should have been covered, months ago, with Tim's blood and brains instead of her own. She was lying cold and dead right now, waiting for spring to come so we could put her in the ground near her mother. Then I thought about Little Miss Seventeen and little Samantha and her mother. The boy who had died of an overdose last summer. And about the families of all those people. Their hearts were aching. Right now. They were lonely and cold and shaking. And they were counting. Days and weeks and months, just like Brian and me. Soon we'd all be counting years. And soon, maybe already—maybe right now—Tim wouldn't be. And he wouldn't be taking them away from anybody else, either.

Not anymore.

And so I smiled. Snuggled in close to Brian. Hoped he could feel my heart beating against his back. Hoped that he knew he was safe and loved. And I fell asleep.

When I woke up there was breakfast and showers and packing and then the drive home. Brian didn't talk much and I didn't talk at all. But I held his hand, even when he was shifting gears. It was warm and strong and I told myself that everything was going to be all right. And so were we. Soon.

We were only home for a few minutes, not even enough time to get the fishing gear out of the truck, when we saw Blue Lights coming into the driveway. Brian jumped when he saw them, the same way he had when I'd driven him home New Years Day and, at 12:26 a.m., he'd learned the truth about Rachel. He recovered quickly and greeted the State Troopers with a nod, polite but confused. And I pretended to be confused, too.

When they left, well over two hours later, he wasn't confused anymore and I stopped pretending to be. Because there had been a brutal slaying in New Mills and Brian had an alibi; someone other than just his girlfriend. A well-respected lawyer and his wife. A clerk from the gas station where Brian had filled up Dave's truck and a waitress from the diner where Dave had taken Brian out for supper. Because Brian had a very handsome face, a face that clerks and waitresses were bound to remember. And there was no physical evidence, even though they had looked. Not in the house or his shed or his truck or on any of his clothes. And so they moved on. Because they had a long list of suspects that included known drug dealers and suspected drug dealers and any one of a number of addicts, desperate for drugs or money or both.

There were other suspects, too. Families of victims we knew about and victims we didn't. Because there really was a rampant teenage drug problem in town. And lots of people who were happy Tim was dead. We all knew that the drugs wouldn't go away just because Tim was gone. Someone else would come in—probably someone else already had—and the kids would still shoot up and smoke and snort and swallow whatever they could get from whoever they could get it from. But we were all happy to see him gone just the same. Happy to know that he wouldn't be able to hurt any more Sweet Young Things. That his ex-wife and daughter with the ineffective restraining order were finally safe. And, mostly, that he'd met with a painful death. A slow death. Stripped naked in the cold and tied up. Beaten. Nearly every bone in his body broken. Sodomized with a blunt instrument. And, finally, his skull was crushed with a rock.

Whoever did it was smart. He or she or they killed Tim deep in the gravel pit near his house. Probably lured him there, begging for drugs. It was a favorite hangout for the local teenagers to make out or fuck or get high, but no witnesses could be found, anywhere. If anyone had been there at the time it happened—and probably no one was, during the middle of the day on a Saturday, which is when the forensic guy said Tim had died—they'd most likely have been either too high or too preoccupied with other business to have noticed. And who among them would come forward if they had been there?

There was no helpful physical evidence at the gravel pit, either. The poor cops who'd had to process the scene had found used rubbers and needles and syringes, lighters and empty bottles and cans—months' and months' worth of litter from dozens and dozens of different people. Some of it on top of the snow and some of it buried underneath. Some of it in layers in between, fossils of loneliness and misery and haze. But nothing useful. Nothing that would lead them to whoever had killed Tim.

Two months, three weeks, and one day after Rachel died I drove into Westville after work, knocked on a door in an apartment building in a very run down part of town, and handed Rick LaChance a business card. It was one I'd filed away in my purse while Brian was fishing because *you never know when you might need it.*

"What's this?"

I cleared my throat. "My brother's a lawyer."

Rick had an alibi, too; the girl he was living with. She was younger than Brian but older than Rachel had been. And she was his third girlfriend in six months. He was sober and he had a job, but he still had itchy feet. And once he left her for the next set of tits there was no telling what her conscience would tell her to do or to say. And the police hadn't found any physical evidence, but it didn't mean that there wasn't any to be found somewhere. And there's no statute of limitations on murder. Even the murder of a vicious, drug-dealing killer.

He filed the card away in his wallet and thanked me. Considered for a moment. Then he asked me about Brian. And I told him the truth: *He's not doing good.* It's all I told him and he nodded. Then we said goodbye and he closed the door.

I didn't tell him that Brian is doing worse now than before Tim died. He's home a little more often, and he's stopped drinking so much. But even when he's home he doesn't talk, except to say, *It should've been me. It was my job to take care of Tim.* But most of the time he just sits there, staring out the window or at the television or at his hands. He doesn't ask me for help. And I don't know how to offer. Don't know what it is he needs me to say. Or what to do.

I tell myself that it will get better, because it has to. It's just the Process of Grieving. It hasn't been quite three months, and what's that amount to? It's nothing, a grain of sand, especially when you compare it to the twenty years he spent with Rachel. And so, I know, it will get better. Soon. And so will we.

CHAPTER 36

The second Sunday in April. Three months and one week since Rachel died.

Brian and I got up early and dressed silently in nice clothes. He'd bought a blue tie and a white button-up shirt and wore them with his good black jeans. I put on a pale blue dress that I'd had forever.

We spent the rest of the morning standing and sitting and kneeling. Watching pretty little girls in white dresses and veils and handsome young boys in their black suits taking their First Holy Communion. I sat with Brian beside the Burkes and all four of Cassidy's grandparents. We watched her kneel in front of the priest and receive—for the first time—the Body of Christ. Then the Burkes and the grandparents and the rest of the believers did the same. Except for me, because I knew: No repentance. No Confession. No Communion.

No forgiveness.

I looked around me. It was a poor congregation, but a beautiful church. Except for the scary statues. Fourteen pictures lined the walls, depicting the suffering of Christ. The Way of the Cross. I studied each one.

1: Jesus is Condemned to Death.

Because Pontius Pilate was too weak to prevent Injustice.

4: Jesus Meets His Blessed Mother.

And I wondered—not for the first time—if Rachel was with her mother. Right now.

12: Jesus Dies on the Cross.

My God…why have you forsaken me?
What were Rachel's last words? Had she called out for Brian? For me? For her mother? Had she said a prayer; begged for her life? Had she said anything at all? Maybe she just went quietly. Just finally stopped fighting.
This is my body. This is my blood. Keep doing this.
In remembrance of me…
And when it was over, we gave Cassidy big hugs. Brian took lots of pictures of her and told her how beautiful she was. Told her he loved her. Then we followed the Burkes' car back to their house for lunch and cake. We even stayed for supper, stayed long after the grandparents had all left. Because we hadn't been to the Burkes' since before Rachel died. And because it felt nice to be in a home with smiles that were real. And before we left I asked Jeff to, please, take a picture of Brian and me because *it's the first time we've been anywhere together all dressed up.* It was true, but it wasn't the real reason I wanted the picture. An image of us frozen forever. The real reason was this:

Right before he stood up and said it was time for us to go, I caught Brian staring at me from across the room. His eyes were filled with tears, but they were more awake than they had been in months. I wasn't sure exactly what he was thinking about as he was staring. But I knew what it meant.

He drove us from the home that was filled with real smiles toward the one that didn't even pretend to smile anymore. But we didn't ride in silence. I talked all the way. Nervous chatter about white dresses and finger sandwiches and pink frosting. But no matter how much I talked about things that didn't matter, it still only took us a few minutes to get home. I grabbed his hand and held it tight as we walked toward the house. Held it, still, as we walked up the porch steps and as we stepped into the kitchen. Even as we walked into the bedroom.

As we changed out of our church clothes and into our comfortable hanging-out-around-the-house clothes I waited, naked, for him to look at me. He didn't until he was completely dressed, in an old T-shirt and a pair of sweatpants, but when he did his let his gaze linger. Everywhere. For a very long time. And that...was when I knew. For real.

He waited for me to get dressed, then he grabbed my hand again. I let him pull me into the living room, even though I didn't want to go. We sat down on the couch, still holding hands and sitting so close together. So close. On the same couch where we'd sat a hundred times at least. Where we'd watched television and laughed and snuggled and fucked. We'd sat here together months ago while Rachel told him a story that began like this:

Once upon a time, there was a girl who lost her way...

As I sat there, still afraid, more afraid than I'd been in forever, I tried to think of something I could say to him, something that would make him change his mind. But there was nothing. No words. Just like always.

He cleared his throat and finally spoke.

"I love you, Tess. I really do."

I believed him. I really did.

But…

He didn't say it. So I did. And then I finished it for him.

"…this is it. It's over."

I gave him a few more seconds. Gave him enough time to say:

No, not over. I just need time. We need time. But we'll be all right again. Soon…

But he didn't. So I finished the rest.

"Because I'm always gonna be the reason Rachel died."

"No." He was adamant. And I believed him. "That's not it. Rachel was…what happened to her wasn't your fault. It's not that."

Then don't tell me. I don't want to know the reason…

"It's just that…I can't do this right now. I can't be with you. Not when I'm like this. I can't do all the things I'm supposed to do, all the things you need me to do. I'm…I feel *dead* inside. I can barely think. I can't work. I just stand there like a fucking idiot trying to figure out what the hell is going on while my guys are doing everything. I can't…damn it, I can't even take care of myself, let alone take care of you."

"Brian, I—"

"Please let me talk. Okay?"

I nodded, even though I didn't want him to talk. Because it didn't matter, after all. He could talk and talk all night long and into tomorrow, and all it would boil down to is one horrible, heartbreaking word. And I didn't want to hear it. Didn't want to hear the way *goodbye* sounded in his voice…

"I've got too much shit piled up on top of me and I need to get out from underneath it. I've been underneath it for too long and I don't know what to do about it, 'cause I never really dealt with it. And now that I don't have Rachel here to distract me from it…I just…I just gotta deal with it *now*. And I'm not dragging you into it with me, Tess. Can you understand that?"

"No, Brian, I can't. If we were married it would be *for better or worse*. Right? And if I'd said yes right away to the saving-for-a-house question, and not hesitated like an idiot, then I'd have a ring right now that would mean I'd *have* to stay. So doesn't it mean more that I *want* to stay? That I'm here because I love you, and not just because a piece of jewelry says I have to be here? I'm here and I'm not going anywhere. And I'll help you with—"

"Help me? Tess…you can't help me. Not with anything. You can't even help *you*. 'Cause you're buried in shit of your own, just as bad as I am. Maybe even worse, I don't know. *I don't know.* Because I don't even know what the hell your problem really is. But if I thought I could…I don't know, make things better for you, I'd try. 'Cause you need it. And believe me, Tess, there is nothing I'd love better. It would be a hell of a lot easier for me to do that than to deal with my own problems. But even if I could…you don't *want* that. You never did, even though I tried. I really did. And even if you started letting me…right now I just can't do it." He shrugged. "Maybe I'm not supposed to. Maybe that's not my job. I don't know. And that's the problem, Tess, the real problem. I don't even *know* what I'm supposed to do. I just...I don't know."

I had never seen so much misery on a face. And I knew he was right. Knew that I was miserable too. Even though I couldn't feel it. I only knew that it was there. Somewhere inside of me. A vague pain. An almost-ache. And I knew that it wasn't ever going away. Not if I stayed with him and not if I left. And I sure as hell didn't want to leave.

"Listen. Brian, I'm okay. I'm fine. You don't have to—"

"Fine? Really?"

"Yeah. Yes. I am."

He shook his head. "You're not fine, Tess. You haven't been *fine* since the day I met you. You weren't fine before that, either."

I pulled my hand away from his. "That is a shitty thing to say."

"Maybe, but it's the truth. Why don't you tell me something, Tess. Why is it you're satisfied to just exist? To live in half a house that's falling apart? How can you paint all these awesome pictures—create all this fucking amazing, honest art—and then just let it rot on the wall upstairs? And why do you lie to yourself and say you don't want kids when you really do? And make just enough money to pay your bills and not any more than that, even though you work your ass off and could make—"

"Money? What the hell does money have to do with anything?"

"It's not the money, Tess. It's *you.* It's...it's about worth. And feeling like you have some. I know you don't think

510

you do and I've tried so fucking hard to help you see that you're wrong."

He sighed. Then he sat up straighter and set his jaw. Determined. Focused. I recognized this look; *this* Brian. Mr. Fix It was back. And even though he had always irritated me before, this time I didn't mind him. In fact I almost smiled because I knew what it meant that he was here. It meant that Brian still loved me.

But then he pulled out his hammer.

"Look. I know your mom was—"

"Wait a minute. You just leave my mother out of this. I fucking hate all that Freudian 'tell me about your mother' bullshit. If you want to talk about mothers why don't you talk about your own. Because she screwed you up pretty bad, too."

And then there was silence. Lots of it. Because it was a low blow and I hadn't meant to say it.

"I am so sorry, Brian. I *really* didn't mean that."

But he only shrugged. "Don't be sorry. You're right. She didn't mean to, but...she did."

Just like that. *She did.* Like it was easy. Like it was no big deal. He held my hand again, looked right into my eyes. His were glowing, almost like they used to before Rachel died. Just like he still loved me. Even though he didn't want me anymore.

"I'm gonna tell you something, Tess. I fell in love with you the first time we met. Right out there in the front yard. You looked so frigging sad and lost that all I wanted to do is to hold you and keep you safe. But there was something else there...something about the way you smiled. There was something going on inside of you that made it so you weren't just gonna roll over and give up. And *that's* what I fell in love with. The woman I saw that first day. But now... Jesus, you're killing her, Tess. You're crushing her and I don't know how to make you stop doing it. And it's not just because of Rachel. I've been fighting this battle with you all along. And I'm too tired to keep fighting. I can't do it right now. Okay? I'm just so...fucking tired."

"I know. I know, I'm sorry. I'll—it'll be different. I promise—"

"No, it won't. And besides, Tess, I haven't got what it is you need, either. Not right now anyway. But I still love you. I love you so fucking much. And maybe...I don't know. Maybe we just need a little time to get our shit together. And after that...maybe someday we can—"

"No. No, Brian. That's not how it works. If we're gonna wait for *someday* then we might as well stay together and fight it out. But if you think this is it...if *you* think it's over, then that's it. Period. Because I can't just sit around waiting to see if *someday* you're gonna come knocking on my door."

There. I'd said it. He'd know what goodbye meant for real and he'd take it back so we could figure out what to do. To make it all right again.

But he didn't. He said:

"You're right. That wouldn't be fair to you. Or to me."

"What?"

Of course it wasn't right. None of it, not a single damn word. Because he loved me, still. I could *see* it. It was right... there. And I knew—I *knew*—exactly how to make him understand. It wasn't over at all.

I let go of his hand and touched his face, gently. It was rough with end-of-the-day whiskers, the kind I loved best.

And I kissed him, just as gently. The kind of kiss that would tell him that I loved him, still. More than anything. And when he kissed me back it was full of tenderness and fire. I opened my eyes to look at his face and saw that his eyes were open, too. They'd been open the whole time. And that's when I saw the sadness again. It was the same way he'd looked at me at the Burkes' house. It was there again because he knew.

It was our last kiss.

No!

I rolled over on top of him. Straddled him. Kissed him again, but it was different now. Trembling lips and shaking, desperate hands. All over him. Everywhere. His face and chest and hair, then his were on me, too, my ass and my back, then underneath my shirt, because he knew—he knew—that I wasn't wearing a bra. I'd done it on purpose. Because I knew it would come to this and I felt a little better, just a little, because it was going to be all right. It was going to happen again, see, Brian? See? Just fine. Both of us are. Because there's passion still, it's there again, finally because I could feel it, feel him, hard underneath me, underneath his sweatpants. It was working and now—right now—everything was all right…

But he broke away. Took his mouth away from mine, took his hands away.

"No, Tess." He took in a deep, shaky breath and said it again. "No."

I didn't move. Just held his face in my hands and looked right into his eyes.

"Yes. You want it, too. You want me."

He swallowed hard, and his hands were shaking. "Yes, I do."

I smiled. "Okay, then."

But he didn't let me kiss him again.

"Brian, you're…why…"

I had to stop, because it was there again, in his eyes. Sadness. More than I'd ever seen, anywhere. A single tear slid down his cheek. And I knew…

I did that to him.

"Because I love you, Tess. I love you."

He cleared his throat to make his voice stop trembling. Then he said it.

"And I'm not letting you leave here tonight thinking that you're nothing more to me than just a fuck. Not like the rest. I don't want you to go away thinking that's all you're worth."

I let go of his face, but stared at him still. Tried to absorb what it was he'd said. But I couldn't. They were words. Just words. And I knew what they really meant.

Goodbye.

So I did the only thing I could do. I got off of him. Pulled down my shirt. Went into the bedroom—the one that was just his again—and got my bra from on top of his bed. Then I grabbed my purse and keys and coat from the peg in the kitchen. And I left him. Alone.

I climbed the fourteen stairs and unlocked the door to the apartment that wasn't Rachel's anymore. Tossed my bra and purse and keys and coat onto the table. Walked into the bathroom, kneeled in front of the toilet, and waited for it all to come up. Vomit and tears and what was left of my soul. But nothing came up. Nothing. Because there was nothing there.

I took quick, quiet footsteps into the living room, because I knew how loud they would sound to him. And

I wondered, for a moment, if he was crying down there. Right now. But I just stood in front of the window without any tears. Stood there and shivered. Even though it was April. Even though it was spring. Even though Brian had replaced the drafty window months ago. I tried to look outside, into the darkness, but only saw my reflection. I relaxed my eye muscles and tried to look through me, but I couldn't. All I could see was me. And I didn't like it.

Why is it you're satisfied to just exist?

I closed my eyes, squeezed them shut; tried to will his voice away. I even covered my ears with my hands, just like a kid. But it wasn't going to work. I knew it.

...I'm not letting you leave here tonight...

I needed something different, something else, and I knew what it was. I needed the Something I always needed to make it go away, all of the voices.

...thinking that you're nothing more to me than...

And I knew it would be easy to go out and find the Something. But I couldn't do it to him. Couldn't force him to listen to the squeaky bed. So I stood there instead, in front of the window, and forced his voice away, forced his questions away with a few of my own.

What the hell happened to us? What did I do wrong this time? How the hell can it be over?

Because there was still love there, love that was hot and beautiful and real. But it was over anyway. Over and he was gone. No more dark, mischievous eyes and soft, deep whispers. No more strong arms around me in the middle of the night, no more heart beating against my back. The heart beat that told me I was safe...safe and loved...

And still I felt nothing. Somewhere deep inside me there was searing pain because it was over. Because he was gone. But it was underneath the ice. Underneath the hard, packed soil. Where I couldn't feel it. Couldn't feel anything.

I let my gaze follow the windowsill and drift over to the wall, to the spot Brian had fixed for me so I didn't have to pay a security deposit. I took three more quiet steps and touched it. Barely visible, just like he'd promised. Then I touched the closet door. I looked at the doorknob for a long, horrible moment. And I knew. If I turned that doorknob and pulled on it and opened that door, I'd find the answer to *what the hell happened to us* and *what did I do wrong?* So I opened the door. Because even though I knew, I still had to see it.

And there it was.

Empty boxes.

...you never know when you might need a box...

They had been waiting here for me. All along.

You knew you wouldn't be holding his hand forever.

I closed the door again so I wouldn't have to look at Fear anymore. But even though the door was closed the Fear was still there. Right. There.

Flying. Falling. Landing hard.

And I knew that it always would be.

CHAPTER 37

Third Saturday in April. Three months, two weeks, and six days since Rachel died.

It was moving day again. It had taken less than a week for me to realize that I couldn't live above Brian anymore. I'd wake up early every morning and watch out the window as he left for work, as his truck grumbled out of sight. And every evening I'd sit on the couch, staring at the floor, listening to the muffled sounds of his television, wondering if he was actually watching it, or if he was staring at the wall or out the window...or up at the ceiling toward me. And every night, as I lay alone in bed, I'd listen to the loud, bubbly pipes that told me he was in the shower. I'd imagine him in there, wet and soapy and beautiful. And I would wonder how long it would be until he was healthy and strong enough to have Someone Else in there with him. A Someone who wasn't me.

But the Saturday after our last kiss was what finally did it. Brian had climbed the fourteen stairs, knocked on my door, and handed me an envelope. It was filled with cash. Because we'd been saving for a house and now there was no more *We*.

"No, Brian...I don't want your money."

He shook his head. "You did that to him, Tess. I'm not letting you do it to me."

I couldn't think of anything to say, so I just nodded. Then I watched him walk down the fourteen steps. And I haven't seen him since.

Two days later I used the money for a security deposit on a new apartment in town. It was within walking distance to Zeke's and the market and the grade school. And a few days after that, Laura told me that Brian was moving out, too. He was going to stay with them for a while, just until he figured out what to do. Because he couldn't bear to live in a house where Rachel's ghost was still hovering. Or mine.

This time it was Jeff and Zeke who unloaded my furniture and boxes. It was easier this time because my apartment was on the first floor, only four small stairs to climb. It was another old house that had been converted into two apartments, just like a dozen others in this part of town. Business men from out of state had paid pennies on the dollar for homes that had been lost by mill families, families who had owned them for generations. I knew I should care, because I knew that it was Unjust that those families were scattered and broken now while the business men were seeing double and triple returns on their Wise Investments. But I didn't care. Not about the business men or about the families. All it meant to me was that I had a place to live. A place with no ghosts.

Zeke left as soon as Jeff's truck was unloaded, because he had to check on the diner and open up the bar, but Jeff took off his coat off and went to work on my entertainment center. I knew Brian had asked him to set it up for me, and

I wanted to tell him to leave it alone. To have him tell Brian to fuck off and leave me alone. But the truth was that I had no idea where all the wires to all the gizmos were supposed to go or how to connect them all together. Instead I surveyed the apartment. It was bigger than the last one, and in much better condition, but the walls were beige. Beige was even worse than white, and I decided to start my unpacking by hanging up my paintings to cover it up. Jeff watched me while he worked, but said nothing until I unwrapped Kineo.

"Did you paint that one recently?"

I shook my head. "I did it about fourteen years ago."

"Really?"

"Yeah. Why?"

He pushed his glasses up a little higher on his nose and squinted to get a clearer view. Then he shook his head and said, "No reason."

He finished up a few minutes later. "You're sure you don't want Laura to come over and help you unpack?"

"No, I'm all set. And you guys are gonna be busy enough today." Because it was moving day for Brian, too.

"Well...give us a call if you need anything."

"I will." I said it even though I knew I probably wouldn't. As I watched him drive away...that's when I knew I was alone. For real.

I took my time unpacking, because there was no hurry. There was no heavy dread either because I knew that if I came across a box that claimed to hold three bottles of bleach then that's exactly what would be inside of it. And when I unpacked my bathroom box I came across a bottle that I'd been expecting to find. It was Rachel's shampoo.

I had packed most of the stuff she'd left behind into three boxes and put them on the porch outside Brian's apartment. By now they were probably sitting in the Burkes' garage, along with Brian's stuff, right next to the boxes Rachel had left there last winter. When Brian eventually got around to going through them he wouldn't miss the half-empty bottle of jasmine shampoo. And I needed it. She had smelled like jasmine that day, a lifetime ago, when we had sat together and frosted Christmas cookies. And I needed to keep that part of her with me.

When I was finished unpacking I took a long, hot shower. Fixed my makeup and hair, just so. Slipped on a short black skirt and my red, low-cut, button-up shirt. Because there was something else I needed. And I had waited long enough.

I drove into Westville, to a bar that was near the hospital. Because I couldn't get what I needed in New Mills. Not without everybody finding out about it. I parked my car, snapped on the interior light, pulled down the rearview mirror, and examined my reflection. Put on a little more red lipstick.

10:02.

And I was ready.

The bar was dark—darker, even, than Zeke's—and it wasn't homey at all. No sports memorabilia, no ancient beer bottles on the walls, no huge television that let us know how Our Boys were doing. Just tacky, blinking neon signs that had seen better days and an old jukebox that played country music. I sat down at the bar and surveyed the crowd. Three couples were on their feet, slow-dancing to a twangy love song. I hated them. So did the three other single patrons who sat at three separate tables: an ugly, puffy-faced woman of about forty-five with bleached-blonde hair; a young guy with piercings in his ears and face and, most likely, his tongue; and a tough, angry guy who looked like a real lumberjack, scruffy beard, flannel shirt and all.

Which made Bartender my only real prospect. He was a nice-looking guy, maybe thirty or so. A carrot top with amber eyes. My stomach gave an excited little flip—the closest thing to a real emotion I'd felt in months—because I'd never been with a redhead before. He watched me closely as I slipped off my coat and set it down on the stool beside me. Then I gave him a pretty smile and started the dance with:

"It sure is chilly out there tonight."

He smiled back and his eyes told me that he'd noticed. "What can I get to warm you up?"

It was a lame line, but I didn't care. Because it meant I could relax. It meant that, in just a few hours, I would get the Something that I needed.

"Why don't you surprise me."

He brought back a sweet, red drink that tasted like spiced rum and I sipped it slowly while we made friendly chitchat. I smiled a lot and didn't flaunt my tits, because I didn't need to. He noticed them because they were there. Genetics. Luck of the draw. Just like straight teeth. Or a handsome, rugged face and eyes that were Van Dyke Brown...

The couples left, one at a time, mercifully leaving the jukebox in silence, and by midnight only me and Ugly Woman were left in the bar. She'd tried, unsuccessfully, to hook up with both Pierced Guy and Lumberjack, and was now working on what was at least her fifth drink. I was still only nursing my second. I looked away from her and took another sip, tried to imagine Bartender without a shirt. Tried to imagine red chest hair. I couldn't do it. I kept seeing Van Dyke Brown.

Bartender cleared his throat. "You okay?"

"Yeah. I'm fine. Why?"

He pointed to my legs. I had them crossed, but my feet were bouncing, tapping against the front of the bar. I managed a smile. "I guess I'm just a little...antsy."

He smiled back and his face flushed, the way only a redhead's can. He looked at the clock, then over my shoulder at Ugly Woman. "Hey, Sharon. You done with that yet?"

She gave him a sullen nod.

"Then get going."

"You ain't closed yet. You don't close till one."

"I'm closing early tonight. And you've had enough."

She muttered something I couldn't make out, then got up and stumbled toward the door.

"Um...should she be driving home like that?"

"She's not driving. She lives right across the street."

"Ah."

I could easily imagine the ad that had attracted her attention to that particular apartment:

Great location. Walking distance to local bar and hospital with detox unit...

I made my escape into the bathroom so he could lock up. Tossed my purse onto the counter. I wanted to wash my hands, but there was no soap in the dispenser. I took a quick look in the mirror. My hair was fine. Mascara was fine. Red lipstick still in place, even after two drinks and two hours of friendly chitchat. The lady on the commercial had been right after all: Long lasting. And I wondered what else it would last through. But I couldn't even smile at that. So I closed my eyes and tried again.

Red hair. Carrot top. On his head. Right. So...imagine it on his chest. It shouldn't be that difficult, Tess. Not really. Not at all.

But it was still Van Dyke Brown.

He was waiting for me right outside the bathroom door. Smiling. I didn't say a word, just grabbed his face and pulled his mouth down onto mine, gave him my tongue right away. Because I needed him to know.

Forget the foreplay. I just want to fuck.

He was willing to oblige. He pulled my skirt up, high above my waist, then yanked my underwear down past my thighs. I wiggled out of them, let them fall to the ground as his hands wandered freely, blatantly groping, rubbing, squeezing. They were everywhere, finally, my ass, my tits, between my legs...everywhere...

But I needed more than his hands. There was a booth a few feet away. I pushed him down onto it and dropped to my knees.

...you just dropped to your knees for the first fresh dick that came along...

Shut up, Jason. Shut the fuck up.

Bartender kindly kicked the table away as I unbuttoned his pants and pulled them down to his ankles. Then I rested my elbows on his knees and lingered there for a moment, staring. Because now I knew what a redhead looked like. And it had been a long time since there was something new.

I couldn't take him into my mouth, though, even though I had planned to. Not with Jason's words still echoing in my brain. I climbed up onto his lap instead. He was probably disappointed, but I didn't care. Why should I care? He was too excited to last very long, and I hadn't driven thirty-one miles just to let some strange guy get off in my mouth. I made it up to him by pulling my shirt off as I straddled him. And just as I slipped Bartender's dick inside of me I remembered:

It was the same shirt I'd worn the first time Brian had fucked me.

He didn't fuck you that first night. He made love to you. There's a difference, and you know it.

It didn't matter now, didn't matter anymore. What mattered was that there were hands and fingers unhooking my bra, pulling it off, and a mouth that was all over me now. Hot, wet lips and hotter tongue and what mattered was that I was fucking someone, fucking someone, finally, thank God, someone who wanted it as badly as me, who wanted me badly. I closed my eyes so I wouldn't see red hair, didn't want to see it, didn't want to see anything. I just wanted to feel him inside of me, feel his hands and mouth, all over me, wanted to hear him, his moaning and grunting and broken, halting words, the sounds that reminded me how much he loved the way I tasted, loved the way I felt, loved the way he felt inside of me and it didn't take me long to get there, not long at all. Because I'd been waiting for hours for him, waiting for months for it, waiting for Brian please, Brian, *please* just one more time. Just once more, Brian, and you'll see, you'll see, you'll fucking see how much you've missed it, how much you'll miss me, how much…

I love you, Tess. You know that, don't you?

Yes. I know. And I love…you…too, Brian…

And then it was over. I was done, Bartender was done. I had driven thirty-one miles and it had barely taken five minutes. And when it's all done, just what do you say to a man whose hands are on your ass, whose face is buried between your tits, whose dick is buried inside of you, whose name you don't even know? I couldn't think of a thing. Unfortunately, he could. He looked up at me, his head still between my tits, and said:

"Who's Brian?"

"What?"

"Brian. You said his name."

"I did?"

He nodded.

"Oh. Sorry. He's…um…"

But I couldn't think about Brian anymore, couldn't talk about him. Especially not while another man's dick was inside of me. So I said it again.

"I'm sorry."

He shrugged. "Why be sorry? It doesn't matter to me."

Of course it didn't. He'd just gotten a good, free fuck. Why should he care what—or who—the woman that came along with it was thinking about while he was getting it?

I'm not letting you leave here thinking you're nothing more to me than…

You know what, Brian? Fuck you.

I cleared my throat. Tried to think of what to do next. It didn't take long to figure it out. What I had to do was clean myself up. Because I hadn't thought about protection. Hadn't thought about anything. And I wanted to ask him if I had anything to worry about now, if he had the clap or AIDS or some other disgusting disease or infection, but why bother? He probably didn't, and he'd probably just lie about it if he did. And I had to get away from him. Couldn't look at him anymore. Couldn't let him look at me for even one second longer.

I hopped off, pulled down my skirt, collected the rest of my clothes, and sped into the bathroom. My purse was still on the counter. I searched inside it with shaking hands, shivering hands, for some change and found a handful of quarters. I used them to buy a pad from the dispenser on the wall. I didn't want him all over my underwear. Then I cleaned myself up as best I could in a public bathroom that had no soap, got dressed, and took a quick look in the mirror. At my mascara and red lips and long, fake-blonde hair. I still looked fine. Just So. Even after I'd fucked a strange guy on a booth in a bar thirty-one miles away from home.

Bartender was already dressed, picking up glasses and bottles and trash. It made me remember that I hadn't paid my bill. I pulled my wallet from my purse, but he waved me off.

"Nope. You're all set."

I plunked the money down. "This is not up for discussion. And…just keep the change."

He chuckled lightly. "Oh, I think you gave me a big enough tip already."

I had to grab tight hold of the bar. Because the room was spinning and nothing was in focus. And I tried to think, through the fog, of some words to say to him, words that were filled with venom and hatred and disgust. But there were no words inside of me, and the only hatred I could dig up from the hard, frozen ground, the only disgust, was for myself. Because, of course, Bartender had it—

You fucking whore.

—exactly right. So I did the only thing I could do. I grabbed my purse and walked out of the bar.

I stood alone in the parking lot, shivering, my teeth actually chattering. Even though it was April. Even though it was spring. I hugged myself tightly, rubbed my frozen arms, and looked across the street, up at Ugly Woman's apartment. The light was on and there was no curtain in the window, so I could see her sitting at her kitchen table. There was an open bottle of Something in front of her. Even though she'd spent all night drinking, she was sitting there drinking some more. Drinking herself into oblivion. Into a haze. Filling her stomach and liver and brain and empty heart with poison.

I looked away from the window, away from her, because I knew. That would be me. When I was too old and ugly and desperate to get a guy to give me the Something that I needed to make the voices go away. To make the godawful ache in my heart disappear.

That would be me.

Bullshit, Tess. That's you right now. Right now. Because you fucked that guy. You know that, don't you? You fucked a man you don't even know. You climbed on top of him and took him inside of you and let him make you come. You let him come. Inside of you. It's still inside of you, right now. And you don't even know his name.

That's what I did.

She's the girl you fuck and toss aside.

I was. I really was that girl. And I probably always would be.

And that's when I heard another voice, a younger voice. A girl who had always just whispered, when what she'd really wanted to do was shriek. She was still whispering, still, and I could just barely make out what she was saying underneath all the other voices. The voices that bellowed—

Two years too late.

—the voices that sneered—

You fucking whore.

—the voices that told me…that told me…

You're just not worth it.

She was trying to tell me something. Something from long, long ago.

Dig out the rock. Fill up the hole. With whatever you can find lying around…

Your heart is like soil and mine was trampled and hard. Packed down tight from a lifetime of pushing it down, all the things that hurt. All the useless emotions. All the things that you can't do anything about anyway. Pack it down tight, so far down that you can't feel it. And when it's hard, too hard to stay, it comes to the surface. A big, fat, ugly rock that you have to puke out, and that hurts, too, hurts even worse, because it leaves behind a crater. So you fill it up with Something, anything, it doesn't really matter what. Fill up the empty, aching, gaping, goddamn fucking hole. Fill it with booze, sex, work, drugs, religion. Find yourself a lover, find yourself a daddy, find yourself a god, find yourself a dick. Just fill it up. Fill it up. Just make it. All. Go away.

Don't fucking do this again. You don't deserve it. You deserve better.

I looked again at Ugly Woman—at Sharon—trying desperately to fill up her holes. I could do that, too. I could go back into that bar, right now, and drink ten of Bartender's sweet, red, rummy concoctions, but it wouldn't do the trick. I could fuck him again, I could fuck him all night, and it wouldn't fill up the hole Brian had left behind. Just like Brian couldn't fill up the one Jason had left. Just like Jason couldn't...couldn't...

"Oh, shit..."

I had to close my eyes. Because the world was spinning.

You're just...

And nothing was in focus.

...not worth it.

It was going to come up. I could feel it.

I stumbled to my car. Opened the door. Fell onto the seat.

Settle down. Deep breath, Tess. Deeper. You can do it. Hold it down. Just one last time...

And. I did.

I started the car, turned the heater on high, and pulled out of the parking lot. Drove past the hospital where Matthew had been born, where Alice had died, where Rachel had spent the last week of her life aching and shaking and puking—

Just so I could sleep, Tess...

—past the woods beside the hospital, where she had died—

Did she cry out? Did she scream? Didn't anybody hear her?

—and toward the middle of town. I stopped at the red light near the interstate. The sign on the overpass reminded me that I was thirty-one miles south of Brookfield and thirty-one miles north of New Mills. It was the sign that meant I had to decide. There was a breakdown coming, that much I knew. And I had to figure out where I was going to have it.

Green light.

I drove the thirty-one miles to the only place I could think of to go. Someplace where I might feel safe and loved. And when I got there I was surprised to see that it was only 12:55. Less than an hour since I'd last done the Something that used to make all the voices go away. The Something that didn't work anymore. So I tried something new. I sat there, shivering, even though the heater was on high, and tried to cry. Because I hadn't done it in such a long time. Not after Rachel died. Not after I'd put all her stuff in the box that meant she was gone forever, or when I'd opened up the envelope with the money that meant Brian was gone, too. Not even when I'd moved into the new apartment that meant that everything had changed. I knew I was supposed to be hurting. I knew that, somewhere, there was searing pain because they were gone. But it was all still buried beneath the hard, frozen ground where I couldn't feel it. It's where the tears were, too.

And that meant that nothing had changed.

CHAPTER 38

I walked into Zeke's, where it was safe. Even though it was filled with people and even though they stared at me—because they smiled while they stared. Sad smiles. I nodded back, because I couldn't smile. Not even a sad one.

The television was on, a baseball game. It would be a late night because the Sox were playing on the West Coast. Our Boys were ahead seven to zero in the bottom of the eighth inning and I didn't care. I didn't want baseball and I didn't need any more alcohol. I needed something here though. And the Something said:

"Tess…I'm sorry, but I'm closing after the game is over. Last call was—"

"I don't want a beer, Zeke. Just…" I fell onto a stool. "I don't know. Maybe a diet soda."

He brought it over, then looked at me closely. At my hair and makeup and nice clothes that were Just So. But he didn't say a word. Even though he knew what I'd been out doing, looking like this. And while he looked at me I looked at my soda. Just looked at it. Because I couldn't drink it. Couldn't even pick it up. I was shaking too badly.

"Tess, where's your coat?"

"My coat?"

"Yes. Your coat."

"Oh…it's…"

I'd left it on the stool at the other bar. My coat and my pin. The three-dollar pin that cost me a buck. The pin that meant, *I love you, Jason, so don't give up. I love you more than anything, so don't let me go.* Filled with colorful stones, except for the fake ruby. All the colors that meant… that meant…

There was never any color in my world, Tess. Not until I fell in love with you.

And I had let it go, just like he had let me go. It was back in that bar in Westville with Red Bartender. And what would he do with it? With a worn-out old coat and a cheap old pin? From the worn-out, cheap old lady who had fucked him in the booth of a bar…

"It's gone, Zeke. That's where it is."

He studied my face again. And I knew that, this time, he wasn't looking at the makeup.

"Uh…Tess, can you hang on for just a sec? I'll be right back."

"Okay."

He went into the kitchen. I looked at my soda. The bubbles were dancing and popping. I tried to listen to the pops but the game was too loud. I could feel it building up. Inside me. Could feel it wanting to come out. Tears and puke and bitter angry sad scared words, all moving up, up, up like bubbles of soda so I closed my eyes, focused. Focused hard on the sound of the soda, tried to make it louder than the baseball game, louder than the stupid announcers and the crowd on the television and the crowd behind me because what the fuck was the big deal? It's just a game, a game, a stupid fucking goddamn game...

Then another sound, my name, so I looked up. Zeke was back. Zeke and...

"Donny?"

"Hey, Tess."

I love his eyes. They smile even when he doesn't. Even when he's tired and sweaty and greasy.

They weren't smiling now. Had they smiled just for her? She had loved him, even if it was just a little, so maybe he had loved her too. I wanted to think that he had. That he'd loved her eyes, those beautiful eyes, and her laugh that was so full of mischief. Just like she was. So full of hurt and longing and fear...

It was easier for me to say goodbye to him than it would be to hear him say it to me later. Because he will.

Oh, Rachel. My poor, beautiful, lost little girl...

"Come with me, Tess." It was Zeke. He said it loudly, like he'd said it already.

"Where?"

"The break room. The diner's closed and Donny's just cleaning up the kitchen. He'll be okay to watch the bar for a bit."

"It doesn't take a whole lotta brains to keep an eye on these guys." Then he gave the boss a sheepish look. "No offense."

Zeke didn't even blink. Just said, "Come on, Tess."

I followed because I couldn't think of an excuse not to. And because I really did need to talk, needed to tell someone everything. Everything that was coming up. I couldn't push it back anymore. There was too much shit. Too much shit buried in boxes in the closet, too many people just waiting to knock at my door. Too much time with my head buried in the sand hoping it would all go away. It was all there, all there. Pain and sadness and other useless fucking emotions. But I couldn't feel them. They were under the hard ground. Covered with ice.

Break room. Very uncomfortable chair. Was it the one Rachel had sat in? *That* day? When she had told us everything and nothing? If I'd known it was so uncomfortable I would've, would've, would've what? Pillow? Cushion? Like I have an extra one I carry around with me, just waiting for uncomfortable chairs? Why does it matter now anyway, and I left my soda back at the bar. Can't drink it anyway but don't forget to pay for it, Tess, don't forget...

And Zeke was waiting for me to talk. Even though his bar was busy and swarming with people who needed him to fill up their holes. He was here with me. But I just sat, silent and still, because I was waiting for the words, too. There were so many of them, so many things to say. To Confess. Because we all get around to it. Sooner or later. The only question was where to start.

Because I could tell him all about Red Bartender, how I'd used him. And about Chris and all the others that had come before Jason, how I'd used all of them. I could even tell him that I'd used Jason, used Brian, too. Because even though I had loved them both—even though I really still did—I had used them. To fill up the holes. To make all the voices go away...

It was the voices I needed to tell Zeke about. One voice in particular, the one that had always been louder than all the rest. And the story started like this:

"When I was sixteen I fucked my mother's boss."

He sat there. Just looking at me with no disgust. That would come later.

"Sixteen?"

I nodded.

"How old was he?"

"He must've been about…forty or so. Mike Poulin. He fucked me right in his office, right on his big, ugly desk."

He nodded. "Did your mom ever find out?"

"Sure did. I got home late that night and ran up the stairs to my room. So she followed me up, because, of course, she had to yell at me for not calling to say I'd be late and letting her know I'd miss supper. For wasting her precious fucking time. And…she knew."

Did she smell it on me? Was it the flushed face? Guilty face? Scared face?

Scared. It scared me. He scared me. And so did I.

"She walked into my room, took one look at me and she didn't know who, but she knew what."

You're shaking. Stop it.

Stop it.

"And she said, 'You need to be careful, Theresa. Everyone's going to think you're a slut if you keep this up.' As if *she* didn't already think that. I mean, she put me on the pill a whole year before that. Not because I asked. Not because I needed it. Because she *knew*. It's what she said. 'I *know* you're going to need these.' She was always just expecting me to go out and fuck everything in sight."

I folded my hands. I had to make them stop shaking.

"And it was all bullshit anyway. She didn't care what anyone thought of *me*. She was only concerned about me putting *her* reputation in jeopardy, about people knowing that *her* daughter fucked around. And she just wouldn't shut the fuck up."

I took a deep breath.

"So I finally told her who it was. Just to shut her up."

That's not why you told her.

"It didn't, of course. But it did piss her off."

"Well, no kidding. Her boss took advantage of her daughter. Of course she was pissed."

"No. You don't get it. She was pissed at *me*. It embarrassed her. *I* embarrassed her."

"Oh." He looked at me carefully. "Is that why you did it?"

"No." Then I shrugged. "Maybe a little. But mostly I liked the attention. He didn't take advantage of me, Zeke. Well, not really. Maybe a little. But only because he knew I'd let him."

Go ahead, Tess. Tell him. Tell him why you fucked the nice boss man.

"He was this big-shot business man in town. He owned most of Brookfield. Gas station, used car place…you know the type. Had his fingers everywhere." I laughed because I had meant it in the clean way, but the other way was true, too. "Pretty much the only thing he didn't own was the café, and his brother owned that. He still does."

Still shaking. Still…

"The office my mother worked in was sort of the hub of Mike's mini-empire. She did his books and ran the office and answered phones and did the filing and a bunch of other shit. Anyway, I went in one day after school for… something. I don't remember what. And he…was there."

Tall. Handsome. Politician's smile. I was so young and so stupid that I thought the smile was for me. Just for me. And I thought that it meant...

"So after that I started going in every day."

Hey, Mom. Just popped in to say hi...

What had she thought? Years of nothing and then all of a sudden...every day. For weeks and weeks. Had she *really* thought I was there to see her? Had it made her happy, even a little, to think that I might actually have wanted to spend my free time with...*her*?

"And Mike was always there. I knew he wanted me, because he'd always make a point to come out of his office, out of his lair, whenever I came in. And he'd stare at me... you know, stare at me *that way* when her back was turned. Or he'd ask her to go get a file and say nice things to me once she left the room."

Goddamn it, Tess. No one can fill out a sweater like you can.

And that's when I started wearing a sweater every day. Even after it started getting warm.

"He did it for weeks. At first it was, you know, kinda creepy."

Liar.

If it was creepy you would've stopped going in. It's why you kept going back there, for weeks, and you know it. So did he...

"But after a while I started to like it. He had lots of money and he was good-looking and he had all these people who answered to him—and he wanted *me*. Sounds pretty stupid, I know, but I thought it was great. I mean, I was just a...girl."

I was. I was just a girl...

"And I was doing that to him."

Look what I can do...

"And so one night I went into his office."

First Friday of summer. A week after Dave's graduation. Because graduation meant college. It meant that—soon— he'd be gone. And I'd be all alone. For real.

"And I knew Mike was there alone, because his car was the only one out front and...it happened."

Big smile. Big politician's smile. No one else was there. He knew why I was. Sixteen years old. Still a virgin. Had he known that, too? Before it happened? Probably he did, but he didn't say a word. He just shut the door. Closed the shades. Cleared off the desk. Not like in the movies. Not a big *whoosh* and papers flying everywhere. Not like that. I helped him clear it off. Five stacks of files. Adding machine. Pencil box. Two small piles of papers. Telephone. We put it all on the floor.

You helped him clear off his desk...

Then he kissed me. First time I'd ever been kissed. He was so gentle and it was so nice, and I didn't want it to ever end. Then his hands were all over me and his mouth was everywhere. Everywhere and I loved it. I really did. Even when the clothes started to come off, I loved that, too. Loved him looking at my naked body. Loved what it did to him. Then he laid me down on the desk, on his big, ugly desk. I thought it would hurt, thought it was supposed to, and it did, but only a little. Not like I thought. And he was so slow, took his time, knew what he was doing. I even came and that surprised me, even though I'd done it myself plenty of times before that night, most of the time while I was thinking about him. And when it happened he knew it almost before I did, and I had never in my life felt so good and so happy and so loved as I did at that moment. Not because I was coming, although that was amazing, but because my ears were full of a man whispering to me, in between his grunts and moans—

...that's it, Tess...come for me, Tess, come for me...

—my name. My name. And then he told me how beautiful I was—

...just look at those beautiful tits...

—and how sexy—

...I could just fuck you forever...

—and it was just what I had always wanted to hear.

Well, not really. But it was close enough.

But when it was all over everything was different. When it was all done I didn't have the power anymore. Because I had liked it. And he knew it. And I was scared. Just like a little kid.

I cleared my throat. "Anyway, my mom really did freak out. Although, now that I think about it, I don't think she was pissed."

I closed my eyes for a moment, and tried to remember her reaction. She didn't yell. She didn't actually say anything. She just stood there, looking at me, her mouth literally open. She started to shake. Couldn't stop...shaking...

"I think it scared the shit outta her."

But whether she'd been pissed or scared didn't really matter. Not back then, and especially not now. And I sat silently for a few seconds, looking at my hands. Because I couldn't look at Zeke for the next part. But I had to say it.

"Not that it stopped her from using it to get a huge raise from the guy."

"*What?*"

I laughed. Laughed. Just like it was funny.

"Oh yeah. She told him that she'd tell his wife, that she'd tell everyone, all about it if she didn't start seeing more money in her paycheck. *Lots* more. Because she knew he wanted to go into politics and that he'd want to keep it quiet. So of course he gave her what she wanted. She told my dad that...she told him that she got a raise."

She called it a raise.

"It's how she paid for my brother's college tuition."

I smiled again, but my heart was squeezed so tightly that I could barely breathe. Because I didn't want to think about how Dave would react if he ever found out that his sister's cunt had paid for his education. And I looked at Zeke again, looked him right in the eye. Because there was something that he had to know:

"Dave's a wicked smart guy. He deserved to go to school and get a good education. And he came back to Brookfield to practice law when he could've gone someplace where he'd make big money. He's helped a lot of people. He really has."

He battles Injustice. Because of me. For me. Because of *two years too late*. Because he'd spent all his life knowing how much she hated me. She didn't love him, and he knew that, too. But she didn't hate him. And he knew that it wasn't fair. It wasn't Just.

"And once he was done with school, she put all that extra money away for herself. And now she's living it up in France. With all that fucking money."

Fucking money. That's just what it was.

"Anyway, when I found out what she was doing to Mike, I went back to see him. Because I wanted to tell him,

you know, that I was sorry and that I didn't know she was…
going to do that to him. I *really* wanted him to know that. It
was very important to me for him to know that."

And I said it again:

"That was very important to me."

I needed Zeke to understand that. Because Mike never
had.

"But when I got there he thought I was there for
another reason. He thought I was there to fuck him again.
Because…"

Yes? Because?

"Because he'd already paid for it. So…I let him. I let
him fuck me. Again."

I swallowed.

"Why not? Might as well. I mean, he did pay."

"Oh, Jesus…"

It surprised me that it was sadness I heard in his voice,
and not disgust. Sadness. Because he loved me. Even
though he shouldn't. Even though I didn't deserve it.
Because what he didn't know, and what I couldn't tell him,
was that I kept going back. Kept going. All summer long,
every Friday night, because it's not like I was doing anything else with my time. What else would I be doing on
a Friday night? What else could I possibly do? And every
Friday I'd walk through the door and help him clean off
a desk. So he could fuck me. But it wasn't his desk. Not
after that first time, that first night. It was my mother's desk
because that's what he wanted. Where he wanted to be.
And what he'd say, as he was fucking me, what he'd talk
about was her. Because he hated her, hated her, he fucking hated, hated, *oh god, I fucking hate her, I hate that fucking*

bitch. He'd say it even louder, so loud, so fucking loud, as he was coming. Inside of me. On her desk. But every Friday I'd close my eyes, close them tight, and try to imagine the words away. Even though in my mind it was still him, still him, still Mike…in my mind he was saying something different. Something else, beautiful words—

    …*beautiful…forever…*

—just like the first time. And I'd come, every time. Just like the first time. Every time. Because—in my mind—those words meant that he loved me. Even though he didn't. Even though I knew he didn't. I imagined it anyway because it's what I needed. To hear. Even though I agreed with the words he was really saying. The ones I heard when I couldn't imagine them away. Because I hated her, too.

    I fucking. Hate. Her. Too…

And every Friday night, after he was done and after we were dressed, I'd look at her desk. Look at it. And I'd leave it so that she could see. It was empty and dirty and torn apart, just like I was. And every Monday morning she must have gone into work and looked at her desk, her empty, dirty desk. Looked at what was dried up on top of it. Because I always waited, always, for a minute or two, waited naked on her desk, and let drip…right…out. Onto her desk. And, of course, she had to clean it before she put all her stuff back. On top of her desk. The files and papers and her adding machine and her pencil box and her telephone. Every Monday morning. All summer long. But she never said a word. Never. The only words I heard all summer, the only words at all, were Mike's words. The words that were real and the words I imagined. They mingled together in his voice until sometimes I couldn't remember if it was my mother he hated...or if it was me. Probably it was both.

And then: the last time. The last Friday night. Hot awful August, right before summer ends. When you don't know, really, what Autumn will bring. Because that last night I found out, for real, what he thought of me. Right after I came I opened my eyes. I usually kept them closed until he was done but I wanted to see, for some reason, his face. To see...something. To see if the Something was there. And, of course, it wasn't. His eyes were open, too, because they'd been open the whole time. Probably he always kept them open, always watched me. To see it happening. And then he smiled, that horrible, cold smile and I saw something else. Something else. The look that was really. A word. And then he said it. He said the word. While he was coming. Inside of me. On my mother's desk.

"You *like* it. You dirty...fucking...whore. You. *Love*. It..."

And I did. So he was right. I really was a—

"No, Tess. You're not."

I blinked. Because the words were real, not in my mind. And I blinked again. Because it was Zeke's voice. And if Zeke had said those words—out loud—that meant that I had said it all out loud, too. And this is what his words meant:

I know. Everything. And it doesn't matter. I still love you anyway.

And so I told him the rest. The other words Mike had said. The ones that hurt worse than anything ever had.

"As soon as he was done he said...I mean, he was only *just* finished. He was actually still...inside me. And he looked right into my eyes and he said, 'Don't bother

543

to come back again, Tess. It's just not worth it anymore. You're just…not…worth it.'"

And I laughed. Just like it was funny.

"He still kept paying my mother, though. Every week. Because it was worth it to keep her quiet. His reputation was worth it. His career. And his family not knowing, *that* was worth it. Even if I wasn't…"

…worth it.

I shrugged, because I was too tired to care. Still. Or too frozen. Because it wasn't gone. It was all still there. Packed tight. Underneath the hard ground. Underneath the ice. Maybe it always would be. And I didn't know what to do about it. What else I could do.

Zeke reached over and held my hand, and it felt like the sweetest thing anyone had ever done. "Tess. That doesn't make you a whore. It makes you a scared, lonely kid. You were searching for something you needed and didn't know how to get. It's what we all do. It makes you normal, Tess. It makes you human. And all the rest… well, Jesus. That wasn't you. Not *you*, Tess. That wasn't your fault."

They were the words I'd hoped he'd say, the ones I'd always wanted someone to say. Even though I didn't know it until he said them. Because I'd never felt normal before. I still didn't. Not quite. But I had to try hard to feel that way, to believe I felt that way. To pretend that I did. At least long enough, maybe, to help Brian. To help Rachel, because please, God, *please* don't let her die…

Tess…she's already dead. She's been dead. Forever. And Brian's gone. He's gone…

Oh. That's right.

And that's when something shifted inside me, ruptured inside me. I knew what it was, what was going to happen, even though it was different than before. It was bigger. The only thing that wasn't different was the fact that I had to do this part in private.

And Zeke had to get back to the bar. Because he was never gone from it this long. He was always there.

Always...

"Zeke. What happened with you and Dean?"

I'd caught him off guard. He sputtered a few incoherent syllables before he managed, "What makes you think something happened?"

I squeezed his hand. "You can't fool the cleaning lady. There's only one toothbrush in the bathroom again."

He shrugged. "It just didn't work out."

"Because you're here all the time."

He shrugged again.

"You gotta cut that shit out, Zeke, because...You know, don't you? She wouldn't want to see you living like this. She stood up to those assholes because of you. She fought for you. Not for the diner. Not for the bar. For *you.*"

Must be nice.

"And she didn't do it so you could waste away in here with no one to talk to except a bunch of drunken assholes and an idiot cleaning lady. She didn't want you to live your life all by yourself and die all alone. So go out and...fucking *live*. Like she'd want you to. Like she *wants* you to. If you can let Donny loose on the public on a Saturday night just so you can listen to my bullshit then you can sure as hell let him go out there a few nights during the week so you can have a goddamn life."

And still he said nothing. So I shot his words right back at him.

"Get him back and love him, Zeke. Love him like it's your last day."

He finally smiled. We stood up and I gave him a hug, one that was as tight as I could make it. And I hoped that he knew it meant *thank you.* That it meant *I love you.* Because I couldn't say the words out loud. If I did I would break down for real, and I still had to do that part in private. Because it was starting to come up, for real. And pretty soon the whole world would be spinning and nothing would be in focus...

I followed him back into the bar. It was empty except for Donny, who was collecting empty bottles from the tables. I stood with my hand on the doorknob for a minute and waited for him to finish. Because there was something I needed to tell him. Something that I knew was important. I knew it even through the fog.

"Donny...you're still with Ashley, right?"

"Yep."

"Well...you be good to her. Okay? Be *good.* She deserves it."

He gave me a big smile. "Yes. She does."

Then it was time for me to leave. Because I'd held it down long enough. And when I got into my car I turned on the heater. Turned it on high. Because I was still shaking. Still.

I probably always would be.

CHAPTER 39

Outside my apartment it was pitch dark. Upstairs Neighbor was asleep and I'd forgotten to leave my porch light on. The only street light was burned out. There was no moon, no headlights from oncoming cars. I'd only been living here for fifteen hours so I was still unfamiliar with the terrain of the yard. I slung my purse over my shoulder and made my way along anyway. Slow, tentative footsteps, up the uneven dirt walkway, arms extended, hoping, soon, to feel the handrail of the stairs. Five wobbly steps. Six. Seven.

And that's when I lost my footing, stumbled over something, I didn't know what—a rock or a bump or a body—and fell to the ground. It was cold and wet with just-melted snow that the lawn was still too frozen to absorb. Even though it was April, even though it was spring. Wet and frozen, just like me. I felt my way along, ran my fingers along the cold, prickly grass, dragged my bare knees through tiny, cold puddles. By the time I found the bottom step my teeth were chattering so badly that my jaw was stiff and sore, and my clothes were soaked with water. Like I'd just crawled out of an icy lake.

...she jumped over the edge, right into the lake...

She jumped off that mountain. That Indian princess. She looked over the edge and into the water and she jumped right in. And I knew why. I'd always known.

I crawled up the four porch steps and finally stood up, still shivering. Teeth still chattering. I reached into my purse for my keys and unlocked the door.

Nine steps into the living room. Still shaking. It was all coming up and I knew I couldn't stop it. But there was something I had to do first.

I snapped on a lamp and scanned the paintings on the wall. Brian had spent so much time staring at them, examining them, searching for clues. Because he knew that these landscapes weren't really landscapes at all. They were people and feelings and moments in time; pieces of me, of my life. Each canvas covered with beautiful, fragile bits of what was left of my soul.

A field of fragrant wildflowers...a muddy brown brook filled with trout...a dark, green forest edged with a solid rock wall. Love and friendship and justice. There were others, too. Anger and laughter and shame... and fear.

Kineo was Fear. I'd sold Hope. And held onto Fear.

I yanked it off the wall with dirty wet hands and ran with it into the kitchen, with no clear idea of what I was doing. I threw it down onto the table, backed up a step, and stared at it. Remembered the bored mindless waitress who thought it was nothing, who told me the story of the doomed princess in that stupid voice, that droning fucking monotone. Just like it was nothing.

She jumped right off the edge there. Drowned, most likely, or died 'cause of the fall.

No. She was dead first. She was dead before she hit the water, hell she was dead before she jumped, before she took her first step toward the summit. She died somewhere between her home and that mountain. Her brain willed her feet to move her shaking body forward. One step then another step and another. But her heart had already stopped beating.

And I was sick of her. Fucking sick of being her.

I picked up the canvas and hurled it against the wall. It fell harmlessly to the floor, face up, staring at me. It was still alive. And I wasn't.

But the fucking thing wasn't alive. Wasn't indestructible. It was just a canvas, and what's a canvas? Just cotton threads woven together and stretched over some wood. Nothing magical about it, nothing special, nothing permanent.

It was Nothing.

I chucked it onto the counter and rooted around in the silverware drawer. Found my paring knife, small but sharp, and it did the trick. Punctured, poked, ripped, hole after hole, one after another, easily—so fucking easily— because it wasn't really a mountain and a lake. Not flint and water and stone and fear and trees. It was just cotton threads woven together. Hanging in pieces from some wood.

I zipped the knife through one piece, then another, and another. I missed a few times, got my thumb and then three of my fingers, until finally there were no pieces of canvas big enough to cut. Nothing left except clusters of ribbons dangling from a bloody wooden stretcher bar. And so I dropped Nothing onto the floor.

But that wasn't all. I knew.

I turned around. Gripped the counter. Dizzy and...

Here it comes.

I leaned over the sink and waited, but nothing came out. There was just a little bit of alcohol inside of me, not enough to vomit. And that meant it was gonna come up for real, for real oh my God...make it stop...

I fell to the floor beside what was left of Kineo, still clutching the knife in my bloody hand. I stared at the sharp, beautiful blade, then at my wrist and I wondered if it would hurt. Probably wouldn't hurt any worse than the cuts on my fingers. And then afterwards...what it was like to feel everything just fading away? Drifting. Slowly. Probably the same way it always had. The way I'd felt all my stupid, miserable, fucking life. Minutes and hours and days and weeks and months and years, watching hope and happiness and love slipping away. Drifting. Slowly. Away...

But how would it be for the Someone who would find me like that? Covered in dried blood and waste, cold and dead and rotting away for real. Who would it be? Zeke probably. Or Laura. That would be unforgivable, because that would mean Cassidy would see me, too. And you just don't do that. Not to anyone. And besides...I didn't really want to die. Even if I didn't want to live like this. Oh, God, not like this...not anymore...

I want. To live. To live for real.

So put it down, Tess. Put it down.

Down.

I opened my clenched fingers. And the knife fell to the floor.

Dizzy, so fucking dizzy, even sitting down. I put my head between my legs and, with nothing inside me to puke, I had to cry. It was all coming out now, fat ugly tears and brutal sobs that hurt my stomach and my head and my neck and my back, but not as much as holding onto it for so long, too long. Holding onto it forever. It was loud and awful, but not loud enough to drown out the voices. So many of them, with words filled with hate and despair and *dirty whore*, and the words were familiar and loud. I listened to my mother and waited to hear my father, but there wasn't much of him there, not the words I'd needed. Not *stop it, leave her alone.* Not *I love you, Tess*, but there was Mike to fill in the hole, I thought, I hoped, and a dozen others or even more of them and they echoed in my brain. The ones I'd let use me, use me like a whore, and all the others, the ones I'd used. And then everyone who knew. All the voices that judged...

But love was there, too, it had always been there, and the kindness seemed greater than the bitterness and hate. But it couldn't get through the hard, icy ground. It just stayed on the surface to be trampled and washed away. Because I never thought I deserved it. That I was worth it. I never let it in.

The tears finally ran out and I was left with an aching head, but not as bad as it had been. I was too exhausted to get up off the floor, so I crawled into the bedroom, climbed onto my bed, underneath the blankets, and slept in my clothes. Slept forever.

When I opened my eyes it was dark and I didn't know why. I looked at the clock. Glowing green numbers.

10:14.

Must be P.M. Sunday night. Because it's so dark. I slept all night and all day, too.

But then I heard it: Rain on the windows. I blinked a few times, and it wasn't as dark as I had first thought. Just cloudy. A storm. 10:14 a.m. Sunday morning.

I made my bed and took a shower. Jasmine shampoo. I threw my old clothes into the trash can, rid my kitchen of the remnants of Bloody Kineo, and ate breakfast. Cereal and toast and coffee. Washed my hands. Brushed my teeth. Lavender and mint. And by that time the storm was done. Outside it was April. Outside it was spring.

I opened my windows and let it in. Took in a deep breath, then a deeper one. Filled my lungs with lovely spring air. And I knew.

It's gonna be all right.

So I said it out loud.

"I'm gonna be all right."

And then I lay down on my couch and cried. Again.

I cried for a mother who hated me and for a father who loved me, but was weak. Too weak to protect me. And for a brother who had seen it all, felt it all, and had taken on the burden of loving me and protecting me. The burden that wasn't his.

I cried for Alice, who had tried to love me, and for Jason, my beautiful friend. The man who really had been the love of my life. Once. I missed him still, so much. His humor and brains and rough, gorgeous beard. Most of all I missed the way he knew me, inside and out, better than anyone ever had; without the words and with them, too. Because there had been a Jason-and-Tess for a long time. Long before I put on a white dress. Before he knocked on my door in the rain. Even before he walked into the store on that cold, perfect February morning. And now there wasn't. And there never would be again.

I cried for Rachel because I missed her, missed her so much. Wanted to go back to that last night, Christmas night. Wanted to run up the stairs and tell her the sweet things that had been in my heart. Tell her I didn't care about the ring. *It doesn't matter, Rach. It doesn't matter at all. You matter, though.* Take back the anger she'd seen on my face, and the hurt. Tell her, instead, about what I'd seen on hers. What I'd seen in her heart. Tell her *I know you're hurting and scared. And I know your heart is tender and fragile and full of beauty and love.* Even if it wouldn't change anything, but especially if it would. I cried because I wanted to tell her that I loved her. And I couldn't.

And I cried for Brian. Because as much as I missed Rachel, as much pain as I was in, his was so much worse. And he was somewhere right now, somewhere on this beautiful Sunday, this gorgeous spring morning, feeling empty and alone and scared. And I wanted to hold him and feel his tears, wet on my shoulder and breasts. To tell him it would be okay—because it really would be, *it really will, and so will you, Brian*—and I couldn't.

I cried because I missed him. I wanted him beside me, right now. I wanted to see his glowing eyes and feel his strong arms around me and hear his sweet, deep voice. I wanted to hear my voice, too, telling him all of the things that had been locked up inside of me for a year. All the things he had been hoping to hear from me, needed to hear, the things he had searched for every time he'd searched my eyes. All of the beautiful, powerful feelings that I could never find words for. *Brian, Brian you are fire. Fire and music and life. You are everything that is good and decent and strong.* I wanted him to know me, inside and out, better than anyone ever had...and he couldn't.

And when I was finished crying I sat up. Took another deep breath and wiped the tears from my face. The sun was still shining. Yellow and warm. And that's when I knew there was Something I needed. And I knew what the Something was.

I put on my light spring jacket and stepped outside. Took a walk through town, down the main road and every side road, too. Even here, away from the woods, I was surrounded by trees. They lined every road and filled every yard and they stretched their arms out to me. Maples, mostly, but oaks and birches, too. The were bare, still, but I knew. Just a few more weeks and they'd be bursting with newborn leaves of the palest green.

And there was a Something that was green and new inside me, too. A feeling that something more had shifted and loosened, just a little. It was even lighter the next day and kept getting lighter, kept getting looser, in the days that followed that. There were more tears, lots more, and sometimes the hurt was almost more than I could bear. But I was still all right, and more alive than I'd ever been. And by the time I looked at the calendar and noted that Rachel had been gone for four months, I knew what had happened.

The rocks were being unearthed, one at a time, all the rocks of my life. The holes were still there, and craters too, and they still hurt. All of them. They hurt like hell and they were going to keep hurting for a while. I knew. The ice had melted and the soil was still hard, but not like it had been, and now it was waiting. Just waiting to be tilled. Because what was underneath, what had been there all along, was lovely and soft and fertile.

Just like spring.

CHAPTER 40

Second Saturday in June. Sunny and warm. More than five months since Rachel died.

I took a very deep breath and walked through the door of Hillside Café. Nodded a greeting to Deb. I'd noticed when I pulled in that the sign was lit up outside and she raised her eyebrows. I shook my head.

Not today. Not anymore.

She nodded. "He's waiting for you."

"Thanks."

I walked toward his table, past nosy diners who stared, and when he saw me he smiled. And for a moment I remembered when I used to live to see him smile.

We made small talk while we waited for a teenaged waitress to bring me my coffee. Because this was private. Our story, not their gossip. He asked me about my new place and I asked him about work. Then he said he was sorry that things didn't work out with Brian, and it almost looked like he was. So I told him I was happy to hear that he'd found someone and I asked him about her, even though I already knew. Kim had told me everything he was telling me now, which wasn't much, but it was enough.

Amy. Guidance counselor. Smart. Pretty. Twenty-nine. September wedding.

And he looked happy.

"Is she upset that I'm here? That we're talking like this?"

"Not really. She knows why you came. And," he gave an embarrassed chuckle, "at least you had the courtesy to call first."

It was my turn to laugh. And it felt good.

"She is meeting me here for lunch, though. She'll be here at about twelve-thirty."

Which meant, of course, twelve-fifteen. I glanced at my watch. I had twenty minutes. More than enough time.

Teenage Waitress finally brought my coffee. Cream. Probably sugar, too, and I knew what that meant. I smiled and looked over at Deb and she smiled right back. He waited until the girl was safely away, then reached for his wallet, took out an envelope and slid it across the table. I looked at it, at my full name and new address in his nice, neat penmanship. And what that meant was, *I could have mailed this and we both know it.* I took a deep breath and braved his face.

"I want you to know that it's not about the money. If it was just that then I'd let you keep it. I only asked for it because..."

I took a quick glance around the café. Staring faces. Still.

He looked too. Then he boomed, "Is there any way you could all just mind your *own* goddamn business? Just this once?" There were nods and smiles all around us. No more stares. And no hard feelings. Of course.

He was Jason Dyer. And he could do no wrong.

I nodded my thanks and continued. "It wasn't fair of me to...leave it with you. To make you hang onto part of us while you were trying to start a new life. And it was wrong of me to say what I did to you about it last summer. I know that's not what this money is. And that was a really shitty thing for me to say."

He shrugged and told me it was okay. Even though it wasn't.

I took a sip of coffee. Another one. Sipped till my cup was only half full. I could have said that over the phone and we both knew it. So I took an even deeper breath and tackled the real reason I'd driven for an hour to talk to him in person:

Sorry.

It was like *love*. A stupid, ineffective word. Too much emotion for just one word. What's a stronger word? A better word? I hadn't been able to find one even though I'd actually looked.

Remorse. Repentance. Regret.

Those words didn't even come close. Because this is what sorry is: deep icy pits lined with spikes and razors that live in your gut and heart and brain and soul. Frigid misery. Sharp reminders of your mistakes and the sadness they've caused people you love. People who love you. And how can you say those words to someone? You can't. And so I was stuck with:

"Jason, I never told you that I was sorry for cheating on you. I was stupid and selfish and I hurt you. I did it like it was nothing. I did it without even thinking about it. Without thinking about what I was doing to you. I was just

thinking about me. And I want you to know that I *am* sorry.
I was sorry even...even while..."

*Even while it was happening, oh God, even before. Before I
ever touched him, before I reached for him. Even when it was only
a seed of an idea. I wanted you, Jason. Goddamn it I wanted you.
I loved you, so much, for so long, before I even knew what the word
meant. Before you taught me what it meant. I was just so scared...
and I should have told you that. So you could tell me it was all
right. Because it would have been. We would have been. I know it.
I know it...now...*

They were the words I wanted to say, but, of course, I
couldn't. There are some things you just can't say out loud.
But I looked at his face again, at his eyes. At the man I'd
held back so much from already. And that's when I knew
I was wrong, that I'd been wrong the whole time. Some
things have to be said. Out loud.

So I cleared my throat and I used those words, for once.
Used the words that meant all of the powerful feelings I'd
held inside of me for so long. I knew it was too late for
those words to change anything. But it wasn't too late for
him to know. And when I was done I asked him for something. It was something I needed, but didn't really deserve.
But I asked him anyway.

"I just...I hope you can forgive me, Jason."

It was probably too late for friendship again. I knew
that and it hurt, but it was my own fault. But maybe—*please,
God*—maybe forgiveness...

"Tess, I forgave you a long time ago. The second I
closed the door behind me that night. I was just too stupid
and proud to open it back up again and tell you." He shook
his head. "It was my own fault. I hurt you first. I gave up on

you…I gave up on *us*. I pushed you away and then I had the nerve to play the part of the injured husband when someone else caught you. And I'm sorry for that. I really am, because…"

He lowered his voice.

Our Story.

"…I loved you, Tess. I loved you so much."

…*and don't ever forget…*

"But I woke up one morning and I was thirty-five. And I felt so damned old and useless, like my half of my life was gone and I hadn't done anything with it. My dad was thirty-five when he died, and I got to thinking about him, and that got me thinking again about starting a family of my own. I wanted it so badly, I've always wanted that, because I thought I lost mine when he died. I grew up feeling like it wasn't…whole anymore. Like it wasn't real." He shook his head. "I know that probably sounds stupid, but—"

"It doesn't sound stupid." But it made me feel stupid, like the biggest idiot in the world. I should have known that he didn't just wake up one morning with a baby craving. I never bothered to find out what was *really* bothering him. Never bothered to look past my own hurt and fear.

"It wasn't until my mom died that I understood what the word actually meant. It didn't occur to me until *that* moment. I had it, all that time. She was my family. And *you* were my family, Tess. You and me. And I blew it. But I thought—I really did—that if I went down to see you and told you all that then we'd be able to pick up again and start over." He shook his head. "But it was too late.

I knew that the second you got out of your car that day, the way you looked at me. The way you *didn't* look at me. Then *he* showed up and...it's how you looked at him. And when I left your house I knew I'd lost everything, because..."

He looked me steadily, with bright blue eyes, the eyes I had once loved more than anything in the world.

"You know that we were all set, don't you? We were set. If we hadn't been so stupid we would have made it all the way. One of those couples who get to their fiftieth anniversary and even beyond that. One of those couples who look back and wonder how the hell it all went by so fast. That was *us*, Tess. That was us."

...I have loved you forever.

I could only nod. My heart hurt too badly to let me speak. Because he was right. That was us. It was what we had let go of, what we had thrown away. Just like it was nothing.

Forever.

And there we were. Jason and Tess. We were sitting less than two feet apart from each other—close enough to touch if we'd wanted to. And each of us was holding inside our heart and mind and soul exactly what it was the other had needed two years before. What we needed right now. That's what our time apart had given us. It had given us everything. Except for the most important thing, of course. The love. That's what it had taken away.

We were sitting there, having our private conversation in public, so Amy wouldn't feel threatened. That was my idea, because I knew the raw, nagging, achy fear that was probably eating at her, the fear that came from that one little word: *Ex*. The word that meant a history of love and passion that had once been strong and powerful and real. But Amy could show up right now or she could wait an hour or she could leave us alone completely and never show up. And the result would be the same. Nothing would happen. Because there wasn't enough love or passion left for the two of us to salvage anything from our history. Nothing left except an occasional, sad flicker of memory.

And a tiny glimpse of the life that Could Have Been. I looked at his eyes and he looked at mine. Because the other thing was there, too. The other part of Us, the one that would never be. We were both seeing it, the first time we'd ever seen it at the same time. Clear and vivid and real. And it hurt so badly that I had to look away from his eyes, because I couldn't let him see mine. Couldn't let him see the sudden, irrational spasm of jealousy that twisted my heart at the thought of him having our family—our beautiful blue-eyed family—with someone else. Someone new.

I looked instead at the envelope, held it in my hands. Concentrated hard. My name. New address. Neat cursive writing. Took another deep breath.

And the spasm was gone.

I looked at my watch. Only five more minutes until Amy's arrival and I had absolutely no desire to meet the woman. Not yet. There'd be another time for that awkward introduction. It was going to happen. But not today.

"Kim's due in December," I said.

"Yes. I know."

I knew he did. It's not why I said it.

"I'll...I guess I'll see you guys at the hospital then."

He nodded. "Yes, you will."

I opened my purse, deposited my new fortune safely inside it. Pulled out my keys and an Abe. A big tip for the teenager who'd brought me a one-dollar cup of coffee. The best coffee in the world.

"Before you go, Tess, there's something I need to ask you. Something I've always wondered about."

"What is it?"

He smiled at me. Smiled. And it was the biggest one I'd seen on him since...I couldn't remember when I'd seen it last.

"Did you really beat my Space Invaders score? Or was that just a pickup line?"

And there he was. Jason Adam Dyer. My friend. The man I had loved forever. The man I had once loved more than anything. And for just that moment he was Mine. Again.

"I really did beat your Space Invaders score."

Damn right I did. January 17, 1982. 3:05 a.m.

I smiled back at him. "And it was a pickup line."

He nodded. "It was a good one."

We both stood up and he gave me a very quick kiss on the cheek, barely enough to give me a hint of his beard. Then we said it. Because we had to.

"Goodbye, Tess."

"Goodbye, Jason."

And I walked away. Without looking back at the diners who were staring once again. I nodded to Deb. Then to Coach. He glared back at me, and I didn't care. Not about what he thought of me. Not about what Mike thought, either. Not even a little.

They just weren't worth it.

I got into my car and drove, but not toward home. I wasn't done with Brookfield yet. My next stop was my dad's new place. It was just a small house but very clean. He asked me how work was going and told me about his. He worked only part time now, even though he didn't have to work at all. Even though he hated it. Because if he retired, he said, he'd go crazy with nothing to do. Then he told me about a woman he'd met online who lived only two towns away. He called her a Chess Friend. He only told me a little, but what little he said let me know that he was happy. Finally. Just like he deserved.

Then he cleared his throat, reached over to the coffee table, and handed me an envelope that had my name on it. Inside was a picture of my mother that he'd taken long ago, during that Summer of Abandon. Nineteen years old. She was surrounded by flowers and trees that were full of color and life. And she wasn't. Her eyes were filled with Pain. Fear. Exhaustion. Even though she was still just a kid. Even though it was summer outside and beautiful. Even though she was. Even though there was no Dave or Tess in her life yet. It was there already, all of it. And I didn't know why.

Neither did my father, even though he'd wanted to. Because he really *had* loved her, once. At least he had tried. She never let him. Never let him in. And I remembered that night, the middle of the night, when we'd been yanked from our sleep by a phone call. A grandmother I'd never met, never known, was dead. *Her* mother was dead and gone. But there were no tears. None. And I still didn't know why. Maybe I never would.

I thanked my dad, then tucked the picture back inside the envelope and put it in my purse. Gave him a kiss and told him I loved him. Told him that he'd been a good dad. Because he had been, even though he could have been a better dad. He could have done more. But he did what he could, which is all any of us can do, and he'd done the most important things. He'd stayed. And I'd always known he loved me. Even if he'd never said it.

He said it to me now.

"I love you too, Tess."

It sounded so beautiful. Sounded just like a song.

My next stop was Dave's house, but he wasn't home. Out battling Injustice, even on a Saturday. I hung out with Kim and we talked about a Christmas baby. She wasn't very far along, just a few months, so there wasn't enough belly for me to poke. She didn't know if the baby was a boy or a girl yet but I called the kid Bertha anyway.

When she asked about Brian I told her, *he's not doing good.* Because just the week before we'd finally buried Rachel, deep inside the cold, hard ground. Brian, Zeke, Rick, the Burkes, and me. We all cried, big horrible tears, and I thought again of all the things, all of the beautiful words, I could have said to her, words that might have made a difference. Helped her to hold on, maybe for one more day. Maybe that would've been enough. I tried saying them to her at the cemetery, silently, but I couldn't. Because she wasn't really there. Just a headstone, beside her mother's, with two dates. The dates that told us she really had been much too young to die. And her name:

Rachel Carson LaChance.

And after the service was done I took Rick aside and said, "Stop at a bookstore sometime soon and buy a copy of *Silent Spring.*"

He nodded and promised that he would, even though I knew he had no idea what I was talking about. But when he read it—if he read it—he'd understand exactly what I meant. And he'd know a little bit more about his wife. He'd know where his daughter had gotten her name.

Then I spoke briefly to Brian. It was the first time I'd seen him in almost two months. He looked worse than he ever had, like he was still buried, even deeper than Rachel was. And I knew he'd be buried for a long time. I gave him a hug and tried not to smell his shirt. But I couldn't help it. And I wanted it to last forever, to just hold onto him and never, never let go; but of course I had to. And even though I wanted to I didn't tell him I loved him. Even though he knew it, just like I knew he still loved me.

And once I got home I cried on my couch for the rest of the day. Because I really had thought, right up until the moment I saw him, that he'd be stronger already. That he'd be better. But he wasn't and that meant that he really wouldn't be knocking on my door. Not any time soon. Maybe not ever.

Kim held my hand and said she was sorry, and I told her I'd be all right. I knew I would be someday. And I spent the next hour playing outside with Matthew. He was fifteen months old now and walking and running faster than ever, with cute chubby legs and a great big smile and big Blue eyes that only hurt a little to look at. When I held him he smiled even wider and when I blew bubbles on his belly he laughed. Then he said my name and it sounded like this:

"Dessssh!"

My name in my nephew's voice. It sounded beautiful.

And then Dave came home. Tired and content. When he gave his wife and son their kisses and hugs he had glowing eyes, and I wondered why I'd never noticed them before. He smiled when he saw me, even though he'd known I was there before he came through the door. Because my car was right out there in the driveway. And because I'd been out in public with Jason. Brookfield was bigger than New Mills, but it was a small town just the same. Then we talked privately in his den. And it started like this:

"I never said thank you for being strong for me all those years," I said. "And for loving me."

He was crying just a little, and it was the first time I'd ever seen it. "I don't think it was enough."

Of course it was enough. More than just *enough*. He'd done a good job, done a job that wasn't his. He'd put down part of the burden already, some of the load that had my name on it, in big, bold block letters. But I knew that he hadn't put all of it down. And he had his own family now. He needed to be free of **TESS** so he could help them with their loads, and to let them help him with his.

So when he asked me how I was doing I told him I was doing good. Because I was, for the most part. And I was getting better all the time, even if it was slow in coming. Then I said *I love you, Dave*, for the first time ever and he said he loved me, too. And then I said, *Oh, there's one more thing.* And he listened and he gave me the Something that I needed.

An address.

And before I left Brookfield I stopped at the post office. It was closed, of course, but there was really no hurry. My letter would get picked up on Monday and it would make its way to France. And when my mother read it—if she read it—she wouldn't see the words *I love you.* But she would see *I forgive you.* Because that was the best I could give her.

I couldn't see her heart, her soul, and I didn't know why her soil was hard ground, too. I didn't know what or who had trampled it down, so long ago, long before there was a John or a Dave or a Tess in her life. But if there was anything left that was soft and lovely and fertile, even if it was way down deep, underneath the hard, trampled path, then maybe my seed would fall through the cracks and land there. And maybe love would grow.

But even if it didn't, what I knew was this:

I was gonna be all right. Either way.

CHAPTER 41

The day after Brookfield I knew. It was time for Change.

I used my new fortune, part of it anyway, to buy a computer. Jeff set it up for me and Cassidy showed me how to surf the net, because I'd never used a computer before, even though Jason and Brian had each owned one. A week later, my dad came down and installed some accounting software. Then he helped me make a spreadsheet with all of my clients' names and how much each of them paid. Yearly, monthly, weekly, hourly. I printed it out and studied the figures. And that's when I knew.

My time was worth more. I was worth more.

And so I sent out a brief, polite letter to each of my clients. Raising my rates. Private homes that paid on time and businesses that didn't. I raised them more than I thought I would, but less than I could have. And then I waited. For the irate calls and letters that said, *we've decided to go with someone else.* But there were none.

So I took the next step. I hit the pavement and got even more work. Office jobs, mostly, and some of them were outside of New Mills. But not just for me. Zeke had told me about a girl he'd hired in the spring. She was a nice girl, he said, and a very hard worker. Honest and polite. But she was slow and his customers were complaining. The problem was that she was too busy cleaning. She cleaned everything. All the time. And I knew what that meant:

Hire her, please. So I don't have to fire her.

And I did. Because lots of businesses are still leaving the state, sending more jobs south and east. So if you have the opportunity to create a new job then it's your responsibility to do it. And even though working for a small cleaning company isn't the same as being a lawyer or a doctor or any of those other professions that make people say, "*Oh...*" in that reverent, awestruck way, at least it's a job. It's better than working for minimum wage and tips that aren't big enough. And maybe—with hard work and Focus—it will lead to bigger and better things.

For me it meant that I still got paid even when I wasn't working. And it meant lots more free time. Time to take walks through town and visit with Laura and watch the sunset. Time to paint and read and play with Cassidy. To watch Red Sox games at Zeke's. Even though Zeke isn't there as often as he used to be. Because there are more than seven mugs in his sink again. Dean lives there with him now, and he really is just as hot as Rachel once said he was. He's like sunlight, like Bo Duke: all blonde and blue. So now Donny pours the beers at the bar two or three times a week, and he's discovered that it really does take some brains to do it. It takes brains and heart and two strong shoulders. He's got all those things, even more so now that he's a married man. He's not as good as Zeke, not by a long shot. But he'll learn. He'll get there someday.

And as July rolled along I felt better with every week that passed. Healthier. Stronger. But I still missed Brian, missed him more with each day that passed and not less. And on those fitful nights when I was wide awake, tossing and turning in my bed, restless and lonely...sometimes I still needed him to help me drift off to sleep. Even if it was only in my mind.

Then came the first Thursday of August, the one that meant it was just over seven months since Rachel died. There was a letter in my mailbox and I had to sit down before I could open it. Because it was from my mother.

It was a brief letter. Dispassionate, but nice. From Nice. In it she told me about The South of France. About wine and music and the *Colline du Château*, about figs that were sweet and water that was Mediterranean Blue. And when, at the very end of her letter, she told me about art she'd seen at galleries she'd visited I wondered if that meant she'd been thinking about me.

After I'd read through it three times I picked up a pen and my pretty, floral stationary and sat at my new desk. I thought about blueberries that were just now ripe and filled with sweet juice. About maple trees that whispered and rustled in the breeze, even here in the middle of town. About a documentary I'd bought recently about Bill Lee. He'd gone to Cuba to play baseball with people who didn't care about money and agents and endorsements, they just loved to play the game. And it was the coolest thing I'd ever seen. I thought, very carefully, about all of those things.

But when I put my pen to the paper I didn't tell my mother about any of them.

I told her instead about Matthew and how big he was getting. Told her that his laugh sounded just like bells pealing from heaven. That I was looking forward to meeting Caleb, his little brother, who would come in just a few months; and I wondered if this baby would get Kim's eyes. I told her about Jason's wedding, in case no one else had; told her that she should have just enough time to send him a nice gift from Nice. *After all,* I wrote, *he's family.*

I told her about Brian and how much I still loved him. And about Rachel. That *when I think about her I sometimes still cry.* And that *sometimes I wonder, even though I shouldn't, what I could have done differently.* Then I took a deep, deep breath. And told her about a warm, clear, beautiful night just the weekend before. *I was lying on the lawn, looking up at the sky and I saw her there, Mother. I saw them. Alice and Rachel and Wendy, winking down at me. Because they're much too restless to stay cooped up in heaven. God has to let them out at night to play.*

And when Laura dropped Cassidy off a few minutes later we walked to the post office together and dropped the letter into the Out of Town bin instead of putting it in my mailbox. Because that meant my letter would go out a day earlier. It meant that she'd get it a day earlier. And that maybe, someday soon, another one would come for me. A letter that was filled with my mother's thoughts, instead of the sights and sounds and tastes of France. Maybe not. And that was okay. Either way.

Two mornings later there was another surprise, but not inside my mailbox. It was the day I ran into Brian. At the grocery store. In the bread aisle. Not that I hadn't seen him around town since we'd buried Rachel. I had, of course, because it's a small town and you can't help it. But it was my first face-to-face, *oh my God, there he is, I can't get away from him* encounter.

We both came to a complete stop and stared at each other for what seemed like an eternity. He was dressed in his work clothes and his jaw was covered with a faint black shadow, with the scratchy early-morning whiskers that I'd always loved. He was a little thinner and a lot darker than I'd ever seen him. His eyes, of course, were still Van Dyke Brown.

I knew a little bit about what was going on with him, because Zeke kept me informed. Brian was so thin and so dark because he'd been doing a lot of extra outside work. Not just for his clients, but for himself. He'd moved out of the Burkes' house in early July, bought Charlie's old place, the house and the ten acres of land that went with it. Charlie hadn't rented it out again after Brian and I left because he didn't have the heart to do it. And because it really was run-down. When he decided to move to Florida he offered it to Brian. Sold it to him at a good price, Zeke had told me, because he'd always liked Brian. And because he didn't want some fucking flatlander getting ahold of it.

Brian bought a mobile home, too, a small, old, cheap one, and moved it in front of where the orchard once stood. He was spending his evenings and weekends tearing the house down, slowly, so he could salvage as much from it as possible. And next spring he'd build a new house right where the old one stood. Because, he'd said, it's still got a good foundation. Even after all these years.

And now…there he was. Just a few feet in front of me. Closer than we'd been in months and it made me wish that I'd put on some makeup before I left the house, that I was wearing something other than my usual T-shirt and jeans ensemble. But one of us had to break the awkward silence. I decided it should be me. And this is how it sounded:

"Uh…hi."

He only nodded and gave me a weak smile. I wasn't sure what it meant so I looked away, let my gaze fall onto his groceries. I let it linger there, waiting for him to speak. And that's when I saw something in his cart that made my heart stop for a moment and then drop into my stomach. I stared at the Something for about three seconds. Then I said, "Uh…gotta go," and walked away. Quickly. Without looking up at him again and without giving him the chance to work up the nerve to speak.

I made a beeline for the checkout counter. Answered *yes* to every question Agnes asked me, even though I didn't hear any of them. And then I walked home quickly. Without any bread. Without half of what I'd written down on my list. I hid inside my apartment for the rest of the morning and spent most of that time crying, face down, on the couch. It was the same couch where Brian and I had spent so much time together. It's where we were sitting the night we were too drunk to even kiss, the night I'd realized that he was in love with me. It was where Rachel had spent so many of her final days. Sleeping. Shivering. Hiding away in a haze.

When the tears were gone I washed my face and walked back to the store to finish my shopping. Because even when your heart is breaking you still need bread and Rice Krispies and orange juice. And when I got back home again Laura's car was in the driveway. She was sitting on my front steps, waiting for me.

"Are you okay?"

"I'm all right. Why?"

"Well, Brian came over this morning. He said you ran away from him at the market."

I grabbed tighter hold of my grocery bags. "I wasn't running from *him*. It was only…it was just the shock of seeing him unexpectedly. I mean, I turned the corner and there he was. In the bread aisle of the market."

It was true, but it wasn't the whole truth and I could tell that she knew it. So we went inside and she helped me unpack my groceries while I told her a little more of the truth. I told her that being so close to him, so close that I could actually smell him, had made me remember that I still loved him, even though—really—I'd already known it. It made me wish that I could be there for him right now, now that I was healthy and strong. Made me wish that I'd been healthy and strong back when he'd needed me to be. Because I had seen in his eyes that he was still in so much pain, and there wasn't anything I could do about it. Not anymore. And that made me wish that I didn't love him. Or that I could turn it off, the way I used to be able to do. That I could make the love just go away.

Then we sat down on the couch—the same one I'd covered with tears just a few hours earlier—and we talked about him. It was the first time we had since the breakup, because we hadn't wanted things to be awkward. She told me, *He's not doing well. But he's doing better.* He still blamed himself for Rachel. Still felt like he'd let her down and that he could have done more to save her, even though he knew he shouldn't. His father had been in touch again, and still called him from time to time, and Brian was trying to forgive him. Because he knew— like everyone did—that he'd made sure Tim had gotten what he deserved. But he didn't know if he'd ever really be able to look at Rick without thinking about how he'd left Rachel all alone and scared. What troubled him the most, though, was that he was angry with his mother for putting all of that burden on him. For not trying harder to find someone else to take care of them. Someone to take care of him. He was angry that she'd left him all alone and scared. Even though he loved her still. And missed her. Still.

Then she said that he'd asked her about me, too. She told him about my trip to Brookfield and the letters I'd written to my mother. She told him that I'd been teaching Cassidy how to paint, and that she didn't know which of us was enjoying it more. And when she told him that I'd expanded my business and hired a local girl to help me out he nodded and said he'd heard about it already, from Zeke. Then she gave me an eyebrow and said:

"But...I didn't tell him about that bartender."

I knew what that meant. So I nodded and thanked her. Before she left I gave her a hug and told her that I felt a little better. Because I did, at least a little bit. Even though I hadn't told her the real reason I'd left the store so quickly. I hadn't told her about what I'd seen in Brian's cart, the something that had left me too stunned to do any-thing more than mutter *uh...gotta go* to the man I still loved more than anything in the world. Because she'd drawn the boundary lines and she was right. Then there was the other thing. I didn't tell her what I'd seen because—really—it was stupid.

What I'd seen was a toothbrush. Red handle, medium bristle; the kind of toothbrush anyone might use. And it made me wonder—for the first time—how many there were in his bathroom at home. How many towels on the floor, how many mugs were in his sink. And even though I knew it was hypocritical—because of Red Bartender, because I was the one who had slammed the door on waiting for Someday—and even though I knew it was selfish, the idea of him being with someone else was almost more than I could bear.

I spent the night crying some more. Spent it trying not to imagine him with someone else, trying not to think that—right now—someone else could be with him. In his bed. The one that should have been Ours. That he might have had other someones in it since he'd moved out on his own, and that there might be even more of them in the future. What I tried hardest not to think about was that someday, maybe soon, he would have Someone in his life. Because it was going to happen sooner or later. Someday, he'd be healthy and strong enough to have a beautiful brown-eyed family. With Someone.

When I woke up the next morning it still hurt; it hurt even worse than it had at first, and there were still lots of tears. It hurt for days and even into the next weekend. But all week long, even through the pain, I knew that it was okay, because it should have hurt. I knew something else: whether or not he had someone in his life right now, or lots of them, and whether or not the Someone was going to be me...eventually I was going to be all right. With him or without him. I really was.

One morning, the last Monday in August, when I knew Brian would be at work, I decided to drive out to his place. Not to look for clues about a someone. Just to see the house, to see how it was coming along. I knew what it meant that he was tearing it down. That it was more to him than just taking apart an old house that was falling down anyway.

On my way there I stopped at the lake, because I hadn't passed by this side of it since I'd moved into town, and hadn't really looked at it since long before then. Not since winter. Even though it was August and even though it was over ninety degrees outside and oppressively humid, I was still surprised to see that it wasn't gray and frozen solid. It's how it had looked in my mind all this time. But there it was, in real life: deep Prussian Blue. Warm and alive, buzzing with motorboats and jet skis. Busy again.

Brian had been, too. The upstairs of the old house was gone. Gone. The roof and the walls and even the plumbing. All of the rooms I'd lived in, and that Rachel had lived in, too. Just like they'd never existed. Like we'd never been there at all. Most of the downstairs was gone, too. Just framing left, mostly, and some very old pipes and some wiring. Between Brian's trailer and what was left of the house stood three piles. I examined them as closely as I could from the safety of my car.

One of them was covered by a tarp, but I knew what was underneath. Anything that was still in decent enough condition to use for his new house, his Spring house. His Starting-Over house. The other two piles were in two separate dumpsters. One was just trash and the other was for the recycling center. And I sat in the car for nine full minutes, looking at the tarp. The dumpsters. The trailer. At what remained of the house.

Then I drove to the other side of the lake. I smiled politely while I cleaned the camps of families who were too busy and too lazy to do it themselves. And I nodded politely while the wives—Mays and otherwise—complained about the stifling heat and oppressive humidity that kept them trapped indoors. Even though they had no right to complain. Even though they were protected from it in air-conditioned comfort while—somewhere—Brian was working outside in it. Working hard. I hoped that he didn't make himself sick again.

When I was done I drove back home and lay on the couch for the rest of the evening. Remembering, without any tears, the night Rachel had moved into my apartment. Remembered the words that I'd almost spoken to Brian about sorting things into three piles: Things that you keep and things you discard and things that you give away. About saying goodbye. And moving on. He wasn't finished with his sorting, not yet. Even though I was. Even though I knew exactly which pile Brian was in. It was the one he'd been in all along.

Because I wanted him. All of him. His mind and heart and body and laughter; his words and smile and soul and life. His life.

I wanted the rest of his life.

And there was only one way to find out if he wanted mine. One way, and it would be hard. Harder than anything I'd ever had to do.

I had to wait. Wait until he was healthy and strong. Wait to see which pile I was in. Even if it wasn't the one I wanted to be in.

I had to wait.

CHAPTER 42

October always begins with a promise. Color and flavor and fragrance. Movement and beauty. Change.

The first Thursday in October I dug out my lime-green sweater bin, unpacked my sweaters and packed up my summer clothes. Then I threw on my favorite red sweater and walked to the grade school to get Cass. On the way back to my apartment she told me all about boy at school whose name was Isaac. He wore *dark, ugly glasses and they make him look like a nerd.* He was *a big, fat jerk* because he always cut in front of her in the lunch line, always aimed for her at recess when the kids played dodge ball, always said her name without the "C" and *you know what that spells, don't you, Tess?* I nodded sympathetically and didn't bother to tell her that he singled her out like that because he had a crush on her. She knew. And, of course, she liked him right back. Because if she didn't she wouldn't have mentioned his dark, ugly glasses that made him look like a nerd. He'd just be a big, fat jerk.

We tossed a Frisbee around the front lawn because pretty soon it would be too cold for it. Pretty soon, I said, there'd be snow. Cassidy smiled and said she couldn't wait, because winter was her favorite time of year. Time for snowmen and snow forts and snow angels. When the ground was covered with a beautiful white carpet and the trees sparkled with icy diamonds. I smiled right back and told her I'd never noticed the diamonds before. But that I'd be sure to look for them. Once it was winter.

And then she said, "Another reason I can't wait is because Brian promised he'd take me plowing with him this year. Even when it storms in the middle of the night."

I nodded and told her that sounded like fun. Because, of course, I knew that it was. It was the most fun I'd had with him with our clothes on. Then she said:

"Did you know that his house is all gone?"

The Frisbee hit my forehead. Because I hadn't thought to catch it. I blinked a few times, then managed: "Oh?"

"Yep."

I picked up the Frisbee and tossed it gently. "So...he'll be all ready to build his new house in the spring."

"Yep."

Laura arrived a few minutes later to pick her up. We made quick, pleasant chitchat and I watched them drive away. Then, after supper, I got into my own car and drove to the lake. Because there was something I needed to know.

I sat alone in our spot, underneath the maples and the birches, on the cold, damp grass. It was almost sunset. The wind blew through the trees, a rough, chilly wind. It blew through the branches above me, behind me, in front of me, through the leaves that surrounded the entire lake. They all shook and rustled and I closed my eyes, let the sound completely envelope me. Took in a deep breath, deep through my nostrils. Someone was burning leaves nearby and the scent drifted over to me on the wind. Lovely, smoldering heat. I sat. Still. Silent. Breathing deeply. Waiting. Finally, I opened my eyes.

The whole world glowed, ablaze with vibrant red and vivid orange; the sky and the grass and the leaves. The hot colors of the sunset and the trees that reflected on the water were caught for a breathless moment of eternity in its ripples; the ripples from the wind. The leaves all around me crackled and sizzled and whispered its message to me... whispered...

I closed my eyes, one more time, took it all in. Because whatever happened tonight I had to remember this scene. Had to remember the lake—just like this. With all six senses. So I waited, seared it all on my brain and heart and gut and soul. Images, flashes of image. Love. Heat. Connection. Fire. Waited until I had it all locked inside, to keep it part of me forever. Because soon, one way or the other, I would pull out my easel and pour it all out onto a fresh, white canvas. This lake. The lake that was really Brian and me.

I stood up with my eyes still closed. Turned around, away from the lake. Opened them again, ran to my car and hopped inside. I was facing Brian's road. Brian's home. I swallowed and took a deep breath, waited for my hands to stop shaking. Then put the car into gear...

And that's when I saw them in my rearview mirror: a pair of headlights. My heart skipped a few beats, then started up again, because it couldn't be him. I would have heard his truck at least half a mile away. But the lights slowed down as they came toward me. Slowed even more. Then pulled in behind me and came to a stop. I squinted my eyes, looked more closely at the reflection in the mirror…and it was him. I could see his silhouette, even with just the dark orangey light for illumination. Because I'd know it anywhere…

I got out of the car and shielded my eyes against his headlights. Then I smiled. It was a brand-new truck, finally—another red one. He opened his door and I saw it, in big, bold beautiful letters:

LaChance Builders–Brian W. LaChance

He banged his door shut, looked at me and nodded. I nodded right back.

Deep breath, Tess. Deeper. Because it's gonna be all right. Either way.

Yes it is. And so am I.

Motion…

I walked toward him, slowly, and came to a stop directly in front of him. Close enough to smell sawdust and heat. His face shone oddly in the combination of colors that came from my taillights and his headlights. It was covered with dirt and end-of-the-day whiskers. Still he was beautiful.

If he'd been with someone new, or with lots of some-ones new, during the summer I didn't care anymore. Not even a little. Because even though everything had changed, nothing really had. Nothing. Not for me. There was only one way…one way to find out…

I cleared my throat. "Hey, Brian."

"Hey, Tess."

I gave him a big smile. Because I loved the way my name sounded in his voice.

"Your hair looks good like that," he said.

I touched it, surprised, because I'd forgotten that it had been getting gradually darker over the summer. "Thanks."

I looked down at my shoes, not quite sure how to begin. Because we didn't have to play the *so what have you been up to* game. We both knew the basics. He was still swinging a hammer, I was still scrubbing toilets. We knew about parents who were trying to make amends and houses that had been torn down and exes who were remarried. So there was just one thing left to talk about. It was my turn to go first.

I cleared my throat again and looked up at him. Looked right into his eyes.

Momentum…

"You know," I said, "I heard about these monkeys once. They live in the Congo. I wish I could remember what their real name is. They call 'em hippie chimps, and I guess it's a good nickname, because all they do—pretty much—is have sex all day long. But, it was kinda sad, too. Because they're almost extinct."

He gave me a big smile. A real one. Then he said:

"Damn poachers."

And there they were. Glowing eyes. I knew mine were, too. And I wanted to reach for his hand but I couldn't. Because he was already holding mine.

Back at my apartment. We were sitting on the couch with no words. Just sitting still. Not even holding hands. Because there was no hurry. But it was still a little weird, sitting so quietly on that same couch where we'd sat and laughed and made love and watched television and fucked and snuggled and talked about The Future. But I'd been there with Jason before there was a Brian, done all those same things with him, too. On that very same couch. And it didn't matter. None of it.

And finally he spoke:

"Beige walls. You must hate that."

"Yep. They really do suck."

"Got that right."

Silence again, but not an awkward one. He was just looking around, scanning the paintings on the walls. Most of them he'd seen, a hundred times at least. But two of them were new. White, starry jasmine blossoms. And a beautiful blue swing set, gleaming in the golden summer sun. He smiled but didn't ask about them, about what or who they were. Because, of course, there was no hurry. And then he noticed.

"Where's Kineo?"

I cleared my throat. "It had to go away."

He nodded. Looked at me. Looked me right in the eyes. And I knew. This was the moment. This was It. But I didn't even hesitate, didn't take a deep breath or clench my toes inside my socks. I didn't have to. Not anymore.

"Can I tell you about Kineo? For real this time?"

He reached over and gently caressed my cheek. "Yep."

I scooted closer to him. Took his hand in mine again, looked at his fingers. One at a time. At the rough cuticles and broken nails and the scratches on his knuckles. Turned it over and touched each callous. Gently. Kissed his palm.

Then I said:

Letting go...

"Actually, I'll have to go back a little farther than Kineo."

And I did, back to the start, to the beginning of everything. But once I started I realized that the beginning went back even further, even before rainbows and soil. And I told him everything. There were things I'd forgotten about, harsh words and sadness and feeling alone. There was longing and shame and other emotions I couldn't even put names to. But I kept talking anyway. Then I told him about safety and home and love, so much love. But that underneath it all there was still fear. And then the fear took over because I didn't fight it. I let it take over and threw away all those things. All the things that were delicate and precious and too rare to be discarded without any thought. When I found all of it again, with him, I was still afraid, too afraid to believe in it. To know that it was real. So I let it go. All over again.

He listened and didn't talk, not at all. Not to ask me anything or to prod me when I fell silent. He just listened and held me and he cried when I did. And when I was done there was still love. It was stronger than fear and harsh words and sadness. There were his arms and his shoulders and they still seemed so strong. I found out just how strong they were, how strong they'd had to be.

Because he talked, too, about sunshine and music and stars and love; of loss that was almost unbearable and burdens that were too heavy; fear and exhaustion and frustration and abandonment. And then he talked about hope, about searching and finding. And losing again, losing it all, and the second time it really was unbearable. A black, cold abyss, with no sunshine and no music. And no stars.

I listened and didn't talk. I held him. I cried when he did. When he was done there was still love, stronger than everything else. It was still there when we woke up the next morning, on my bed, in the clothes we'd slept in. My head was on his chest and I could feel his heart beating against my cheek, telling me that I was safe and loved. When I looked up I could see it in his eyes, and I knew he could see it in mine. We didn't have to say it but we did anyway.

This is how it sounded:

"I want the rest of your life," I said.

"Tess, it's yours. It's *always* been yours."

We made love in our bed. Hot and slow and beautiful and wild, hearts bursting with fragile emotion. Two souls touching, closer than two bodies ever could…

Outside it was October. And that meant Autumn. Color and flavor and fragrance. Movement and beauty. Change.

And inside my apartment, lying in each others' arms, it felt just like Spring.

EPILOGUE

The middle of May. Newborn leaves of the palest green, everywhere. Tulips and daffodils in the front garden. Dozens of birds at our new birdfeeders. Finches and grosbeaks and chickadees. Others, too, birds whose names I haven't learned yet. But I will. They sing to us, every morning. It's the best alarm clock in the world.

We can't forget, of course. Every month we look at the calendar and still take note. Remember her. Miss her. Every month it still hurts. There is still sadness. But now that it has been almost two and a half years there are other dates to take note of, too. Like this:

One week and three days since Brian and I celebrated our first wedding anniversary.

But some days, even though I'm happy, even though I'm happier than I've ever been in my life...I'm still not feeling so great.

Wednesday. **11:52 a.m.** Another countdown.

One minute forty-six seconds.

Standing. Aching. Waiting. Facing the counter, tapping my foot. Impatient. I looked at the wall and it was a good distraction. Cherry Tomato Red. Brand-new, just like the rest of the house. I'd chosen all the colors, even though I hadn't done any of the painting, and it cheered me up to see it. Made me forget that I was aching.

Brian burst through the door and I turned with a sharp cry of surprise. Because his new truck—that wasn't really new anymore—was too damn quiet.

He smiled. "Sorry I scared you. How are you feeling?"

"Sore and tired."

He kissed me. "And cranky."

"Just a little. You're home...uh, early."

"Just passing through real quick in between jobs."

I nodded. Backed up a step. Closer to the counter. He fished around in the fridge for a can of soda, cracked it open, guzzled about half of it. His gaze fell on the kitchen table. Sketchbook open. Spring orchard. Beautiful, out-stretched branches, thick with bright green leaves. Glowing with pink, starry blossoms that held a secret. He smiled. He didn't have to ask. He knew.

"I haven't been painting today. Just sketching."

He nodded. He knew that, too. Finished his soda. Chucked the can into the sink. Cocked his head. "Something smells good."

I shrugged. Casual. Hands clasped behind my back. Nothing odd going on here.

But the microwave beeped and gave me away.

He gave a small chuckle. "What've you got in there?"

"Oh...just lunch."

He smirked. Took a step toward me. "Really? Lunch?"

"Yep." Then I backed toward the microwave, slowly, try-ing for nonchalant but not getting anywhere near it. He nodded. Stretched. His turn to try for nonchalant. I didn't buy it, either. He sidestepped, quickly, tried to go around me, but I had anticipated the move. Blocked him cold. He leaned to the right and when I blocked him again I dis-covered—too late—that he'd faked me out. He went left instead and charged straight to the microwave.

"Wait…"

It was too late. He exploded with laughter. "You're eat-ing Chef Boyardee?"

I folded my arms as best I could. "It's not my fault."

"Yeah, I know."

He poked my big fat belly and was rewarded with a kick. Kissed me again. Softly.

Glowing eyes. Van Dyke Brown.

Because there was another date circled on our calen-dar. Another countdown.

One week, two days.

That's when our daughter is due.

Her name is Spring.

ACKNOWLEDGMENTS

Without the following people, *Waiting For Spring* would be sitting on the top shelf of my closet right now, in between my box of baseball cards and my husband's 8-track tapes:

My kids, who didn't complain when the muses whispered to me while I was supposed to be making supper. Mr. Jim Reed, my high school English teacher, who always expected me to write a book. Amy Rogers, Linda Bennett, and Alice McCreary, my first readers and editors, whose honest feedback and unfailing support I can never repay. Stan O'Donnell, who taught me what it means to be a lumberjack. Matt Vaughn, my favorite Son of the Midwest, who battles Injustice and who helped me with the boring legal stuff. Henry Lambert, whose knowledge of all things guns helped me from making an idiot of myself.

And a special thanks to Terry Goodman and everyone at AmazonEncore for all of their hard work and support in introducing my novel to a whole new audience.

ABOUT THE AUTHOR

R. J. Keller lives in central Maine with her husband, their two children, and the family's cats. She enjoys gardening, rooting for the Boston Red Sox, and watching other people cook. *Waiting For Spring* is her first novel.